THE
ELEVENTH
YEAR

By the same author

The Four Winds of Heaven
Encore

THE
ELEVENTH
YEAR

Monique Raphel High

GRANADA
London Toronto Sydney New York

Granada Publishing Limited
Frogmore, St Albans, Herts AL2 2NF
and
515 Madison Avenue, New York, NY 10022, USA
117 York Street, Sydney, NSW 2000, Australia
60 International Blvd, Rexdale, Ontario, R9W 6J2, Canada
61 Beach Road, Auckland, New Zealand

Published by Granada Publishing 1983

British Library Cataloguing in Publication Data

High, Monique Raphel
  The eleventh year.
  I. Title
  813'.54[F]   PS3558.I3665

ISBN 0–246–11807–5

Printed in Great Britain by
Richard Clay (The Chaucer Press) Ltd, Bungay, Suffolk

Granada ®
Granada Publishing ®

For my mother, Dina,
dearest of friends,
most beautiful to me

How is the faithful city become an harlot! it was full of judgment; righteousness lodged in it; but now murderers.

ISAIAH 1:21

Whose solid virtue
The shot of accident nor dart of chance
Could neither graze nor pierce?

SHAKESPEARE, *Othello*, IV, 1

Prologue

To every thing there is a season, and a time
to every purpose under the heaven.

ECCLESIASTES 3:1

The immense reception rooms of the Varenne mansion glittered with the refractions of emeralds and diamonds, of the cut crystal of the antique chandeliers and of the perfect Venetian *coupes* that guests balanced in their adept fingers while immaculate waiters in dress uniform filled and refilled them with vintage champagne.

Alexandre stood half listening to the words of congratulation that were being offered to him like so many trays of hors d'oeuvres, toast laden with Beluga caviar, smoked salmon, truffled pâté from the province of the Perigord. It was an odd victory he was celebrating. Once again he would have his seat in the Chamber of Parliament, but by this time he had few illusions about being able to straighten out the politics of Europe. He smiled at the plump little

7

banker next to him, wondering just how drunk he might be. How many times had the butler filled his *coupe* with Dom Perignon?

He touched the front of his frilled shirt, the fine fabric of his dinner jacket. The soft hair at his temples was turning grey. He was thirty-eight, a mature man. His grey eyes scanned the room for Lesley and, when he saw her, he felt relieved. What was it she had said to him earlier that evening? That love, intimate love, was painfully wrought from the shared years of joy and pain, not just from those first sparks of electricity that gave off a sometimes artificial glow mistaken for fire. Did it mean that she loved him then? Or had those merely been a string of words as pretty as the costume beads that women sported in Paris these days, coloured beads that, beneath their attractive veneer, were worth less than the string that bound them together? For a moment his oval face clouded, and then he saw her turn slowly to him and smile.

Lesley, her red hair fringed and bobbed, wore a low-necked satin dress of the same brilliant green as her eyes. The three-quarter sleeves hugged her arms, and as a low-slung belt she had looped some beads around her waist. The dress hung loosely around her boyish hips and narrowed, so that her ankles showed in their dainty green pumps. Emeralds, always her stone, covered her hands and ears, and she wore one large, tear-shaped one between her breasts on a gold chain. The effect was of high, fashionable sophistication. She moved in a single sweep with her dress, a flapper of utmost taste, the most glamorous of the jazz-age girls. But you aren't a girl any longer, he thought, his throat tight. You are a woman of thirty, and I have known you for ten years . . .

'Excuse me, please,' he murmured to the little banker, aware that he was cutting him off in mid-praise. He would have to make amends for this later; politicians always did. Especially politicians of the rightist minority, who needed bankers. Then he caught up with Lesley just as she was explaining something to the two servants at her side, in the carved entrance to the hall.

She turned at his touch, smiled. 'I had to send down to the cellar,' she said to him ruefully. 'We were running low on brut.'

'At this point, Madame la Marquise, you could bring out hock and they wouldn't notice. The guillotine will spare you, darling.'

It was a moment caught in space, and neither of them paid attention to the liveried servants at their side. She rose on tiptoe to finger his cravat. From the silk, her hand moved to the tip of his chin. Such a small gesture, yet such a fragile one.

Then the moment dissolved and she was gone, between the two waiters. He stood alone for a few minutes, scanning the room. The Paris giants were there, Hélène Berthelot laughing with Cécile Sorel, the Quai d'Orsay meeting the theatre with complete ease. And there was Gabrielle Chanel, spare, thin, dark, with her friend the voluptuous, overdone Misia Sert. He had never liked Misia and so he simply nodded in her direction. An egotist of the first order, he thought with some disdain.

He could hear laughter, he could hear French, he could hear English. Now and then there was a hard, raucous word of Russian, and he thought: What an odd mixture Paris has become . . . and how far we have travelled from the early post-war days of Clemenceau, our 'Tiger,' our *Père la Victoire*. Someone was touching his sleeve. A deep, throaty, well-known voice was saying: 'You never did like strange women to approach you, did you, darling?'

He blinked. From head to toe, Elena Sergeievna Egorova was sheathed in black. Her tall, Minerva figure was encased in velvet, and diamonds and rubies adorned her magnificent white neck and shone again from the tiara set against the thick swirl of her long black hair. She is my age, he

9

thought, yet still she manages to stun by her appearance. She so rarely did anything with that mane of hair except to let it hang, perfectly straight, down to the middle of her upright, majestic back. She said, to cover the uncomfortable silence: 'Do you feel a winner yet?'

'And what, Elena, is a winner?'

'One who survives. Look around you at the sea of faces that have already drowned, and you'll understand exactly what I mean.'

He could not help but follow her gaze. His plump banker, red-faced, was trying to make a point with a sad-eyed man who looked amazingly like James Joyce. Lesley had read Joyce to him aloud, but one had to have been born to the English language to capture his bizarre imagery. There wasn't any life to it, he reflected, all at once aware of what Elena had been driving at. 'I think I see,' he murmured.

'Proust saw it all so well. What a shame he died, isn't it?'

Alexandre smiled. 'Yet he was unquestionably a survivor. He'll survive us all.'

'I have often wondered if he patterned Madame Verdurin on your mother.'

This made Alexandre laugh. 'I hope so. She richly deserves it! And you? Were you a younger version of the Princess Yourbeletieff?'

She shrugged, and he was conscious of her white breasts rising and falling like twin Alps above the black décolletage. 'I wasn't part of the *ne plus ultra* of Parisian society in those days. I had . . . barely made my appearance.'

'But an appearance nobody is likely to forget.'

She looked at him levelly from kohl-ringed dark eyes that seemed somehow soulless in their abysmal depth. 'Old age makes you gallant,' she commented, and then turned around to mingle once more, a tall black exclamation point among the shimmering soft colours of the other guests. He remained in place, still watching her. Old age! She's exactly as old as I, he thought with wry amusement.

10

Elena was linking arms with a tall, exquisitely tuxedoed man with brown hair that gleamed under the chandelier, a man with large brown eyes who was slipping his arm possessively around the black velvet shoulders. Alexandre winced. Damn Paul! He hadn't wanted him to be there, not on this night, *his* night. But to keep his brother away took more than the lack of a personal invitation. Damn, he thought again – and where is Jamie?

On the small love seat next to the bay window, he saw her. Soft brown hair swept into a knot, soft blue dress to match her eyes, those eyes that said – Forget me not – the eyes of the seeress, Cassandra. They had so teased her about that in the old days. Jamie Lynne Stewart, so earnest, so pure, so direct. He made his way toward her, and when he reached her, she rose, excited, pinpoints of red on her cheekbones. 'Oh, Alex! It's such a wonderful evening!'

He took the proffered hands, kissed them gently. 'Do you really think so?' He could not help but sneak a sideways glance toward the woman in black velvet and the man with the brown hair.

'It's all right, really,' Jamie said, oddly reassuring, making him sit down beside her. She had not touched her champagne.

'I didn't want – '

'I know. But the circles of our lives cannot help overlapping sometimes. He's your brother, Alex.'

'*You* shouldn't be defending him.'

'I'm not.' There was a hard note to her voice. She cleared her throat. 'But writers need to go out once in a while. Otherwise, where would we get our inspiration?'

He was thinking of Elena Egorova, talking of Proust, comparing his own mother to Madame Verdurin. But his mother had, in spite of everything, been an aristocrat. Did that matter? Did any of this matter in 1928? He was sitting next to Jamie Stewart, recalling that her beginnings had been very humble, that to many she had simply been a

11

'nobody'. But she was no longer a nobody. She'd pulled herself out of anonymity, and not by selecting for herself the best stable of lovers Paris could provide. That had been his mother's particular achievement. He could feel the acidity in his stomach, the rancour. Jamie's eyes had filled with tears that she was fighting to hold back, and suddenly he kissed her cheek. 'Don't cry,' he said.

'They aren't tears of pain. Only of regret. One has to cry at what might have been but never could be.' She had swallowed her tears, however.

He sat there with her hand in his, feeling warm, feeling at odds within himself. She was no longer speaking. Then all at once he heard the commotion, and a footman was coming toward him across the reception hall. Alexandre rose instantly, drawing the liveried man off to one side, away from the sofa.

'Monsieur le Marquis!' the servant whispered urgently. 'Madame Stewart's nursemaid – '

Although the two men had moved to whisper alone, they had not managed to avoid Jamie's sudden rising to join them. She had heard everything.

'My daughter's nanny? My God – ' and Alexandre felt her body swaying, her knees starting to give way.

'Is the nursemaid *here*?' he asked.

The servant nodded. 'Madame la Marquise has put her in the study. She came all the way from Louveciennes – '

In an oddly calm voice that chilled Alexandre, Jamie said: 'Tell me at once what's happened to my daughter.'

Alexandre was conscious of voices stilling around them, of pairs of eyes riveted to Jamie's blue gown, to his reassuring hand on her arm. His own mouth was dry. Jamie insisted: 'You must tell me.'

'Someone has kidnapped Mademoiselle,' the footman answered, and it seemed as if all ears in the large room were straining to hear his discreetly murmured message, as if every glass of champagne had remained poised in mid air.

12

Alexandre saw, out of the corner of his eye, the athletic figure of his brother rushing toward them, but at that moment Jamie collapsed, her face white, and he had barely enough time to catch her before she fell. His brother was tugging on his arm and asking urgently, over and over: 'What's this all about? Why is Jamie ill? What is going on?'

Alexandre's grey eyes narrowed, and he glared at Paul's handsome face. Behind him stood the black velvet figure of Elena Egorova. Placing his fingers on Jamie's forehead, he whispered to Paul: 'This isn't your business. I don't know what's happened – but whatever it is, it hasn't a goddamn thing to do with you!'

Book 1
Springtime

A time to be born, and a time to die; a time
to plant, and a time to pluck up that which is
planted;

A time to kill, and a time to heal; a time to
break down, and a time to build up . . .

ECCLESIASTES 3:2–3

Chapter One

Emily was always perfect. As a child, Lesley could remember her older sister's pink and white beauty, the ribbons in her blond hair that gently curled, that never rebelled. Em the Gem. The wide house near Central Park held an entire suite of rooms for the two of them, Em the Gem and Les the Mess, and their Swiss governess, Mademoiselle Blanchard, Zelle. Zelle used to irritate Lesley so, with her dry accent, with the tuft of hair sprouting from the mole on her chin, with her dull chignon. But Emily, three years her senior, never seemed to mind. Holding hands, Lesley and her sister would take their daily walk in the park, while Zelle pointed out a flower by its generic name, or explained a rock formation. Lesley never listened to the dry dull voice, but Em did. Lesley knew she did. Em never faulted anyone for being boring, because she had been born that way herself. Poor old Em the Gem. It wasn't always fun being the little golden princess, the one who bobbed the perfect curtsey to Papa's clients and Mama's august relatives from England.

Lesley loved New York City with its wide avenues, its marble houses. Fifth Avenue was where they lived, behind elegant iron-grilled windows. Slowly during Lesley's childhood the carriages and prancing horses had begun to make way for cars, and the pretty ladies who drove by no longer warmed their feet under quilted blankets but wore goggles beneath wide-brimmed hats tied down by chiffon scarves. A new era. Papa owned several wonderful machines, as Mama's relatives in Great Britain called them. At first he had had them shipped from Europe. Then she could recall the large Packard – with twelve horsepower! – and its high steering wheel and deep leather seats. Some time later he had bought Mama a tiny motor car, which she had called a 'horseless carriage': the Kiblinger Model N. Such odd, coded names. A delicate covered wagon on four frail wheels, with a tooter that resembled a French horn in an orchestra. Lesley had wondered where all the horses had gone and missed them. Later she would be taught to ride and to jump, but even when very young she had liked to draw the horses in the park, with their flowing manes and dainty legs. Les the Mess, because there was always a paint spot on her clothes. Zelle didn't understand.

It wasn't that Lesley disliked Emily; it was simply that they were too different to understand each other. Later Lesley ascribed that essential difference to the two sides of their family: the English and the Irish. Em was like their English mother, blonde and white and porcelain pink, and tall and therefore pretty; Lesley didn't wonder whether or not she was pretty too, with her red hair and green eyes. She was the different one, the one who was always asking 'Why?' while Emily did what she was told. About her colouring, her father used to say: 'It's the Irish in you', although Lesley hadn't known what he meant. For after all, Papa had been born in Chicago, and that was part of the United States. Mama had been born in England, spoke with a crisp new accent like a dollar bill, and that made her a foreigner.

Lady Priscilla Aymes had come to New York for a visit and had met the eager young advertising executive who had made her want to stay. Priscilla was the daughter of Arthur Stephen Aymes, Earl of Brighton. Edward Franklin Richardson was the son of an Irish meatpacker, who had come to New York with ideas for promoting products. In those days at the end of the nineteenth century, advertising agencies had been very crude shops that printed simple pictures with simple slogans. Ned Richardson had begun by selling his ideas, by placing better pictures with more clever slogans and charging the merchant company bargain prices. Now he was chairman of the agency he had founded, Richardson and Associates, and he was a legend in New York like his competitors, J. Walter Thompson and Roy Durstine. Lesley thought he was handsome, with his reddish-brown hair and his rich brown eyes, and with the dimple in his chin – a burst of colour. When he had married Lady Priscilla, society had ceased to consider him merely a creative young genius on the rise. He had become a man never again to be discounted. People had forgotten his plebeian origins and had even been willing to overlook his Catholicism. He and his bride had built the white marble mansion on Fifth Avenue, and he had revolutionized the concept of advertising. Em had been born in 1895 and Lesley, born three years later, was like Ned Richardson. The Irish side. Later she would learn that the English had never been able to understand the Irish, nor the Irish the English, and then she would accept the differences between her own nature and that of the cool, diplomatic, calm Emily.

After a while Zelle had become more of a companion and chaperone, less of a governess, and the girls had gone to the Clara B. Spence School. It was small and exclusive. The girls wore uniforms and came in chauffeur-driven motor cars, such as the turquoise-canopied Pierce-Arrow that drove Lesley and Emily up town. Emily was good at everything and wrote essays in her lovely script that brought praise from Miss Spence herself. Lesley's essays brought questions. Where was the girl getting her bold opinions, on labour unions and the rights of women? But Lesley wasn't really a rebel. She was quiet enough, and ladylike, and had many friends. It was simply that she felt the world around her more deeply. She read the newspapers and wondered – about the miners in Pennsylvania, about the Hungarian illiterates, about the rising tide of bad feeling

19

among the countries of Europe. 'That's because you haven't forgotten where you came from, lass,' her grandfather Sean from Chicago had told her. After that she hadn't seen her grandfather and grandmother much at all – and then they'd died, and she hadn't even been told about the funerals. That was certainly strange, considering Papa's friendship with the monsignors in Boston and New York. For Papa was still a Catholic, and although Lady Priscilla didn't go with him, being herself a member of the Church of England, he attended mass at St Patrick's Cathedral whenever he could. The girls went with him, and nothing was ever stated about Mama's absence. 'Whenever he could' might be twice a month, or it might only be on Christmas Eve and for Easter – but Papa would go, the blonde sylph that was Em on his right, the smaller, pert Lesley on his left, holding his hand. And the elegant ladies would raise their gloved hands to him and the men would incline their heads. People always noticed Papa wherever he went, and sometimes the monsignor would come to the marble house for a reception, in his special, festive robes. Papa wasn't ashamed to be a Catholic. But he'd gone alone to his parents' funerals, and the newspapers hadn't carried the obituaries, and the Society sections hadn't printed a photograph of Papa at the cemetery. Yet when Lady Priscilla's mother had died at her country estate in Yorkshire during Lesley's third year of high school, black had been hung from the windows of the marble house on Fifth Avenue.

Growing up. Emily Jane, well trained like a racehorse. A glowing debut in New York, another in Washington, DC. Graduation from Spence. Lesley, at fifteen, had wondered what her sister would do. But Emily was sensible – another good, healthy trait. Emily had met a young stockbroker in Newport, Rhode Island, and George Brandhurst had proposed marriage to her in the magnificent drawing-room of the marble mansion, all decorated in blues and greys and

delicate Louis XVI furnishings. Lesley had seen the two
young people from the hall. George had wanted to take Em
in his arms, but she had resisted – 'Now *really*, darling . . .'
– interposing her white hands between him and her and
laughing that rather high, shrill, quick laugh of hers, so like
a filly's whinny. George, poor George, had shrugged and
accepted instead Em's long, strong fingers, with the large
platinum ring, its emerald-cut diamond sparkling like the
embers in the fireplace. Lesley had felt – she didn't know
why – that somehow George had been cheated. But George
had married Emily, and Lesley had been her maid of
honour, and the couple had gone to England for their
honeymoon, to visit their widowed grandfather, Lord
Arthur, who would arrange for a presentation at Court. On
their return Papa and George's father had set up the young
couple in a smaller version of the Richardson mansion, only
this one was of fine red brick, with grillwork. Lesley hated
it. Lady Priscilla gave Em some of her august family's bone
china, and Lesley hated that too.

At some point Lesley had decided that she wanted to take
hold of her own life as she would the reins on a headstrong
thoroughbred. She couldn't recall when the vague ideas,
more like auras and colours, took root in her conscious
mind. Perhaps they had always existed, lying in wait, fallow
during childhood. She read a lot, but mostly she was a
visual person. She loved the outdoors, the seaside resorts
where they spent holidays, Long Island Sound. She liked
the oranges and golds and purples of the sunsets. God was
not the Host but the rays of an early-morning dawn,
spreading coldly over green lawns. He breathed life into the
lonely moorhens searching for breakfast in the tall reeds.
God was in the animals and in the wildflowers. Lesley
sketched and painted and took long walks. And she
watched and listened.

Papa spoke of business. His marvellous laughter was a
sensuous delight, full-powered and rich. He would some-

21

times take her to lunch when she had a school holiday. She would meet him at the office, she in her trim little good-girl outfit picked out by Zelle, he dressed in a well-cut suit of flamboyant tones and the office all desk and glass and charts and posters. She would look through *Harper's Bazaar* while she heard him giving specific instructions to his assistants as to the copy of a certain advertisement: Bruce's Peppermints, which were to emphasize their medicinal value, as opposed to Caraway's after-dinner mints, which were to capture the essence of a fine Cognac. 'And don't forget the key thrust of our business: You sell them on the single differentiating point, John. Don't hit them over the head with all the marvels of our product – one will do, thank you, if it's what makes it unique. We want to be *recognized.*'

Yes, Lesley thought, I too want to be recognized. And she said to her father: 'Women are more intelligent than men, if they use their brains. I'm going to be a suffragette.' And then, calmly, she bit into her pineapple salad. He stared at her and then shook his head, and laughed – but he wasn't angry, and he didn't disagree. 'I don't want to have children,' she then declared. 'I'd like to travel through Europe and visit the museums, and really learn how to paint.'

'You're not strong enough for that kind of life,' he replied seriously. 'It requires an inner core of survival that you don't have, Lesley. Maybe I should have seen that you got it. I had it, God knows, and your grandparents on my side had it too. As for your mother, she can survive any storm. And Em will go along with the crowd, so she'll be all right. But you – you're the mystery among us, girl. There's something there, a particular need, that isn't going to let you alone. You want – I don't know – you want a *connection.*'

'We all want a connection, Papa. That's simply being human.'

22

Ned Richardson smiled. 'Then you're too human to be a barren woman. Maybe that's why I see you surrounded by little children.'

Lesley's eyes filled with tears. 'I'm disappointed how poorly you know me,' she stated.

'Time will tell. Time alone will tell.'

She would never forget that conversation at the Waldorf-Astoria. She had thought her father a religious old fool and herself invincible and modern and brave. She was sixteen and it was the year the war had started in Europe.

Later that autumn she told her father that she had thought things over and that she wanted to go to college. Em was expecting her first child, and the house was in an uproar, maids running in and out with piles of infant linens and elegant maternity clothing. Her mother and sister had been on a shopping spree. 'I don't want my daughter to be a school-teacher,' Lady Priscilla said. Coolly, in the midst of all the confusion.

'I don't know what I want to be. Probably a painter, or a sculptress.'

'Oh, Lesley.'

'Higher education is very much in fashion,' the pregnant Em said, falling back against lace pillows. 'You can meet fine fellows there, Mama. Yalies. Mmmmm . . .'

'Emily. Georgie went to Harvard.' Mothers always remembered.

'Yes. I forgot.' Stifling a yawn.

'You don't really love him, do you?' Lesley cut in. Her tone of voice was anything but hostile – it was simply curious, as if suddenly she had realized something of import. 'Why'd you marry him, Em?'

Emily smiled. 'We were suited to each other. And of course I love him, Les. It isn't like Romeo and Juliet, but then neither are we. We're grown-up, sensible people.'

Something rebelled inside Lesley, something turned over. She could feel the tightness in her throat. Her father said,

23

saving her: 'So. You want to go to college. I don't think that's at all a bad idea. What does Miss Spence think?'

'She agrees with my choice: Vassar.'

'So you've already decided?'

'Yes.' Lesley waited quietly, her hands folded in her lap. She wasn't so sure of him any more, not since that discussion about her need to 'connect'. She wasn't sure of him, and she didn't really know what her mother thought. Nobody ever knew, for sure. Lady Priscilla seemed conventional enough, but in her day she'd done a most unusual thing: She'd married an American of dubious family and the Catholic faith. That was why Lesley, although she didn't want Mama for a friend, still felt, at odd moments, a kind of bond – tenuous at best, but nonetheless existent.

'Well, then,' Ned said brightly, 'there's no more to be discussed.' And he watched as the muscles in Lesley's arms relaxed, as the scene shifted once again to the boxes of eyelet lace and trimmings that had been set down by his wife's feet. Lesley turned round, very quietly, and left the room. She didn't belong there any more, not any more.

Cincinnati was a city of German immigrants, mostly Catholic. The Reverend Stewart felt them around him all the time. *His* people were those who had come from the farms, west, in the flatlands. Thin, with wire-rimmed spectacles and a pronounced Adam's apple, John Stewart always sensed his own difference, his own 'foreignness' in this city to which he had come as a young man, to help civilize it and render it more godly. He had been born and reared in Scotland, and had left when the spirit had moved him, when he'd thought it was time to leave his village and spread the gospel. His father, a tanner, had laughed at him, but John had come nevertheless, with his small earnings and his minister's education. He had come to New York and left at once, horrified: a city in which to drown, in

24

which to give in to perdition! And so he had arrived in Cincinnati. But still, he did not like it. He had stayed because he'd felt needed, and because of Margaret, the milliner's daughter, plump and friendly and shy, whom he had met at church and married not long after. He'd married her to stave off loneliness and to make roots. She'd kept the loneliness away but had not succeeded in turning the angular Scotsman into a regular American midwesterner. She'd given up trying, but she liked her life, liked her city. She also liked her husband but could not understand him. A rare bird . . .

John Stewart liked to read. The house smelled of beeswax, of lemon oil, and his study smelled of old books, even of the old people who came there to see him. They always brought their own scent of unrinsed soap, of dry saliva. Margaret accepted their intrusion into her neat parlour because she had no choice: John was as he was, he was a quiet philosopher, and the old people were drawn to him because he seemed more mature than his years. He'd been like that as a young man too: twenty-three going on fifty!

Margaret spoke to her neighbours and baked cakes and helped set up the women's group at the church. She didn't believe in this nonsense of the suffragettes. It was better to leave the thinking, the serious ponderings of state, to the menfolk. But it was lonely sometimes when John was in the study, writing his sermons, and she was the only one in the parlour except for the girl, Emma, who came in two hours a day to help with the cleaning. John had found her: A German Catholic, if you please! But he'd given her the job in spite of this, because she'd needed it, he'd said. Needed it for that child of hers, the one who had no father, who sometimes hung around the kitchen. Three years old and still a mess . . .

It wasn't that way with her own daughter, Jamie. Jamie Lynne, clean and well scrubbed, plump and rosy like her mother. Jamie Lynne, named for Margaret's parents, the

25

Jamisons. She was a joy, but too quiet, like her father. One could learn to overcome timidity, as she herself had; one could never overcome innate quietness. It was in the disposition.

But Jamie confounded her mother: She read. She found her father's old, gilt-edged Bible in his study. She read of Isaac and Jacob, of Ruth and Esther. What marvellous stories! She didn't like Sundays in the gloomy old church, musty and brown. She liked to walk in the park, or to climb in and out of ditches near the university. Some day, she thought, she would see what really went on in a university. She was so small and didn't understand. But as she grew, the fascination remained. Sundays were liked boiled cabbage: One had to swallow them. Papa behind the pulpit, describing things that only she, Jamie, could understand. For the farmers he was a saintly man, because he was good, in his reserved, unsmiling way, helping where he could. But they did not know, nor did they care, that he was also a poet. Jamie cared. She cared about the cadences of Papa's phrases, about his choice of images. One day he told the people that they were the salt of the earth and the light of the world, and she thought that was wonderful. Later he showed her where it had been written in the Bible. The Bible was beautiful, as beautiful as the church itself, with its rancid smells, was an eyesore and a depressant. Why had Papa become a minister? He should have written poetry, like Wordsworth, about the scenery and feelings and ideas. In her own little room, before going to have her hair washed and plaited, Jamie sometimes wrote lines of images that came to her in the afternoon: 'golden mirror of the sun', 'small slender leaves of fall', 'red and green cabbage like the rose and its leaf'. Simple things. She was only ten or twelve then. Papa was over forty and should have done better. His farmers wouldn't have missed him. Half of them didn't even understand his accent!

She was sent to public school with Emma's son, Willy.

Willy was a year and a half older than Jamie and, really, a lot prettier. Nobody knew anything about Willy's father; Emma had always pursed her lips proudly and refused to reveal a single thing. The church women wondered. He must have been part Irish, with his dark hair and blue eyes and his white skin. Not at all German, like Emma. Willy was skinny and she, Jamie, was always round. Her eyes were blue too, but of a different shade. His recalled the depths of the ocean and hers a spring sky. They went to school hand in hand, the quiet little girl with her neat brown plaits and the tallish, skinny boy with his black curls. He spoke all the time, the words tumbling out rapidly. Perhaps he spoke so much because in the house it was gloomy and his mother felt embarrassed; or perhaps it was because *her* mother, Margaret, never paid him the slightest attention and treated him as if he were an object to be stepped over on the carpet.

Jamie listened to Willy. He talked to her of his dreams, of his crazy ideas. He wanted to go to China and kill dragons. He wanted to go up in the sky in those funny air balloons. He would skip and jump and his dark eyes would sparkle, and small points of scarlet would rise to his high cheekbones – and Jamie, her face amazed, would look up at him, bewitched. How unlike anyone she knew Willy was! He was not like her quiet, bookish father; he was not like his own illiterate, hard-pressed mother; and he certainly was the opposite of Mama, her mama, who took her ideas from readers' suggestions in the brightly illustrated *Good Housekeeping* magazine. He was quick and voluble and very sensitive. Jamie could feel his sensitivity as though it were an integral part of her own: How he bristled when people looked oddly at him because he had no father. How he almost never smiled, except when they were alone. Sometimes, as they grew into their early teens, she would gently tease him and call him Heathcliff.

Margaret and Emma did not approve of their being

27

friends. Margaret did not approve of him at all – of his existence. Emma worked for other families besides the Stewarts, and surely, some must have paid her better wages. Sometimes Jamie would hear Willy repeating, in angry German, to his mother that she had no pride, remaining where she wasn't respected. Jamie didn't speak much German, but one could not help but understand a good bit of the language, growing up in Cincinnati. Emma would do that special thing with her lips, tightening them, and toss her head at her son and reply: 'But the reverend is a good man. The reverend needs me as I once needed work, and he gave it to me.' But she too felt uncomfortable that her son spent his free time with Jamie Lynne.

When she was fourteen and Willy nearly sixteen, Jamie decided that she held the key to the enigma: Willy must be her own brother. John, her strict, austere father, must have 'done something' with Emma before he'd married Mama. The notion set her mind and heart on fire: how absolutely romantic, and how dramatic for her and Willy! Brother and sister, with only the silent John and the proud Emma as witnesses. Brother and sister, growing up as daughter of the master and son of the housemaid. It would explain her own mother's disdain and literal ignoring of Willy. It would explain why Emma stubbornly remained their servant. How wonderful! She told Willy, her face aglow and her wide-set eyes a sky of shimmering stars. She did not anticipate his reaction.

They had been walking near the university, where the city merged into the hills. Suddenly he stopped, facing her, his young body taut from head to toe. She knew then that she had made a terrible mistake, telling him. He frightened her. 'Don't you understand anything,' he merely said, a spiteful statement, not a question. She shook her head: No, she really didn't understand, not this, not this look of such rage and compressed hatred. He *hated* her!

28

Very quietly, his voice shaking, he said, not looking at her: 'If it's what you think, then he simply used my mother and kept her around for years to torture her, to humiliate her. A married man can fall in love with another woman. But if a free man allows a child of his to be born without claiming it and then marries someone else, that's criminal, Jamie. It's an *insult*! My mother isn't an old garment that can simply be put away when the fashion changes! No man can exchange her so casually – especially not for someone like Miss Margaret, who thinks she's better than we are because she was born here!'

A deep flush passed over Jamie, and her eyes filled with tears. 'I'm sorry,' she whispered. 'And my papa isn't like that either. I was wrong.'

Willy shrugged. He chewed on his lower lip, looked over the curve of the hills at the city below. 'It's all right. You're just a girl.' And then he allowed his restless eyes to come to her, and she could not look away. 'A girl. It's okay, Jamie.'

'I just so wished for you to be my brother.'

'I know. But it will never be. Nothing good will ever come to me, Jamie. I'm a bastard. That's an ugly word – they don't allow it in your father's church. As for me – I don't really have a church. My mother can't go in to light a votive candle without somebody's bad thoughts reaching out to her. How do you think it makes us feel?'

'But I love you,' she said quietly, her firm young body still and strong, not moving away. 'I love you, and you and your mother love each other. My father loves you too – I know it.'

'Your father loves only his books. Not even you.'

Jamie bit her lip. 'Yes, of course he loves me.'

Willy laughed then, a mirthless sound that made Jamie feel goosepimples growing over her arms. 'Nobody loves anybody,' Willy finally said. 'I care for my mother: I respect her, for bringing me up in a rotten world. But how can I love her for allowing me to be born this way? And how can she love me, for having brought her the stares and smirks of a whole town of busybodies?'

She could not answer him. She could hardly see for the mist of tears, and so she simply laid her hand on his elbow and held it there as they resumed their walk. A beautiful dream had been splintered into glass shards, and it was difficult to avoid stepping on them.

Afterwards they did not spend so much time together. Jamie read a lot in her father's study and Willy took an after-school job in a bakery. Margaret seemed relieved. Jamie was developing into a beautiful girl, in that under-stated way of hers: curves, softness, and yet those direct blue eyes, brown hair that had hints of gold. Her mother dreamed of sending her to finishing school, but a minister did not earn enough to put money aside for an education. Jamie, meanwhile, dreamed of a *real* education, not her mother's kind. She was the brightest student in her school. All the others were the sons and daughters of German immigrants. Willy was bright too, but where would he go after he graduated? She tried not to care. It was his life, and he'd made it clear that she was no longer to meddle in it.

In the autumn of her senior year, when she was seventeen, Jamie was summoned to the principal's office. 'If you are interested,' Mr Hoffmann said, 'we could arrange for you to obtain a scholarship to a college or university. This would be a most serious step for you, Jamie. But think what it could mean! With your excellent standing, you could enter any good school.'

Jamie could feel the breath stopping in her, the ecstasy – the fear. 'What do I need to do?' she asked.

'Fill in some forms. And take a competitive examination for an honours place. Tell me – the thought had occurred to you before, hadn't it?'

She nodded. 'Yes. I'd thought of Vassar, Bryn Mawr. Maybe Barnard.'

'Good choices. But it would mean hard work, my dear.'

30

'I'm not afraid of any intellectual work. Of any sort of work. I don't want to be like my mother – ' She caught herself, suddenly ashamed. 'I didn't mean – '

But, tactfully, Mr Hoffmann was dismissing her. She floated on air. College! Just like the envied girls whose families could afford to send them. Learning . . . Papa would be pleased, so pleased. Mama would be horrified. But . . . who could turn down the offer of a scholarship from an exclusive institution? Mama would have to give in, she'd *have* to!

And Willy? Suddenly she felt sad. Willy had graduated two years before and refused to take any of the competitive examinations. She'd so hoped he would be admitted to the University of Cincinnati. Instead he had increased his job hours at the bakery to full time. She hardly ever saw him any more. People said he'd taken up with a German girl, a pretty little blonde. She was angry, then, and resentful. Willy had disappointed her. He had done everything to prove that what people said was right; that he would indeed amount to nothing. He had turned away his best friend, Jamie Lynne. Well, if that was how he was going to be, then she would certainly not tell him of her own glorious plans. They were too good to be shared with someone who had lost all his own dreams. One afternoon, after school, she stopped in the park with a book of medieval romances. She had never been in love and imagined it ardent, overpowering, tempestuous – a revolution. And then she saw the shadowed form of someone above her, and hastily, almost guiltily, she set her book down, looking up. Of course it was Willy. It had to be. She was moved and thrilled and then angry again. He had intruded.

'You still write your own poetry?' he asked.

'You're off early?' she countered.

'Boss shut down the shop. Has some kind of influenza.'

'Oh. That's nice.'

He threw back his head and laughed, that raucous,

31

mirthless laugh of his, and she could see his Adam's apple. He was tall and thin: wiry, really. He smelled a man's smell, and she could sense it from below, and it was exciting. He said: 'For him it isn't so nice. Sweet little Jamie.'

He had embarrassed her, and now she wanted to find an excuse to leave. Years of resentment welled up inside her: sweet little Jamie, indeed! He'd rejected her as a sister, as a friend. Now he sat down beside her, and her first reaction was to pull away. But he was wiping his brow, sighing. 'I'm so tired,' he said simply.

'You don't like your life?'

'I don't like it, and I don't *not* like it. It's just a life.'

'But life is supposed to be joyful – if you can learn to take hold of it.'

'Straight from the lips of her papa, the good reverend.'

'I'm quite serious. Don't waste it.'

He narrowed his eyes at her and said tersely: 'Don't lecture me, Jamie. I don't need it and I don't like it.'

'No, of course not! You're wiser and more intelligent than us all, and you never need anything or anybody!' Now the anger came tumbling out of her, and her surprise at its vehemence was as great as his. She moved closer to him, took his chin in her firm young fingers, looked hard into his eyes. 'You're nothing but a loser,' she finally stated with disgust.

The muscles tightened in his shoulders, in his arms. 'So. After years of friendship, it all comes out. You're ashamed of me too, because of what I am.'

'Not of what you are – of who you've become! What do I care who your father is, or if your mother scrubs floors? But I can't be friends with a fellow who won't respect himself. Does she let you do this – what's her name?'

'Eva. No. Eva and I don't talk.' He laughed a little, but this time in a more private manner, a low chuckle. 'Talking was with you.'

32

'And you got bored and threw me away.'

Willy noticed for the first time that she was still holding him by the chin, and she dropped her hand, embarrassed again. But this time he picked it up with strong, blunt fingers of his own. 'Oh, Jamie,' he murmured. 'Jamie, Jamie. I never threw you away. We drifted our separate ways, as people do when they grow up.'

'Why must they?' she asked earnestly.

'I don't really know.'

In the stillness that followed, there was awkwardness, sadness, and a hint of something else. Jamie wanted him to leave and wanted him to stay, and could feel the pulse beating in her wrists. When he bent toward the round softness of her neck, above the white starched schoolgirl collar, she was not really surprised, and wanted to feel his lips on her skin. She made a little sound and lifted her face to his, and then he kissed her. She wanted to weep, she wanted the release, and yet her tongue wanted the taste of more, and it was as if she were being sucked inside a marvellous deep velvet cave. It was hot and warm and burning and lovely, and it was the spring sunshine on her naked arms, on her naked limbs. If there was pain when they finally came together, when they had made sense of all the buttons and hooks on their respective clothing, the pain was welcome too, although unexpected. He knew what to do although she did not. He wanted her not to know. He had entered a hidden place where none had come before him, and she understood that he wanted to explore it with the miracle of discovery. 'I love you,' he said, and she nodded, because they had always loved each other, because it was right.

During the next month Jamie and Willy made love again, many times, whenever and wherever they could. She hoped that he would reconsider taking the exams, but she dared not ask him to do it for her sake. Changing a person was an intrusion and an error: You were who you were, true only to yourself. And she did not tell him about her own plans. She had no real reason for not telling him, except that, somehow, inside, it felt right not to speak. And so when he finally said, a month later, 'Marry me, Jamie,' she knew. She knew with certainty, and she knew with pain, and she knew with numbing fear.

'I can't,' she answered.

'You can't? But why?'

She then turned aside, weeping. 'Because I'm going to Vassar in the autumn. I'm going East to college.'

'Then – I suppose I'll wait. You'll come back, won't you?'

She felt as though she were being torn apart. 'No. I can't return here, Willy. I don't want to live in Cincinnati. And you – you don't have your magic dreams any more, and without them we wouldn't have the right sort of life together.'

His fury did not surprise her. 'Dreams! *Dreams?* This is a rotten life, Jamie, a life of lies and cheating. But I love you. Why should you leave me after this? Don't you know how much my mother would have envied you? That man, whoever he was, simply took what he wanted and vanished, but I want you to be my *wife!*'

'I know. But that isn't the right reason either, Willy. You wanted to prove that you were different and better than him, and I want something else. I don't know what. Maybe independence. You can't be independent in the American Midwest. Of course I love you – I always have.'

He was standing up, red in the face, and brushing off the burrs from his clothing. Oh, she thought, I hurt too! I don't want to give you up. I don't want to lose what we have either! And yet . . . marriage . . . It didn't matter any more, because he had left, and she could see his footprints in the soft green sward.

Jamie Stewart wondered then when the pain would go away, or if it ever would. Love. It didn't make sense. Nothing made sense. But at the same time, she knew that she had made the only possible decision. For that very morning Mr Hoffmann had announced to her that Vassar had accepted her as a scholarship student. There was no turning back, not from this.

Place de l'Etoile was called the Barrière de l'Etoile, and beyond it Paris ended. Several of the twelve avenues bore different names. Avenue Victor Hugo was called Avenue de l'Impératrice, after the beautiful Eugénie, and its left pavement was three feet lower than its right one. The road itself was bisected lengthwise, and the right half a yard higher than the left. Six of the elegant town houses between the avenues had already been erected, and it was there, in the sixth, that the Marquis Adrien de Varenne had settled with his family. Adrien's son Robert-Achille was born in it in 1855.

But the house, for all its stateliness, was not large enough. Adrien made a petition to build a seventh mansion, between Avenues Wagram and MacMahon. Yes, the authorities told him, he would be able to do so, so long as the new façade matched the other six. And so, in 1867, the Varenne clan moved to grander quarters. From the road people saw three storeys in white sandstone, simple and streamlined, with different masonry around the windows of each floor. The ground floor was all bays; the first, rectangular panes topped with a decorative triangle of Greek style; and the second, a series of shorter rectangles adorned with curlicues of scroll-like appearance. Then came a double parapet, and highest of all the 'attic', in grey-blue tiles, its square windows jutting out, protected by triangular eaves of the same stone. Each storey possessed at least twenty windows, some with grilled balconies, others with pillared, Doric ones. The first and the second became living quarters; on the ground floor were the ballroom and reception halls; and in the attic, the servants slept.

35

The main entrance was on the dark, circular street behind the house. On the Etoile side the ground fell abruptly, and there were two enormous rooms facing a garden. On the street side this apartment was a basement without windows. It provided the ideal 'bachelor's quarters', and the Marquis Adrien reserved them for his son and his son's tutor. The young Count Robert-Achille was most relieved that his rooms faced the sunny Barrière, so that he could watch the dainty carriages that drove by Napoleon's Arch of Triumph; especially he loved the pretty ladies inside the carriages. Tall plane trees bordered the pavement beyond the iron grillwork that protected the garden, and pigeons settled around them, completing a picture of peaceful harmony.

A Renaissance man, the marquis had placed a copy of Michelangelo's Moses in the vestibule, between the two circular staircases that wound to the first floor. He was a tall man, well built and imposing, and had connections in high finance and government. Long ago the Varenne family had been intimates of the Bourbon kings; he himself, though disdainful of their plebeian origins, had befriended Napoleon III and Eugénie; or so he always phrased it, conscious that his was the truer blue blood. For he never hid the fact that he was still a monarchist: The Varennes had been royalists for centuries, since the days of the Crusades.

Robert-Achille did not resemble his father. From the start he had been a disappointment to Adrien. He was, first of all, short – too short for a Varenne. His head was round like a ball, and his small nose pointed upward like a trumpet. His lips were thickly sensual, and a weakness in the eyes made him blink too much. He was not handsome, to be sure; but he was well dressed, and in his high-buttoned frock coat trimmed with braid and heavily starched choker collar and silk cravat, he seemed aristocratic in spite of his ugliness. What distressed Adrien more was his

36

son's predilection for not studying and for carousing in Montmartre with the sons of other noblemen, similarly disinclined to be serious. Robert-Achille went out every night, drank champagne and gambled, and often the next day a bill would be delivered for broken furniture and windows in an establishment of ill repute. Adrien paid it and hid the fact from his marquise.

In the eighties a Baroness von Ridenour arrived from Vienna, with her daughter, Charlotte. Charlotte was twenty-one and a rare beauty. Her hair was thick and black, her face pale and narrow, with azure eyes under arched brows. Her nose was regular and fine, her mouth well drawn, with small white teeth and a pearlescent skin. She was tall, shapely in a slender fashion, and her bearing was regal, almost arrogantly so. Adrien de Varenne fell in love with her by proxy – that is, she was too fine a lady to be made a mistress of his own, but she appeared perfect as a prospective wife for his wayward son. The fact that the Baroness von Ridenour had lost her fortune did not disturb the marquis: Charlotte's beauty, her poise, and the obvious strength of her character impressed him sufficiently for him to overlook the matter of dowry. And for Charlotte's mother, this was an opportunity not even hoped for. How could she have thought to marry off a daughter without the appropriate wedding monies?

Charlotte was not so eager to marry the unattractive Robert-Achille, but he did present her with a luxurious alternative to her previous life of quiet retirement in Vienna. He had a name and a fortune, and that was infinitely preferable to a name without means. Besides, he had fallen totally in love with her: she, a foreigner whom nobody knew in the elegant Parisian circles. She was excited at the notion of being at last a rich and independent woman. For Robert-Achille would not restrain her: He would be too busy with his disreputable friends, and besides, she was the dominating partner, without a doubt.

She accepted his marriage proposal. Time was of the essence. At her age one had to grab one's opportunities without weighing them too seriously. Beautiful though she was, there were others as lovely who possessed large dowries.

This union was to be one of the most disastrous of the century.

Proud of his wife, whose smile was a veritable enchantment, whose ways were so engaging and sweet, and especially proud of the fact that she had accepted him in spite of his size and lack of distinction, Robert-Achille, Count de Varenne, took Charlotte every night to Montmartre to show her off to his dandy friends. Robert-Achille was not very bright and had little ability to think things through. Charlotte, on the other hand, was a remarkable opportunist. Admired and courted for the first time in her life, adored by her husband's friends, she suddenly became aware of her extraordinary beauty and of how she might gain from it. The finesse, charm, joyful spirit that were lacking in Robert-Achille, she soon found elsewhere. Life could be a never-ending diversion. On the one hand she was wealthy and lived as a queen; on the other there was love and intrigue. Happiness made her even more beautiful.

She came to hate her husband. Robert-Achille irritated and disgusted her in so many ways that she could barely tolerate to be in the same room with him. Whenever the Varennes were invited to a château for a weekend or a hunt, she never accepted a room with him, but would upset the plans of the hosts by demanding quarters as far away as possible.

Some years later she became pregnant. Fear overtook her. First of all, the child might look like her husband. Of course, the Marquis Adrien was a most distinguished-looking specimen. She had often noticed him, and knew that he was not indifferent to her either. But, second, who would want her now, *enceinte*? She would have to hide herself

38

for the last few months. Rage shook her. Life had grown too pleasant to suddenly have it change, and all because, out of ridiculous duty, a woman had to submit several times a week to the disgusting ministrations of the man whose name she bore. But when the child was born, in 1890, it turned out to be a slender, elegant baby boy, and for a while she was pleased with him. She called him Alexandre. The name rang regal and sounded good in every language. She was pleased also to have finally delivered him and to be once again young, shapely, and available.

The following year a second son came. He did not look like her, as Alex did, nor did he look like anyone in Robert-Achille's family. He was plump and strong and bold-featured, and his hair was glossy and richly brown. She name him Paul, a name that suited him by its shining brevity. Adrien de Varenne watched this new grandson carefully. He seemed almost British in his appearance, a small Lord Fauntleroy.

Charlotte said nothing, but at Maxim's and in Montmartre, others talked. And everyone remembered that the Prince of Wales, Bertie, had made a sojourn in Paris and had resided on Avenue Foch, only a mile away from the Varenne mansion. Had he come alone, or with a friend? No one could quite recall. Charlotte, wise woman, let the rumour run its course. If she ever cared about Paul, her conscience could rest assured of her utmost selectivity in the matter of her lovers. Perhaps she should have felt more guilty toward Alex. For, after all, she had handed down through her own body the seed of the repulsive Robert-Achille.

It was obvious to everyone that Charlotte de Varenne cared only for herself. Her children were a nuisance, but it was unbecoming in a lady to admit this to her friends. And so, in front of society, she paraded the little boys, impeccably dressed and coiffed, and made motherly noises. They were beautiful children: Alex, tall and quiet, resembled her, and Paul was a plump, rosy, happy boy. The fact that she had produced such comely offspring was an asset to be displayed at the right moments, like precious but bothersome accoutrements worn to enhance her beauty.

From the beginning the boys reacted differently to their mother. Her temper tantrums with the servants flared up almost daily. Alex would watch her from his crib, where he was tentatively attempting to stand up and appraise the world around him. Screams were physically painful to him. He was a sensitive child, aware of changes in smells from the kitchen, in voices when nurses left and were replaced. Paul, on the other hand, made a great deal of noise himself, banging on doors and tables, trying to imitate, with ferocious glee, the shouts and screams that emanated from his mother. He did it to be like her, because she was beautiful; he also did it because from the first moment, he realized how much such behaviour offended his brother. And although Charlotte bestowed her few kisses on him rather than Alex, Paul nevertheless wished that his brother would disappear and leave him alone with his mother. Their father was such a nonentity that even as babies they both ignored him.

Alexandre admired his grandfather, and was sad for the first time when Adrien died. But amid the mourning he was aware of a certain contentment. For, as in all French families of high lineage, with the old man's death his title would be passed on to his son. Count Robert-Achille became a marquis. Alex himself went up a rung, from viscount to count, and his little brother from baron to viscount. Charlotte was delighted to become a marquise, but irritated that it was her elder son who was entitled to the higher title. But for little Alex, who was five, the ceremony was imprinted on his overdeveloped conscience. If he was now a count, he would one day rise to be a marquis. And the family name would rest on his shoulders, as a mantle of responsibility. He was a child who was

40

careful never to spill a drop, never to forget to put away his toys. This way his mother – so beautiful, and so impossible to please! – might perhaps remember him when it was time for the good-night kiss. But so often, no matter how hard he tried, she forgot nevertheless.

On the night after the burial of Adrien de Varenne, little Alex came up to his mother, alone in her boudoir, and said seriously: 'Now that I am a count, Mama, I'll take good care of you.' She smiled, unexpectedly. He would remember that smile during the whole of his adolescence. She, that angel with the black hair and scintillating blue eyes, she whom all men bent over in their haste to kiss her jewelled hand, had smiled at him, Alex, the one she didn't love. Then, maybe, after all, there was a small reserve of affection somewhere in her heart. The key to producing it seemed to be to take care of her. He would be sure to do that. He would be sure to honour her, to guard her, as God had told him in his sacred commandment. For he believed that God was watching him at every point and was recording his doings in a neat ledger. He would do good things, so that God would reward him with one of Charlotte's kisses.

When he was six, a good thing happened, although for years to come he was not able to remember why. His father had been away on a hunting expedition and the governess had been ill with influenza, in a separate wing of the house. A sudden storm had broken out, and Alex was rudely awakened. Paul was still sleeping, impervious to the thunder and lightning, as he always was to any great noise. But Alex felt tremors passing through his small body, and even though big boys who had started school were not supposed to cry, the tears sprang to his eyes, and he jumped out of bed, his heart pounding.

No one was there. He began to panic and to sob. In his bare feet he padded out of the nursery. Mademoiselle – the current one – was ill, he remembered. He rushed out into the corridor and was even more scared by the lighted oil

41

paintings of his forefathers. All at once he stopped, hearing laughter. The low, gentle laughter of a woman. His mother? But Mama never laughed, not with him and Paul, and amongst her friends her laugh was brittle as she hid half her face behind an antique fan. This laughter was so attractive, so charming, that Alex wanted to be part of it, wanted to see who was laughing so generously, so merrily. He walked on tiptoe to a closed door and stopped. The laughter came from behind that door.

Dare he enter? Suppose his mother found out? Yet he was only six, and the mystery was too appealing to be left alone. He tried to turn the knob, but it resisted. Silence replaced the laughter, and now the old fear took possession of the small boy. A voice that was hard and shrill, his mother's voice, said: 'Who's there? What is it?'

'It's me, Alexandre,' he replied, starting again to sob. He was bewildered. The laughter and his mother were together in that room. Yet the one could not possibly belong to the other. And now he would be caught, and punished. The door swung open, and the child fell back, stunned. An elegant gentleman was leaning out, peering at him. Alexandre didn't think he'd ever seen him before.

The man, unlike his father, was tall and smart, with shining brown hair and a fine face with twinkling eyes. 'Well, young one,' he declared, 'what seems to be the problem?'

The gentleman was wearing a silk kimono open around his chest. Behind him Alex could see his mother, in her nightgown, pink satin trimmed with lace. The gentleman was holding a brandy snifter in one hand and the door with the other. He was smiling. Yet Alex was terrified.

'I – I was scared,' he stammered. 'The storm woke me up – '

'Send him back, for God's sake, Bertrand,' Charlotte was saying with annoyance. 'Can't you see the little fool's a coward?'

42

But the man's eyes were gentle on Alex, who was shrinking away from his mother's voice. He said, looking only at the child: 'I myself used to be afraid of lightning when I was small. And nobody has ever dared to call *me* a coward. Come in, young man.'

'Are you out of your mind, Bertrand?' Charlotte screamed, rising in a fury.

The gentleman placed a protective hand over Alex's head and looked directly into Charlotte's angry blue eyes. He said: 'I'm sorry, darling, but I don't like the thought of frightened children. He can come to bed with us for a while, until the worst of the storm is over.'

Alexandre was flabbergasted. This was such a nice, friendly man, and even his mother wasn't shouting any more. She didn't want to argue with the nice man, was perhaps afraid her tantrums would drive him away. And he *was* such a nice, handsome man that Alex could well understand her. He too wanted him to stay in the house.

And so, for two hours, little Alexandre was permitted to lie beneath the satin sheets and the great quilt, and the gentleman held him close. Alex's mother remained quiet. The child wished that she too would hold him, but this was the nicest thing that had ever happened to him in his entire life. He wanted to remain there all night, breathing his mother's perfume and the scent of brandy and cigars on the gentleman's breath.

Later, when he was nine years old, he was leaving the Lycée Condorcet when he saw that same gentleman again, riding across the avenue on a fine black stallion, a gold-studded riding crop in his hand. The current governess was not a mademoiselle, but a German Fräulein, and Alex, tugging at her sleeve, said to her: 'Who is he? I know him!'

'Yes, who is he, who is he?' Paul took up as a refrain. 'He looks like the King of England!'

The governess laughed. 'No, he's not British,' she answered. 'He's a friend of your parents, I believe. All of

Paris knows him. He collects beautiful paintings, and they say his apartments are a thing of wonder. His name is the Chevalier Bertrand de la Paume. I've never actually met him, but – '

'*I* have!' Alex suddenly cried, the blood rushing to his cheeks. 'When I was little,' he broke out excitedly, his eyes shining like Charlotte's, 'he took me into bed with him and my mama!'

All colour drained from the Fräulein's face, and at once Alex realized that he had committed a grave error. He didn't understand what he had said that was so wrong, but knew only that it was an irreparable gaffe. Fräulein was bending down, taking his shoulders in her firm hands and whispering. 'Alexandre, you must never, never repeat this story. To anyone, do you hear? The honour of your family is at stake. Your mother's – your father's!'

'What has any of this to do with Father?' Alex asked.

'Everything!' Fräulein retorted, and now her cheeks were bright red. She hustled the children along and refused to exchange another word on the subject. Alex felt deeply ashamed. Somehow he had threatened the honour of his mother – and he had promised her, and God, that he would always take care of her. What had he done?

From that moment Alexandre was careful never to speak before he had thought everything through. He saw the gentleman again, but never dared to look him in the eye. He knew, somehow, that this man, whom he had thought so kind and friendly, was in reality a danger to his mother, to his whole family. Later Alex grew to hate the Chevalier de la Paume, who had brought such pleasant laughter to his mother. He grew to hate him and also to be a little afraid to talk openly to anyone about anything. If the family could be hurt through one innocent phrase . . .

As he entered adulthood and the pieces of the puzzle became clear to him, he became afraid to look at his mother, for what she had done had been very wrong, a

44

cardinal sin. But still, she was his mother, and try as he might, he could not abandon her.

A short time later, in 1902, it was eleven-year-old Paul who stumbled into Robert-Achille's study and found him dead, his head bleeding upon the desk, the blood seeping into the Aubusson carpet. It was Paul who stood clutching the wall, vomiting; it was Paul whom everyone pitied for years to come, who described the revolver on the desk, who saw the letter but could not read it for the blood. Charlotte read it. While the scandal erupted, she wore black and kept her eyes downcast. Robert-Achille's suicide was a mystery to no one, least of all to his elder son.

The family honour was at stake, centuries of Varenne blood, spilled now so wretchedly, yet once spilled in the great cause of the Christian Crusades. Adrien had died, and Robert-Achille was better off dead. Now the only Marquis de Varenne was a twelve-year-old boy called Alexandre.

As for Charlotte, she had new calling cards printed, which read: 'Marquise de Varenne'. As a widow she no longer needed her husband's first names as marks of identification. She shed them gracefully, as easily as she shed her widow's weeds the following year. Of that fact, some men were sorry, for never before had a woman shown such elegance in mourning. But Charlotte was at last free, and rich in her own right.

Chapter Two

She was tall, statuesque like Minerva, with thick black hair that fell straight down her back, uncurled by the Marcel wave. Her high white brow, her full lips over strong white teeth, the prominent cheekbones tinged with red from the Siberian cold, all were characteristics of a Tatar maiden, willing to take all risks and laugh defeat in the face. Or so people said in the small Siberian village when first they laid eyes upon Princess Elena Sergeievna Egorova. She was nineteen years old, and it was 1909.

It had not always been this way. Tears of anger burned on the edge of her eyelids when she remembered the Nevsky Prospect, the balls, the Mariinsky and Alexandrinsky theatres: St Petersburg. She, the only daughter of Prince Sergei Egorov, had been treated like a young queen then. He was the chief aide and confidant to Peter Stolypin. In 1904 Stolypin had been Minister of the Interior, but in 1906 the Tsar, Nicholas II, had appointed him premier. Prince Sergei had been his closest friend and associate. Elena could recall so well every article in the study where the two men used to confer, and which she alone was allowed to enter, bearing the tea tray. She listened, and she never forgot. She had been, even then, a young woman of rare mettle.

Elena had gone to Paris with her family, to add to her wardrobe for the coming winter season. At eighteen, she had recently made her debut in the elegant society of the Russian capital and had been ready to conquer the Parisian capital too, much to the distress of her paid companion, Fräulein Borchner. Elena was so much taller, so much more striking than other girls her age, and when men turned round in the street to watch her, she would smile widely and

46

tilt her head charmingly to one side. It was deliciously brazen. She was easily bored, courtly life became dull after a few dances. She wished, more than anything, that she'd been born a man. How she envied her father! He played with continents and moved soldiers around the map like pawns on a chessboard. But she'd been born a woman, and a beautiful one at that. And so she thought: Let them love me. Let them work for me without knowing they are.

Upon their return to St Petersburg, the Egorovs were informed that revolutionary anarchists had set a bomb to Stolypin's villa on the suburban isle of Elaghin. All had perished, but their friend had not been in his home. Elena's mother, the fragile Princess Ekaterina, wanted to leave the country for good. The Prince hesitated, profoundly shaken. Elena persuaded them to stay. She cried out, her eyes wide with outraged pride: 'We are Russians! We cannot also be cowards!'

But the bomb had been merely the beginning. It was followed by a series of unexpected government shakeups, and then, all at once – disaster. Her father was seized in the middle of the night and thrown into the Fortress of Peter and Paul, the strictest of all Russian prisons. Suddenly the telephone no longer rang. Elena was not invited to cotillions, she was snubbed in the street. 'High treason!' people whispered. Elena heard everything yet kept her elegant head high. She was angry and she was humiliated. Most of all she did not understand. Stolypin no longer came to the beautiful palace where Prince Egorov lived, not far from the Tsar's own Winter Palace. Stolypin refused to save his dearest friend, and Elena realized they had been betrayed.

In winter there came the official judgment. Prince Sergei Egorov was condemned to exile in Siberia for having revealed matters of state of the most secret kind. Elena stood in the courtroom and wanted to scream. She did not, but her eyes revealed her anger and her pain. She said nothing, but gripped her mother's cold fingers in her own and vowed that never again would anybody get the better of an Egorov. Never again. *She* would bleed *them*, all of them. Their friends had deserted them. The three young men who had proposed marriage to her had announced their engagements to three other young beauties of St Petersburg. No one would ever slap the face of Elena Egorova again: She would see to that.

She was pleased then with her resilience. Had her little brother survived the spinal meningitis that had felled him ten years before, she was certain that he would have been weaker, like her parents. Prince Sergei, however, was broken. And the Princess took to her little house and became a recluse, prostrate in her degradation. They'd been sent to Minusinsk, a miserable village near Krasnoyarsk, in eastern Siberia. The two princesses had never handled physical work before. Now they hired a young peasant girl to clean the rooms and cook. But the first time that Liza served them a chicken, she boiled it without removing either its organs or its feathers. Elena saw the horror on her mother's face and the disgust on her father's. She knew what they were thinking, but she refused to give in to the temptation of 'going back'. The only way they would survive would be to grasp strongly onto the present: They were still alive. The Tsar might have condemned Prince Sergei to death. So Elena took an empty plate and used it for discarding the feathers. She carved the bird, dug out the gizzard and entrails, and deftly stuffed them behind the feathers so as not to turn her mother's stomach. Quickly she sailed into the kitchen and showed an astounded housemaid what one did with such unwanted materials, and then she returned, triumphant. 'I'm starved,' she announced. And she began to cut into her meat. Her parents remained staring, open-mouthed. But Elena knew that one ate to survive, especially in the depths of Siberia where water crystallized into shards of ice as one washed one's face.

The Prince was soon playing cards with the mayor, the pharmacist and the teacher. But Elena and her mother embroidered silently in their house. Sometimes the young woman went for a long walk. In winter the snow was so thick that it almost prevented one from going outside. The cold was intense, but the sky was blue, the sun shone, though without heat. Yet there was absolutely no wind and so one could brave the low temperatures more easily. Elena found the houses overheated. In the spring the village became a muddy cesspool with puddles. Summer, however, turned the country into a fairyland for four months. The peasants tilled and sowed, the wheat grew and matured, and there was time to reap and make hay twice before autumn came. The wind caressed the steppe, bearing its scents of sweetness. It was dotted with a multitude of diverse flowers, bursting with colour, often overpowering in their perfume. Besides the daisies, goldenrod and red, white, yellow, orange, pink and blue flowers unknown to the rest of the European continent, there were wild lilies and gentians. Elena escaped from her mother's hermitage by exploring the surrounding nature. She was not searching for God but for a way out.

After a year the Prince's situation improved. He was transferred to Krasnoyarsk. It was a true city. As with all the rivers of Russia, the eastern bank of the Yenisey was flat, while its west was a high cliff. Sharp rocks fell into the water, scarlet and green rocks, for these were mountains of porphyry and malachite.

But, as with most provincial Russian cities, the pavements were made of wood, the houses only had a single storey and there was neither electricity nor a sewage system. There were schools, however, and literary clubs, a theatre, artistic circles and a piano in almost every home. Mail arrived daily, the public library was well furnished, and several nations had sent their consuls to this Siberian city. For the Prince, this meant a greater intellectual life;

for the Princess, an ability to socialize if not with her peers, then at least with women who knew some of the ways of the world. But for Elena, this represented only a continuation, an underscoring of the injustice that had been levied against her family. Krasnoyarsk might have been more bearable physically; but emotionally it was no different from the village of Minusinsk. She was twenty years old, and her old friends were all making brilliant marriages in the capital; she was vegetating in Siberia.

When Elena was twenty-four, the war broke out. In the remote parts of Siberia, it was hardly felt. She watched her father as he rather pompously 'broke off' relations with the Prussian consul. Prince Sergei fundamentally still felt a part of his country's government. Elena's heart constricted for him – but she had also begun to despise him. She thought: I must get out of here.

She was surprised that she felt no pain from her decision. She sensed relief, even exhilaration at the notion of change – but not the hurt of previous times, when she had felt herself growing detached from her parents. She was a woman now, and on her own. There could be no last-minute hesitation – she'd have to leave Krasnoyarsk for good. The only unresolved issue was how to accomplish this? For she possessed no assets but her striking looks, and no talents but her will to survive.

One day she was passing the time in a small teahouse on the edge of town when the thick outer door swung open and gay voices filtered through the tearoom. Elena looked up, gasped, and looked again. Two pretty women in their thirties, wrapped in furs, were shaking the snow from their coats, fluffing their hair under their elegant toque hats and sitting down at a small table toward the front. Elena was mesmerized. These women, with their bright faces, the diamond pendants on their ears, didn't belong in Krasnoyarsk, let alone in this godforsaken teahouse. They were from St Petersburg, or Moscow, or, at the very least, Kiev.

Elena wanted to be with them, to breathe their French perfume, to hear what it was like in the city that they had obviously so recently left. Unable to resist, she stood and moved across the room toward the women.

And then Elena was near them, speaking to them, her voice trembling slightly. 'I am Princess Elena Sergeievna Egorova,' she said to them, conscious of the tilt of her head as she pronounced the noble name and of how she herself, with her marvellous black hair loose over her shoulders, contrasted with the outdated seal pelisse that she was still wearing – a remnant of better days. She could taste the salt of her own bitterness but also the excitement of having found these women, who belonged to that past, perhaps.

The younger one had lovely brown eyes, soft brown hair and fair skin. The two resembled each other, but the other woman, whose nose was a tiny bit larger, had skin that was darker, more sultry. It was she who looked up first, who smiled, whose face mirrored the apparent pleasure of this aristocratic introduction. She replied in a gentle voice: 'We are the Adlers – Evgenia Borisovna, my sister; and I am Fania. We're from Moscow – you may have recognized it by our accent.'

The other said: 'Please, sit down and join us for a glass of tea. Do you live here?'

The intense humiliation with which Elena had learned to exist, returned in a flood. She cleared her throat, swallowed back tears of remembrances. 'Yes,' she answered.

'You're very beautiful,' Fania commented frankly. 'Like a rare painting. Our father had a most wondrous collection at home. There was a French painter whom he had discovered in Paris, drinking himself to death – Modigliani, was it, Genia?'

'I believe so, Modi-something. But you are embarrassing the Princess, Fanny.'

'No, please. It was a great compliment. I haven't been

51

to France for several years. I miss it very much. I used to go each year, of course . . .'

'Of course. But Genia and I are tired of the usual travel routes. We're on our way to China this time. The war – Europe seems blighted now, all the men dying on the fronts . . .'

'Yes.' Elena fidgeted with her fingers and a piece of lace on the tablecloth. How did one avoid telling them about her father, when any stranger might inform them the next day? She knew she couldn't lie. But she also couldn't admit the truth. She felt hot waves of shame and realized that she was growing to hate the man she had so loved, this father whose exile had so shamed her and her mother. She wasn't sure he'd done what he'd been accused of. It didn't matter. What mattered was that he had been caught and sent away. Therein, more than in the dubious question of guilt, lay the shame.

Adler, Fania Borisovna had said. Adler – a German name. Or a Jewish one? From beneath lowered lashes she examined her companions. Yes, they might very well be Jewish, with their noses curving delicately down. Rich Jewish women from the gold ghetto. Slowly, realizing that if indeed these were Jews, they would have a common ground – that of being forever on the outside looking into society – she murmured: 'We suffered a terrible tragedy in our family. My little brother died. My parents were never able to recuperate from their loss. And so, although my father had a most important job in one of the ministries in St Petersburg, he couldn't face the capital any longer. He's happy enough here – but I am very much alone. There is no future in Krasnoyarsk.'

'Oh, my dear, how simply awful,' Fania replied. The waitress brought Elena a glass of tea, removed the Adlers' empty ones. Everyone was silent. Elena thought: I have said too much. They will suspect me. One doesn't spill so intimate a story to two strangers on first sight.

'It's really amazing,' Genia was commenting, 'how when we suffer, we hold it in so well in our natural surroundings. Then, suddenly, when we're out of our element, the truth comes flowing out of us. It's so much easier to tell one's problems to a total stranger – someone who has no place whatsoever in our lives. I can empathize so acutely with the Princess's story. Do you feel it too, Fanny?'

I've won! Elena thought, turning red from her unexpected joy at Genia's thoughts. Fania was saying: 'Yes, absolutely. The Princess lives her tragedy – her dreadful isolation – daily, with the same anonymous crowds around her. The way we did during Papa's lifetime. And look at us now . . .'

Elena didn't understand, and so she was quiet, sipping her tea. The Adlers didn't continue, didn't bother to elucidate. Theirs was the real truth, and therefore they were more reserved, more guarded. She looked directly at Fania, asked: 'Will you be here long?' She could feel the tightness returning to her throat and wished she could cry out: No, you must stay! You are my past, my future – My *future*? But how?

'A few days. Then we go to Irkutsk, and then to Harbin. We're on our way to Shanghai, where we hope not to hear the word "war" mentioned. Actually it's peaceful here – '

'But too much peace can dull the mind, the senses. Allow me to call on you at your hotel – ' I mustn't beg. Elena told herself. I must seem in control . . . She clenched her hands into fists on her lap, but kept her eyes clear, her smile perfect.

'Wonderful! Here's our address. Would you care to meet us tomorrow for tea? But not here. We shall take it in our rooms, which are infinitely better decorated than . . . this.' Genia moved her head, encompassing the room in one gesture. She took out a piece of paper from her fine leather bag, extracted a small silver pen, and wrote down the information.

53

Elena took it. She felt, in the instant of contact, a shock close to electricity, as if something beyond her scope was warning her that this was the way out of exile, out of the Siberian wasteland. She stood up, hoping the Adlers wouldn't stare too much at her old coat, and extended her hand, first to Fania, then to her sister. 'I shall come. It was so delightful to meet you. We shall talk of Paris and of Moscow. But perhaps not, because the war is so much on all our minds. Instead we'll talk about your trip, we'll feast on pagodas and rickshaws – '

'Yes, we shall!' Fania agreed warmly. Neither of the Adlers was even looking at her pelisse, and inwardly Elena sighed with relief. She inclined her head, smiled once more, and departed, striding as was her custom. Her heart was knocking inside her with suppressed excitement. Yet she couldn't explain her feelings in any concrete, reasonable terms. The Adlers were the opportunity seized on the cuff, the shower of gold captured in an instant – a propitious instant. When Fate extended her hand, one had to grasp it without a second's hesitation . . .

The next day she dressed carefully, simply but well. She had never worn the frills that women had enjoyed in the past, because she knew she looked better in clothes that would offset her unusual beauty without offering competition of their own. The Adlers were waiting for her, and there was a marvellous array of cakes in the salon of their suite. Elena began to talk, pleasantly, of teas she had attended in the past, of the Tsarina Alexandra, of her sister, the Grand-Duchess Ella, who had become a nun after her husband's vicious murder. But she skipped quickly on to the subject of art, of concerts, of dances, for the Tsar was not only a sore subject to her, but also surely to her hostesses if they were Jewish. She asked questions, laughed, ate, but all the time she existed outside herself, watching herself consciously pretending to be carefree. At the end of the afternoon she consulted a small gold watch that was

54

pinned to her jacket, and she murmured: 'I must go! I hope that you will still be in town tomorrow?'

'Oh, certainly. Will you come back, Princess Elena?'

'It would be my pleasure.'

Outside, hugging her old coat to her sides, she wondered: But how much longer shall I be able to act the part of Scheherazade and detain them from leaving? She thought of the bureau in the bedroom of their hotel, and of the fabrics and jewels literally spilling from its drawers. Her mouth was wet with hunger, and her nerves were on edge.

Jamie felt immense peace of mind at Vassar. From her room in Main Hall, she could see the autumn leaves gathering in romantic piles over the hills. She liked to walk to class past the old stone buildings. There was security at Vassar, security in its past, security in its own future and, therefore, in hers too. She had felt closed in by Cincinnati, by the world of her mother and father. Now she felt free, limitless, like a blank page on which anything could be written.

She was rooming with a girl who was as different from her as anyone could ever be, Jamie thought. Lesley Aymes Richardson was so small, so elegant, so utterly graceful in the simplest movement she executed – in hanging her fox cape in the wardrobe, in pulling down the cuffs of her starched bishop sleeves. Sometimes Jamie envied her. Lesley was so perfect, like a doll that sits on top of a musical box, turning and turning, without fault unless its owner forgot to wind the key underneath the box. Lesley was a quiet girl, reserved yet friendly. She had beautiful skin, the translucent skin of natural redheads, and long, silky hair that every morning she parted with her silver and ivory comb, let fall over the ears, and swooped in one single gesture into a knot at the back, secured with pins and flowers. Her eyes were a brilliant green, flecked with gold,

55

and she wore a large emerald on her left ring finger. She moved her hands, fluttered them in the air, when she spoke. And sometimes when Jamie returned from class she would find Lesley sketching by the window, a look of absorption on her triangular face. It was difficult to guess what she thought, or where she wished her life to proceed.

Lesley didn't talk much about her family, but everyone at Vassar courted her, wanting her to join the most exclusive sororities, because her father was a millionaire in New York City and her mother was the only daughter of a British peer of ancient lineage. Yet Lesley seemed to float above this, smiling slightly at Jamie and saying almost apologetically: 'It's all such nonsense, isn't it? Everyone wants to "belong". It's the country-club syndrome all over again. We all think we're so much better if we can say that So and So belongs to the same institution as we do – but that has no meaning.'

Jamie wondered what did have meaning for this pretty girl. She went to Yale and Harvard and Williams just like the other rich girls, and there were letters from young men in the mailbox several times a week. There were telephone calls from her mother, and Jamie noticed that every time they came, Lesley's face would close into a tight, hard line. Those from her father produced an opposite reaction. Oh, well, thought Jamie, I can't stand Mother either, but Father is of a different breed. Perhaps, after all, she and her roommate weren't so different beneath their appearances.

Jamie didn't much care how she dressed. Skirts had risen in 1915 to reveal the ankle, and women's dresses were of a loose, ample style that suited her own voluptuous build rather well. But she possessed only a few outfits. She didn't want to be introduced to eligible young men, because she wanted above all to earn her degree. Willy remained an ache in her heart. It was difficult not to give in to the desire to write to him. I wonder if I was really in love with him, she thought, or if we were simply so used to each other that things just developed the way they did because that was the logical outcome. She felt a certain detachment from Lesley and the other girls, because she had slept with a man, and, for the most part, they hadn't. They did everything *but*, Jamie decided, rather nauseated by their lack of honesty. I'm not ready, she thought, to play the games that are required of women today. At least with Willy I wasn't wasting our time being a flirt and a tease.

The truth was too that Jamie didn't have the necessary knowledge of society games. The 'country-club syndrome' of which Lesley had spoken so casually was something with which she was totally unfamiliar. The country club at home was far away, in Indian Hills, ensconced among the palatial grounds of the very wealthy. At the country club the girls and young men went riding. Lesley had her impeccably fitted riding attire, of course, but Jamie had never even been on a horse. There was a world of difference between them that could never be crossed.

Jamie worked, too, to supplement her scholarship, while others sat on the grass and talked about conquering the most outstanding Big Man on Campus from Harvard or Princeton. Jamie did research for Gertrude Buck, one of the English professors, and she loved her time in the stacks of the Thompson Memorial Library. She could lose herself in old manuscripts, wondering what it must have been like in Thackeray's England, in Chaucer's. She was so hungry for the written word that it hardly mattered whose word it was so long as it was well turned out. She wished beyond anything that she possessed the talent of a Virginia Woolf.

When Lesley went back to New York for elegant parties thrown by one or another of the matrons of Fifth Avenue Jamie stayed alone, appreciating the narrow room with its simple wooden furniture. She also liked the dignified professors, women in long ungainly skirts, their hair in simple buns, and men with clear, intellectual brows, moustaches and beards. But when she imagined herself acting the role

57

of Professor Buck, something made her draw back. First of all, there was a sexlessness about her that was sad. Life had to be a passion play, didn't it? At some point a woman met the ideal man, someone of equal intellectual bent, and something happened. Besides, Professor Buck studied the words of others. Jamie wanted to write her own words, to break through to some sort of discovery, to some sort of verity that she and she alone could impart to her readers. The writer, she thought, was like a fine funnel. Life poured experiences haphazardly into him or her, and it was then through the writer that these experiences were ennobled and tragedy and comedy emerged from the natural chaos of everyday existence. She envied Theodore Dreiser, who could write about a young man's desire to conquer the world and how one false move turned this ambition into a disaster. She herself wanted not so much to conquer the world as to reach men's souls – the very heart and guts of them. She felt dwarfed by those who had succeeded in reaching hers – yet also impelled even more to draw up the juices of her own creativity, pouring them out into a finished product that would strike each reader in the deepest part of his own being.

It was difficult to get to know Lesley, and Jamie had to admit that she wasn't quite sure she really wanted to know her. There were conflicting elements about her roommate. She read Freud, Maria Montessori and the newly published *Education and Democracy* by John Dewey. But at Vassar there were other girls who affected interest in psychology and a writer-philosopher who was clearly in vogue. Afterwards when no one was looking, they reverted to their diet of *The Atlantic Monthly* or that staple of middle-class gentility, *The Ladies' Home Journal*. Jamie wondered what Lesley understood beyond the obvious fact that Freud was obsessed by sex. How profound was she, after all? She drew good sketches but not outstanding ones. Yet how could one exist

58

merely to exist, without pursuing a lifetime ambition, without wanting to distinguish oneself?

In November Lesley joined the Women's Suffrage Club, and it was then that Jamie dared ask, piqued suddenly by new curiosity: 'Do you think that women are more intelligent than men?'

Lesley had just walked in, and she removed her hat, hung it on a hook, and threw herself like a graceful ragdoll on her narrow bed. She was thoughtful. '*Some* women,' she finally replied. 'It's hard to tell. Men are out in the world and their wives aren't. So it's difficult to judge the intelligence of most women. But if we had the vote, if we were given confidence – then perhaps we'd come out of our shells and be our real selves, and then test the intelligence we're not supposed to be allowed to use.'

Jamie nodded. That was an excellent, perceptive answer. 'If you were to choose the ideal way in which to exercise your own intelligence, what would you do?'

Lesley smiled – that remote, dreamy smile that was at once so reservedly British and so vulnerable in its fear of appearing ridiculous. 'I'd be Rosa Bonheur. I'd paint the most glorious paintings a woman could paint. But Professor Chatterton doesn't think I have much talent.'

Jamie winced. Clarence Chatterton was the artist in residence at Vassar, and she thought: How horrible to have your dearest illusions crushed before you even have a chance to test them out! How dreadful to be told there isn't enough in you . . . Dr Buck always commended Jamie, read her poems and prose pieces, criticized them, certainly, but never without encouragement. How did one go on *living* when a 'superior' being – one who truly possessed the talent to which you yourself were aspiring with tears of desire and frustration – informed you, point-blank, that you were never going to have it?

'So, if you're not going to be Rosa Bonheur,' she plunged in, feeling such compassion that she put forth the most

59

positive front she could muster, 'what *are* you going to be?' She could not recall Lesley's expressing an enduring interest in any other subject besides art.

Lesley looked at her gravely. 'I don't have the slightest idea.'

Jamie was disappointed. 'Then ... you want to be married, I expect.'

'So far I've not met the man to make me think so. No, I don't want that.' She leaned on her elbows and said, 'What I'd like to do is travel! I want to see something of the world. I've thought, now that there's a war on, of going to England and becoming a nurse. Or to France. There's such a great need for nurses – for committed women – '

'You'd put yourself right into a war zone?'

'Well, the boys do, don't they, over there? My father says it won't be that long before America has to enter into the conflict. I feel . . . strange about that. I don't believe in war. But on the other hand, if the fellows are out there dying, we should be doing our share. I mean, if we want the vote . . .'

'Nobody seems to care much about the war, here at Vassar,' Jamie reflected pensively.

'Nobody cares much about *anything* here. Except the latest movie! Sometimes I can't stand it. Everyone wants to be just like everybody else. That's why I like Chatterton so much. His ideas are different, and he doesn't give a damn whether anyone agrees with them or not.'

Jamie was silent. She was thinking what it must mean to live in an artistic community where others shared your passions and your ideals, where convention was laid at the doorstep like a pair of shoes in front of a house in Tokyo. She said softly: 'It would be wonderful to travel. Not to be in the United States.'

'My father claims it's the only free country in the world. I don't agree.'

Jamie was remembering Willy. 'I had a friend in Cincinnati,' she murmured, 'who was of German descent. His

60

mother was an immigrant. They all made fun of her accent. He was as American as you or I – but not American enough.'

Lesley asked, 'Was this someone special?'

'Very special. He was my brother – my first love. He's bitter because he's never been treated with any decency. He was born illegitimate.'

'And he wanted to marry you?'

'Yes. But I didn't think it would work. There's so much I want to do, and he saw life as encompassed by our home town. He never wanted me to go to college.'

'Would you want children, some day?'

'How can I tell? I don't see myself tied down, but then perhaps that's because of Willy. Married to Willy, I would have had no other option. He's the type of man who'd get a job somewhere, earn his weekly salary, come home, eat his dinner, read his paper, make love, and go to sleep snoring. I'd be lying awake in the darkness, feeling like a trapped animal.' She looked away, her eyes filling with tears. She'd worried, once, about becoming pregnant. She'd sat up praying for her period to come, for fear of being caged by force into a marriage she had no wish for. Then she added, somewhat coldly: 'But you wouldn't understand that sort of life, Lesley. The life of a day worker in a city like Cincinnati, Ohio.'

'It isn't so different from the life my sister leads in New York City. She has luxuries that a day worker would never even dream of – but basically, there are no vistas and she has no horizons. George comes home every night and insists on seeing the same parade of couples every weekend. No one looks her in the eye because she's a matron, a married woman with a child. There are no possibilities, no risks, no miracles for Emily. She must lie awake in the dark too, unless she's anaesthetized her mind to such an extent that she can't see her situation clearly any more. I don't want to end up like her. It's the nightmare I've been staring at.'

61

'Whom did she marry?' The description sounded horrible, and Jamie pictured a fifty-year-old man with a pipe and a paunch.

'A very nice young Harvard graduate. Handsome, funny. I can't stand being with them!'

They were suddenly laughing, laughing over George who was so nice and bright and who could be compared to Willy who had never been to college; George who was a bore and Willy who might not have been, if he'd been born into a luckier family. They laughed, understanding each other, and all at once they were friends, and the room had become smaller, more cosy, filled with warmth. Lesley in one movement was unpinning her hair, letting it flow unimpeded down her back, shaking loose the waves.

'God,' she said. 'I wish we could be in Paris drinking wine.' Then she looked at Jamie, and her eyes were serious, wide, and striking. 'Are they drinking wine in Paris, do you think? I read that the government had fled to Bordeaux.'

'That was last year,' Jamie replied. They stared at each other, wondering about this war that neither of them could imagine, could understand. 'Now the elegant folk have come back to the capital from their hideaways.'

'Then the French don't care either about their own men?'

Jamie didn't know what to answer. 'I can't really believe that,' she finally stated. But what was death from the vantage point of the living? 'This is my first trip away from Ohio,' she admitted. 'All I know of Paris is from the books I've read, and from the newspapers.'

'Why is it,' Lesley asked bitterly, 'that we can't even be entitled to a dream? I've so often pictured myself in a garret somewhere on the banks of the Seine, watching the barges moving slowly down the grey waters. But in my pictures there have always been young men, and wine, and roses.'

62

'And love?'

'And of course love. But not the love of pessaries and condoms, and of coy petting in the back seats of cars. Real love, like Natasha and Prince Andrei in *War and Peace*.'

'He died,' Jamie cut in. 'From his battle wounds.'

'I want my money back,' Lesley said, watching a brown leaf fall twisting onto the hill below the window. 'I bought the book thinking he would survive, because she was by his side, loving him, nursing him. And Anna Karenina threw herself in front of a train. Is that love? Would you have done that for Willy?'

'I'm here, no?' Jamie retorted. 'I think maybe I didn't love him. Or maybe just not enough.'

'But at least you've had something close to the real thing. To me it's still Anna and Natasha, never me.'

Jamie started to laugh. 'I'll write about you. We can make each other famous. You live the romance, and I'll be your biographer.'

'Oh, Jamie,' Lesley said gently. 'You were the first to be kissed, and I'm still waiting, so to speak.'

She rose and went to shut the curtains on the dismal twilight of autumn. Jamie sighed and turned on a lamp. Its pale-yellow glow spread over the room, making odd patterns on the spread on Lesley's bed. Soon, again, it would be Christmas, and she knew she didn't want to go home. 'Let's go to dinner,' she said, 'and pretend we're painting Paris from the rooftops.'

Charlotte von Ridenour, Marquise de Varenne, was, in 1914, fifty years old. Only the wrinkles on her neck betrayed her age. She was very thin, more than ever before, but her thinness added to her distinction. She had allowed her hair to turn perfectly grey, knowing that to tint it would have made the years all the more apparent; and still, for her, nothing was more important than men. She dressed in

63

black, white and grey, to set off her extraordinary face, with its brilliant blue eyes and fine bone structure.

The death of her husband in 1902 provided one unexpected shock: He had left behind a most confused estate. Adrien de Varenne had bequeathed lands and the châteaux to his only son, but Robert-Achille's affairs were riddled with debts. His gambling and general heedlessness had depleted the family fortune. Charlotte felt the hysteria mounting within her. She had married him for his position but also for the funds behind that position. To be left with nothing . . .

'But it's hardly nothing, my dear,' the attorney informed her sympathetically. 'If you sell the house on the Barrière and find yourself a more modest residence, you'll be able to keep the castle in Beauce, with a smaller staff.'

Charlotte was appalled. She had known the relative poverty of coming to Paris without benefit of dowry. To give up what she had so struggled to attain . . . and all because of that repulsive, cowardly fool! She looked at her sons, twelve-year-old Alex and eleven-year-old Paul, and thought: Some day the older will save me. He must. It is his duty. But Paul, now . . . He was different. He was . . . not Robert-Achille's son and had been conceived in an act of pleasure with someone unconnected to the Varennes. If Alex had to suffer because of present debts, that was only right. Justice demanded that he should correct the mistakes of his own father. She said to him coldly: 'I am not accustomed to being poor. You must decide on a career and make a brilliant marriage. Your grandfather would not want the great name of Varenne to go hand in hand with restrictions and parsimony. He was a *grand seigneur*.'

'Yes, Mama.' What did one do when one was still so young? But Alex had lost his childhood when he had faced the truth about Charlotte. He was afraid now to express his desperate need for his mother's affection. Paul was caressed. Alex, never. And so he closed off his emotions even

more, guarding the tenderness of his heart from the coldness of the marquise.

She purchased a spacious ground-floor apartment on the
Boulevard Saint Germain, which she decorated sump-
tuously in the finest Oriental styles: rare carpets, turquoise
vases of the Chinese Ming dynasty, silk screens bordered in
black lacquer. Every month she had to change *maîtres
d'hôtel*; for if anything went wrong, she blamed the major-
domo. Alex was growing accustomed to his mother's bitter
scenes with her servants. And he swore never to marry a
headstrong woman. He dreamed of finding a gentle soul,
who would soothe him and make him forget that he had
never been loved. Paul, on the other hand, found his mother
a source of amusement. But Alex was ashamed, and hurt.

Her exhortations did not go unheeded. At the Lycée
Condorcet, he was an excellent student. In 1908, Alexandre
obtained his Baccalaureate with the qualification of honour,
Bien. It was doubtful that Paul, the following year, would
pass the dreadful test at all. But Charlotte said, her voice
suddenly most Germanic in its dryness: 'You missed *Très
bien*. A Varenne must always be the best, Alexandre.' A
Varenne: Then why was Paul not expected to succeed, to
bear the double-edged responsibility of the ancient name?

Alexandre thought he knew the answer, one day, when he
was eighteen. He looked quietly at his mother, who was
forty-four, and at his seventeen-year-old brother who resembled no one in the family. His brother who laughed at
life, who took nothing seriously. And he knew what he had
always suspected was true. And felt hatred for the two of
them. Charlotte and that other son of hers, the one who was
exempt from all the troubles. The one who was not a
Varenne.

He studied for the bar and did his military service. In
spite of Charlotte's evident disdain and lack of concern, he
did well at the Sorbonne. His professors had been impressed. There was even talk of a career in politics. He had

65

listened, interested. Maybe. But he held back, afraid that elected officials could not earn enough money to keep his mother happy.

When he met Yvonne, Alexandre had just opened a small but distinctive office with a ready-made, choice clientele. Charlotte's own attorney and dear friend had recently retired, and she had persuaded him to recommend her son to certain important people. Alex resented her for this, because it meant that he was in debt to her, that the cord would take even longer to cut. But he also knew that her help in Parisian circles was a *sine qua non*. He wanted to be free of her, because he wanted to forget the shame of her adultery and wanted to erase the pain of not being loved. Yet only by work would he succeed in 'buying' her out of his life for good.

Yvonne de Larmont was not particularly beautiful. She was tall, slender, with a narrow face and attractive hazel eyes. Her father, Henri de Larmont, was a well-known surgeon whose business Alexandre had been asked to handle. The professor, as he was known to his associates, was a somewhat formidable man with a wry wit. Alexandre liked them both. For the first time in ages, he was able to relax.

He began to invite Yvonne to the opera, to hear Caruso, and to sessions of Diaghilev's Ballets Russes. He was not a ballet aficionado, and neither was she. But afterwards, in the quiet little restaurant booths where he took her for a late supper, they laughed about it together. 'Why have you never married?' he finally asked, blushing, one evening.

'Why? It's very simple. On my wedding day I shall receive a great deal of money – call it a dowry, or a trust. Papa believes that an intelligent married woman needs her own funds, although until then her parents should take care of her. Just now my life is good. Marriage is a big responsibility. I don't want to go into it lightly.'

Later that night, without warning, it was she who kissed him. She cupped his face in her hands, rose on tiptoe, and kissed him full on the lips. Alexandre was startled. For a moment he could not respond, and then he seized her slender form and crushed her to him, driving his tongue into her mouth, tasting. Then, embarrassed, he stepped back. Yvonne smiled and said nothing.

But the next day he was strangely restless. He cared for Yvonne. He would propose to her. By doing so he would of course be playing right into his mother's hands. Charlotte would be thrilled by the dowry, but Yvonne would understand. They would do for Charlotte what had to be done, and then they would bar her for ever from their lives and the lives of their children. Charlotte would be rescued by Yvonne's money. Then life would begin.

When Alexandre went to the Cité to make his formal proposal, he was met in the entrance hall by Yvonne, her hair in disarray over her shoulders. He was surprised, but she gave a little cry and held her hands out to him, her face aglow. She knew why he had come, and she was glad.

'It's all right, dear, we shall be very happy,' he heard her answering moments later. She had accepted and so quickly! He touched the fineness of her hair, the fabric of her blouse. And for once he felt happy.

Paul de Varenne was handsome. His skin was ruddy, and his brown eyes ringed with curling black lashes twinkled with an ironic merriment that, even as a child, drew attention. His body was powerful. He was well aware of his virile good looks. Nature had blessed him, and he knew it. From his earliest moments, he had seen through his mother, recognizing in her a kindred spirit. But he would succeed where she had never even tried. Charlotte von Ridenour de Varenne was a charmer by temperament; early on, Paul de Varenne had resolved to become a charmer by profession. He watched his elegant mother and was amused.

He liked people, but Alexandre was a bore, his mother unpredictable, and his father . . . Later he would begin to wonder. Robert-Achille was so unlike him, in every way. Except of course that he too had never much liked work and had loved to gamble and run off to Montmartre.

At the Lycée Condorcet he was an abysmal student. Alex did brilliant work, whereas Paul was lazy. He only enjoyed the occasional class. Things to do with art. He went to the Louvre and the Musée du Jeu de Paume with his governess, and he could hardly tear himself away. But he could not draw, oddly enough. He could only appreciate.

And then, when he was eleven, catastrophe hit. He would never forget finding his father, dead, in the study. This mass of blood and brains could not possibly be *his father*. Paul's head had reeled and he vomited, and then he screamed, screamed for someone – his mother, a servant, anyone! Later, to his own surprise, he did not feel sad, only horrified – and a little disgusted.

He failed to pass his Baccalaureate examinations two years in a row. His mother shrugged the episode off. He thought he knew why: His father, his real father, the one whom everyone in Paris guessed to be his father, must have been a poor student too. Paul was very curious, and also embittered. To have been conceived out of wedlock, never to have met one's true father – this was unforgivable. His mother, the elegant charmer, was also a whore. All women, Paul felt, were whores. He decided that women were like extraordinary flowers, each more lovely than her neighbour. But women were also deceitful. The world needed them; but like flowers, they should be picked with impunity, for some had poisonous blossoms. This had been Charlotte's legacy.

He was not particularly disposed to work. He was an expert in nothing save bridge, dancing and horsemanship. Alexandre had passed his examinations, was going to law school. Paul spent his days amusing himself. His mother had made it clear that the saviour of the family was to be Alex. Paul occasionally felt a sadness, an emptiness, nagging. There was no centre to his life – only a void.

Nothing caught his emotions. He flailed about, trying one thing after another. Life seemed boring. And then Paul made a friend. He was an older man, whom Paul met one day leafing through a book of Sem's sketches in his mother's drawing-room. He was dressed in a Norfolk jacket and sported a fashionable pompadour of grey hair. He looked every inch the sportsman, and Paul said, advancing into the room: 'We've never met, have we? I'm Paul de Varenne.' Yet the man looked familiar, a face from his childhood dreams, perhaps, or an album of photographs.

The other smiled broadly. 'How do you do. Bertrand de la Paume. I've been hearing much about you from the ladies of the city, Paul. You break hearts the way another man looks through his morning paper. Fitting for the son of Charlotte von Ridenour!'

'Yes, isn't it? Mama broke quite a few hearts in her day, it would appear.'

'It would appear.' Bertrand de la Paume sat down familiarly and patted the other side of the sofa for the young man to join him. Deftly he extracted a gilt-tipped cigarette from a leather case, inserted it into an ebony holder, and lit it. Then he passed the *étui* to Paul, who took one for himself. The Chevalier lit it for him with a natural ease. Paul was conscious of being covertly examined, but, oddly, he did not mind the scrutiny. The man intrigued him too.

'I have also heard of you from your mother. Our lovely Charlotte thinks that you are gifted in the arts. I wonder . . .'

'I can't draw worth a *sou*,' Paul stated honestly, motioning toward the book of famous sketches that the other had been looking at when he had interrupted him.

'That isn't what Charlotte meant. You see, I'm an art dealer. I go to the provinces and purchase paintings that are on sale there, and resell them to collectors. But for years now I've been feeling the strain of all this coming and going. Tell me – how would it strike you to work for me?'

69

Totally taken by surprise, Paul felt his body go rigid, taut. 'But again, I am not an expert. I couldn't tell you what to sell a Matisse for, or a Bonnard. I'd have no idea whatsoever!'

De la Paume shook his head. 'No, no. I'm the expert, remember? What I need is a young runner – somebody with impeccable taste who'd do the travelling for me. You would bring home the paintings, and I would judge their worth and sell them at the proper value.'

'Still – I might come back with something of no value at all!'

Narrowing his brown eyes, the Chevalier slowly shook his head. 'I very much doubt that,' he concluded.

Paul suddenly felt excited. No one had ever thought him worthy of anything – and now this stranger was offering him a job.

Looking up, he found the other still smiling at him. There was a touch of irony in his expression. 'Come now,' the Chevalier said. 'Put on a coat and let's go. We'll go out to dinner, the two of us. Then I shall take you to meet Martine, my lady of the moment. You'll enjoy her company.'

'Wouldn't you rather – be alone with her?' stammered Paul.

'Heavens, no! Martine is an interesting specimen. In her day she gave pleasure to all the golden youth, to all the men of Parisian society. She made her rounds, fairly and equitably. Now she's being frightfully faithful, and it's starting to annoy me. Please – come with me. You need to meet one of the genuine charmers of the Belle Epoque!'

Paul breathed deeply and looked away. 'But I already know one,' he declared. 'My mother – remember?'

There was a small silence in the Chinese sitting-room. Then, casually, Bertrand de la Paume acquiesced with a nod of the head. Paul rose, his legs weak. All of this had been too much. But he would follow. He would let Bertrand, Chevalier de la Paume, carry out his education.

Chapter Three

Elena wasn't at all surprised at what Fania had to propose. Her only question had been when the sisters were going to come round to asking her. They were once again eating, this time a fine luncheon in the hotel dining room, when the older Adler sister said:

'We'll miss you, Princess. It's been a joy to have these conversations. You're younger than we are, but Genia and I haven't had many friends of our own. Mama died when we were children, and when Papa passed away this year, he left us without human ties. Our father was very possessive. We had our governess, and later on a paid companion – another Jewish girl, of the same background as ours. Whereas you are somehow different.'

'The Prince was one of the Tsar's own men,' Genia reminded her. 'Papa was just a businessman from Moscow. There are entire continents the Egorovs have travelled that you and I never shall. Balls at the Winter Palace, intimate teas with the grand-duchesses . . .'

'But lately,' Elena said sadly, 'there's been none of that.'

'Had there been, you might not have given us a second look,' Fania commented astutely. Elena looked at her and smiled. Had she been that obvious? But it was true, and there was a naïve but perceptive quality in Fania that was touching. Elena had lost her naïveté so many years ago that it gave her a jolt to watch a woman ten years older practising guilelessness without embarrassment.

'I've changed,' she said. 'I know where I'd like to be, and it isn't here. I shall never go back to Petersburg. My friends have all given me up as a lost cause. All my suitors and my best friends have married. Married couples have nothing in common with single women, do they?'

71

It was Genia who took the bait, almost eagerly. 'Nothing at all! We were never permitted to encourage young men. The ones with enough money weren't Jewish; the Jewish ones were either frightfully unappealing or anarchists, or not to Papa's liking as business partners. And now Fanny's thirty-four and I'm thirty-two. Who would want us? We're two old maids of the wrong religion.'

'But you're so beautiful – both of you! It's me no one would want. I've forgotten how to dress, I haven't been to Europe in ages, and my own companions have been a housemaid and my mother's seamstress. Widowers would look to you as mature enough to handle the children of their first marriage, yet still young and attractive for their own pleasure. But I'm too old to be someone's first wife, and too inexperienced to be a second. So what's left? In this godforsaken town, there isn't even a dandy to keep me as his mistress!'

Fania had blushed and was saying anxiously: 'Oh, Princess, you can't speak this way . . . If either of us were only as lovely as you, with that marvellous hair, those glorious eyes – and the proper background! Somebody's "mistress"! What a revolting thought.'

'One's thoughts turn very bitter after enough time alone.'

'Then come with us!' Fania's face was filled with a sudden animation. 'We'd love to travel with you!'

'Have you ever been to China?' Genia was asking.

Elena opened her mouth, shook her head, appeared bewildered, shocked, joyful, and yet regretful. 'But I can't . . .'

'What's to prevent you? Your father?'

'Yes. Among other things. Our family assets are tied up in the capital. My passport is out of date. Thousands of valid reasons.'

'We have sufficient money for the three of us. And you wouldn't have to feel under any obligation to repay us. Your experience is something Genia and I would treasure.

The two of us have never been anywhere alone, but you – you've learned the ways of the world.'

'And if we bribe the border authorities, no one will even glance at your passport.'

'Your parents would want you to go abroad, since they haven't sent you for such a long time! Unless . . . unless, Genia, it's the fact that we're Jews. The Prince and Princess might very well object to their daughter travelling with two Jewish women.'

'Don't worry,' Elena said softly, laying a hand on Fania's arm. 'It will be all right. My father, as you say, will want what's best for me. And now, at twenty-four, it's to leave with you as your paid companion. I am a very capable person, who can organize, who understands how to run the operations of a voyage. If you invite me as someone in your employ, I shall accept. But if you simply treat me as charity, you'll have to understand my refusal. It has nothing to do with your religion. It has to do with my pride. I've never taken anything without giving in return. I couldn't, now, change my principles.'

They were exclaiming with excitement, rising to kiss her, and Elena felt a burst of pleasure, a knowledge that hope still existed. It lay beyond the border, perhaps in Harbin, perhaps in Shanghai. She was somehow going to make the break, now that she'd seized the golden rod thrust at her by the two attractive Adlers. She closed her eyes for a moment, to let everything sink in. She would be going to step toward freedom, finally.

There was only her father left to stand in her way.

When Alexandre returned to the apartment on Boulevard Saint Germain, his heart was filled to the brim with inexplicable emotion. His head was swimming. The next day he would be married at the Madeleine to the sweetest girl in the world. Early that morning, Yvonne's father had

73

signed her trust fund over to her in acknowledgement of her mature new position as Marquise Alexandre de Varenne. But for everyone, tomorrow was the ceremony that counted, and only in the legal sense had the civil wedding of that morning held any significance. Yvonne and he had signed some papers, and the professor and Charlotte had witnessed them. It had been simple, quick – and then Yvonne – his wife yet not yet his wife – had left for a final fitting of her gown at the *maison de couture* Poiret. He had rented a flat on rue de Passy, in the select Sixteenth *Arrondissement*, not far from the Trocadéro and the Bois de Boulogne. Together they had chosen the stark fifteenth- century furniture that they both liked, had added gay touches with colourful Persian carpets and emerald-green velvet curtains. His study was upholstered in leather, and already his legal books lined the walls. He looked forward to living there with Yvonne.

After the civil wedding, the professor had made his hospital rounds as usual. When he arrived at his penthouse flat in the evening, he saw the welcoming light in the foyer and looked for signs of Yvonne's being still up. She had gone to bed. There was her coat on the small sofa, and her hat on the side table. He sighed. He wished he might have been able to speak to her on this eve of her marriage – might have spoken some few words of fatherly wisdom. He smiled wryly at his own sentimentality and walked into his library, to clear his mind.

The letter was on his desk, propped up by a medical encylopedia.

My dearest Papa,

There is so much you never understood. To you I was always the girl of peace, the girl of the hearth, Mother's replacement. You never really wanted me to marry. You made that very clear, by not letting me touch my own funds until I was ready to become another man's wife. You wanted me to pretend I was *your* wife, your lifelong companion. And when you watched me growing

74

older, you decided that I should marry your perfect counterpart, Alex de Varenne, because he would never take me far from you.

Do you remember Mother's hat? She used to have a marvellous hat, a hat I never saw her wear all the days of our time as mother and daughter. It was a hat of the *Belle Epoque*, with plumes and flowers and an enormous rim, and ribbons. The sort of hat the Marquise de Varenne surely wore in those grander days. But Mother never did. She'd take it out of its tissue paper when she thought nobody was looking, and she would touch the velvet ribbons, the silk flowers, the feathers . . . with longing. I never wanted to be like my mother – to have such a hat and know that I could never wear it, that it was my forbidden apple. I liked the plumes and the posies even though you didn't. I wore my hair in tight braids because that was how you approved of it. But I wanted to let it stream down my back. You wouldn't have understood, and neither would Alexandre.

But there was someone else. He paints. We have been seeing each other in our quiet way, and I love him. I could never have brought him to you. You would have thought he was a fortune hunter. I wanted to marry him, but there was no way. I could never have convinced you. So I did the only thing I could think of: I married Alex today at the city hall, so that I might take the funds that are rightfully mine as someone's wife. In a legal sense I am his wife. But I shan't live the lie. Papa, I'm not going through with the religious ceremony: To God I shall not lie. My friend and I are going away together, to live in a foreign country where no one need know whether we are married or not. Do not mourn for me. I am happy, and I love him, and he loves me. You can do me one favour, however: Apologize to Alex. And tell him it is really for the best, for both of us.

Your daughter,
YVONNE

The professor felt paralysed with grief and bewilderment. But he knew that he must notify Alex right away. In the morning there would be the Mass at the Madeleine, hundreds of guests . . . and the Marquise Charlotte, dressed in splendour . . . He put his coat on and left at once.

In the Varenne apartment Henri de Larmont greeted Charlotte curtly and went alone into the study with Alexandre. The young man read the letter, once, twice. It made

75

no sense. He sat down. In his dressing-gown he seemed younger, more vulnerable. Henri de Larmont felt more discomfort than he had felt in a lifetime of medicine, of hospitals. Alex laid his head in his hands, numb with sickness.

His mother burst in, and Alex simply handed her the letter. She perused it rapidly. Then she began to scream.

Alex stood up, trembling. 'Mama,' he said quietly, 'no one has the right to pass judgment on Yvonne. Tomorrow I shall go to the Cardinal of Paris, to discuss the situation. The marriage was never . . . consummated, and we were never married in the eyes of the Church. Perhaps we'll only need a civil annulment. Or I shall set the wheels in motion for a divorce. I'm sorry – '

He could not continue, and abruptly left the room. Charlotte de Varenne's mouth opened incongruously. The professor, who had been standing awkwardly in the corner, turned to her. 'Madame – ' he began, but then words failed him too. He quickly strode out of the house, grief-stricken.

Alexandre sat in his bedroom, shaking. He thought of Yvonne's story about the hat, and tears now came. He had not seen that side to her – but there were sides to him she'd failed to see too. He rose and began to pack his bags, his fingers stiff, his stomach in knots. On the morrow, while his mother dealt with the ridiculous horde of guests she had insisted upon inviting, he would quietly move, alone, into the new apartment on rue de Passy. He would face the emerald-green curtains and learn to adjust. There was no choice.

In the summer of 1916, Jamie and Lesley parted after the end of their freshman year. Lady Priscilla wanted to take her younger daughter to England. Lesley could not really imagine a Europe torn by war. She only remembered the Europe of her grandparents, of other trips. But this time,

Ned had been adamant in forbidding his wife and daughter to go. Lady Priscilla had insisted: 'In Yorkshire there is no conflict. And as for Paris . . . it is so far from the front!' Ned had finally yielded; in the United States one heard reports, but as the distant whispers of another world. He had questioned associates, been reassured. The war was being fought in the north and east sectors of France, not where his wife and daughter were going to travel. A pressing advertising campaign would keep him glued to the office all summer. Was it fair to let the holidays go by without a trip for his family?

Lesley was eighteen. At Vassar, and in the ballrooms of Fifth Avenue, the war in Europe seemed far away. President Wilson had been speaking about the need to negotiate for a peace without victors. Yet no sooner had they arrived in Paris than the Richardson women were confronted with the nearness of the war, with what it was doing to France. Verdun had been won from the Germans, but at what cost! This was the start of a third year of battles for the French. Marshall Joffre's dictum, 'To be killed rather than step back,' represented the French mentality, from the richest aristocrat to the smallest shopkeeper. And Georges Clemenceau, 'the Tiger', detested by members of all political parties yet the most dreaded statesman in the country, had been named President of the Commission for the Army and had pushed his way into the very trenches of his soldiers, to breathe courage into each man from on high.

Paris society had reintegrated the capital. In 1914, faced with losses so serious that all fronts were giving way, the French government had fled to Bordeaux, and the elegant folk had gone to Deauville to gamble and to Biarritz to sunbathe. Now the war seemed sufficiently removed they had returned, but many of them had been forced to leave their homes, for coal and servants were almost unavailable, and tearooms had had to be closed. The rich had been forced to move to rented suites at the luxury hotels.

Gabrielle Chanel was the *couturière* of the day, for Paul Poiret had thrown all his energies into clothing the armed forces. Lesley wanted to meet her and to buy her entire autumn wardrobe from her, because, earlier that year, a sketch had appeared of one of her dresses in *Harper's Bazaar*. Entitled 'Chanel's charming little chemise dress', it consisted of a most avant-garde outfit: slim form-fitting sleeves, a plunging V-neck, and . . . no waistline whatsoever. The hat had neither egrets nor flowers – only a small border of fur around its crown. Simplicity had rendered the design a marvel of good taste and comfort. Lesley had immediately picked it out, adopting it for her slender figure.

So they went to rue Cambon to be fitted for a series of such outfits, and Lesley professed herself delighted. More of the calf showed than in America, where a display of the ankle was still considered mildly risqué. Lesley bought clothes for the coming term made of the new material, jersey, invented for Chanel by Rodier. And she admired the dashing, pencil-thin Frenchwoman, who dressed with the flair of a distinguished hermaphrodite, her clothing always borrowed from the best of male attire, because it was comfortable and useful. Yet on the inside one felt her a true woman, who breathed sexuality.

They saw Cécile-Sorel and Sarah Bernhardt on stage. Bernhardt had been on tour in New York, but here, in her own ambiance, she exuded the 'something extra' that turned some actresses into legends. Lesley loved Paris but was a little ashamed of enjoying herself. The shadow of the war hung over the city, and almost no young men remained there. That young men her age were dying – for no reason! Yes, surely President Wilson was right: Peace was worth any price. Peace, and the breath of life. The promise of the future. How could one be young and ignore tomorrow?

But in Paris, everyone was vilifying Wilson and glorifying the *poilus*, the soldiers in the trenches. War was seen as a holy crusade, and the Germans were the *Boche*, the most despicable of infidels. America, safe and hedonistic, seemed like a faraway land of make-believe, where reality was not allowed to enter. Lady Priscilla and her daughter did not remain long in Paris. They sailed for England, under a stormy sky.

Arthur Stephen Aymes, Earl of Brighton, was ill with arthritis in his summer home in Yorkshire. Lesley was bored. The days were monotonous, the guests full of dire predictions about the conditions in Europe. In the vast stone mansion where Cromwell had stayed, the young girl missed the elegant boulevards of Paris, the picturesque, green-grey Seine winding around the city like a sensuous, loving arm wrapped in an embrace. One afternoon, looking for a novel to read, she walked into her grandfather's large dark parlour, and there, in front of the fireplace, stood a young man she had never met. She hesitated briefly on the threshold – he seemed so absorbed! – but his beauty caught her. He was tall, slight of build, with fine black hair that curled gently over a thin, oval face. His eyes were dark too, and he might have been Italian: All that was missing was a *moustache en pointe*. He was, she thought, perhaps twenty-three. She touched the pearl comb in her hair and felt her fingers trembling inexplicably.

'Hello,' she said softly. 'I'm Lesley Richardson – Lord Brighton's granddaughter.'

'And I'm Justin Reeve. Did I startle you?'

His voice was deep, melodic. It went with his Byronic bearing. He was wearing a dark suit from Savile Row, and a black pearl gleamed from his cravat. She felt stupid, disconnected. 'I suppose you did,' she admitted.

'My grandfather and yours went to Oxford together. They were great friends. So now that Adele and I are alone, Lord Brighton is most kind and invites us sometimes for the weekend.'

Adele. Then he was married. She could feel the colour rising in her cheeks. An awkward silence followed, and

Lesley realized with sudden panic that he was waiting for her to fill it. She cleared her throat. 'That's . . . very nice.' She asked nervously: 'Do you ride?'

'Of course. My sister and I both do.' He smiled at her.

Lesley's tautness dissolved with absurd relief. She went to him and pretended to become interested in the andirons of the fireplace. 'It gets so cold in England,' she said. 'In the middle of summer we suffocate in New York.'

'Ah.' Clearly he was not interested in her chatter. She could hardly blame him. She should have excused herself and left him alone, but she could not move. And so, quite gently, totally unexpectedly, he took her hand and brought it to his lips. Amazed, she turned her face to him, her lips parting. Then, casually, he dropped the hand and smiled. 'Hello, Lesley Richardson,' he murmured.

She knew her face betrayed her rush of joy, the tingling sensations inside her body when he touched her. Lesley remained speechless, staring at Justin. She was eighteen years old, in a world at war. And her own world, hitherto a crystal fortress, had only just begun to crack.

Elena's father was, like her, tall and broad shouldered. The natural stateliness of his bearing was in marked, painful contrast to the nervousness of his hands as he rubbed them together over and over again. He had developed this habit since his exile from Petersburg, and as she watched him, pacing the floor and rubbing his blistered hands against the cold of his Siberian banishment, she wondered suddenly whether she possessed the heart to reject him too.

'Just imagine,' he was saying, 'how much Nicholas Alexandrovitch is underestimating von Hindenburg and Ludendorff! After Tannenberg, the Second Army will never recover. Ninety thousand prisoners on the eastern front. God knows how many dead . . .'

'Father,' Elena countered, 'there is Galicia that we won

from the Austrians.' She was wondering how he could still care, after what the Tsar had done to him. She wet her lips, looked away, and asked: 'Why not go away?'

His dark eyes widened with sudden anger. 'Go away? Elena, you were the one who urged me to stay, in 1908! You were the one telling me what it was like to be a Russian! Could it be possible that you've forgotten – the lecture I received from my eighteen-year-old daughter, as well as the message it contained? Lenya – look at me, for God's sake!'

She raised her face, unable to resist when he called her by her child's name of endearment. 'Much has happened between then and now,' she said with a rush of blood to her cheeks, a quickening of breath. It wasn't going to be easy at all.

'But we're Russians, more than ever! Our country is at war, and we're needed!'

'Papa, you haven't been needed for five years.'

He blinked, and a shocked silence stood between them. She cried out: 'Haven't you any pride left in you? Look at us! We're hardly better than the peasants! Don't you ever see Mama! She's grown into an old woman, and she's not even fifty!'

'Your mother vowed when she married me to go wherever I went.'

'But I didn't.'

She saw the purpling of his cheeks and refused this time to avert her eyes. 'What does that mean, Elena?' he asked.

'It means, Father, that I'm twenty-four now, and that I don't want to die an old maid with an empty life behind her. And that I'm not going to marry the first secretary at the British consulate, or the headmaster of the gymnasium. Six years ago you refused to give your daughter to the son of Count Andrei Branilev, because he is not descended from one of Tsar Ivan's boyars. You wanted me to fall in love with Grand-Duke Dmitri Pavlovitch! And now? What future do you wish for me?'

81

He couldn't reply. Tears had filled his eyes, and she thought: If I give in, I'll remain here for ever. She made herself stare at the blisters on his hands and made herself think: I am a winner, he is a lost man. She then said softly: 'I can't stay, Papa. Tomorrow I'm leaving for Irkutsk, with some new friends. The Adler sisters of Moscow. They're charming women who are making a tour of China.'

The purple was draining from his face, to be replaced by a sick pallor. She took one step, stopped. Her eyes burned from the tears that she was forcing back with sheer will-power.

'Papa – I'll be back. Soon.'

'Yes, Lenya,' he repeated, like a dumb animal. 'Soon . . . The Adler sisters? Who are *they*?'

'They're heiresses from Moscow.'

'Jews.'

She nodded. 'It doesn't matter, really, Father. Jews or Christians, it isn't how we worship that counts. You know damn well there isn't any God. If there is, He certainly has let us down, and for no reason that I can understand.'

'So you're going to blaspheme too, Elena . . . What's come over you?'

'Reality. I'm not going to allow them to beat me any longer. Not the way they've beaten you and Mama.' She knew how hard she was beating him now, but she refused to let up, refused to give in. 'You don't really want me to stay, do you?' she persisted. It was high drama, and she was playing it for all it was worth. 'You always wanted me to strike gold, to ride atop the tallest stallion. You made me into what I am, so now you've got to accept your own creation. I'm not like Mama, I'm like you – as I remember you, in Petersburg. You haven't been yourself for a long, long time, Papa, and I can't bear to watch you die on your feet. I can't talk to you of the war, and of the Tsar, as if nothing had happened!'

His eyes filled with tears. At length he said to her:

'Lenya, perhaps you're right. You were right in 1908, when you told me to stay. But I can't leave now, I'm too old and too broken down. You asked about my pride. I can't remember what it felt like to be an Egorov. It was a past life, not my own past history.'

She came to him then, falling into his arms, and he held her tightly against his chest. Elena began to sob, and her father kissed the thick dark softness of her hair. But all his strength would not keep her with him, and reality, at that moment, struck him as viciously as the Germans had hit the Second Army at Tannenberg. And she knew how much she still loved him, and that the rage inside her would never kill the love that remained inside her heart.

Paul de Varenne felt a new sense of purpose. Until his meeting with Bertrand de la Paume, he had lived each day in boredom, in a cynical search for pleasure. At twenty he had reached such a point of disillusionment with human nature that nothing seemed worth the effort of being honest. Charlotte had shown him by her own behaviour that one took from the weak and the blind in order to succeed. He had never once opened his heart to another being. He had never trusted anyone else, and never trusted himself.

Bertrand de la Paume was not a god, but he was someone who, on occasion, listened. Paul saw in him a man who had made a connection with life. He was a cynic: he took people for what they were, expecting no miracles, yet accepting their foibles. He enjoyed life because it fascinated him. And Paul looked at him and was filled with admiration.

The Chevalier loved Beauty first: Whether it lay in a work of art or in the eyes of a handsome woman, he sought it and made it his, until he was no longer absorbed by it. Then he would simply pass it on. Paintings would be sold, women would be gently but firmly removed from starring role to chorus line. But those around him seldom suffered from his rejections. He had ways of making people and possessions seem all the more precious for having once been his. A painting that had hung in his study became a work of greater merit to its next owner; and a woman once adored came to her new lover with the secure backing of the Chevalier's good taste.

Because of Bertrand de la Paume, Paul de Varenne had ceased to fritter away his time. He had made an entry into a new world. At first he had not known how to behave among the art collectors and the painters. He had gone with the Chevalier to the house at 27 rue de Fleurus, in the Sixth *Arrondissement*, where Gertrude Stein and Alice Toklas lived, an odd couple if ever he had met one. They were both Americans; Gertrude was heavy and masculine, with short crisp hair and a stentorian voice. Alice wore gypsy clothes and looped earrings, and on her upper lip grew what appeared to be a moustache. They were intellectuals, and Paul had never before encountered any of this species – particularly not one who took herself as seriously as Miss Stein. She had once studied medicine but had instead become a writer – in English, of course. Alice acted as her secretary and as buffer between her and the rest of humanity. They were known to every artist of note in Paris, and to every art broker. For it was Gertrude and her brother Leo who had discovered many a painter and enhanced the reputation of many others. On Saturday nights they held open house, and every literary and pictorial luminary knew that his status depended upon an occasional attendance.

Paul was fascinated. For the first time in his life, other people truly interested him. There was Picasso, the dapper little Spaniard, and the woman he loved, Eva. She seemed quite ill but very beautiful. There was Juan Gris and his wife Josette. He was a man of changing moods, a womanizer. There was the elfin Marie Laurencin, who painted in delicate pastels and had been the mistress of Guillaume Apollinaire, poet and critic. The great master of Fauvism,

Matisse, still came, although it appeared that Cubism had replaced his style. He was a nice middle-class professor, Paul thought, taken aback by the master's bourgeois appearance. But he himself still loved Matisse's odalisques, sprawling naked women with bodies that looked like real bodies. That, he thought, was life.

Bertrand de la Paume explained Cubism to him. Paul saw that this encompassed a whole philosophy; there were the Cubist painters, such as Picasso, Braque, Gris – and the Cubist 'thinkers', such as the poet Jean Cocteau. Theirs was a parody of life. Monsters shaped like cubes embodied their sense of mockery. How different from the rounded, thick-ankled women sculpted in bronze by Aristide Maillol! And the individual interpretations of simple, casual scenes by Edouard Vuillard and Pierre Bonnard: They attempted to grasp the intangible, through their renditions of colour and line. But always with grace. Their women were extraordinary, like poems. Paul watched and learned and asked questions.

Some people in this world are born with charm. Charlotte had acquired it to survive. Paul had possessed it from the cradle. The fitting comment came to his lips without effort. He could charm his way into a gallery and talk the owner into relinquishing a dusty canvas or a yet untested one. And he was discriminating. Once he had mastered the market, he could predict which artist would rise next to the forefront. And in the background, the Chevalier de la Paume watched, wryly smoking cigarette after cigarette.

The canvas trade was not accustomed to aristocrats of the calibre of Varenne and de la Paume. Mostly it was comprised of fat little round men with moist hands, such as Adolphe Basler, who had sold the first Utrillo. Once the entire industry had been housed on rue Laffitte. Now the price of paintings was going up, and up – and as it rose to new and dizzying heights, the tradesmen left their old shops and moved to grander quarters. Rue La Boëtie displayed works offered by Chéron and Paul Guillaume; Ambroise Vollard possessed more than three hundred Renoirs in his ancient house on rue de Gramont. To these people Bertrand de la Paume had been an anomaly; but to the society queens such as the Comtesse Greffuhle, or the Princesse Murat, he was one of their own clan. And they accepted Paul at once, having known his mother and his grandfather Adrien. Of his father no one spoke.

Something else happened to Paul. He fell in love. Until Martine, Paul had loved only himself, beautiful *objets d'art*, and horses. At times Paul felt despair at his rootless existence. Bertrand de la Paume had opened up new worlds, allowed Paul to breathe and live by providing him with work that tied in his appreciation of art and beauty. But on the night of their own meeting, he had also introduced the young man to his current mistress, Martine du Tertre.

She was certainly fifty. Next to the elegant Chevalier, she appeared, in fact, older. Her complexion was not milk-white like Charlotte's, nor was her hair the magnificent thick, even grey of the marquise's. Martine du Tertre was in no way stately. She was of medium height, her brown hair was touched with henna, and her cat eyes, turned up at the corners but always half closed, were painted on the outside with kohl – merely a trace, yet enough to strike the young man Paul as quite exotic. She had a plump pigeon breast that was always propped upward and out so that it was inviting as it peeked up from the low bateau necklines that she often wore. But she had a smile, warm and genuine and full of the joy of living, that actually made her imperfections amusing additions to her fascinating personality. For Martine du Tertre had been a reigning courtesan of the turn of the century. She had broken hearts and mended them with the grace and vitality of a Liane de Pougy or an Emilienne d'Alençon, the queens of the *Belle Epoque*.

'You see,' Bertrand de la Paume had said to Paul, 'one of

86

the tragedies of today is that all the *grandes dames* of the *demi-monde* have retired. Most of them have made brilliant marriages. After a while it ceases to matter that a woman has sold herself to the most distinguished bidder, and she acquires a style, a fortune, a manner that transcends social prejudices. That is Martine's situation. She was a mason's daughter in Lille and came to Paris as a very young girl. She met people. She met men. Each kept her for a while, until she chose to leave, with wit and charm, for the bed and board of a more enchanting lover. Her canny sense of business stood her in good stead. After a point she was richer than her first protectors, and then she bought herself a marvellous house on rue de la Pompe and "retired". She could now choose her lovers according to the dictates of her heart.'

'So . . . you don't keep her, then?'

'No. She loves me, you see. Long ago I suppose I succumbed to her personality, but then, so did the rest of Paris. Every man of note has at one time been her lover. She's proud of that fact. You'll like her.' He had smiled then at the young man and dropped the subject.

What struck Paul about Martine during their first evening, when the Chevalier took him to meet her in the house on the aristocratic rue de la Pompe, was her own appreciation of *him*. She moved with small easy steps, pouring him brandy, pouring him tea, stopping in her tracks to tilt her head to one side the better to appraise him. Then she would smile. 'Bertrand,' she would say, 'what a lovely young man you've brought! Such a magnificent young man, with such colour and life to him! You don't find lively ones like that any more, do you?' And then the frank laughter. No mockery, no coyness.

He returned home unable to sleep. Until then he had possessed any girl he pleased. Paul thought of Martine du Tertre, absurd with her hennaed hair, a woman thirty years his senior. She might have been his mother. She made no effort to hide her reputation: She'd been a simple girl from

87

the North, who had warmed her heart and the soles of her feet within the charmed circle of Paris's most eligible bachelor apartments. These *garçonnières* had sometimes been occupied by married men. She had not cared. Free, and richly rewarded, she had enjoyed all her protectors and made herself unforgettable to each one.

The next day Paul received a note from her. 'Would you consider dropping by for a sip of the finest Napoleon?' she had written in curlicued script. He laughed. She had made the first move. He would go.

In the arms of Martine du Tertre, that night, he found such voluptuousness as he had never imagined possible. She was not, in bed, a fifty-year-old woman propped up by corset stays. She was a woman who relinquished herself to him with a fervour and passion unknown to inexperienced young girls. Paul was beside himself. She kept a scented candle on the nightstand, and in its flickering light he thought, amazed: She's beautiful! And then he touched her face, her eyelids – gentle movements not characteristic of him, that made him suddenly shy.

In the morning she brought the breakfast tray herself and served him his *café au lait* in bed, ministering to him with the deft soft grace of femininity. 'So many have loved you,' he murmured.

'Yes. I offer what I can.'

'And you love . . . Bertrand?'

'Bertrand is unique. His intelligence and his wonderful taste make the days seem brighter, more finely tuned.'

'Then – if you love him – why?'

She smiled at him. 'Life is too short,' she stated simply, shaking her head. And once again he thought her beautiful. He was also aware of a new sensation: jealousy of the Chevalier. And then a sadness: I am only an unformed youth, and this woman has lived fully. What could I possibly mean to her? He had never felt insecure before in the presence of any female.

88

But what to do about Bertrand de la Paume? It was she who finally resolved the situation. One evening when the two men had dropped in to visit her together, Paul uneasy in his role of young friend to her acknowledged lover, she came to them in a flowing satin gown trimmed with fur. She came to them on her tiptoes and settled herself on an ottoman by Bertrand's feet. Looking up at him frankly, she declared in her blunt fashion: 'My dear, it's over. I've fallen in love with Paul, and it can't be helped.'

The young man swallowed and turned crimson. His stupefaction was so total that while he recovered, Martine took Bertrand's hand and began to run her index finger lightly over the knuckles. 'We've always been friends. As lovers we ran our course. You prefer younger women, and as for me . . . I've had the marvellous good fortune to find Paul.'

'It's as you wish,' Bertrand replied. A half smile came to his lips. 'And I'm not at all surprised. Love him. He is shallow and self-centred, an egotist and a user. But he is also an original and not half the idiot he's taken for. Enjoy him, Martine. He is my present to you, my way of bidding you *adieu*.' And he brought her hand to his lips and kissed it. Then he stood up, summoned the footman, and walked out.

On 1 August of that year, when mobilization was declared, Charlotte von Ridenour sat numbly at her dressing-table, remembering when she had been young and beautiful. Her sons, through their ill-conceived involvements, had made her the laughing-stock of her peers, and who would want her now? Two days later, the Germans declared war on France, and Alexandre immediately enlisted in the infantry. Paul followed, reluctantly deciding that if there could be no escape from combat, he wanted to be a flyer. But Charlotte heard the rumblings and saw the gatherings in the street, and thought of Alexandre's broken marriage to Yvonne, who had taken her money and gone to live in Florence with her lover; and of Martine, *née* Marie Leclerc, whose affair with Paul was making the rounds of Paris gossip. The world was setting up its battle lines, her sons were going to fight. Charlotte closed the door to her bedroom and pulled down the blinds, in order not to see her ageing face reflected in the mirrors and the windowpanes.

Jamie had returned to Cincinnati. Her father had found her a job in the public library, writing out file cards in the stacks. She needed the dollars.

The moment she came home, her mother said: 'Willy is married. Did you know that?'

'How could I, Mother? Willy and I haven't been friends for years.' Still, she felt a kind of shock.

'Made a girl . . . with child. Can you imagine?' Margaret's piercing blue eyes drilled holes into her. Jamie panicked: She knows! Oh my god – she knows! But no, I must be dreaming, she's just . . . Mother.

'Who – who was the girl?' she asked, trying to let her breath out normally. The unbearable heat was suffocating her like a pillow over her face.

'The same one. Probably the only one who'd have him. Eve – Eva? An immigrant, naturally.'

Jamie couldn't help it. 'Daddy was an immigrant,' she reminded her mother. Then, touching the redness of her cheeks, she couldn't bear it any longer and left the room. If she had to, she would still defend Willy. She had been the one to leave; he had done nothing bad to her. Only one year ago they had sat in the park, under the flowering trees . . .

But she didn't want to see him, especially not now. And yet, of course, she knew she would, some time when she was least expecting it. It happened after work one evening, when she was leaving the library. She walked out into the balmy air of summer, feeling tired of the white lights in the stacks, of all the old dusty books with their fine print that hurt her delicate eyes. And suddenly he was beside her, carrying an absurd metal lunch pail, wearing absurd olive-green overalls. His black curly hair, his blue eyes – those were unchanged. His expression was sullen.

'So. My darling sweet Jamie. How was your great year at the bastion of all learning?'

She looked down, wet her lips. 'Must you talk like that?' she asked in a hushed voice.

'Why not? The world knows you've come home. All the minor dignitaries have been alerted by that *grande dame*, your mother. The church is buzzing.'

'She tells me you and Eva have married, and are expecting a baby.'

'Always the direct little Jamison. But you're wrong: We've already had the child. She's a month and a half.'

'What's her name?' she asked. 'Your daughter?'

He shrugged, looked bitter. 'Emmeline Jamie. Can you believe it? I couldn't resist.'

She was stunned. And then, somewhat delighted. 'Eva – doesn't mind?'

He stared at her then and said: 'She doesn't *know*. She thinks, you see, that you are like my sister. She doesn't hate you. You've been gone, exploring the great horizon. Why should she fear you?'

'Why, indeed? I'm not a threat because you and I finished long ago. I wish you well – all three of you.' That sounded hollow and insincere, and so she finally raised her head and looked at him. He'd been examining her all the while. She blushed and stammered: 'Are you happy? I mean – what are you doing with your life?'

'I'm working. At a construction site. And I have a family to support. I don't mind the kid. Of course I wasn't going to let her down – Eva, that is. You know why I couldn't.'

'You really needed to be married, Willy. I don't think you would have let her become pregnant if you hadn't also wanted a family of your own. It isn't *all* because of Emma that you made things legal with Eva: You must be honest

91

with yourself. It's also because of you. Some people need to be solidly anchored to another person.'

'Is that what they teach you at Vassar? Freud – or is it Jung? I do read, you see. Even if I'm not a college boy.'

'Do you wish you were?' she asked abruptly, searching his face for clues. A hope that maybe all was not lost, for his own future. She still cared. Jamie said: 'Willy – why can't you try a summer school? Or night classes? You can do all the reading you want, but a good teacher – '

'I don't need any professors,' he cut in angrily. 'Tell me – do you have someone, an Ivy Leaguer or something? Don't you ever want to get married, Jamie?'

She shook her head. 'Not now. And I love what I'm doing. I have a roommate, Lesley. She and I have become quite close. I'm not looking for any great romance. I have no money to fall back on, like most of the other girls there. So I need to work toward a career, prepare my life.'

'Yes. I'm thinking of going to Germany to enlist.'

She drew back, the wind knocked out of her. 'What?'

'Nobody cares here about the war in Europe. I don't like America. My mother and I were never accepted. What is it your ma always called us? "Immigrants". A step up, but only a small one, from the coloured folk. We're still Germans to everyone. Well, then, if that's what we are, we should fight like Germans. I've come to that conclusion. Maybe we should even move back there.'

Jamie was horrified. She cried out: 'But if America joins the war, we'd be fighting against the Germans! Boys you grew up with would be fighting you! I don't believe in war! There's no reason for it.'

'Somebody has to do something,' he answered, looking away. He fidgeted with his pail, then with a button on his shirt. 'I don't really know,' he murmured uncomfortably. 'But I've sure been thinking about it. I hate it here!'

She heard the passion in his voice and saw that he meant it. He had always hated the United States. Could she really

92

blame him for wanting to hang his hat in a country that might, because of his roots, greet him with more friendship? Filled with sadness, Jamie placed a hand on his sleeve, kissed his cheek. 'Oh, God, Willy,' she whispered. 'I wish I knew what to tell you. It's such a confused world. And I'm such a fool, I can only repeat what other people say. I'm sorry.'

As he walked away, breaking into a run across the street, she felt the desolation of his life and was sorry for him. He had locked himself into a way of life for ever, a way of life now totally removed from hers.

Some day, she would meet someone, but not a Yalie or a Harvard boy at somebody's house party. She would meet a man of consequence, who would accomplish something. But first she had to weld herself into a 'somebody'. She had a special quality inside her, regardless of her mediocre family background and her lack of funds, that was going to prove to be great. But she needed to develop it into a real talent. And she already knew what this was: She could write.

Jamie Stewart crossed the street in the shadows of dusk and thought of the trees and the asphalt and the hot summer flies. It was better than thinking about how far she had yet to go, to prove herself. Or about Willy and the war.

Chapter Four

Harbin. A city turned inside out, upside down. By the time Elena had reached it, she felt burned out. They had gone from Irkutsk to Chita, then crossed the border into Manchuria, she and her elegant Moscow Jewesses. Genia was the more beautiful of the two Adler sisters and also the more unstable; Fania was poised and likeable, a solid person. Elena found them both, however, naïve and childlike. For the odyssey of their existence was only just beginning: But it was 1915, and she had been fending for herself since 1908!

They knew of the world only what had been taught to them by their governess. Of men they knew nothing. Well, thought Elena, and what do *I* know? A bitterness flooded her then. She was twenty-five and had never loved. Genia and Fania were after the easy adulation of flatterers: she, who had nothing to offer save herself, no money with which to lure admirers, was after so much more! And yet, she thought, I do not trust men.

Her role had been quickly defined as the leader. The Adlers paid, gratefully, whatever gratuities needed to be issued; but it was she, Elena, who managed their comings and goings, who made certain that Genia was not forgetting her hat nor Fania the passports. She had assumed the part of a paid companion. It was only a temporary measure to get her from one place to the next, and the Adlers treated her with kindness and thankfulness. 'What would we ever do without you?' one or the other was for ever repeating. Usually it was Fania, looking at Elena with her large almond eyes and smiling that slow, lazy smile of hers, like that of the Gioconda.

Harbin. The clocks seemed turned around. People breakfasted at noon, had lunch at five, and businessmen returned home at eight in the evening to have their high tea, English fashion. Nightclubs did not open until one in the morning, and dancing took place till five or six. It was an interesting city, built in the 1890s at the eastern end of the TransSiberian Railway to Vladivostok. So essentially it was a railway centre, with offices conducting railway business. Its inhabitants were mostly Chinese and Russian, and there was an ancient flavour to the city. Yet its construction was modern in a western European way; there were luxury hotels and nightclubs with dancing girls who did the tango with their rich customers.

How much more advanced Harbin was than the true capital of Manchuria, Chang-chun to the south! This city was composed primarily of Chinese, and to collect taxes, platoons of soldiers marched from shop to shop. Genia and Fania were mesmerized by the primitive quality of this Manchurian city. They could not associate this sort of life with the one they had led in their genteel Jewish quarter of Moscow. But in Harbin the Adlers began to come out of their shells. In the centre of the town were a dozen nightclubs, with boxes around the dance floor where the wealthy came to dine and observe. The Adler sisters, blushing, took Elena with them and scoured the floor for potential admirers. There was always a British officer available to do the honours. But, more often than not, his eyes would remain riveted on Elena.

But she saw the larger picture: It did not behove her to alienate the Adler sisters. And so, humbly, she would cast down her black eyes, flutter their heavy lids, and murmur: 'I'd rather not dance, thank you. In Russia I left behind a fiancé.'

At those times Fania's gaze would encounter hers and a slight tremor would traverse Elena. She would feel the blood pounding at her temples and would hold herself quite still in her chair.

Elena looked around, watched the hostesses in the night-clubs, all well-bred girls whose money had run out for some reason or other. And she wondered! What would happen to me if the Adlers left me? Suddenly, for the first time in her life, she felt unsure of herself.

One evening after Genia Adler had met a dapper Englishman, and he had swept her off for a tango, Elena noticed that Fania stayed ill at ease at the table. Genia was laughing, on the dance floor, a hysterical note to her mirth, and Fania frowned. Genia had consumed altogether too much champagne. Still, the man was pleasant, courtly. Fania loked away, and Elena saw that her eyes had become full of tears. She reached over and laid a hand upon the other's arm. 'Thank you,' Fania whispered. 'You are such a sweet girl, Elena. I feel so . . . alone.'

'I too feel alone,' Elena admitted candidly. She felt depression settling over her like a shroud but could not shake it off. 'Harbin does that, don't you think? It's four in the morning and we haven't even begun to think of sleep!'

'I miss my father,' Fania said, bending foward.

'I miss mine too. He was once a remarkable man.'

Despair knotted itself around Elena's throat. 'He was so brilliant, so worldly, such a witty man,' she murmured. She could see Prince Sergei in his study, conferring with Stoly-pin, and then again, bending over the hand of the Tsarina Alexandra . . . And she had sworn never to look back!

'My father was strong-willed and stern, and very religious,' Fania said. 'We used to tremble before him, Genia and I. He kept us little girls and made us unfit for other men. He shouldn't have done that. Look at Genia now! She is exactly like a fifteen-year-old girl, who has not yet made her debut! Blushing and tipsy and flirtatious. You know how to hold a man, Elena: We don't. This one too shall go his own way. Genia does not know how to be a woman.'

'But one doesn't have to learn. It comes to us all, naturally,' Elena countered gently.

'Oh, to you it may. You, my dear, are special. We are merely provincial girls, barely a step removed from the Pale of Settlement. Come – let us go home now to the hotel. He will bring her home later. There is nothing more to be done, and I am exhausted.'

She stood up, and Elena did likewise. It had been a long evening. Genia waved at them from the dance floor, but Fania was too demoralized, too drained to return her sister's gesture. Elena put an arm around her and they took a taxicab back to their suite. Neither said a word. Around them floated the unreality of the Orient, the reality of their personal dilemmas.

In the small but lovely room that was hers, Elena brushed out the long thick strands of her black hair and massaged her temples. Her head felt tight, tense with dull ache. She looked at the mirror reflection of her face, noted the mauve circles under her eyes. Then the door opened, and Fania stood on the threshold, in her nightgown. She was holding some flowers, flowers that the maid had put out that morning in the ornate vases of the sitting room. 'For you,' Fania said.

Elena's eyes, inexplicably, filled with tears as Fania's had at the nightclub. She took a few steps, held out her hand, received the bouquet. For a second their fingers touched, and Elena's lips parted on a sudden intake of breath. Then she turned away and placed the flowers in a bowl, busied herself by pouring in some water. Fania waited.

Silently, then, Elena left the bowl of flowers on her dressing-table and followed Fania to the other bedroom. Fania removed her peignoir, and Elena sat very still so that Fania could lower the straps and place soft fingers on her shoulders. Very tentative fingers. 'You are so beautiful,' Fania murmured, her voice barely audible. And then Elena burst into tears of fear and misery. She wept and sobbed until Fania's arms were around her, cloaking her from the world. And Elena cried in Fania's arms and then received

97

Fania's kisses, the first that had ever tasted her firm, virginal body. She went to sleep in the crook of Fania's arm, like a lover, and Fania watched her sleep until it was time for breakfast. Genia had not come home, but Fania did not care: Let Genia have this Englishman and all the rest, if she so chose! Her sister would have Elena, the most exquisite, the finest. 'I love you,' Fania said to her sleeping form. 'I shall love you for ever.'

But Elena never heard her. She slept like a small child, after a storm.

Three weeks later, when Genia announced that her British friend wanted to take a drive to Chang-chun with them, Elena declined the invitation. It had been evident to her that this man too looked first at her, then at Genia. She would pretend a headache and thereby avoid the jealousy of both Adler sisters. Fania should not see her drawing a man's attention, and Genia should not see her drawing this particular man's. She watched from the window as he helped first the younger, then the older sister into his Rolls-Royce. Fania was adjusting her goggles, and Genia struggled for a moment with an elegant scarf to protect her from the elements. Then Fania raised her face to the air, scanning the window for Elena. She lifted a hand, smiled. The door closed, and the car took off. Elena remained standing by the lace curtains, looking out at the motes of dust and sand raised in the wake of the car. She sighed and turned away. There was nothing to do in Harbin before eight at night, tea time. And then, with whom? The Adlers were really the only ones she knew there.

The next day she was still in the suite, all alone. It was there that the attorney reached her with the news. The Englishman's car had lost a wheel while making a precarious turn around the side of a cliff. The Rolls-Royce had somersaulted over the edge and burst into flames. The three passengers had been killed.

'The Adlers made a will a few weeks ago,' the man told

98

Elena. 'They bequeathed all their goods to you, in the event that neither outlived the other. Most of the funds, and the real property, are in Russia, but the sisters did establish a small bank account here in Harbin, for convenience. It's yours.'

He left his card for her. Elena sat in stunned silence, her strong hands clenched in her lap. She was trying not to think of Fania, or she knew she would crumble. So she concentrated instead on the harsh realities of her financial situation. The lawyer had mentioned funds, in Russia. But she would never return to Russia. Some day, when the Harbin money ran out, she would send someone – this attorney, perhaps, for he looked trustworthy – to sell the land and bring her the proceeds. For now – she was not sure what she would do.

The white sun, with its blinding glare, lay over the city of Harbin like a bride's veil. Elena could not weep. It was 1916, and she was in the middle of a no-man's land.

One of Lady Priscilla's most serious desires had always been for both her daughters to be presented at the Court of St James, as she once had been. Blonde, lithe and elegant, the only child of Arthur Stephen, Earl of Brighton, she had been presented to Queen Victoria, imposing and triple chinned, during the summer following her eighteenth birthday. Emily Aymes Richardson had come in 1912 and been presented to King George and Queen Mary. Now it was Lesley's turn. Lesley regarded her court presentation much as she had viewed her New York debut. She went dutifully to the rehearsals, wearing the gown that they had bought for her in Paris, but her eyes were turned inward. Her mother noticed that she seemed nervous. During the week she was her normal self, but toward the weekend she would fret, hardly touching her food.

'Did you leave a friend at Vassar?' Priscilla asked

99

carefully, keeping her voice evenly modulated to show she didn't really want to pry.

'A friend, Mama? Jamie?'

'No, darling. A young man.'

Lesley's eyes widened, her face drained of colour. 'At *Vassar*? In the States? No, Mama. I haven't any boyfriends. Escorts, yes, but no one I like.'

'I see.' Lady Priscilla thought: I shall have to watch her more closely. And then she began to search for meaningful signs among her father's guests. It must be someone there, because in Paris, they hadn't met anyone new. All the young men were in the front lines.

Lesley, if aware of the parental scrutiny, seemed unconcerned by it. She was thinking: Why isn't he coming back? Am I just someone he saw in a room at his host's summer house? And then she felt the sense of anger, first at herself for being so foolish, then at him for not rushing more quickly back for another weekend, to renew his acquaintance with her. 'I have a crush on a man I've seen only for two minutes,' she wrote to Jamie, her cheeks red with shame. She worried much more about when and if Justin Reeve would return than about how to address the King and Queen of England. She could do the latter, she knew without doubt: but Justin Reeve filled her with *such* doubts that her stomach knotted and her throat tightened, just in the hope that he would come and in the fear that he might not care to see her again. And so her presentation to King George and Queen Mary went by almost as though it were a routine event.

Then he came. Not the first weekend, but the second one. Lesley, from her window, saw him and his sister, Adele, stepping out of a shining black Rolls-Royce, laughing together. I wish *I* could make him laugh like that, she thought jealously. Adele was so different from Justin. He was all finesse and darkness, all sharp-edged glamour, and she was British tweeds and had the long face of a mare, pleasant but undistinguished. Lesley rushed to her cupboard, pulled out her new clothes from Paris, and kicked off her shoes. One had to prepare for him – but so casually that he'd never know she'd thought even once of him since their encounter.

Lady Priscilla, embroidering on her *chaise longue*, looked up sharply, noticing the array of clothes heaped on her daughter's bed, and felt uneasy. She'd been right. Tonight she'd know who.

But it wasn't obvious. Lord Brighton, now rotund, but still a most outstanding man, reigned over his guests with the usual flair, drawing young and old about him, recounting stories of the hunt, of past adventures in the Far East. He'd kept up the British tradition his wife had so treasured of inviting guests of all sorts – but only of the top social echelon – from Friday to Monday. The rest of the week he rested, like a replete god, and to his family he seemed introverted, an old man with asthma and arthritis who sat by the fire even in summer and sighed a lot.

That weekend there were several couples Lady Priscilla's age, two young girls Lesley's age, another young man, and the Reeves. Justin Reeve. Lady Priscilla saw him with her father, a slender figure but very tall, with pronounced cheekbones and deepset eyes in a long, delicate oval face. She walked over to them, smiled, and said: 'Sir Justin. What a pleasure to have you with us again.'

He was bowing over her hand with continental poise – too much so, Priscilla Richardson thought. Her memory of this young man was slight. His father had been a contemporary of hers, a baronet, but he hadn't possessed his son's charm nor those good looks. He'd resembled the daughter – Adele, with the horsey laughter. Whom had he married? She was trying now to remember.

'Justin brings me the pleasure of his visit about once a month,' Lord Brighton was telling her, his hand proprietorially on the young man's arm. 'He's very busy these days, you know, Prissy. He's opened an art gallery in town, and he's quite the boy, quite the boy. Makes me think of his grandfather, sad to say. A friend I deeply miss.'

Priscilla thought she remembered that Justin and Adele had lost both their parents in some sort of dreadful accident – a horse overturning their carriage, something like that. She had no recollection of the boy's mother. She'd have to ask her father. Better to know. Because, she thought sharply, he was obviously the one.

Lesley was sitting with the two young girls, her hair in a topknot with fresh flowers in it, her dress one of the Chanel wisps of nothing that she'd adopted. She was wearing no jewellery except a string of pearls and matching pearl studs on her ears. She looked, her mother thought, almost too young. And she was laughing, not looking at Justin and her grandfather, but every now and then fingering the trim of the sofa or biting her lip. Lady Priscilla thought: Now I remember! It was an Italian girl – a contessa, delicate and frail.

Sir Justin Reeve had finally left Lord Arthur and was coming to the sofa. Lesley felt his presence, looked up. He said, 'Miss Richardson. How nice to see you.'

Is it? she wanted to ask, thinking angrily: Of course he knew he'd see me. I'm living here all summer! But instead she cast her eyes down and answered, 'Thank you.'

The other girls must have sensed that their presence was no longer required, because as soon as he had greeted them, they stood up and found an excuse to go and speak to Adele Reeve. Justin sat down next to Lesley, and she didn't know what to do.

'Your mother is charming,' he said at length.

'Mama? Yes. She's in her element here. I wonder if she doesn't at heart wish she'd never left England. New York is ... different.'

'Is it? You must tell me about it. I've never been there.'

'But there's so little to tell! I don't like it. I don't think

102

I'm going to live there when I finish my studies.' She was speaking too quickly, not looking at him, but at her feet, at the dark Persian carpet below them.

Justin was saying: 'I came back because I wanted to see you again. I had to drag Adele. She thinks once a month is often enough, and she had other parties to go to this weekend.'

'And without your sister, you don't go anywhere?'

'Oh, it isn't that. We're used to each other. I suppose we're what people term "close". We've been on our own since I was eighteen and she, seventeen. And since she's had the good sense not to marry . . .'

'Well,' Lesley murmured, 'I wouldn't marry unless everything were just right. If all you think of is the final step, it can take the joy out of loving someone. Later, the rest will fall into place.'

Justin smiled at her.

'You don't agree?'

'It's not that. But to me, your words are a delightful change. Usually I find that girls are *only* after an engagement ring. They don't care what's beneath the person. So long, of course, as he's from the right background!'

'Then England is hardly different from New York, or Vassar College.'

'It's very dull,' he stated. 'How could a man decide to marry a girl who hasn't cared enough to understand him? Are you engaged, Miss Richardson?'

'You must call me Lesley. And no, I'm not engaged. Last week I was presented at Court, but that was only to please mother. It was a lovely ceremony, but to her, much more important than to me. You see, since I'm *not* engaged, I have to do these sorts of things to make it up to her!'

She had succeeded in making him laugh. She felt the warmth in the room, the redness in her cheeks. 'And you?' she asked. 'What do you do during the week? Surely you've finished your studies?'

103

'Two years ago, at Oxford. Now I've opened a small art gallery. But it isn't doing too well. The brilliant artists are all in Paris, and this isn't the ideal time to travel across the Channel.'

Adele was coming over to them, her cheeks ruddy with good health, her large hands chapped from many Sundays of early-morning riding. Lesley was resentful of the intrusion, yet grateful too, because she had run out of intelligent things to say. It was only Friday. What would she say to him tomorrow?

'Well, now, my dear brother, I finally put two and two together, I daresay!' Adele was remarking brightly. 'You didn't want to spend another weekend with Lord Brighton. It was his granddaughter who caught your fancy!'

She was laughing, heartily, in her blustering, friendly fashion, but Lesley turned scarlet from confusion, and Justin's face looked amused. She was averting her eyes when she felt his hand briefly resting on one of hers and then its soft pressure. 'My sister is a bit indiscreet,' Justin said quickly, and then he added, more gently, for Lesley's ears alone: 'But she's also far from being a fool . . . And he stood up, took Adele's arm, and made his way to a group of people who had gathered around the grand piano. Lesley sat alone, watched him walk away, noticing his graceful small waist and broader shoulders, the slim hips in the fine fabric of his suit.

The next morning there was a hunt, and when she awakened, everyone was gone. She'd asked her grandfather to be excused from this event. She dressed, but lightly, because of the heat, and kept her hair coiled in plaits around her head. She wanted to draw, and declined breakfast, accepting only a cup of tea and a slice of toast and marmalade. The morning was clear, with small white clouds above, clustered in a hyacinth-blue sky. She walked through the front gardens, filled with summer blooms, and wended her way toward a white gazebo some distance from the main house, near the stables. She was going to sketch bits and pieces of the woods as they blended into the cultivated land and perhaps one of the mares grazing in the field to the far left. Only in England did one find such pastoral scenes, she thought, and sudden pleasure flooded her heart.

A light wind was blowing her hair around her ears, over her forehead. All at once she felt that someone was approaching, and raised her head. It was Justin, in riding attire, crop in hand. She felt blood rush to her temples. She asked: 'Is the hunt over so quickly?'

'Of course not. At the last moment I told Lord Brighton that I had a headache. I was certain you'd be there, and when you weren't . . . Your mother told me that you would probably come out to draw. I didn't realize you were an artist.'

He was sitting down beside her, and instinctively she covered her sketch with her sleeve. 'I-I'm no good,' she stammered.

'Who told you that?'

'One of my teachers at Vassar.'

'That's cruel. He's only one man, and he's already persuaded you to be a defeatist. Let me see.'

Unwillingly, she relinquished the sketch and watched as he examined it cautiously, then with a smile. 'It's not bad at all,' he declared. 'I like its pure lines.'

'You embarrass me. But . . . thank you.'

They were looking at each other, and gently he laid aside the sketch pad and pulled the pencil from her fingers. He cupped her chin in his hand, and in this moment she felt the sun on her skin, the breeze in her hair, heard the mare braying, and thought: I'm going to capture this instant for the rest of my life. And she raised her lips, and he kissed her, softly at first and then parting her mouth to find her tongue and taste it. She raised her arms, wound them around his neck, abandoned herself to the delicious sensations that were making her entire body quiver with pleasure.

Then he was drawing away, saying quickly: 'I mustn't, Lesley. I mustn't be with you alone too much, or I shall want more.'

'What do you mean?' she asked, disappointment in her voice.

'You're innocent. I don't want to take advantage of this innocence.'

'I'm eighteen years old, Justin. Doesn't that make me old enough for you not to treat me like a little girl?'

'I didn't mean to be insulting.'

She was confused and angry, angry at her odd array of feelings and at him for not understanding them. She said, turning away: 'I've never kissed a man the way I've kissed you. I don't kiss somebody simply because he takes me to a dance, or because he brings me flowers. In America I've gone to countless functions with what my mother calls "eligible young men of standing". I've kissed one or two, but never like this, never . . . with my whole being. Don't . . . make it cheap.'

'I didn't mean to. Forgive me, Lesley. The girls here tend to act just as you describe: They kiss not for the man, but for the occasion. I wasn't kissing you for any reason other than desire, the desire to be with you. I'd wanted *you*.'

Was this what had propelled Jamie into making love to Willy? Lesley wondered. She imagined the act and then couldn't complete the picture. Yet with Justin it would have to be a beautiful experience. He was such a beautiful man . . . and so kind, so gallant and sensitive. She found that suddenly it was too warm, that she was perspiring, and she whispered. 'I'm going back inside. Any moment now my grandfather will return with the others. I must change for luncheon.'

'Lesley,' he said. 'Any day now I may have to go into the armed forces. I wish I could promise you a future – '

'Don't even speak of it. We hardly know each other.'

'But when love comes, it comes like this, in a flash. Real love is born like an electric spark. I don't believe that it can ever take place between two friends of long standing. That's contentment, that's brotherhood, but not passionate love. Could you love a man with an unclear future?'

'I don't look to the future,' she replied, standing awkwardly in front of him, wanting to weep from the fear and the excitement mingled inside her.

He stood up too then and took her in his arms, and she slid closer to him, trying to fit into the crevices of his body. She felt the hard bump on her thighs and was tempted to step back. But she didn't pull back, not this time. She didn't want to hurt him, and then suddenly there was a responding chord, and she *wanted* to feel his hardness against her. She was pressing herself closer, without realizing she was doing so, when he stopped and put his hands cautiously on her shoulders. 'Lesley. What are we doing?'

She shook her head, ashamed then and frightened. 'I must go inside,' she whispered again, and this time she turned from Justin and broke into a run toward the house. When she reached her room, she threw herself on the bed. I don't know whether this is good or bad, she thought with apprehension. And then: Is this how all women feel when it happens? She wished that she had the courage to ask her mother, or that Jamie were close by.

The Cromwellian mansion was spread out over several buildings, and Lesley's small suite overlooked the trim formal gardens with the circular gravel driveway from which she could see guests as they arrived. Beyond the garden stretched the hills of Yorkshire, grey-blue in the distance, and at night the sun set behind them, its molten orb disappearing in a magnificent range of colours that spilled out over the adjoining countryside. She loved the

107

dusk, and now, this Saturday, it moved her deep inside. She thought of the ancient druids who had worshipped nature, who had felt within them a respondent chord. The sharp cry of a night bird sounded, eerie and unseen.

I don't want to go to dinner, she thought, and went to the adjoining double door that connected her sitting room with her mother's bedroom. Lady Priscilla was already at her dressing-table, twirling a piece of blond hair back into a knot. 'I'm tired, Mama,' Lesley announced.

'You haven't done anything today. You missed the hunt.'

'You know why I didn't go.'

'Do you want supper in your room?' Lesley could read the concern in her mother's tone.

'That's too much bother.'

'Then I'll ask them to send up some tea and toast, and perhaps some soup.' Lady Priscilla smiled briefly, and Lesley suddenly felt immense relief at her mother's discretion, at her reserve. Could she have guessed what I feel for Justin? she wondered.

'Well, then, it's all settled.' Lady Priscilla stood up, sighed, and wrapped an evening shawl about her dinner gown. If she knows, what does she think? Lesley asked herself.

Alone, she sat by the window, and presently the servants came out to turn on the front lights, and the gardens were bathed in a yellow glow. Her grandfather's house breathed comfort, a word so terribly at odds with war that it made Lesley feel almost sinful.

A small knock sounded, and she answered, 'Yes, Sylvia.' The chambermaid with her tea. The door opened, and Lesley thought: I should have turned the lights on in here for her. But outside there are such lovely colours . . .

The tray moved forward, and she stood up to help the girl. But to her amazement, it was not Sylvia who was wheeling the trolley, but Justin Reeve. Lesley felt the beating of her heart and a sudden tensing of her body. She

108

hadn't pinned her hair up since her bath, and was wearing her lace-trimmed housecoat, with no jewellery at all. She hadn't even splashed Shalimar behind her ears.

She wanted to ask why he was there, doing the maid's job, but it was so obvious that she said nothing, her tongue dry between her parted lips. For a second she remembered how shocked anyone would be at his presence in her room, particularly considering her state of dress. Then she was excited by it. Her first time with him alone in a room that was private . . .

He was laughing and coming to her, extending his hands. 'I gave Sylvia a gold coin and said "Happy Christmas!"' he stated. 'You should have seen the look on her face . . . Then I gave her another coin to make her swear that no one would share her Christmas news.'

Lesley didn't have time to think about how incongruous they were, he in his dinner jacket, she in her mint-green housecoat, her hair undone. He was pulling her toward him and wrapping both arms around her. Beneath the housecoat she wore nothing, and his hands wandered up and down her back, exploring. She allowed her mind to float from reality to give herself up to the dream of her senses, those fingers caressing the soft material covering her bare skin. Beneath her room resounded the muted laughter of dinner-table conversation – beneath them, and continents away.

'We're all alone, Lesley,' he was whispering into her hair. 'We're going to close the double door and lock it, and your mother will assume you've gone to sleep.'

She could smell him, feel him, more than she could distinguish him in the dark room illumined only from the outside. He seemed haloed by the golden glow of the garden. She clung to him, frightened. What had he said? What was he intimating? She wasn't sure now that she was ready for this, because there was still so much they didn't know about each other, so much of their past that they hadn't revealed.

'Justin . . .'

109

'What, darling?'

He was unbuttoning his jacket, and she felt the tensing of her own body. He was behaving as if this were his room, their room, a wedding chamber. But what do *I* want? she asked herself, panic-stricken. She wanted him, she wanted to be near him, to hold him, never to let him go. Did she want him to marry her? Yes, she thought, I suppose I do. Yes, *yes*, this moment was right, and she did want what he wanted, right now.

'Help me,' he said to her. His voice didn't sound the way it normally did, but was low, tremulous, throaty. She reached out at that moment toward the appeal of his voice, because it made things happen inside her, sending her stomach into knots, her heart racing. She went to him as he was sitting on her canopied bed, a young girl's bed, and he took her numb fingers and placed them over the buttons of his dress shirt. She understood what he was asking her to do, and felt embarrassed at her ineptitude in these matters. So she concentrated on the buttons, small pearls, easy to slip behind the eyes of the buttonholes.

When she had finished she stepped back, but he put a hand on her wrist, and she stayed near him as he shook the shirt off and looked at her. In the half-glow of the room his irises seemed black coals, burning with intensity. Then she looked at his bare chest, at the two dark nipples surrounded with black tendrils, at the line of fine hairs that went from his chest to his belt. At the belt her eyes stopped, and she swallowed, afraid of his nakedness, wanting now to ward it off.

Seeming to sense her hesitation, he unbuckled his belt and shed his trousers in one swift motion, and she turned away. When she felt his hands on her shoulders, she leaned against him, closing her eyes. *Now*. Did he think she was being shy, or coy? They had never discussed making love, it was simply happening; so maybe he thought that she was more experienced than she was and simply being a tease.

But her heart was pounding, and she didn't dare speak. Whatever she said was bound to be the wrong thing at this moment. She would have to trust him.

From behind he was undoing her housecoat, and small goosepimples prickled her skin. Tiny little electric shocks were taking place all over her body. The satin gown fell to her ankles, and then he turned her toward him, and she wasn't sure whether to be embarrassed at her own nudity or afraid of his.

He wasn't speaking. She wished he would break the awful silence of their naked bodies, but he didn't. His hands cupped one breast, played with the nipple until it stood erect, then let go, went to the other. She knew that he was examining her, measuring her. Was she as he'd envisaged?

Then he was carrying her, laying her on the coverlet like a precious package, and he lay down beside her, on his side. One hand played over her stomach, which contracted. Relax. Don't let him know you're so afraid. She shut her eyes, but he was taking her hand and placing it over something she had never felt before: his own hardness. She felt the shock, sensed the tears almost ready to spill. Oh, Justin, please – Please *what?* She didn't even know. Please *do*, and also, Please *don't*.

Something was rebelling inside her now, and she almost gave in to it and pulled away. But she thought: Nakedness shouldn't frighten me. He was kissing her breasts, and she concentrated on the curls of his head, on the smooth line of his muscled back.

He was going to realize she was a virgin, if he hadn't thought so before. His kisses wended their way southward, his tongue flicked around her bellybutton, continued down, stopped at the red curls of her pubis, then he buried his head in their female softness. Dismayed, Lesley writhed away. He stopped and looked at her in the semi-darkness. 'No,' she stammered.

'But it should give you pleasure.'

111

'Please, Justin, don't.'

He stared at her, his eyes unblinking. She thought: But Jamie never told me they did *this*. His fingers were gently opening her sexual parts, where he had placed his tongue a moment ago, and she had made him stop. She felt dirty. Why would a man want to do a thing like that?'

'You mustn't ever be ashamed, Lesley,' he said slowly, and then he bent his head over her again, and she thought, wildly: I guess they do much more than what it takes to make a baby. She was afraid to ask him again to stop, and so she endured the soft thrusts of his tongue on the outer lips, on her clitoris – parts of her body for which she'd never even had a name. Then he kissed her stomach and her shoulders. The hard part of him lay pressed against her thigh, insistent. He, for one, was definitely not ashamed.

'I want you to enjoy it,' he said.

'But Justin . . . I don't know *how!*' She knew the tears were there now because her eyes stung from them. Did he think she was accustomed to sexual matters? That she'd known all along what he would do? 'Justin,' she whispered. 'Maybe it's wrong . . . I've never – '

'You've never been with a man?'

'No.' Should she have told him before?

'The first time is always difficult, darling,' he replied very gently.

So he wasn't going to get up and leave just because she was a virgin. She felt oddly relieved. He kissed her cheek, almost like a brother, and then she knew that she was crying, because he was licking the tears away with soft flickers of his tongue. 'I love the taste of you,' he was saying. 'All the different tastes of you.'

She thought that she was going to die of shame. Why weren't there courses and books on what men did with women during their intimate moments? Why did one always have to enter into sex knowing less than nothing? She thought, wildly again: But there *is* something I know,

112

and I haven't done anything about it! After Mary Rose, Emily had begun to use a pessary –

'Justin,' she said, 'what if I have a baby?'

He laughed. 'Then I shall marry you.'

Oh. Her forehead was drenched with perspiration, and she couldn't think any more. He caressed her temples, her chin, kissed her on the lips. 'I love you, Justin,' she whispered.

'And I love you too, Lesley Aymes Richardson.'

They lay quietly side by side, and she was almost relaxed. He threw one leg over her thighs and pressed his penis between her legs, where he had kissed her before. She put her hands on his shoulders to ward off the pain, and he said: 'It won't be so bad, sweetheart. After a while it will be good.' And then he pushed himself into the inner parts of her, soft pushes, trying to make her accept him without so much pain. But there was pain, burning pain. 'Don't fight me,' he said, his voice tender and reassuring.

She was reminded of being in a doctor's office. She'd been three. 'Don't cry, Lesley,' the doctor had said. 'It will only hurt for one second.' And then he'd thrust the needle into her arm, and she'd cried out at the suddenness of the jab. She wasn't going to cry now because she wanted him, and she didn't want to send him away. And what he wanted, she wanted, because she loved him.

Why did people make such a to-do about sex, as if this forbidden apple were such a desirable experience? He was all the way in now, and still she was feeling only pain. Then he kissed her mouth, and in the moment of kissing she forgot the pain and relaxed. Yes. I love him. I love his mouth over mine. I want to learn about these things – yes. She wound her arms around his neck and let him move inside her, until he slipped his hands beneath her buttocks and raised her toward him. It was better this way. Oh, God, I don't want to become pregnant . . .

113

'Then I shall marry you.' 'And I love you too, Lesley Aymes Richardson.' He was thrusting harder, and she felt better, realizing that they were as close now as any two people ever could be, that this was a kind of consecration, the most precious gift between a man and a woman. He made a little sound against her neck, and she felt him letting go, the part of him between her legs withdrawing, pulling out. She wondered if she'd bled, and if so, what Sylvia would say in the morning. Oh, God –

'I love you so much,' she said to him, hiding her face in his chest.

Would he understand? He was winding strands of her hair onto his long fingers, and in this tender moment between them, she heard again the laughter from below, and the hoot of a night owl.

She was silent, and he whispered: 'Tomorrow we shall ride, and then we shall make love behind an abbey that is almost as ancient as time itself.'

She wanted to hear him say he loved her again, and as she reached toward his cheek to stroke it and ask, she heard his even, measured breathing. He was asleep. Gently she disengaged herself, checked the locks on the double connecting door and on the one leading to the corridor, and then went to the window and closed the curtains. She wanted to wash, because she felt sticky and uncomfortable, but at the same time she needed to be with him still, holding him, warding off the outer world. So she climbed into the bed and pulled the covers over both of them, and pressed against his sleeping body.

But for hours she couldn't sleep. In the night he moved, groaned once, reached over, touched her. She heard her mother coming into the neighbouring suite. Then the sounds died. I am a woman now, she thought. 'Then I shall marry you.' 'And I love you too, Lesley Aymes Richardson.' Dawn slowly rose, piercing between the curtains, and she felt him stirring. He sat up, rubbed his eyes.

She loved him so, and there he was, like a small boy brushing the sleep from his eyes . . .

'Darling,' he whispered, 'I'm going to have to leave, so that they don't catch us in the morning. Sleep a while longer.'

He was struggling into his clothes, and she watched, propping herself on an elbow. Such grace, such beauty. No one would ever be able to paint such complete loveliness. He placed a finger on his lips, blew her a kiss, and softly unlocked the door, opened it, slipped outside.

He was gone, and only the pillow testified that he'd been there next to her for so many hours. The pillow smelled like him, a scent like no other, and she buried her face in it, suddenly very happy, ecstatic, because they had made love and they loved each other. This, then, was *it*: a miracle, a joining. 'After a while,' he said, 'it will be good.' Yes. she would go with him to the abbey, and she would be less shy. 'I love you too, Lesley Aymes Richardson.'

Chapter Five

Jamie read the letter again in the peaceful stacks where she was sorting out new books, and where time was endless. She wondered whether her face reflected the fact that, at nineteen, she felt old, undiscovered, forgotten, like the oldest book in the stacks, which nobody ever borrowed any more.

The stationery was lightweight but embossed with the Brighton seal, dragons meeting over a lion's head. Suddenly Lesley's world and hers seemed very far apart, and the Brighton seal was the symbol of the invisible partition separating them — that, and the ocean, and a war.

Yorkshire is sprinkled with old abbeys, fallen into ruins. We drove that Sunday to Fountain's Abbey to see the façade, which has remained intact, with ogival windows peering at us hollowly from centuries past, when other wars shook the soil of England. There was no floor. It was a carpet of grass, young grass, impervious to war, to us, to the passage of fashions and mores. Justin does odd things in the abbeys: He gathers dust. Sometimes he climbs over the stones to the highest points, and there he scrapes up old dust into envelopes, to keep. I asked him why. He replied: 'Because God lies in these corners, and the God of old England was a different God from today's.' I don't always understand Justin.

I wish he'd talk a little bit about the future. He knows I'm going to go back to Vassar. Grandfather used to think the world of him, but the other day I overheard him say to Mother: 'He'll have to enlist. It's the only solution to his predicament.' Everyone seems to be talking in tongues, around me. What predicament, do you suppose? Do you think it's money? I doubt it. Grandfather never even alludes to money — it's taboo, like sex. He spoke as if it were a question of honour. To do with *me*? But then his enlisting would make no sense, so it must be something else, and it worries me. I

116

wish Justin would talk to me about his life, about his problems. Because now I'm sure he has some, and that they run deep.

Jamie folded up the letter, thinking: She wants more than anything to get married in Westminster Abbey and become Lady Reeve. And she would enjoy it. She'd be the focal point of artistic gatherings, where it wouldn't matter whether Clarence Chatterton approved or disapproved of her skills as a painter. She'd be the new Vanessa Bell, and everyone would come to see her because of her charm and her charming young husband. She closed her eyes, picturing Lesley in a sitting room filled with Impressionist oils, drinking tea spiked with whisky in Sèvres china cups. The old, the new, the risqué, the traditional. All were part of Lesley Richardson, whose grandfather was an earl and whose father had come from the South Side of Chicago.

Jamie put the letter carefully back in her bag and rose. It was time to lock up the stacks and go home. Justin Reeve's behaviour worried her too. It didn't seem to make sense. She wished she could meet him and judge for herself whether he was right for Lesley. Jamie walked home pensive and troubled.

At the start of September, the entire household of Lord Arthur Stephen Aymes moved back to the tall, red brick mansion in Kensington that had housed the Earls of Brighton for several centuries.

The head butler and cook, most of the ladies' maids, and Lord Arthur's personal valet always came with him from house to house; there remained only the shadow of a staff to take care of the empty Yorkshire mansion and its gardens. Lady Priscilla supervised the move and thought that some time in London would be good for Lesley before having to return to Vassar.

Lesley felt empty. She wondered when Justin would say

something to her. What he did say was: 'We'll go to Covent Garden together, darling, and walk through Soho. London in early autumn isn't so romantic as Paris, but I like it well enough.' She thought his tone was too cheerful; she felt miserable, because the notion of separation was bad enough, but without a commitment, it was unimaginable. She simply didn't want to think about any of its ramifications.

Her mother was watching her cautiously. And several days after the move back to London, she said offhandedly: 'My love, summer romances are wonderful if one puts them in their right perspective. They're a bit like shipboard flirtations. One shouldn't take them too seriously.'

Lesley felt the shock at the pit of her stomach. She blinked, speechless. Not take Justin seriously? They'd made love in her bed, on the green grass behind age-old abbeys, in inns and hotels. She'd given him her body, allowed him to teach her how to touch his, how to respond. She *loved* him! Not take him *seriously*? He was the only young man she had ever encountered who could fill her needs, who understood her. She spoke to him as she had only dared speak to Jamie. With him, her usual reserve could fall, like an unnecessary cover, and she could glow as herself, without fear of ridicule or judgment. She could not answer her mother.

But nevertheless, Lesley felt humiliated. If Justin had only spoken, said one single sentence about their future, she would have been able to reassure her mother. Justin had said he loved her. He was of impeccable lineage, so that even her grandfather would find him a good match. Justin would come through, and this was absolutely the man she wanted.

There was nothing lovely about London in September, she thought with rancour. It rained almost daily. And daily she counted the remaining hours until departure time. She dressed three times every day, putting fresh flowers in her

118

hair, buffing her nails – hoping that he would call in unexpectedly, or telephone or send a note. After the first few days it was becoming uncomfortable to sit with her mother having tea; they both skirted the subject with painful awareness. Lesley could feel the rage building up inside, like a tidal wave; but there was no outlet for her to express it. With the rage came a tremendous bewilderment. His absence didn't make *sense*! She smiled and pretended to eat, getting up in the night with intense nausea. Anything would have been better than this silence.

I must do something, she finally decided. She put on her simplest outfit, a little Chanel suit of dove-grey jersey, and tied a silk scarf around her neck. Her burgundy boots matched her leather bag, and the small grey hat matched the suit. She went downstairs and called the chauffeur. He would drive her in the silver Bentley to the town house of the Honourable Adele Reeve, on Upper Brook Street. She wondered what she would say, appearing unannounced at their house at five o'clock. That was teatime. If he and Adele were entertaining . . . But at least he'd be home from the gallery.

The chauffeur opened the door, and she walked up the porch steps to the old stone house, narrow and tall, bordered by roses. She was suddenly very much afraid. But better to face him, once and for all. She rang the doorbell. A young maidservant answered. In a high-pitched voice, Lesley said: 'Please inform Sir Justin that Miss Richardson is here to see him.'

The uniformed girl, about her own age, led her into a small sitting-room. Everything was decorated in Louis XVI furnishings, and as she sat down in a small chair with dainty legs, she thought that Adele must have felt awkward in this environment. Probably the contessa, their mother, had selected everything, and Justin, who was rightful heir to the house, had kept it intact. She loved the ensemble of rose-coloured materials, all in varying shades, and the

119

magnificent oil paintings on the wall: Vermeer, Hals, the old Dutch masters. In the corner was a gilded medallion with a madonna and child by Raphael. A different world. I wouldn't have thought it of Justin, she said to herself. He belongs better with the Bloomsbury set, in furniture that's more comfortable, less old-fashioned.

She went to the window. It overlooked the back garden, with trimmed hedges and beds of autumn blooms. A young man she had never seen was sitting on a wrought-iron bench, just below her, holding what looked like a canvas on his lap. Curious, Lesley stepped toward the window, opened it to let in the air and take a better look at the man.

Then she saw Justin. He was walking out of the house into the garden, toward the young man. She hadn't seen him for ten days, not since she'd come back to London. She could picture what he looked like beneath the dark-blue suit, his muscular shoulders, the small, firm buttocks . . . She shut her mind against the memory and listened instead.

'Well, Thomas, let's see this marvel of yours,' Justin was saying, sitting down on the bench next to the young man. Lesley could see them perfectly, though she was partially hidden by the rose damask curtain of the window.

'I used that mixture of yours for the patina,' Thomas replied, handing over the canvas. Lesley, intrigued, bent over, and as she did so, Justin lifted it up to get a better perspective for himself. She was amazed. The image was a different version of the medallion on the wall of this very sitting-room: a perfect Raphael madonna, holding the Christ child, looking down upon Him placidly. This madonna was tilting her head the other way, and the child's clothing was folded differently and of another colour.

'You did a good job, old boy,' Justin stated. Lesley wet her upper lip, blinking. But a Raphael . . .? She'd studied

Raphael so thoroughly for her course with Professor Tonks, head of the Art Department at Vassar. Justin was holding something from the Italian Renaissance, and yet their words . . .

'What sort of price do you think you'll get for it?' Thomas asked.

'Oh, I'm not sure, these days. I must find myself an aficionado of Florence in the fifteenth and sixteenth centuries. Just now the fashion seems to be moving toward the modern. There are new trends in Paris that are putting Matisse behind the times, and he's no longer considered the Master.'

'Still, Justin, for a Raphael . . . time is endless.'

The phrase seemed to amuse them both. Justin tapped the other on the shoulder, laughed. 'I worry sometimes that dust from old English abbeys won't do the trick, because the air must have been somewhat different in Tuscany. But the period's relatively similar. You mixed it up with that linseed formula I blended for you? Let me see the cracks . . .'

'It's in the cracks: old dust from ancient times, my friend. I worked on this one very hard – I think it's perfect.'

'Still, things are getting too dangerous, Tommy. The problem I had with the Blake you did for me, which that god-damned American in Paris thinks is a fake – '

'But my work was impeccable.'

'Yet Gertrude Stein's brother, Leo, is an expert. He knows a good deal about art – and he claims William Blake never did such a piece.'

'Of course he didn't. We wouldn't ever be stupid enough to do a reproduction – that's child's stuff! Any idiot could catch that. Among the collectors, it's known exactly who possesses which masterpiece on record. But what we've got to offer are recently discovered works that have been dug up in small-town auctions . . . that sort of thing. Any connoisseur would want a hitherto-unknown Blake – or better still, a Raphael. It will become the talk of London . . . or Paris.'

'Or whichever jail they place me in, old chum. It's getting very hot here. You're all right. But I'm not. I come from old stock, Tom. My sister means the world to me. She'll never marry if our name is tarnished. And I really am afraid. This last affair with Stein has made ugly noises in Paris. With echoes across the Channel. Even in Yorkshire, some of my father's oldest friends looked at me very strangely . . .'

'You're becoming unhinged, Justin.'

'No. Simply realistic. I'm going to enlist, Thomas. And ask to be sent far away. The Far East. So that people will forget the Blake and this can die down and Adele can live freely while I'm out of mind.'

'And you can die, full stop.'

'Perhaps. But the honour of my family still means something to me.'

'You have an odd code of values,' the other man stated, shaking his head.

Lesley slowly pushed the window back into place and groped for the nearest seat. She removed her hat, felt her cheeks, which were burning. She felt intensely sick, and the room was reeling around her. She had removed her gloves, and now she found a small silver bell. With a clammy hand, she agitated it several times before the young maid returned. She looked apologetic. 'I'm so sorry, milady, but Sir Justin had an important business meeting to attend to, and I wasn't able to catch him in time. He should finish any moment – I saw the gentleman fetch his hat and coat from Smithers.'

'It's all right, thank you, but I'm going to be sick, and I need a bathroom,' Lesley cut in. Together they hurried into a small corridor, and then the girl opened a door and Lesley saw a marble and blue-silk bathroom, with monogrammed linen towels hanging from silver racks. She nodded, and the girl shut the door behind her just in time for Lesley to bend over the basin and vomit. Finally she finished, ran water from the taps, washed her face, rinsed her mouth. In the mirror her face looked puffy, her eyes bloodshot. She sat down on the toilet seat and held her face in her hands, trembling. But who am I to judge? she thought. He's the man I love. Who knows what's pushed him to do these things? Perhaps it's worry over a dowry for Adele. Perhaps there is no family inheritance left, and he doesn't want his sister to pay for any wastefulness on his father's part. Or perhaps it's for me – so that he doesn't have to marry a girl who's richer than he is.

But that didn't make sense. She'd only known Justin six, seven weeks. He and Thomas had evidently been associates for much longer than that . . .

'He's not dishonest,' she said aloud. 'He can't be.' She was remembering everything they had talked about together, countless times.

For the first time in her life she was intensely grateful for being rich. Security was important, after all.

She took a small vial of Shalimar out of her handbag and applied the perfume on her temples and behind her ears. Then she resolutely left the bathroom.

In the sitting-room, he was pacing the floor, and when she entered, he looked up, smiled. His smile transfixed her with its strength and power. She wanted to run to him then, had all but forgotten the scene in the garden. She smiled back hesitantly. 'I'm glad you came,' he was saying, taking her hands in his and kissing each one in turn.

'I came,' she stated, looking down, 'because you didn't.'

'Darling, my letter?'

'I never received one. Why a letter, and not you?' She hadn't meant to sound so clinging, but the words simply came of their own accord.

'I sent one over with Smithers – '

'It's not important. I'm sorry. What did the letter say?'

'That I'd come just as soon as I could. That I had a client here from France, and that he and his wife were taking up

123

undue hours of my time . . . And that I missed you, dreadfully.'

'Oh, Justin.' She laid her head on his shoulder, and there was peace. Then she raised it and asked: 'You know we leave in four days?'

'So soon?'

'Yes.' There was a silence, long, uncomfortable. She said: 'Justin, what about our future? Tell me, please.'

'Our future? Lesley, my dear, the world's at war. I can't continue to remain a gentleman without also becoming an officer. When I return from my first tour of duty, I shall formally propose, send a letter to your father to ask for your hand in marriage.'

'But Justin, tours of duty last at least a year, eighteen months!'

'We could win the war sooner than that.'

'Justin – I understand this is no moment to get married. But why couldn't we at least become engaged? You could speak to Mother and my grandfather. We have . . . four days.'

Her earnest green eyes searched out his dark ones, held them. She could feel the tension in the muscles of his jaw. 'Justin, why not?'

He stood up abruptly, sighed, raised his shoulders, let them drop. 'Lesley, what can I tell you? I'm about to embark on the most terrifying experience of my life, and you're pressing me for a commitment. I love you, you know that. Isn't it sufficient for the moment?'

His face was red, his nostrils moving like those of a stallion in anger. Was it so unreasonable to want to know that he loved her enough to make their union public knowledge? Suddenly she felt numb. A woman should not have to beg the man she loved for a commitment. It should be his choice too. Only a man inconsiderate of a young woman's feelings wouldn't care to make such a commitment, after the one she'd made, giving herself freely.

124

'It isn't as if you were pregnant, darling, and couldn't wait,' he was saying, and the tone of his voice was placating, gentle but also patronizing. She began to feel anger.

'And if I were? You'd do what, then?'

'The honourable thing. Don't be silly, Lesley.'

'So it's honourable to marry a pregnant girl, even though you're going off to war, but you don't feel honour-bound to marry that same girl until two years later if she's been lucky? And you don't feel the least bit honour-bound to become engaged before your enlistment?'

'God damn it, Lesley! What if I died? You'd have wasted two years of your youth waiting for a man who'd never return!'

'That's ridiculous! You didn't think of that when you were making love to me, over and over again. You weren't thinking that you might die and leave me with a child, unmarried. Then what would my life be? You make no sense whatever, Justin. You seem to do only what pleases you on the moment. How many other girls have you deflowered with empty promises?'

She had spoken the unspeakable. She wanted to swallow back her words, yet knew she couldn't. She had meant what she'd said. He was staring at her with disbelief, and she still wanted him to tell her that she was right, that he would speak to her mother. What had his accomplice in the garden said? 'You have an odd code of values.'

She repeated the sentence, slowly, measuring every word, looking at him with her wide green eyes without flinching: 'You have an odd code of values.'

He drew in his breath, appeared to blanch.

He was holding himself at rigid attention, and all at once she knew that she was facing a stranger. She whispered: 'There are so many truths you didn't tell me, Justin, and so many lies you told . . . or implied.'

'Lesley – ' He was reaching out to her, but she stepped aside and his hand fell back.

125

'I was very angry, Justin,' she said. 'And since I thought you were my friend, I came to you today. I'll know better next time. I used to have a French governess in New York who used to say: "*Les hommes, ce sont tous des porcs.*" Pigs. She should have known. She did know. That's why she never married.'

'Lesley, please . . .'

She was running out now, blinded by tears, running past the butler, Smithers, and past the young maid. Justin's steps sounded behind her, then abruptly stopped. She opened the door herself and dashed out into the slow drizzle of rain. 'And how is the Honourable Adele, milady?' the chauffeur was asking politely, as she tried to hide her tears.

'She's very well, thank you. Please, Higby, tell my mother that I had high tea with the Reeves and shan't be wanting supper.' They drove home to the red brick mansion in the rain.

Four days later she sailed for the shores of New York, and her mother asked her no questions. It was a rough voyage, and everyone was seasick, including Lesley and her mother. But never, never shall I be this sick again, she thought, remembering the bathroom on Upper Brook Street.

The return to Vassar was an anticlimax for Jamie. Lesley wasn't at all herself. At the beginning Jamie had asked her about Justin: Lesley had shaken her head quickly, and tears had clouded her eyes. 'It's over.'

'But . . . why? He seemed so "right" from your letters.' Jamie felt then the renewal of the fears she had experienced after receiving Lesley's letter about the abbeys. But she couldn't pry into her friend's suffering. All she could do was ask this single, tentative question.

'I didn't know him then, and I guess I didn't know much about myself either. Typical isn't it?' But the brave little smile banned further intrusion. Jamie felt a bit hurt by this

126

rejection of her help. Lesley was barricaded in her own misery.

A war effort was being started at school, to raise money for an ambulance for the Allies and for the funding of a tuberculosis hospital in France. President Wilson, re-elected, was showing every sign of wanting his country to take sides against the Germans. Lesley, discarding her peg-top skirts so that others would imitate her and save cloth and materials to supply the armed forces, had joined the publicity campaign to obtain more relief moneys. Patriotism had become a fad at Vassar, and the rich girls looked to Lesley Aymes Richardson for guidance: She was half English, therefore already committed to the side of the Allies.

Lesley had also been gaining weight. For someone who ate as little as she did, and who was as nervous as she'd been, with dark, purplish circles under her eyes and hollow cheekbones, Jamie found the midriff bulge incongruous. But Lesley rarely dressed up these days, and never went to parties. She said: 'Why bother? We have too much to do for this sort of nonsense.' But it wasn't like Les to turn herself overnight into a spinster, she who had loved life, had breathed in jokes and food and the wonders of the changes in seasons. There was no joy left in nineteen-year-old Lesley: only a grimness that repelled Jamie, that she couldn't understand at all.

And then, during exam week, in their room, she caught Lesley staring blankly at her desk, her hands clasped before her. Jamie looked up from her book, saw that she was about to cry. She rose, went to the back of Lesley's chair, put her hand on her roommate's shoulder, and said: 'You've got to tell me now. *That*. And also why you keep refusing to go home to visit your family. Your sister called again, about the Christmas holidays. She wants you to go to a cotillion with one of George's friends – '

'Stop it, Jamie! I'm never going to go out with any man ever again!'

127

Her vehemence made Jamie draw back. 'But Les . . . one love affair . . .'

Lesley wheeled about. Her intense eyes drilled into her friend. She stated, barely above a whisper: 'It wasn't just one love affair, Jamie. I'm pregnant. I'm into my fourth month.'

Jamie could feel prickles rising on her skin. She sat down, feeling out of breath, and said. 'Why didn't you tell me earlier?'

'At first I didn't want to face it. And then . . . what could *you* have done about it? What could anyone have done? I was such a fool!'

'Les. Do you still want to marry Justin?'

Lesley didn't cry. But her chin began to tremble uncontrollably. For a moment she couldn't make a sound, and her white face seemed bruised around the eyes. Jamie said, very softly: 'If you still love him, you know he'd marry you. He told you he would, didn't he?'

'Whom do you take me for, Jamie? To marry a man who didn't even want to get engaged . . . To marry a man who makes his living selling fake art works . . .'

'I didn't know. I had no idea.'

'You know what that's like, Jamie! Look at Eva! Willy's still in love with *you*, but he married *her* and only because he "had to". I'm never going to do that to myself or to any child of mine. What kind of marriage would exist for us? He'd never respect me, never feel he acted out of choice. I don't love him any more anyway, Jamie.'

'Do you want to have this baby?'

Lesley said, to the air as much as to her friend. 'What are my options? I don't want to be a mother – I'm not even sure I'd ever want to be one, if I were *married*! But to have the child, in a family like mine . . .'

Jamie was thinking quietly. She declared: 'Then you must get rid of it. There are ways.'

'But where? It costs a fortune! And if I asked my father

for that much money, I'd have to give him an explanation! He'd insist on seeing me! It's a wonder everyone hasn't guessed by now – especially you!'

'It's this whole war craze. Vassar isn't the place to expect people to be aware of others. As for me – since you told me nothing . . .'

'I'm sorry, Jamie. I should have told you. But I was so ashamed – '

'Ashamed? But it's not as if I were some virgin, for heaven's sake! The same thing could have happened to me last year! Why on earth ashamed?'

'Because Willy was in love with you, he wanted you; you were the one who rejected *him*. With me it was so terrible – to be thrown away, abandoned.' Then she burst into tears, sobbing, and Jamie came to her and held her. Lesley wept for several minutes, pouring out four months of misery, four months of shame and fear and abject loneliness. 'Yes!' she finally announced, looking up at Jamie. 'If I could somehow find the money, I'd have it taken care of. I don't want his child! I hate the man! He humiliated me and lied to me – And he's a thief!'

Jamie stood up, chewing on one of her fingernails. 'Then we're going to have to work something out. Let me find out what I can.'

Lesley's eyes expressed such childlike hope that suddenly Jamie felt almost trapped. There was no way she could let her down now. There were girls who knew about these matters . . . It wasn't the first time this had happened at Vassar. In every college town there were people – nurses, laymen – who helped girls out who were in trouble. Missy Brookhouse, one of the seniors in Main, knew everything. She'd go up to her room and talk to her tomorrow.

'Jamie,' Lesley whispered, 'if you speak about this to anyone . . .'

In a flash Jamie pictured Missy's eyes widening: Lesley

129

Richardson, pregnant! It would take maybe two days to spread like wildfire throughout the campus, and the following week everyone would know at Yale and Princeton and Harvard, at Williams and Haverford: All the young men who might one day be expected to propose to Lesley. In less than a fortnight the Richardsons and their Fifth Avenue friends would be informed of the unmentionable fact. Jamie pressed Lesley's hand. 'It's all right. I know just how I'm going to handle it.'

For no one would care if Jamie Lynne Stewart were pregnant and then had it taken care of. Missy would be sympathetic for one minute, pretending to be shocked. 'Just trust me, will you?' Jamie said.

'There's nothing else for me to do.' Lesley replied lamely. And then she whispered: 'I'm so scared . . .'

The next afternoon Jamie Stewart, bundled up in an old cloth coat, was making her entrance into a small side street of Poughkeepsie, holding five hundred dollars. She had no idea where she would go to replace this money, put aside for the coming semester at Vassar. But Lesley's predicament had to take first priority. Missy had told her about the woman, Marcia Preiss, who performed on pregnant girls in her kitchen for half a grand. Jamie didn't want to think of how hard she had worked for the money. Somehow, when a person wanted something as badly as she'd wanted an education, help appeared on the horizon in some form or fashion. One had to have faith. Missy had told her what to ask, what to watch out for.

Marcia Preiss was small, fat, and unkempt. 'It isn't for me but for my best friend,' Jamie stated uncomfortably. 'But you can't let anyone know . . .'

'If I let them know, d'you think I'd still be here? I'd be in jail, sweetheart. How many months is she along?'

'It happened late in August.'

The Preiss woman cocked her head to one side, let out a low whistle. 'That's what I call "along". That's very

130

dangerous. Sure she isn't going to change her mind and bolt out of here like some of 'em do?'

'Absolutely sure. And . . . I brought the five hundred dollars.'

'She's a rich one, then. Only the rich seem to get pregnant.' The woman held out her plump hand and Jamie gave her the crisp bills. The woman smiled, like a greedy child as she counted.

Jamie watched, and felt such intense loathing for Marcia Preiss that had she not thought quickly of Lesley, and her scared eyes, she would have stood up to leave. The apartment smelled of boiled cabbage.

'Do you sterilize your instruments?' Jamie asked instead, remembering Missy's instructions. Missy's father was a surgeon, in Atlanta. He had told his daughter a great deal about botched operations like these where the uterine lining was perforated, or where unsterile conditions caused fatal infections. She was terrified for Les.

''Course I do. Never had a patient die on me yet!' 'Patient.' This horrible person was now speaking as if she were a doctor.

'Are you a nurse?' Jamie questioned.

'What is it you want, honey? My diploma? No, I'm not a goddamned nurse, but I'm a good midwife. For a regular living, that's what I do: deliver live ones. Is that enough?'

'One last thing. What about the pain?'

Marcia Preiss shrugged audibly. 'Look, angelface. If you're going to go and do it, you know there's bound to be some danger. What can I say? I use ether. I pack 'em well afterward. You'll come with her, won't ya? You look like a good kid to me. Put her to bed. The lining of the uterus will fall out later, same as if she'd had the kid.' She stopped, regarded Jamie strangely. 'What happened? Mind telling me? Fella run out on her, or what? Married man?'

Jamie rose and replied in a steady voice: 'It's not that at all. He's an officer in the British navy. He doesn't even

131

know about the baby. They're engaged to be married. That's why it's important – *essential* – that you do a clean job. She's going to want other children when all this is over.'

'Baby doll, when it's over, you can bet your sweet ass she isn't gonna wanna get *near* a man – him or anyone else. And you won't either. It takes a tough old cookie like me to stomach this sort of thing. But stop looking so worried. Your friend'll survive. A week later she'll be dancin' the foxtrot.'

Jamie walked out into the snow, and as it fell about her, she could only remember the smell of cabbage in that dismal apartment. When Lesley asked her how the interview had gone, she answered brightly: 'Perfectly. She's a nice lady. Fat, but nice. We're going tomorrow.'

'And the money?'

'Don't worry about it. Take a bath, Lesley, and try to get some sleep. Tomorrow everyone's going to be taking exams, and no one will notice we're gone. I'll have to find some excuse for Professor Buck . . .'

'Oh, Jamie,' Lesley burst out, 'this whole thing is ruining you, ruining your career – '

'Just take your bath, Les, for heaven's sake. And please shut up.'

In the blizzard of snow, that Wednesday, the two girls fought their trail through to Marcia Preiss's house. The woman opened the door, stood back. The apartment was perfectly clean, smelled of cleansing liquid. A flood of relief washed over Jamie. Marcia said, peering at Lesley: 'You shoulda come earlier, sweetie. Fourth month is pretty late.'

'But – you can still do it?' Dismay was painted over Lesley's constricted features.

''Course I can. Now get undressed, get under this sheet, and get inside that kitchen. Up on the table, like a good girl.'

Lesley looked mutely at Jamie, and Jamie nodded. It was

132

Jamie who unbuttoned the back of Lesley's dress, who eased her out of it. Lesley stood petrified and white, unable to think past the terror of death. That table . . .

The indignity of lying there, naked under the sheet, her legs parted, like a parody of the act of sex that had brought her there, made Lesley close her eyes. She opened them for one frightening instant when she saw the knife and the cup, and her mouth widened in horror. She knew then what the boys must feel when they were ready to shoot or be shot at in the trenches, and for that blind second she remembered Justin, the father of this baby that was going to be cut out of her. She wanted to scream, but couldn't and there were no tears to weep with. And then Marcia Preiss laid the ether-soaked cloth over her face, and she lost consciousness.

Suddenly it was over; Marcia was washing her hands after having discarded the thin rubber gloves. Lesley was moaning, coming to her senses in pain, vomiting into a bowl that Marcia was holding up to her. Even as she was vomiting, she continued to moan.

'She won't be able to walk home,' Jamie whispered, appalled.

'Not right away. Give her half an hour.'

'I'm going to call a taxicab.'

'Thattagirl. Good thinkin'. It went pretty well, all things considered. But tell her next time, not to wait so god damn long . . .'

During the night Jamie couldn't sleep, watching over Lesley. She had given her veronal cachets that she had obtained from a girl who suffered from migraine headaches. Lesley was drenched with perspiration and was making groaning sounds as she tossed and turned. But she was alive. The placenta had come out, but she wasn't bleeding very much now. 'A week later she'll be dancin' the foxtrot.' Jamie laid her head in her hands and wept, for Lesley, for herself, for all the girls who had loved and *not* survived, as her roommate had. It was then that the housemother knocked on the door, and in a panic Jamie rushed to open it. Had word leaked out?

'What's wrong with Lesley?' the housemother was asking with concern.

'Nothing, Mrs MacCarthy. A bad case of influenza. I've been watching her.'

The woman stood in the doorway, and her look of anxiety made Jamie suddenly very nervous. 'Did you come about Les's flu?' she asked. But if she hadn't known about it . . .? Jamie was perplexed.

'No, my dear. I came . . . because of you.'

'*Me?*' Jamie stared at her in disbelief.

The housemother took her hand, pressed it gently, and shook her head. 'My poor dear girl,' she whispered. 'We've just received word that your father died. His heart – '

Tears were streaming down Jamie's cheeks, and the housemother was holding her. She let the tears fall for her father. They had been so much alike and she had loved him very much. 'I'm going to be all right,' she murmured. 'Thank you, Mrs MacCarthy.'

'Your mother said not to come home for the funeral. He would've wanted you to stay and take your finals. He left most of his savings to you.'

Several hours later, as Jamie watched the sleeping Lesley, she remembered what she had thought the previous day. One did what one had to. Fate was strange.

In April 1917 the United States entered the war on the side of the Allies, and the President of Vassar College, Henry Noble MacCracken, urged a crowd of panicking young women not to lose their sense of decorum. One had to remember the reputation of the school: It was a ladies' college. Jamie turned to look sideways at Lesley. And she knew that, whatever had happened on that kitchen table in December, Lesley still cared for Justin Reeve, as she had cared for Willy. But all that was over.

Now, in the months to come, hundreds of thousands of

human lives would be lost, and for what purpose? The college chaplain was leading the girls in prayer now, prayer for the living and for the dead, prayer for the United States of America. Jamie saw Lesley's lips moving, and she reached for her hand.

And she chanted along with hundreds of bareheaded young women: 'I said in mine heart, God shall judge the righteous and the wicked: For there is a time there for every purpose and for every work.'

Chapter Six

April 1917 was the moment of climax when the French army in the north collapsed. Joffre had appointed General Robert Nivelle, proud and vainglorious and highly eloquent, to be his successor as commander of the armies. Nivelle presented his plans well but had had little experience at a position of such strategic importance. Aspiring to be the new Napoleon, he risked everything, as had Bonaparte; and, as with the Emperor in his retreat from Moscow, his losses were complete and cost him not only his command but hundreds of thousands of French lives.

The plan was for the French and British troops to close upon the bulging German front between Arras and Craonne, just west of the ridge picturesquely named the Chemin des Dames. But the Germans anticipated this and fell back to the Hindenburg Line, pulling their forces east into a taut, well-grouped stretch that ran north-south. There was no longer a bulge for the Allies to crush, and now the enemy was fortified by the thick, high ground. The British in the north were separated from the French in the south, but the Germans were more reinforced than ever. Filled with fear, the three French armies that were to attack on the sixteenth of April looked up to the ridge and quaked; the government vacillated in its support of the commander-in-chief; and General Pétain forecast the plan would fail: but one man's vanity overrode the objections, challenged the Ministry of War, and triumphed. It was Robert Nivelle or the French troops; nobody dared to champion the men for fear of their commander.

Alexandre de Varenne had joined the ranks of the Sixth Army, under General Charles Mangin. As soon as war had

136

been declared, he had enlisted. The blow dealt to his pride and his vulnerability by Yvonne de Larmont had created in him a certain change. When war broke out he knew that his country would not betray him, that in this matter there could be no grey areas. In the realm of patriotism there was no alternative: One had to believe and to give one's all. France was his, and would always be.

Captain Alexandre de Varenne discovered that the army was not bad for him. His men, from the start, gave him immediate respect. He felt a confidence with them that he had only experienced in court. One followed orders, one was fair, one dispensed orders with clarity and as much charity as one could. He had suffered through the devastation of 1915 with other officers and formed a camaraderie with them.

Paul had become a flying ace. He had waited until the last possible moment to enlist. Then, when the draft had closed in on him, he had become a flier. With Martine, he had begun to experience moments of boredom. She did not understand the fine points of a painting. He loved her and he wanted to experiment with life, enjoying her; but the idea of living the rest of his days apart from the mainstream of Parisian society was no longer so appealing. Flying, suddenly, became a way out. He would fly for his country and be thought a dashing hero. And he would take risks again and feel the exhilaration of being at the razor's edge.

Alex heard that his brother had scored many victories and a bitterness filled him. Alone in his cockpit, leaning out of his aeroplane, Paul would shoot at a lone opponent or engage in dogfights with several. He was taking risks because he had never truly valued life. Neither, thought Alex, have I. But I value my country and feel responsibility for my men. Paul doesn't have to feel responsibility beyond himself. And yet to the young women of France who counted the exploits of their favourite aviators, the Comte Paul was always at the forefront, for they mistook his recklessness for courage. Alex could not have afforded recklessness, or his men would have been killed.

On the afternoon of 15 April another captain, Jean d'Artois, took Alexandre aside. 'You know that I have leave this evening,' he told him, slightly embarrassed. 'But I am due to return in the early dawn. Just now everything is calm on the front. But I have the opportunity to ... remain longer with my wife, who is waiting in Reims for me in a hotel. The colonel is new, and he doesn't know me yet – nor does he know you, for that matter. Could you possibly take my place from four until eight tomorrow morning? If the colonel should check, he would see a captain with his men and would proceed no further. And of course I should be delighted to return the favour any time. My wife is pregnant, and I haven't seen her since we were married six months ago.'

Alex thought for a moment. 'We're due to attack in the morning, Jean. Will you be back on time?'

'Without a doubt. You can count on me.'

'Then, gentleman to gentleman, I shall do it,' Alexandre replied. But he felt ill at ease. He needed the rest before facing the enemy with his own soldiers. Jean d'Artois was placing his personal life before his country, before Alex's own priorities. But he understood the man's desire to see his wife.

In the early morning, then, Alexandre reached the trenches amid the prepared, massive armour. He made a sign to the sergeant below, lifted his leg to avoid a large stone. All at once the dark sky exploded above him from the direction of the promontory of the Chemin des Dames. Alexandre threw his arm across his face to shield it from the bursting German shell. He could not breathe. His heart was pounding and he realized that he was alive, in spite of this near disaster. And then he was on the ground, unable to move. His thigh was spattered with red, and there were no sensations in it. In the numbness he watched his own blood

138

and heard the screams from the trenches, and blinked incredulously. And then the pain attacked every nerve ending. He vomited.

Alexandre de Varenne felt himself slip away into blackness just as one of the major disasters of the war was beginning. When he regained consciousness in the military hospital, he was told that the battle for the impregnable Chemin des Dames had raged for ten days, and that the Hindenburg Line had remained virtually intact. Fury mingled with the searing physical pain, and Alexandre felt the futility of the foolishly planned endeavour. He was not surprised when the government replaced Nivelle with Pétain, nor even when the army rebelled and a series of riots broke out. He wondered where his men had been, who had died. He had survived, although with shrapnel in his thigh. But if his life had gone, who would have missed him?

He knew then that he had acted correctly, for Jean d'Artois had a pregnant wife who loved him, and it was shrapnel meant for him that now lay embedded in Alexandre's leg.

Elena knew that there was little time to grieve over Fania. At the beginning, she spent her nights at the same clubs as before. She tipped lavishly. But she soon realized that the Adler funds were limited. Genia, especially, had exercised her newfound freedom with no thought for the future. Clearly the two sisters had planned to return to Russia to sell their property and had not left the country with a particularly large sum of money.

As the inheritance dwindled, Elena's sense of panic mounted. What to do? She had no professional skills. In Harbin she had been a rich woman. No one would believe that her wealth was running dry. She would have to move.

One evening, watching the Eurasian hostess deftly placing drinks in front of two beribboned British officers, she thought, in a flash: This is what I can do. But not where they know me as the Princess Egorova.

And so, steeling herself, she packed her bags and moved to Shanghai, an international city made up of settlements in which the Chinese were only allowed in by special permit. She found work at the Little Club in the British quarter. There were big gamblers in Shanghai. With her regal looks and her dark, impenetrable eyes, she encouraged them to spend, and spend more. But she would not leave the club with any of the customers. She was still the Princess Egorova, whose body was intact, whose mind was still clean, clear.

In March 1917 she received a shock. She had been seated at a small, exclusive table, entertaining two British men with stories of Russia, when a tall man behind her suddenly interrupted her. 'Haven't we met?' he asked. She searched his face, felt slight tremors going through her. Yes, they'd met: He was the cousin of one of the men who had once proposed to her in St Petersburg. A cousin from Kiev, but still someone she had known, someone from her past. One of the customers said: 'This is the Princess Egorova.'

'Elena Sergeievna?' the man asked.

She shook her head, her smile remote, her eyes cold. 'Another Egorova, I'm sure,' she murmured. 'The name is common enough.' But she knew that he wouldn't believe her. She stood up, picked up the empty glasses and walked quickly away, feeling as though she'd just escaped from a ghost. Her own ghost.

When she left the club in the early dawn, she heard a noise and saw that the Russian had followed her. 'I knew it was you,' he said. 'Why did you deny it?'

She hastened her pace, but his strides were longer than hers. He stopped her in a small alley near her rooming-house, his hand on her arm. She looked up into his face and saw the Russian lust, the greed, the anger. Russians were always angry, angry at the world. She tried to push him off, but instead he smiled. 'I could return home and speak about you,' he whispered.

There was no choice. She dropped her chin, resumed her walk. He walked beside her in heavy silence. In her small, stark bedroom, she took off her clothes mechanically, her eyes unseeing. She lay down and let him make love to her with her lids tightly shut against the light he had left on, the better to admire the awesome curves of her body. In the morning she rose and went into the bathroom to wash herself.

When she returned, he had left. Crisp bills lay on the bed, sole reminders of the way she had just lost her virginity. She felt no horror. The outrage had been burned out of her during the night. She took the bills, counted them, laid them on her dresser. Then she packed her few belongings and buckled shut her suitcase. Time to move on.

As her ship was raising its anchor, she saw a young Chinese man running onto the pier brandishing a tabloid, screaming something to a group of Europeans gathered not far from her. She strained to hear. He was saying: 'The Russian government's been overthrown? The Tsar has abdicated!' Chills penetrated her. She wondered whether her night-time visitor would ever return home, and whether she had bought his silence with her action. She thought of her father, of what the news of the Tsar's abdication would do to him; and of what the news of his daughter could do. The 'working girls' in the clubs went from Harbin to Shanghai, and if their luck ran out, they went to Singapore. She was twenty-seven. Had her luck run out, or would Malaysia be a new beginning?

Singapore was the centre of steamship traffic in the East. It was a port, with as many Chinese as native Malay. The city was different from Shanghai, although both were very English in flavour. But Singapore was under British dominion. Singapore proper was filled with open spaces. There were cricket grounds, large luxurious hotels. Like most ports, it was cosmopolitan, and the clubs were French, English, American. The British had kept the Germans out because of the war, and had an army headquarters in the city. Their officers belonged to cricket clubs and played golf. At the Seaview one could dance right on the water-front, and the tall diving board stood right above a pool of sea water. Elena was intrigued by the different populations: the various Europeans, held together by a common herit-age; the wealthy Chinese; and finally, the haphazard native population. They mingled, but separated as oil from vine-gar in the same bowl, each keeping to his own.

Once again she found work without difficulty. But she was growing tired, heartsick. Never anyone to talk to; never anyone to understand. She'd been alone, she thought, all her life – at least the last nine years of it.

She saved her money, and at night she danced with the Europeans and smiled mysteriously, playing her best role. But it was ugly to dance with them, because it wasn't the dancing of before, of St Petersburg, where she had filled her little notebook with eligible men's names, counts and princes and barons. Then they had courted her with the ritual of elegant mating birds, dancing circles around her as if she were out of reach in her perfection. Here they purchased champagne and thought that they had also purchased her. She could tell by the direct, unequivocal expression in their eyes. They drank too much and then draped themselves around her sturdy body. The British officers were of course the most controlled, because of the standards set by their headquarters. But to Elena each man was like the next, and boredom was only equalled by the despair of going home to the empty room in the dingy boarding house, the only one she could afford. It smelled of urine and lavender, scents impregnated into the walls from long before her tenancy.

On 16 July 1918, the entire family of Tsar Nicholas II was massacred at Ekaterinburg. Elena remembered the faces of the young grand-duchesses, and then the face of her father. A raking emptiness took hold of her, but she fought it away. Her father would still be in Krasnoyarsk, pompously expounding on theories of government now dead. No one ever really changed, except for the worse.

There was a parade of never-changing British officers, drinking to offset their boredom at not being more involved in the actual conflicts of submarine warfare. Instead they were stationed in a colony that simply supervised the procurement of raw materials for the mother nation. They passed through the club where Elena worked with the regular monotony of toy soldiers. And then one night she saw a young lieutenant whom she'd never seen alone, but whom she'd noticed before. He intrigued her, and tonight he was unaccompanied by the older officers who usually surrounded him. She'd seen him make them laugh, had noticed the melancholy expression on his face even while his superiors chuckled at his easy wit. And, of course, she'd wondered. He didn't seem to belong in the British navy. He had the good looks of a Spaniard or a Florentine, and she'd told herself wryly that Machiavelli, a man she'd always admired and whose works she had memorized as a young girl, must have looked like him. So she approached him, snapping her fingers for champagne, and sat down before he had the chance to refuse her company.

'I didn't think you'd mind,' she stated, smiling, as he raised his eyebrows with amusement. 'It's my job, in any case. The champagne must flow or I shall be fired.'

'There isn't a remote chance of that,' the man replied, laughing. 'You're the most intelligent woman in this place. Who are you, truly?'

'Who they say I am. Princess Elena Sergeievna Egorova.' He wasn't Russian: He couldn't be dangerous. No one from

143

here could ever report back – especially now that the court had dispersed.

He allowed the waiter to pour champagne into two fluted glasses, then tipped him a carelessly large sum of money, a gesture that intrigued her. He remarked: 'A princess from St Petersburg – Leningrad, our former ally. A fairytale princess or a real one? These days Russian princesses float in like tinsel queens, and it's hard to tell which ones are the real ones.'

She bristled inwardly but displayed nothing but a sudden hardness in the eyes. 'Does it matter, then? I'm a real one. My family dates back to the days of the first Tsar, Ivan of Kiev. But no Englishman cares about Russian history, so I could be inventing all of this, couldn't I?'

He inclined his head, raised his glass. 'Indeed. But somehow I believe you. You're not here by choice. A displaced soul, as I am, thrown onto a hostile and distant shore. Why? The revolution?'

She answered as she always did. 'Yes. My parents were murdered in their palace. I was sufficiently lucky to escape with my life, but without the funds to get me very far. And in a world at war, I may as well be here as anywhere else. At least Singapore is civilized.'

'Too much so. It's a mini-London without the excitement of Soho. And there are no interesting women – except you, of course. I'm Ashley Taylor, by the way.'

'Our names are the few possessions that will never leave us, no matter what occurs to strip us of everything else.' She smiled: 'Tell me about yourself. What have *you* left behind, Lieutenant Taylor?'

'I was a naughty boy,' he replied. 'I'm afraid my youth was clouded under a shadow of scandal. I must redeem myself before I return home. A typical soldier's tale, don't you think, Princess?'

'But scandals are the spice of life, Lieutenant. At least they were in Russia. No good count or prince ever survived

144

without his share of naughtiness. They were all bad boys. It was part of the tradition.'

'Russians are known for their outrageous behaviour. Britons are known for their reserve. I wish I'd been born in your country, my dear.'

'No, you don't,' she retorted bitterly. 'You'd be dead on the battlefront, or penniless and in exile. Today's Russia isn't my Russia any longer. It's Lenin's Soviet Republic.'

'You're right. I'm sorry. I was a thoughtless boor. Forgive me. Let me take you out dancing after the club closes, to make my stupidity up to you. You are so beautiful, and we are both alone. Boredom becomes you as little as it becomes me.'

She smiled. 'Thank you – for seeing the truth about us both and for recognizing your own weaknesses. Englishmen usually are insensitive to everything but the honour of winning at golf!'

Then they were laughing, draining their glasses, and through the golden bubbles she saw his eyes fastened to hers, searching for something. She liked him better than any man she'd met since Petersburg.

After the club had closed, in the early hours, they went to a French bar that stayed open later and ordered in rapid succession two bottles of Mumm's Cordon Rouge. He told her little about himself, she even less about her own past. But in the gay atmosphere of couples swinging to the tango, he saw the hunger in her eyes and stroked her cheek. 'My country has turned to dull porridge,' he remarked softly. 'The landscape is Gainsborough instead of Cézanne, under King George and Queen Mary. I wonder if there is any going back for me? There isn't any for you, because the great nation where Bakst and Benois and Diaghilev conceived the ballet revolution has now been broken by a real revolution of politicians. Where is your horizon, Elena?'

She shrugged. 'Paris. But those are dreams, and I've long since realized that my dreams don't ever come true.'

145

'Why so harsh on yourself?'

'Because I'm a realist. What have I to offer? Physical assets. Others possess great talents, on which to build. But the days of the *Belle Otéro*, of Liane de Pougy, of the courtesans of the *Belle Epoque* are over, Ashley. Today there's a war. Women work. I was reared to marry a grand-duke and gently push him into world politics. Had I perhaps been reared to be a politician in my own right, I might have received more thorough training to make a career for *myself*. That isn't the case.'

'There are very few great talents in this world. Some of us must learn to barter our values for opportunity. You've done that. How you spend your nights would make your mother faint. But it keeps the bills from piling up. No one who has an easy time of it can understand that for some who don't, the choices are not so clear-cut.'

'You are speaking of yourself now. What, exactly, do you mean?'

'There were things I did that others termed dishonest. To me, they were performed to earn a better dowry for my sister and to allow myself a life that, frankly, had it been less luxurious, would have been a death-in-life. I *needed* the good life. I went about obtaining it as expediently as I could. I never murdered anybody, and I didn't cheat those poorer than myself. Beyond that, I thought to each his own. All's right in love, war, and the earth's good things. If a jury can forgive a man for killing a faithless woman, why can't they just as easily forgive the sensualist who wanted to live the existence of a gentleman, tasting good foods and being served in style?'

'But what, precisely, did this sensualist do that was so unforgivable?'

He saw the dark eyes turn brilliant with curiosity and an odd sort of empathy. Slowly he nodded. 'Yes. You'd understand. If I can accept that you are still the same Princess Egorova who existed before she sold herself for a

146

more comfortable bed, why shouldn't you understand what I've done? I had a gallery in London. In order to make a go of it, in order to rise more quickly at a very bad time for British art collectors, I sold some fake masterpieces. A friend and I devised a formula whereby he painted a landscape or portrait exactly in the genre of one of the great dead artists, and I sold it as a recent "discovery" of some hitherto unmentioned work found by chance at some remote estate auction. No one really suffered from this scheme, Elena. Richer collectors thought they were in possession of something so new and brilliant – an original painting never possessed by anyone of note until them-selves – that they willingly paid me huge sums of money for it. But Tommy *was* an artist. He may not have been Van Gogh or Turner. But what he did, he did supremely well. He never copied any existing masterpiece. Perhaps we deserved to be paid so highly. We were doing something truly original!'

She was smiling. 'Undoubtedly you were. A clever idea. I can appreciate a good confidence man. I admire your strategy.'

'There were some who didn't. I might have been thrown in prison, if we hadn't been in the midst of a war. And there was a girl – a nice girl – '

'Someone you loved who was too honest to accept this?'

'I never said I loved her. Love is a big word.'

They laughed again, and she could feel the sadness rising to the surface with the bubbles of champagne. She blew gently into her *coupe*, chasing them, making them pop. For the first time in her life she wanted a man to take her home with him – wanted to spend the night in his arms. She stood up, a little dizzy from the drinking, and he followed suit and offered her his hand. There was comfort in that hand, so beautiful and delicate, the hand of a Renaissance artist. Perhaps Leonardo had been a scoundrel and a cheat but lucky enough not to have been found out . . .

147

That night she discovered what it meant to be with a man, how it felt to rouse and be aroused in mutual pleasure. In the early hours of the dawn she fell asleep before him, against his chest. When she awakened, the day was bright outside, and she blinked in bewilderment. He was gone. The luxury hotel room where he had taken her was only that: a luxurious hotel bedroom, with a vase filled with red roses on the bedside table. His uniform was gone, his cufflinks, even the odour of his body. She shook herself to full consciousness, got up. And then she saw it propped against the chest of drawers: the most exquisite enamel medallion by the Florentine sculptor Luca della Robbia.

She went to it, took it in her hands, brought it to the window. In relief three children stood out, singing. The enamel work was chipped in tiny places, because della Robbia had lived and sculpted in the fifteenth century. She ran her fingers over the faces, marvelling.

There was a note on the dresser. 'Dear *Principessa*,' Ashley Taylor had written. 'Take this in remembrance of our night together, as a token of my infinite admiration and hopes for your future. There is an old woman in the British district called Lady Blyford. She lives alone and receives almost no visitors. Her only love is art – in particular, art of the Florentine Renaissance.' He had signed it: 'Your partner at heart, A.T.'

Hopes for her future . . . Lady Blyford. Elena could feel herself flush with an excitement so great that it was difficult to dress with concentration. A della Robbia! Or a Tommy? She wondered how much to ask for it. How much did a passage to France cost? And she'd need to live once she arrived, and, of course, to live here until it was safe to travel to a country now in the midst of war. And Ashley? Would she see him again, or had this just been a one-night adventure?

She went downstairs, hugging the medallion, and was astonished to see a group of hotel employees in excited conversation around the front desk. She hesitated, approached them cautiously. A chambermaid turned to her, her face alight with joy. 'There is an armistice!' she said shyly.

'You mean . . . the war is really *over*?'

'Yes! The officers are going home! Some of the ships left this morning! We're several days behind . . . The armistice was signed on the eleventh, and this is the fourteenth!'

Stunned, electrified, Elena walked out into the sunshine. She wanted to speak to someone, a person who would know. At the club people were bound to know. She wended her way there, her heart beating rapidly.

At the club the manager hugged her, tears in his eyes. Yes, it was true. The great world war had ended. She asked, carefully, about the two regular customers who had come before with Ashley. 'Their ship left this morning.'

So he had gone, only hours after leaving her bedside. She wondered what he would do once he returned to England. But that was his business – his problem. Hers was to go at once to Lady Blyford with the medallion. There was no God to watch over humans, but sometimes a twist of fate occurred to change the affairs of men. Ashley Taylor, she thought fervently, I shall never forget you. You have marked my life as no other man. You I shall remember with gratitude, and with fondness, and with 'infinite admiration', as you wrote in your note. For it took a scoundrel to detect another of his own kind.

A couple of excited French businessmen were running past her, waving their hats in the air. '*Vive la France, messieurs!*' she called after them. And then, to herself: '*Vive la liberté!*'

Jamie had submitted her play as one of many offered to the workshop for competition during her junior year. Only one would receive the prize, but the three best ones would be

149

acted out in front of all of Vassar. Although she didn't win, she felt a moment of unequalled elation. Her work had been chosen as one of the three best and was going to be read, heard, enacted! She hugged Professor Buck, who added, smiling: 'Next time you might try for something lighter, more whimsical. We're in the middle of a war, and people want to forget sadness.'

'I'm not sad,' Jamie countered. 'I'm just not light and whimsical.' She felt hurt, somehow, in this moment of glory. Hers was an important work, and it had been passed over because the world wanted amusement.

Lesley brought them a bottle of champagne. 'The point is that you're going to be a celebrity!' she said brightly. 'You're going to have an audience.'

Because of the play, she *was* in a sense a celebrity. The other students were a little in awe of her. The few boys left from conscription weren't sure how to take her. In the spring of their junior year, her mother wrote to tell her that Willy Künstler had been killed – just that, no details. She wept for him, and for the daughter he had left behind, who would never know him. It seemed that the war would never end.

Then, in November 1918, during the autumn of their senior year, the armistice was signed. The Vassar girls rushed out to Sunset Hill in a tumult of joy, and there, like Greek nymphs, they made a ritual of burying a German helmet as the sun rose. They sang, lifting their voices to the gods of peace and victory, and they hugged one another and danced in their bare feet. Suddenly there was no difference between scholarship student and rich debutante: Everyone was proud, everyone was happy. In unison they went to chapel for a victory service.

France and England had been liberated, the doughboys would come home. Lesley and Jamie sat together on the grass. All at once they turned to each other, and Jamie said: 'Why don't we pack our bags and go somewhere?'

150

'To Paris. Chatterton always speaks of the Parisian artists. But Daddy would never let me go.'

'I have my inheritance. I'd like to live there and write.'

'And it would be a wonderful change after Vassar.'

'Why don't we do it?'

Lesley stood up, stretched her small arms into the air, made a pirouette. 'Paris. Chanel, the Seine, the riverboats. Painting in a garret.'

'Sunsets over Montmartre. Gertrude Stein.'

'We'd have to get an introduction.' Lesley picked up a leaf, turned it over in her hands. 'To meet Picasso . . .' she murmured dreamily.

They were so caught up in their reverie that neither considered graduation, the shedding of parents, means of support. Victory had set a mantle of unreality over Vassar College. Jamie and Lesley, the odd ones, the writer and the would-be painter, remained in their own trance, hoping and making plans.

They were twenty and they didn't want to 'settle down.' They didn't want to have to settle for anything not of their own choosing. Perhaps the war had made the choices clearer. Men had lost their lives, and life, therefore, seemed more precious than it had ever seemed before. They felt its excitement in the air. They felt it with mystical joy, and together they welcomed it.

Victory. Paul was twenty-seven when the armistice came, and while processions filed down the Champs Elysées, he was preparing to relinquish his fighter plane and re-enter civilian life. While eager young women threw bouquets of flowers into the air and danced through the streets of Paris, he sat quietly in the barracks and reflected on what was to come.

Others, like Alexandre, had gone to war for their country as a matter of course. Paul's motives had been at once more

151

and less ambiguous. Flying was exhilarating, and he had submerged his life in nonsense for so many years that putting it to the test of his skill and the Fates had seemed to give it a meaning it had never possessed. He wondered what life would be like for him when he returned. More of the same? He enjoyed the art hunts, bringing home intriguing new pieces for Bertrand. Bertrand might even make him a minor partner in the business if he played his cards right. But apart from that, what was there? Martine.

During his last resting period, a leave that had been granted after several astute victories in the heavens, he had not written to her about it but instead had sneaked off to London. He had been put up at the Kensington town house of a young Englishman he had befriended, had been wined and dined, and had been taken out to meet presentable young ladies and also those who were reputed to be less presentable. He had been to Soho and Bloomsbury, had enjoyed his visit; and he had spent his last night amusing himself in the bed of a lusty young Englishwoman.

None of this had meant anything, he'd reasoned. So why should he have bothered to inform Martine of any part of it? She was happy in Paris, he believed. He had committed no greater sin than the one of omission. And which was better? To tell all and hurt someone, or to hold one's tongue? Still – at one time he would have rushed to her home, to be clasped to her small frail body, to bury his face in her red hair, to make passionate love to her for three days on end. Now he was about to be sent home permanently, and the thought of Martine left him tepid. What did one do with an ageing mistress?

Then, to Paul's surprise, Martine made it all so easy. One day they were spending the afternoon together in her apartment on rue de la Pompe.

Warily, she asked: 'You seem tired, listless. You're not the war-hero type, my angel. It must be something else.' She closed her lips together, bit them from the inside

152

pensively, and continued: 'You must be tired of me. Is that it?'

How ever did she always manage to understand him? Just now, when he would have welcomed hating her, she was doing it again. The most perceptive woman in the world. He took her hand and caressed it with absentminded fingers. He still felt gratitude for her love, but she might as well have been his aunt, his surrogate mother.

'I understand,' she said slowly. In the candlelight her face looked haggard, but her eyes gleamed marvellously, her beautiful eyes. There were tears in them. 'I shall do as you like. You can come and go, my love, and lead your own life. You needn't feel that I'm a burden.'

'What do you mean?'

'I mean that you don't have to stay faithful to me, and you don't have to wind your life around mine, around this place. I shall stay here, and you can be your own man. Come to me when you want. Try not to forget me too fast.'

'But – why are you saying this?'

'I've lived my life, and I love you. I'm not going to be thrown out like an empty bag yet, but I shan't make you miserable either. You're young, and you've been good to me. And the love I feel is enough. If yours has died – then all I can tell you is that I'd always hoped it wouldn't. But it has.'

He had expected anger, tantrums, rage – tears – but not this. She held her arms out to him, and, from custom, he came to her. Then she pressed his head against her bosom.

She was releasing him, and the terms were fair enough, he thought as a flicker of passion animated him for a moment. She was murmuring in his hair, and he felt her tears and wondered why he did not feel more guilty. But she had chosen him, had known what might happen. This, then, was intelligent choice. They had both got wonder and magic from the relationship, and he had loved her. She had made him feel more virile than ever before. They still cared for each other. The rest . . . If she'd suggested it, then that too was a conscious choice on her part, something she could live with.

And she had given him back his freedom, or at least a great part of it. She was opening the cage to let the bird fly out.

154

Book 2

Summer

A time to weep, and a time to laugh; a time to mourn, and a time to dance;

A time to cast away stones, and a time to gather stones together; a time to embrace, and a time to refrain from embracing . . .

ECCLESIASTES 3:4–5

Chapter Seven

Jamie thought that Paris was the next logical step in the ladder of her life. She had arrived with her small inheritance hugged tightly to her. When one has never possessed much, one places great value upon one's choices. She had decided to go there, an ocean away from everything she'd ever known, to develop her mind. She was an artist; in America there was no room for artists to breathe freely. Others were fleeing to the city of light, where art flourished and was appreciated. American writers and poets were leaving their country in the hope that the atmosphere in France would be different from the staidness of the United States. Jamie felt that she and Lesley were part of an exodus spurred on by the end of the war.

Lesley, on the other hand, had had greater difficulties. Jamie remembered staying at the marble mansion on Fifth Avenue, listening to the endless discussions among the Richardsons: Lesley, in her armchair, hands laid rigidly over the armrests; Lady Priscilla, crisp and blonde and distant; Ned, his face reddening, sensing that something essential was eluding him. He hadn't wanted to lose his daughter. Lesley had said, her voice strained, 'But I'm not leaving *you*, Daddy. I'm going to take a trip and learn to paint. You know I want to become a good painter, and a change of atmosphere may make the difference.'

Eventually Jamie and Lesley had been seen off on the big white steamship, where dozens of yellow roses had greeted them in their stateroom. Les had had bright red spots on her cheeks. Jamie had looked out to sea, her beautiful blue eyes intent on her own private thoughts. There was a fire inside her that seemed to be let out only through her writing

157

and through her eyes when she was self-absorbed. Then she became lovely: rounded, like a Rubens, with a gentle earnestness that gave her a grave maturity.

They had sat at the Captain's table, had drunk champagne, had danced in the ship's ballroom. At Vassar Jamie had always been the scholarship student. On board she was travelling first class. She'd wanted to book a tourist passage, but Lesley wanted to be with her, and the Richardsons insisted that their daughter have the best. They had offered to pay for Jamie's trip, and she had refused; to please Les she had finally accepted the difference between first and tourist classes as a gift from Ned.

It felt good, being on their own. Lesley felt less independent than Jamie. Jamie had her own money, whereas Lesley still depended on her parents. In Paris, however, one forgot who manipulated the strings. They were alone in the city of their dreams, and they felt excited and rich and free and talented.

Paris was so beautiful, with its manicured gardens of the Luxembourg, its avenues lined with maple trees, its lazy, indolent Seine. One could become overwhelmed by sights and sounds. Lesley's mother had told them to stay at the Ritz, on Place Vendôme, but they knew that the opulence of the luxury hotel was not what they wanted. They would rent somewhere, something small and charming, to be redone by them. But to start off, they settled at the Ritz and began their endless walks to all parts of Paris, to explore their surroundings.

Paris was still afflicted by wartime shortages. The Louvre museum still had not regained the Venus de Milo and the famed Victory of Samothrace, which had been sent to Toulouse for safekeeping. But there was a calm in the city that was different from the fever of 1916. If there was panic at all, it rose when people talked of Lenin and the Bolsheviks: The French were terrified of the Reds, of upheaval. They had suffered losses of a million and a half men, and from being world creditors they had become debtors with an internal debt of two hundred and seventy million francs. People wanted a return to the status quo: anything but new upheaval, now that peace had come.

Lesley had arrived armed with the names and addresses of people to find: her mother's friends; her teacher Chatterton's contacts; associates of Ned Richardson who had set up business in Paris. Jamie was amused; she really had but one desire, to meet Gertrude Stein. For the rest, Lesley could do as she pleased. Jamie wasn't particularly interested in meeting eligible young American boys here in Paris, or in being dined at the sumptuous town houses of elegant French matrons.

Lesley enrolled at the Académie Julian. She was serious about her painting. Jamie had recently resumed writing poems: formless thoughts encased in strange rhythms. She read and she wrote, and she ached to have someone of note read her work.

It was wintertime. Paris lay beneath a thin coat of powdered snow, and it was very cold. They were still alone and Jamie was becoming worried that her money would run out. It was time to look for a small apartment. And yet she was oddly inert. She didn't feel like being constructive. Solidarity had been Cincinnati, maybe even Vassar. But Paris . . . She wanted the luxury, unparalleled in her life, of being a lady of intellect and leisure.

And this was how, one Saturday, they decided to call on the odd couple at 27 rue de Fleurus, in the Sixth *Arrondissement*. Lesley held in her hand a note of introduction from Clarence Chatterton, the artist-in-residence at Vassar; Jamie had a similar paper from her favourite teacher, Gertrude Buck. The girls had been in Paris for a month; it was late December 1918. Suddenly it had seemed imperative to mix, not just to stay together exploring. They missed the excitement of being with people, and Jamie had been so interested in this Stein woman that Lesley gave in

159

and passed over Anna de Noailles, the famous poet and hostess, who had met Lady Priscilla years ago in London.

They'd been told that Miss Stein held open house after dinner on Saturdays, and so, feeling shy, they dressed the part. Lesley donned a green dress with a cowl neckline and a loose belt encrusted with beads, draping around her neck a string of coloured beads. She wore her looped gold earrings and gold bangles at her wrists. She was stunning, her red hair and emerald dress points of high colour to catch the eye, her skin pale and pure by comparison. Jamie was more modest, in an ashes-of-roses silk blouse, a string of fake pearls and a woollen navy-blue skirt. Their legs in silk stockings showed beneath the edge of their skirts.

A maid answered the doorbell and stared at them. 'We're here to see Miss Stein,' Lesley said bravely, in her impeccable French from Miss Spence and Vassar and other trips abroad. The woman nodded and darted inside. Presently someone else came to them. She was thin, with dark short hair and loops around her ears, just like Lesley's. She wore a dress of flowered print, and above her upper lip was the hint of a moustache, a sombre shadow. A strange thin woman with the colouring of a Jewess or a Mediterranean.

Lesley repeated, her voice more shaky now: 'We've come to see Miss Stein. Are you she?'

Unsmiling, the other countered: 'Who are *you*?' She spoke perfect American English.

Jamie said: 'We're from Vassar College. I'm Jamie Lynne Stewart, and my friend is Lesley Richardson, of New York. We've only just arrived, and we have notes of introduction.'

'Oh? Please, let me see them.' The woman extended a thin hand, and Jamie complied. Lesley was standing quietly at her side. Jamie admired her. She herself was beginning to perspire, but Lesley's poise was such that no one, not even the thin brown woman, could have guessed at her nervousness.

160

'Well,' the woman was saying: 'I'm Alice Toklas. Come in, we're having an open house.'

Alice Toklas. Lesley looked at Jamie, who nodded: Stein's companion, from San Francisco. They followed her into a house with Florentine furnishings, paintings spread over every wall. Lesley's eyes widened. There was a Matisse, a Picasso from the Rose Period, one from the Blue. A soft pastel that must have been done by Marie Laurencin. People stood talking together with animation, a gusto that she could not remember ever having encountered. It was as if Vassar were millions, not thousands, of miles removed from this eclectic company.

At the centre of the most vociferous group stood a very small, very stout woman with hair so short that it appeared barely longer than a crew cut. She had a large, hooked nose and a mountainous breast. Her outfit was a kind of loose caftan that draped to the floor. Lesley was amazed, mesmerized. But Jamie whispered: 'That's her: Gertrude Stein.'

Lesley was a little afraid of the formidable woman, but it did not seem that she was even going to speak to them, so she felt a wave of relief. It had been silly. They should have sent a note to Anna de Noailles, reputed to be a worldly woman of brilliant spirit. This person was bizarre. But Jamie admired her books, books that it appeared no one wanted to publish in America, because they were impossible to understand. Her prose a mindless blur. Jamie read them aloud with great delight, but Lesley found them much too hard to follow. What had intrigued her about Stein was her reputation as a collector of artists and art works – a trendsetter in the visual arts.

'Miss Stein doesn't speak to newcomers, she sends the good Alice,' somebody said in the lovely French of the upper classes, and Lesley and Jamie turned to face the speaker. He was tall, with broad shoulders and very handsome features. He had thick brown hair, and his large, intelligent eyes were riveted on Lesley. They gleamed with

161

a touch of irony. Jamie stood back a pace. This was the most attractive young man she had ever seen. She blushed. He was like a work of art, hewn out of ivory and walnut. But Lesley was appraising him with greater detachment. She nodded, smiled back. 'This is Jamie Stewart and I'm Lesley Richardson,' she was saying, 'and there's no doubt that we're newcomers. Our French is redolent of Poughkeepsie.'

'What's a "Poughkeepsie"?' The young Frenchman asked, laughing.

'Oh, it's a small town in upstate New York, and Jamie and I went to college there.'

'I'm Paul de Varenne,' he said, and took Lesley's small hand and raised it elegantly to his lips. Jamie was watching him. He then dropped Lesley's hand after holding it lightly for a moment and took Jamie's. 'You're Jamie?' he asked. 'Is that really a girl's name in the United States?'

'It's *my* name. Not many people have it.'

Paul de Varenne. Lesley was standing to the side, looking at his large hands, at his athletic body. He said: 'Miss Stein has an excellent collection of wines. Would you like a glass of Bordeaux *graves*? You, Miss Richardson?'

She nodded, grateful for the lack of Prohibition here, and followed him a few steps to a large table laden with drinks and food. Jamie was asking: 'And what do you do, Monsieur de Varenne? Are you an artist or a poet?'

'Neither. I'm an art dealer,' he replied pleasantly, pouring the wine.

'Do you ever go to England?' Lesley asked lightly, accepting the glass from his fingers. 'I ask because we're so new here, and England is such familiar territory to me. I'm half English. My grandfather is Arthur Stephen Aymes the Earl of Brighton – you know? He's very old now.'

Jamie stared at her friend, dumbfounded. It was the first time that she had ever heard Les drop the name of her illustrious relative. And beneath the sweet beguiling femininity was a nervousness that Jamie sensed. The good-

162

looking man made Lesley deeply ill at ease. He raised his eyebrows, made a mock bow. 'Ah, yes, the noted peer. No, I don't go to London very often. Now and then.'

'Do you like it there? Do you have friends?'

'Some. But enough about London. I'd rather hear about you. You're very appealing, Lesley Richardson. Too appealing for this salon. And *la bonne Gertrude* – God help it if she hears me! – won't speak to you on a first visit. You're only women. How about coming away with me to the Closerie des Lilas, for a glass of absinthe?'

'Oh, yes, we'd love to,' Jamie said eagerly, and now it was Lesley's turn to be astounded. They'd passed over the lovely Anna de Noailles for this apparently essential meeting with Gertrude Stein, and here was Jamie, willing to give her up in an instant for an absinthe! It didn't make sense.

She looked at her friend and saw the high colour, the sparkling eyes. She turned to Paul de Varenne and shook her head.

'Thank you,' she murmured, 'but I'm exhausted. Why don't you both drop me off at the hotel and go together from there? Jamie isn't tired, but I'm not so strong, I'm afraid.'

'We'd miss you,' Jamie stated.

'Then drink to my health. Come on,' she added, looking around. 'Even Alice Toklas is too busy to notice if we leave: her two most insignificant drop-ins!'

Paul de Varenne did not look happy, but he escorted them to the door, and when they went out into the cold winter air, Lesley felt his hand on the back of her coat. He was holding Jamie's arm, saying something that was making her laugh, a nervous excited laugh. But while he was speaking, Lesley could feel the very slight pressure of his fingers running circles on the material of her coat. She could feel every muscle resist his obvious sexuality.

There, in the star-brushed Paris night, she decided that

163

she'd stay away from Paul de Varenne. And, at the same moment, Jamie knew that she was falling madly, irrevocably in love with him.

Elena remembered Paris with the excitement of remembered glory. She had loved Paris during her adolescence. She had admired its beauty, been enthralled by its wickedness. For Paris, like Naples, had its seamy underside, its decadence and corruption. And Elena, though still whole and virginal at eighteen, had already possessed inside her soul the seeds of her own corruption.

Paris, with its stately buildings, had appealed to her aesthetic sense of balance; but architectural beauty was unsurpassed in St Petersburg, with its golden spires and onion domes. What really fascinated Elena, however, were the whores of Clichy, waiting under the streetlamps, the open-air cafés and bistros, filled with odd conglomerations of poor students, artists and the well-heeled members of the upper classes stopping for a quick chat and a *café express*. She loved the mixture of rich and poor, of voices with the pure accent of Tours and the argot of the Parisian alleys. She found there a thrill that, as a protected little Russian princess, she'd never tasted during the normal course of her existence. And the naughty and bizarre were more intriguing than the proper and the clean.

Elena arrived from the Orient with enough money left over to settle at the Ritz. It lay in the heart of the most opulent block of the city; Van Cleef and Arpels, the jewellers, were across the square, and elegant arcades housed the most magnificent displays of clothing and furs. Galleries exposed Gauguins and Cézannes and the newest works of Pablo Picasso, the Spaniard who had become, even before the war, the rage of Parisian collectors. She took the smallest room available, but felt that from there, as an eagle from a high rock, she was overlooking the Paris in which she planned to make her life. Fate was smiling at her again. The possibilities were endless.

The first week she merely strolled about, crossing to the Luxembourg Gardens, looking at the distinguished women who walked by. She was thirsty for civilization, for style. Fashions had changed radically since 1908; now, with the end of the war, women once again thought of their clothes, but the shortages and restrictions had for ever altered modes of dress. Loose, short chemise dresses abounded; coats were eight inches from the ground; hats were small toques instead of the wide-brimmed extravaganzas to which she had been accustomed. She wondered how she, so statuesque, would look in clothes made for women with sloping shoulders and tiny bone structures. At first she was dismayed: How to compete in a world of formless young hermaphrodites? For the first time in her life, her Amazonian proportions seemed unsuitable – and for the first time, too, she felt unsure of herself.

She went down to the lobby of the hotel and stopped in front of a display window and peered at a red velvet cushion on which had been propped an enormous sapphire surrounded by rubies and diamonds. The jewels were almost blinding. Elena hugged her cape of zibeline fur, which she had brought with her from Krasnoyarsk and had somehow managed to hold onto from city to city. It was, she knew, hopelessly out of fashion. But it was winter and better to go out in sable than to go out in cloth, no matter how used the fur.

She saw, through the reflection of the glass pane, two figures making their way through the lobby from outside, and, without much thought, she turned around, curious. Two young women, laughing, shaking the snow from their boots. Elena watched them as if in a trance. One was taller, voluptuous, pretty but without distinction. She had brown hair, thick, pulled into a knot at the back of her neck, and soft wisps had blown around her face with its straight nose,

165

unpainted mouth and blue eyes. Her black blouse coat had dolman sleeves cut in one piece from the rest of the material and was open to reveal a lavender shirtwaist blouse tied at the throat. The skirt was navy-blue, tailored, and the boots were black leather. She was certainly fashionable enough; but something about her was ungainly. Perhaps, thought Elena ruefully, it was the sensuous curves of her body, which no longer went with the times.

Idly her eyes went to the other girl. Suddenly Elena came awake. This one was small-boned, with bobbed red hair that fell in bangs over her forehead. Bright-green eyes, catlike, and a pert upturned nose made her resemble a fairy or a woodland nymph. Her three-quarter coat of deep emerald wool matched the little suit beneath it, and the boots were of maroon leather. A woman-child. Elena was bewitched, admiring. This, then, was the French girl of 1918. A hint of naughty freckles shone on her nose. The two young women were laughing, and then Elena heard them speak in English, a strangely accented English that made her blink for a moment in astonishment. Then they were *not* French! But not British either. Americans? She was intrigued.

The two girls hastened towards the front desk, and the small redhead asked in perfect French: 'Do we have any mail, Jean?'

'Not today, Mademoiselle Richardson.'

'Oh, well, it doesn't matter.' They were turning away, going to the lift. Elena felt like following them but remained glued to the floor. Lucky young girls, travelling, at ease in this luxurious hotel. She was suddenly jealous and angry. Once she'd come to Paris with her governess, and she'd gone to the Opéra. She bit her lip in frustration.

Suddenly the redhead was stopping, looking back, a perplexed expression on her face, and without warning, she ran back to where she had been standing. She was looking for something. Her friend joined her, and they scanned the carpet. 'I don't understand,' the redhead was saying. 'I must have dropped it, or left it in the taxicab.'

'I can't remember,' the tall one said.

Suddenly Elena approached the redhaired girl and asked in English: 'May I help you?'

The girl was startled. Her small hand went to her throat, and she laughed, embarrassed. 'Oh, it's just that I can't find my glove. Neither of us seems to be able to recall when I had it last.' She glanced down at her right hand, neatly clothed in tan kid leather, and shook her head with self-conscious amusement. 'It's silly, isn't it? But they match, and I like them.'

'You didn't have it when you walked in,' Elena told her. 'You weren't holding anything but your small bag, and one hand was ungloved. I know because I remember your ring: It went so perfectly with the rest of your outfit.'

The girl laughed. 'Oh. My emerald! My father gave it to me on my sixteenth birthday.' She shrugged. 'So I guess the glove is somewhere in the catacombs of Paris. Too bad. But it's not the end of the world.'

'Thank you for helping us,' the tall one said, smiling shyly. Her eyes were actually quite beautiful, an unusual forget-me-not colour, pure and direct.

The small girl extended her hand and said. 'I'm Lesley Richardson, and this is my friend, Jamie Stewart.'

'I'm delighted. Elena Egorova.'

They shook hands and then an awkward silence fell upon them. Elena was opening her mouth to invite them to tea, when the redhead said: 'We really must go. A friend is taking us to dinner, and we've got to change.'

'Perhaps we'll see you again, Miss Egorova,' the tall one stated.

Elena nodded. 'Certainly. Have a pleasant evening, Miss Richardson, Miss – Stewart?'

She watched as they moved away, forgetting her immediately. Elena felt suddenly empty, without purpose. She

167

sighed, hearing them laugh as the lift man helped them into his cage. Somehow she had not wanted the tall one to stay, only the small redhead. She wouldn't have minded chatting with her a bit. There was an air of distinction about her that meant breeding. Most Americans didn't have it: her friend, for example. Elena, in fact, had already forgotten what she looked like. But the other one – Melissa? Lissy? Lissy Richardson, it was worth learning who she was.

Elena straightened her cape, took a deep breath. There was work to be done in this city, if she wanted to meet the right people.

Charlotte von Ridenour de Varenne sat back on the velvet cushions and propped a small embroidered pillow between her sacroiliac and the back of the sofa. This made her feel better. Lately pains had come and gone: arthritis. She closed her eyes, opened them again, and declared: 'It's annoying, Paul. I have no reason to receive these upstarts.'

'Oh, but you do, Mama,' her son replied, and there was a glint of humour in his eyes. 'Miss Richardson is well worth knowing. Her maternal grandfather is an English peer, and we all know how much you love our British allies.'

Charlotte wet her upper lip with great, precise care. 'Lesley Richardson is part English?'

'Yes. And her father has a most amusing job: He makes what they call "advertisements". Propaganda, you know.'

'Oh? That's quite the coming thing. What is she doing in Paris, this new discovery of yours? And . . . Paul . . .'

He had stopped smiling, and a hard expression crossed his face. He knew she was thinking of Martine, condemning his affair with her. 'Lesley is an art student, and Jamie, her companion – her friend – is . . . I can't really remember.' But he could, of course, Jamie's red cheeks, her bright eyes, the way her breasts rose and fell when she laughed – that nervous laughter. He remembered Jamie as one does a

168

captured bird. He remembered Jamie and the memory appealed to him, whetting a certain appetite. But Lesley was different. An odd girl. Passionate, or cool? Intriguing.

'Anyway, I've invited them, Mama. I'm taking them both to the Tour d'Argent for dinner. But I'd like you to meet them first. They'll be arriving at any moment.'

'You're most cavalier with my time and my residence.' Irritable, she looked away. Then he could feel the anger subsiding. Lesley: Think of Lesley, the lively red hair, the small, well-formed body. Or . . . Jamie. He dismissed this thought as he took a drink from his cut crystal glass. His mother. They had their moments, neither ever really giving in. He sometimes hated her. The one who really hated her was Alex, of course. It was obvious to everyone and seemed almost to amuse Charlotte. Paul sometimes enjoyed her. He wondered, once again, who his father was. It was a never-ending charade that sometimes obsessed him. But he knew that he would never ask, and that she would have refused to tell him. He admired her great airs and her still remarkable beauty, more striking now that she was fifty-four with white hair and white skin, blue eyes and black, arched brows. She'd never been ashamed, and he envied her. She was a woman without a conscience.

They heard the *maître d'hôtel* letting in two ladies, and Paul relaxed, preparing to enjoy himself. It was only later that he tensed, when Charlotte announced that his brother was going to join them. He hadn't wished to share his American discoveries with Alexandre, and when the sound came of the front doorbell ringing again, he could not hide a frown of displeasure.

Emotionally, Alexandre had been at a loose end. Paris was changed. The war had rallied the conservative elements that made him feel secure. He had found his business flourishing. French industrialists wanted to conserve their assets. Now that the war had transformed France from a creditor nation to that of a debtor, the rich were afraid of an

169

inevitable income tax. Anything was better than that. Alexandre, always afraid to lose that which he had acquired with such difficulty, guarded his money carefully. One would have to make certain that the Bolsheviks, who had overthrown the tsarist regime, would stay as far from France as possible, and prevent the Socialists and Communists in his country from forming an alliance and winning seats in next year's elections. Alex felt confident that the conservatives would win; and, like his clients, he believed that France would prosper. If she owed a national debt, this had nothing to do with personal gains on the part of private capitalism. And besides, the Treaty of Versailles had clearly delineated the enormous reparations that would have to be paid by the *Boches* to replenish the coffers of France, whose east and north sectors had been almost totally devastated.

Alexandre paused at the door to the vast living-room, where he heard his mother's voice mingling with other unfamiliar voices. He swung open the large screen doors and saw Charlotte on the sofa, her feet propped up by an ottoman. Her white hair was swept into a chignon, and she wore her most magnificent string of diamonds around her long neck. Her hands were covered in rings. She turned to him and smiled, the brilliant smile of a young woman. It didn't fool him: If she was making him welcome, it was for a reason of her own.

He bowed, walked in, took his mother's hand and brought it ceremoniously to his lips. 'Alex,' Charlotte was saying, 'I want you to meet Miss Lesley Richardson, from America. And Miss Stewart.'

Alexandre allowed his eyes to meet those of the redhead, and he saw her delightful smile. She extended a small hand with an emerald ring. He took the hand, brought it to his lips, met her eyes. She was beautiful, precious. 'Miss Richardson.'

'How do you do. And my friend, Jamie Lynne Stewart – '

If she hadn't reminded him, Alexandre would have all but forgotten the other girl. He saw the teasing in the green eyes, as if she understood. But the teasing was soft, amused, not hurtful. He went to her friend and introduced himself, and then took a seat on the sofa beside his mother, on the side nearest to the girl in green and gold.

'Paul is taking us to the Tour d'Argent for dinner,' Jamie was saying.

'It's the best restaurant in town.' Alexandre wondered which of the two was Paul's latest interest and felt sorry for Martine. But then again – it wasn't his business. He'd heard so many rumours.

'Perhaps you could join us for supper,' the other girl said in a lovely, engaging voice. She wasn't smiling now, but had an air of gravity that moved him. He wanted to take her hand again. A good feeling. He could remember it from Yvonne. But this girl, with her green eyes, was creating for him delicious sensations of joy, of wanting to belong.

'I should be delighted,' he replied.

This girl did not belong to Paul. Alexandre, realizing this with relief, moved closer to her, admiring the cut of her dress, the small breasts, the slender throat. He had just accepted a dinner invitation when he'd had the intention of returning to the office and preparing a legal brief.

He turned away and looked at Lesley's friend. She was so innocent, so pretty in her quiet way. On second glance her beauty became apparent. Her eyes were the key, revealing her soul to the object of her glances. This one was Paul's girl?

For the first time since his brief courting of his wife, Alexandre thought of his own looks, worried about the conservative cut of his suit. The redhaired girl was tilting her head to the side, looking at him. He blushed. The whole thing was stupid; he was twenty-eight-years-old but he felt like the child he'd never allowed himself to be – not even with Yvonne. He sat back and began to look forward to the evening.

171

La Tour d'Argent, 15 quai de la Tournelle, was a splendid establishment. Gaston Masson had taken them to their table; André Terrail, the new owner, had come to speak to Paul and Alexandre. Jamie had sat there, glassy-eyed, her *magrets de canard* untouched on her plate. Lesley had felt annoyed at her for looking at Paul with such candid, open eyes. He was absolutely the wrong man for Jamie.

Alexandre de Varenne was different. Not your usual sort of man. He was attractive. He was even handsome. She liked his quiet ways, his seriousness. As different from Paul as she herself was from her own sister.

Paul was telling Jamie that he wanted to go to La Boule Blanche, where there was Negro dancing. Lesley saw her friend's nod, the eagerness in it. Jamie was almost straining toward Paul, as if he were an irresistible magnet. Lesley glanced surreptitiously at Alex and saw the stiffness of his face. He shared her concern. But Paul was his own brother.

And then Alex turned to him and said: 'Perhaps you and Miss Stewart will go dancing. But Miss Richardson and I are going to go skating at the Palais de Glace. Aren't we?'

Lesley was enchanted. She almost laughed. 'Of course!' she cried. There was an excitement in her voice that sent thrills up and down Alexandre's spine. He had made the proposal as a pretext not to accompany his brother. He had never skated in his life. He must learn to dream up diversions that were not of the usual kind, for Lesley Richardson was an original.

Nobody opposed the plan. Paul helped Jamie into her coat, and she took his arm. They disappeared into the night, in Paul's car. Lesley shivered and drew her white mink coat more closely around her shoulders. Alexandre and she stared after Paul and Jamie until long after their car had departed. Then he said: 'Your friend shouldn't be getting involved with my brother.'

Lesley looked at him. 'Why not?'

172

Grimly, Alex shook his head. Who was he to warn a grown-up young woman? But he was upset for Jamie Stewart, who had obviously no experience with men such as Paul. He took Lesley's arm, and they entered his Bugatti Royal. He was glad he'd bought it on his return from the war, for she was a woman made for luxuries, and it was evident that she was accustomed to them.

They rode in silence. On the Champs Elysées they stopped and an attendant parked the car. Lesley's face was flushed, from the excellent Moët et Chandon at the Tour d'Argent, from the cold of the winter night. They entered the Palais de Glace where a myriad of ice skaters had gathered for their after-supper exercise. They went to the register and rented their skates, and he kneeled down and gallantly fitted hers on, tying the white laces. She giggled. Alex, so grave, was so out of context! She felt a tenderness at his effort, at his touching awkwardness.

She wanted to get to know him, to ask him personal questions. But perhaps he would resent her. Suddenly, as they hit the ice, he wobbled and fell. She laughed. He stood up, steadied himself, and made a gesture of helplessness. 'Come,' she said. She took his arm and propelled him forward. She'd been on skates many times before.

And then she asked: 'Why is it that you don't like your brother?'

'Why is it you invited me to supper?' he countered.

'I'm not exactly sure. I didn't want to get in the way of Jamie and Paul. But also – I suppose, to tell you the truth, I wanted another man around.'

She laid a hand gently on his arm, pressed it. 'I mean nothing bad toward Paul,' she said. 'Mainly I was thinking of Jamie. She wanted to be alone with him, and with you along – ' She blushed, suddenly embarrassed.

'I understand.' But did he? She was afraid that she had broken the mood of the moment. She realized, searching the fine features of Alex's Grecian profile, that she wanted to

173

please him. She hadn't wanted to please a man for more than three years.

'*I* wanted you along, Alexandre,' she said in a low voice.

He stopped, abruptly, clumsily. His face was drawn and tired, and she remembered the war injury to which his mother had alluded. 'Let's take these off,' she suggested. All at once she wanted to leave, to go into the starlit freshness of the night. Too many people were milling about, red skirts and blue blazers and shrill laughter. They left the rink and turned in their skates, subdued.

Outside he wasn't certain how to proceed, where to take her. It was close to midnight. He thought: But I know almost nothing about her! She was the daughter of someone wealthy and powerful in New York; her mother was English; she liked to paint. She sat turned toward him, and he admired the triangular face with its wide-set eyes.

'Have you ever been in love?' she was asking him, sitting in the car. She had shrugged her coat off, and he felt her nearness, her vitality.

'I think so,' he answered carefully. Something about her made him want to be more open than he'd ever been. 'I thought so. Now I'm not so sure. I was married, you know.'

She was startled. 'I had no idea. When?'

'Before the war. It was very brief, you might say. She left with another man between the civil and the religious ceremonies.' He laughed bitterly. She laid a hand on his hand. The story touched her.

'Love is very cruel,' she commented. She looked away, removed her hand.

He was silent. She opened her bag, extracted a cigarette, a small lighter. Her fingers slightly shaking, she flicked it on, missed the tip of the cigarette, gave up, and tossed both cigarette and lighter back into her bag. He was conscious of wanting to do something for her, to make her happy again.

'The war has warped so many values,' she said, and there were tears in her eyes. 'Do you know why I'm here? Because

174

in the United States, people think only of the next product to buy, of the next movie star to imitate. Jamie wants to be the next Sherwood Anderson, *femme*, but I have no such illusions. I'm not a bad artist – but not quite good enough, as they say in my country, to "hack it".'

'Who says you aren't?'

She turned to him then, and he took her hand, raised it to his lips, kissed it reverently. Lesley was a challenge, yet an inviting one. The exhilaration of clear cool water on one's feet, the fear and the anticipation and then, finally, the plunge. Lesley was the turning of a page, the turning back of his past. He held her hand to his lips and then took her small chin in his fingers and kissed her lips.

She let Alex kiss her, and then she wound her arms about his neck, surprising him, and she pressed herself softly into his arms. The car smelled of her perfume and of the new leather. The sky was black, with an occasional spark of a distant star, and it felt good to be in his arms. He kissed the top of her head, protecting her, and she closed her eyes. The mysterious connection: Alexandre de Varenne. Now everything made sense, came together. *He* would never hurt her.

He held her and felt the soft points of her breasts against him, the vague stirrings, the joy of her presence. When he lifted Lesley's face to his, he kissed her with a new passion, furious and sudden. Henceforward only he and Lesley were important: no one, nothing else. 'I think I love you,' he murmured, amazed. 'I know I do.'

In the early-morning hours, while Lesley and Alexandre were walking hand in hand, feeding the ducks in the lake of the Bois de Boulogne, Jamie Lynne Stewart held the body of Paul de Varenne close to hers, greeting the thrust of his maleness, feeling the power of him inside her. She relinquished control and gave in to the ecstasy, the red and purple joy of two bodies in one, and held him fiercely. She lay back on the pillow, drenched in perspiration, and wondered how she had survived without such sensations, without such perfect mutual giving. Paul de Varenne.

She wondered if he could love her. As she watched him fall asleep beside her, she thought of the vast differences between them. They possessed virtually nothing in common. Did it matter? She'd given herself up to him in an act of supreme voluptuousness. He'd accepted her easily, joyfully.

Jamie pulled the covers closer around Paul's shoulders, to protect him from the cold, and then she pressed her large soft breasts against his back, to protect herself from too much thinking.

Chapter Eight

Beauce was undoubtedly the most enchanting château that she had ever visited. Like Chenonceau, it was made of grey stone, with simple turrets that gave it graceful curves. The green trees and the moat and the small bridge, the rose garden to the left where she was now walking with Alexandre, were throwbacks to the Middle Ages. Romance hung heavy in the air. Wives and mistresses of kings had fought over it; she'd heard Charlotte say that Henri II had given it first to his mistress, Diane de Poitiers, who had been evicted upon his death by his widow, the embittered Catherine de Médici. Sixteenth-century politics had been played out in its shaded alleys, famous children had been conceived in its arbours. Lesley, in the early spring of 1919, felt part of this romantic bygone era. She felt exhilaration and fear at what she sensed was on Alexandre's mind.

He looked at her, and she felt his delicate blue-grey eyes upon her. He had eyes that expressed what he felt, unlike the hard compelling gaze of Justin Reeve. She had felt as if Justin, through his eyes, had drawn her inexorably toward a precipice. With Alex, the feeling was different. She felt caressed, as though by rose petals or the soft feathers of a bird's wing. He brought her hand to his lips and kissed it, then turned it over and kissed her palm and each one of her fingertips. 'Lesley.'

She was so much smaller than he, and so perfect. Her teal-coloured dress had a low round collar, and around her neck she wore two gold chains with coloured green and pearl beads falling at different lengths down the front; her slenderness was underscored by the loose belt and the straight, simple skirt. Her forest-green cape was trimmed with strips

177

of ermine and matched the small green hat. She dressed with such easy grace, he thought, overcome. Never in his existence had he dreamed of possessing a girl like this. She was too precious for him. She needed someone gallant, witty, extravagant, and yet good enough to understand the vulnerability that lay behind the façade of the glamorous flapper.

'I wish I could tell you how deeply I love you,' he murmured. 'I'm not a poet. You're a painter, you're fanciful – I'm not. I'm hopelessly prosaic, and what I feel is so grand that I am dwarfed by it – and by you.'

She laughed, reassured. 'You're a war hero, Alex. There must be hundreds of young heiresses throwing themselves at you. I'm really not what you think – ' She let her words trail off, suddenly chilled by the past. 'It is I who am not worthy of you,' she said, and tears came to her eyes.

'But – why?'

'I'm just not.' This was not the sort of man who would ever accept what had happened. She'd been with another man enough times to have become pregnant. Alexandre was old-fashioned. She had to stop him before he went too far, before it became too painful for her to resist what he had to propose. He didn't know her – didn't know what her past contained. She was all at once ashamed as she had never been before – ashamed, and filled with anguish. He was so fine, so good. Her throat was dry. Justin had betrayed her; God knew where he was now, but she had given the most precious part of herself to the wrong person, and he had maimed her for ever, making all future unthinkable.

'You don't love me?' Alexandre was asking softly.

They had been walking away from the rose garden, and now stopped by a small bench under a lilac tree. She couldn't meet his eyes. It was the shame and the fear. She pressed her other hand on the one that held hers. 'Oh, Alex . . . You say "love". I'm afraid of the word. I'm afraid, period.'

'You're afraid of my hurting you?' He cleared his throat, looked away, said: 'Lesley, I wouldn't ask you to marry me if

I intended ever to harm you. I believe in outdated ideals: in the sanctity of marriage vows, in God, in my Church. My brother laughs at me. But when I went to war, I fought for my country, not for medals. You ask me about young women throwing themselves at me. I don't ask to be thanked for what I did, because it was right. And if now I want you to be my wife, it's because what I feel for you must be sanctified formally. Any man could smile at a pretty girl and make love to her. I want so much more for us!'

If he knew, she thought, sweat breaking out on her palms, under her arms. If he only knew, he would shy away from me and call me a whore. He wouldn't understand, and perhaps he'd be correct. Justin and I behaved recklessly, and I thought I'd paid through the pain I had to undergo. It's not true! I've not finished paying! I'm going to be paying for the rest of my life, every time I meet someone I might love, every time the future opens up its possibilities . . .

'Lesley,' he was saying, his voice more even now, but still with that tone of grave tenderness. 'You're a wealthy woman, and I'm not yet a wealthy man. My father left us riddled with debts. This château itself is heavily mortgaged – the château of my ancestors . . .'

She saw the hard line of his jaw suddenly. 'Please, Alex,' she whispered, touching his face. 'It's all right.' She added: 'I understand – truly I do. You come from such an old, noble family – like my grandfather's. You believe in preserving the château not simply because it's so beautiful, but because it housed generations of Varenne men who had the same ideals as you – who fought for their country and perhaps died for it.' She'd taken a human life as much as any warrior, and only for a selfish reason.

'You *do* understand,' he was saying. At that moment she yearned to show him how much she respected him, how much his fine loveliness of spirit moved her.

'But still, I must explain. Your father would want to know everything. Lesley – my mother is a very selfish woman, and

179

my brother . . . You know him a little, enough to see him for what he is. I've had to work very hard to support their extravagant life styles. Paul works, but what he makes isn't nearly enough to keep him safely away from bankruptcy.'

'He doesn't deserve your sacrifices,' she stated bitterly, thinking of Jamie, who was spending night after night away from the suite, arriving in the early-morning hours like a guilty husband.

'If I didn't pay his debts, our family would acquire a bad reputation,' he answered her. Again she noticed the tautness of his expression.

'What is it?' she asked, stroking his hand.

'I was only thinking of things better left unsaid, Lesley. You are too pure to be mixed up with us. We are a family of bad seed. You're right. A marriage would be wrong between us. You're too good to become one of us.'

'Alex,' she cried, 'what has your family to do with *you*? *You* are the one I care about! You are a man with feelings, with self-respect. I don't give a damn about the other members of your family!'

'Then – you'll marry me?'

His face lit up with joy, the eyes all at once bright, hopeful. She felt trapped. Part of her wanted so much to take his face in her hands, to kiss his mouth, to feel his joy and to share it. But the other part pushed the idea away, with fright, with shame, with confusion. 'You're not the first man I've loved,' she said, her voice shaking. She looked down.

'You're speaking to a man who was once married – even if in name only.'

And I, she thought, was married in everything *but* name . . .

'You *don't* understand,' she whispered miserably. 'You don't *want* to understand, do you, what I'm trying – have been trying – to tell you?'

She was now staring at him with a new insistence. There – she'd practically admitted everything, and if he backed away, that was only to be expected. She waited, unsmiling, almost angry for having had to lay herself out in the open this way. But he only coloured slightly and cast his eyes down. She could see the wheels turning in his mind: She's not who I thought. She's just another easy woman . . . like my mother. Lesley had heard all about the marquise.

Instead he asked in a low voice: 'Do you still love him? This other man?'

Her heart was beating very quickly. 'No.'

He'd been afraid she was still in love with Justin and hadn't understood at all! And then, suddenly, she thought. To hell with it! I don't know if what I feel is love. I was so sure I felt it with Justin – and it was only lust. This is a person with whom, truly, I could make a life . . . And if he won't look at the picture the way I've obviously painted it, perhaps it's because God wants him to believe in me. Perhaps God wants me to have a life, after all, and happiness. It was so incredible, imagining happiness . . . She was twenty-one years old, and for three years she had lived as a nun, condemned to loneliness.

She needed it to be all right with Alex now, needed him to accept her, and if she had to skip over the bare facts, then she would.

'Maybe,' she said with hesitation. 'Maybe we could be married. But – '

'Lesley – '

'But I don't want to have any children.'

His eyes became opaque. 'Why not?'

'I can't explain. Either you accept this, or I shall refuse.'

'But you were just speaking about generations of noble individuals, and you would not want for us to continue their line? For us to have a son – or a daughter – to carry on our ideals, a wonderful tradition?'

'I don't want children.'

She was speaking with such intensity that he felt her fright and took her in his arms. He knew what she feared – all women did. Eventually the fright would dissolve, because he would treat her so gently, like the softest of flowers . . . Thinking about this brought a sudden, almost shameful feeling of lust. He was a twenty-eight-year-old man, and she was the most beautiful woman he had ever seen, and he wanted her. He wanted her now, in the garden of his ancestors, he wanted to feel her body beneath his, he wanted to possess all of Lesley Aymes Richardson, the woman he wanted to marry. He wasn't going to hurt her, because in a short while they would be man and wife . . .

He had never slept with Yvonne, but he needed to touch the wholeness of Lesley, to feel her his woman. She was trembling against him, and for a moment he felt that it was wrong. But it didn't matter now. He would make it all good, somehow, because *not* to have her would be refusing a gift he had been offered by Fate: This girl, in his life.

He was kissing her, his kisses travelling down to her throat, and for a moment he was deeply remorseful when he felt the tears on her cheeks. 'Darling,' he whispered, 'don't cry – I love you so much – '

The words were lost in the fragile fabric of her dress, and the magic that happened when the beads fell on the moist earth, and he felt her, naked, in his arms. Her face was closed, like a statue, her eyes shut too, and he kissed their lids, kissed the tears. He wasn't going to hurt her, was never going to hurt her. And then he put his jacket on the ground for a bed and lifted her below him onto it. She didn't cry out, didn't sigh, didn't make a sound. Lesley was going to be his wife, and he told her so, after his ecstasy had drained him and he lay against her soft breasts that tasted like sweet spring apples. 'You are my wife. You are the only thing of worth in my entire life . . .'

Still she did not speak. Guiltily he brushed his lips against her tear-streaked cheek, thinking that he had committed the greatest sin of his life. And then, finally, she opened her green eyes and something between fear and hope shone in them.

She said: 'I love you, Alex,' and buried her face against his neck.

Now, she thought, it would be all right. He had had her and hadn't stopped in midstream, wondering. Either he had chosen to accept her lack of virginity, or, in the power of his passion, he had passed it over. Perhaps his experience with women had been minimal. But after what she'd been through, how could he not have felt it? And she thought of the knife that had scraped out the tiny foetus.

And she knew in that instant that she would fight for ever against his ever learning of it. But no one knew, except Jamie and the woman in Poughkeepsie. She was in France now, an ocean away.

'Yes, Alex,' she cried, hugging him tightly. 'I'll marry you. I'll marry you as soon as you want to. I will never betray you.'

'Shh,' he whispered, drawing a piece of his coat over them. He had never felt such joy coursing through his body, through his heart. Lesley Aymes Richardson, Marquise de Varenne. He would make himself worthy of her love.

No American girl of good family and cultural bent could have resisted the magnetic attraction to the pavilion on 20 rue Jacob. It was the abode of Natalie Clifford Barney and her friend, the painter Romaine Brooks. Natalie Barney, at forty-three, was still a remarkable classical beauty, who had been born in Dayton, Ohio, and had made a brilliant debut in Washington, DC. Then she had come to Paris and given free rein to her predilection for lovely women. She had had a notorious liaison with Liane de Pougy, the most famous courtesan of the *Belle Epoque*, and with the poet Renée Vivien, who had died young. Now she shared her life with Brooks, two years her senior, but it was rumoured that she still could not resist a new and fetching female. For good reason, then, Paris had named her 'the Seductress'. But she was also known as the Amazon and had recently published a volume of epigrams, mostly on love, called *The Thoughts of an Amazon*. She wrote in French; yet she exemplified the culmination of the American liberation that Frenchmen most admired in their allies from across the Atlantic.

The pavilion where she lived she called the Temple of Friendship. But unlike Gertrude Stein, she was more wary of men than of women, and opened her house to welcome those who might be added to her gallery of artistic friends. Her family, in Bar Harbour, had known the Richardsons. And so Lesley, filled with a new desire to see all and indulge her hunger for new experiences, declared that she and Jamie must pay a call on Natalie Barney.

She played with outfits, decided finally on a dress of soft yellow, made of crêpe de chine by the Caillot sisters. She put daisies and buttercups in her hair, securing them with combs. And then she dressed Jamie, discarding the severe pleated skirt and sailor top and instead selecting an aquamarine cotton dress, belted with gold and turquoise braid, that showed off the voluptuous curves of her body. She was angry because Jamie still refused to cut her hair. Jamie was altogether too modest, not sufficiently with the times. Jamie wanted to live contained within her writing. Lesley felt that the world was waiting outside, and that one must see it.

Twenty rue Jacob was like a small enclave of pastoral life. They entered through a garden, and Lesley stopped, enchanted. Voices floated through the opened windows and birds sang of spring. Paris, it seemed, had been left behind, but this was merely an illusion. They were in its heart. The girls were let in through a hall with a three-panelled mirror, where hung portraits of the hostess as a young girl. The salon was walled in pink damask.

This time the young women were noticed. Natalie Barney remembered Lesley's mother, seemed somewhat surprised that she could have had a daughter like Lesley. 'I thought you would be like the other one,' she announced unceremoniously.

Lesley laughed, delighted.

'You are a dream – a red and green vision.' Natalie was tall, with thick, straight brows, a stunning woman. She ran her eyes appreciatively over Lesley, then over Jamie, who turned red with confusion. 'Your friend is shy,' she stated.

Then she introduced them to her other guests. One was a dark beauty called Lucie Delarue-Mardrus, a poet whose doctor husband had translated the *Thousand and One Nights* into French. Another was Elisabeth de Clermont-Tonnerre, whom Natalie affectionately called Lily. She was a writer, daughter of the Duc de Gramont. Intelligence shone from her strong features. And there was Romaine Brooks, sitting at a small table speaking to a tall, attractive man in his mid-fifties, with greying hair and the demeanour of a dandy from the *Belle Epoque*. 'This is Bertrand de la Paume,' Natalie said.

'We've met,' Jamie stated, regarding him with some timidity. She had seen him once or twice when Paul had taken her to some public gatherings. Lesley had only heard of him. He now took one girl's hand, then the other's. He had an ironic smile that was somewhat disconcerting. A wave of embarrassment washed over Jamie. Naturally, he knew everything. He was Paul's mentor, his best friend.

Of course he, the art dealer, would be talking to Romaine. She was a painter. Lesley, unaware of Jamie's uneasiness, sat down and listened. They were discussing new openings, galleries that they both shunned or cared for. Romaine was also an American, and she spoke to Lesley about painting, about her plans. 'I wish that I were more original, bolder,' Lesley said. She was twisting her emerald on her finger. She didn't want to say that she was going to be married. In this sitting room, such mundane happenings seemed out of place. Jamie noticed but didn't comment.

And then a flurry at the door; a familiar voice sent thrills through Jamie. Paul de Varenne, splendidly clad in creamy

beige, entered, and Jamie steadied herself on the back of
Lesley's chair. He hadn't seen her, was making introductions. On his arm hung the dark beauty who had once
addressed them in the lobby of the Ritz. 'Princess Elena
Egorova,' he was saying, and now Jamie recalled the name.
Lucie Delarue-Mardrus was kissing Paul on the cheek. All
the *literati* of Paris seemed to know him.

The voice, so unmistakable, had interrupted the conversation among de la Paume, Lesley, and Romaine. At first
Lesley felt a coldness at the bottom of her spine. Then she
looked up cautiously. At precisely that moment Paul's eyes
rested on her. He raised his brows, smiled. The woman next
to him was magnificent, an ebony statue, black silk dress
with black velvet cape flung over her square shoulders. He
whispered something to her, and they both came to the small
group. 'So,' Bertrand said. 'You decided to join us after all.'

'Certainly, I brought you Elena. Elena, my dear, this is
quite a select company we have here. My sister-in-law-to-be,
the lovely Lesley Richardson; her equally enchanting friend,
Jamie Stewart; Madame Brooks; and my holy patron saint,
Bertrand de la Paume. This,' he added very proudly, 'is
Princess Elena Sergeievna Egorova, of St Petersburg.'

'I share the same hotel with Miss Richardson and Miss
Stewart,' the dark woman said, and she inclined her head.
She was truly a spectacle of beauty. But it was an unusual
beauty, Olympian, foreign. Lesley remembered the encounter vaguely. She smiled, not quite at ease. And Jamie's heart
kept pounding. She hadn't told Paul she would be there. He
had brought another woman, one far more splendid than
she. Suddenly she felt ugly, provincial. Cincinnati couldn't
possibly compete with St Petersburg.

'I brought Elena along especially to meet you, Bertrand.
She's new to Paris. I met her at a friend's. She wants to know
the heart of Paris, its intellectual pulse. What better guide
than you?'

De la Paume nodded. 'You yourself?'

Paul smiled. 'Ah. But Princess Egorova is too sophisti-cated for me.'

'Indeed? Then she must truly be worthy of your praise. Princess – a cup of tea, perhaps?' And the Chevalier, his eyes twinkling, bowed once to Romaine and Lesley and made his way to the woman in black. They moved off to another side of the rose-damasked room and Lesley thought that an odd drama had just taken place, one she hadn't quite understood. But Paul was still with them.

Jamie waited, positioned behind Lesley's chair. She felt vaguely humiliated by the presence of the woman in black, but Paul had made the introductions in such a casual fashion that she might in fact have been a mere friend. She could remember that at the Ritz, Princess Egorova had hardly noticed her but had looked at Lesley with a great deal of interest. She glanced at her friend, saw her eagerly engaged in conversation with Romaine Brooks. Lesley had turned her head away from Paul, chin resting on palm, elbow on the arm of her chair. Finally Jamie stepped forward.

'Do you come here often?' she asked Paul somewhat awkwardly.

'Oh, now and then. They're amusing too, these women of Lesbos. They find most men a threat.'

'I don't agree. They simply prefer a company of women. Not all of them are – Lesbians, anyway.'

'You find the word offensive, Jamie? Or merely the concept?' He was amused and made her blush.

'I don't find anything offensive. I just didn't agree with you, Paul.'

For some reason her level gaze, her tone of quiet rebuttal, annoyed him. 'Jamie. It doesn't matter who is what and with whom – right? Then there's no cause for disagreement between us.'

She blinked. There was a coldness to him today that was

187

so different from the way he spoke to her when they lay entwined together in her bed, or in his. She had read him sonnets she had written, and he'd played lightly with her hair while she read aloud, an expression of rapt attention on his handsome features. Now he appeared bored, irritated at finding her there. Suddenly she wanted to leave.

'We've been here long enough,' she murmured, awkward again. If only she didn't love him so much, so devastatingly much, and if only she could know for sure who this princess was!

'You want to leave already?' Lesley asked, bewildered. Then her eyes once again were met by Paul's, and all at once she understood everything. She was angry. Jamie should never have been subjected to this.

'You're right!' she exclaimed, holding out the small watch that was pinned to the yellow dress. 'We're going to be late.' She turned to the surprised Romaine Brooks and added: 'I'm terribly sorry. We'd made another appointment – '

'I quite understand. You'll come again – both of you?'

'Of course. And thank you.' Lesley looked around for their shawls, saw them in a corner, and walked over. Paul raised his eyebrows questioningly at Jamie and laughed, a light, low laugh. Then Romaine Brooks asked her something and Jamie was forced to answer her, turning away from Paul because she had to.

In one gay corner stood Elena Egorova with Bertrand de la Paume and Lily de Clermont-Tonnerre, and in another Lesley holding their shawls. Paul walked deliberately over to her, so that she could not escape. He held her white knitted shawl out, letting the gold threads fall gracefully into place, and, without a word, positioned it around her shoulders. She stood stiffly for him.

'You have no sisterly feelings toward me,' he chided her. 'Why is it you dislike me so?'

'Because you're a hypocrite,' she whispered back, not looking at him. 'And because you're going to hurt Jamie.'

'Oh? What makes you think that? What if I were in love with her?'

'If you were, you wouldn't turn up at a well-known salon with another woman.'

'Ah . . . so it is Elena that bothers you. Elena is Elena. She is nothing to me but an acquaintance.'

'Have you mentioned this fact to Jamie?'

'Jamie isn't jealous, as you are, dear little sister,' Paul said lightly. 'I didn't find it necessary to dot my *i*'s.'

'Then perhaps you should reconsider. And leave her alone from now on. She doesn't need someone like you!'

'*She* feels she does. Are you your friend's keeper?'

'I should be.'

'And should I be my brother's? Alexandre would find it bizarre that you and Jamie go from salon to salon all day long, and that you find Madame Brooks so fascinating. Or perhaps it's the enchanting Natalie. Romaine, at least, is faithful: but Natalie's roving eye is more than rumour.'

Lesley finally looked at him, and her pallor struck him. Quickly he peered around, saw everyone engaged in animated discussions. She was standing close to him, defiant, her green eyes wide open, angry, her small determined chin pointed upward. With one quick movement he bent down, pushed her face back, and found her lips with his own. He parted them, thrusting a strong tongue into the cavity of her mouth, and then let her go. She was so astounded that it took her breath away.

'Jamie Lynne should have found Alexandre,' he whispered, and walked away. Still she stood in the corner, holding Jamie's shawl, her cheeks devoid of colour. She saw him walk toward Romaine Brooks, saw him raise Jamie's hand to his lips, watched as he escorted her to the door, holding her gently by the shoulders. Lesley was so shocked that she could not even move.

'I'm so sorry you must leave now,' Lucie Delarue-Mardrus was saying to her, and then, at last, Lesley reacted.

189

She smiled perfunctorily, said a few words, and left as quickly as she could. Paul was at the door, grinning at her.

As she closed the front door behind her, she heard Bertrand de la Paume telling Elena Egorova: 'Then it's all set. Tonight, *Tartuffe* at the Comédie-Française. And then supper at Weber. The Beaumonts will join us. You'll like them both . . .'

Lesley strode through the pretty garden, her cheeks aflame. She wanted to scream, to tell Jamie, to tell Alexandre. And yet, of course, she knew that she could not, would not. Jamie was waiting for her by the postern, and she looked forlorn. Lesley's heart softened.

'It's all right,' she heard herself say. 'Our princess from the fallen empire has just made a rendezvous with Paul's boss. They appeared quite thrilled with each other.'

'Thank you, Les,' Jamie replied softly, taking her wrap from her friend. She couldn't meet Lesley's eyes. As they walked away, Lesley wondered, brutally, how far she would have to go to protect Jamie from Paul.

It was one morning at dawn, stealing down from Lesley's suite of rooms where he had just left Jamie asleep, waiting for her roommate to return from a weekend in Beauce, that Paul de Varenne had run into the most startling woman he had ever seen. He was still half asleep after a night of lovemaking, his hair still rumpled. In the front lobby was a woman of his own age, sitting, reading the early-morning edition of *Le Matin*. She was alone, perfectly content in the enormous lobby by herself. She seemed to sit like an Egyptian queen, Cleopatra without her entourage. He stood by the lift cage and literally stared at her.

At length, like a feline, she sensed his presence and raised her eyes to meet his. What eyes! Large, slanted at the corners, almost Oriental – and of the deepest, most disturbing black. Her face was white, her hair black, long and

190

straight. He couldn't concentrate on what she was wearing. It paled next to her beauty. He wanted to approach her but dared not.

She finally smiled. Only her lips smiled, not her eyes. Those remained still, like two black ponds. He knew that either he would have to speak or leave the hotel. He thought somewhat guiltily of Jamie. But this woman! She defied sexuality.

It was she who broke the silence. 'Good morning,' she said. 'Or is it still "good night"?'

He walked over to her, straightening his cravat. She began to laugh. 'You've had a long session with a lovely lady,' she remarked. 'So for you it is "good morning".'

He felt himself colouring and smiled back. '*Touché*. And for you . . .?'

She shrugged with a hint of something like regret. 'In my country, no one goes to bed till dawn. And in the winter – for four whole months – there is virtually no sunrise.'

'I take it that you are a Russian, then. I am Paul de Varenne.'

'Elena Egorova.' She held out her hand, a man's hand, but smooth and white, with nails that were even, beautiful, and unpainted. He took the hand and brought it to his lips. Her fingertips smelled of musk.

'You are a guest at this hotel?'

'Not, like you, somebody else's guest. I have a room here, yes – My own!' She was laughing at him again, and he found her laugh contagious and a bit embarrassing. He wasn't accustomed to being seen in such fashion, except by Bertrand. There was no softness to *this* female.

'Are you against a man having *amours*?' he asked, making himself comfortable in an armchair near hers.

'Never. These things amuse me.'

'But you're beyond them yourself . . .'

She raised her eyebrows. 'Ahh . . . the man has not yet come to turn my head completely. I doubt, my dear sir,

191

whether he will ever come. In the meantime, I look around me: I observe. I am observing Paris again, after eleven years of enforced absence.'

He noticed that her fur coat was out of date but said nothing. He asked: 'You are a political exile?'

'You might say that. Like Prince Yussupov and the Grand-Duke Dmitri. And every other taxi driver in Paris. The French consider themselves impoverished by the war. Our country has vanished for ever. My sympathy, therefore, is perhaps not as deep for your great countrymen as it should be.'

'You are speaking to a flying ace, madame.'

'I beg your pardon, monsieur.'

Simultaneously they started to laugh. Then he stood up. 'It would hardly be fair to leave you on such a note, to bore yourself to tears with *Le Matin*. Would you, instead, accept an invitation to drink with me at le Boeuf sur le Toit?'

She stood up too, swinging her coat from her shoulders like a simple wrap. 'Le Boeuf sur le Toit? I've never been there. What is it? The equivalent of our Aquarium, where gypsy girls dance while rich men drink champagne?'

'And nice girls never set foot inside the premises?'

'Of course not. Is it?'

'This is Paris, Madame Egorova. Our nice girls go everywhere. There isn't a girl in Paris who isn't nice. Some are too fat, others too stupid. But all are nice, I assure you. The intelligent ones haunt Le Boeuf, as I do. If you like black jazz bands, alternating with Mozart and Schumann? And Dadaist songs?'

'Da, da, which means "yes, yes", in Russian, I *do* like. Jazz I know little of. But what I've heard has pleased me. So unlike Tchaikovsky!'

She had a sense of humour. He wondered about her. Where had she lived for these eleven years? Most of the Russian immigrants had left their country later and were

192

more up to date. This girl – this woman – had come out of nowhere into the Ritz: a vision, an atavism. She took his arm and he led her to a waiting taxi.

Sex hadn't really entered his mind. He had seen her as he did rare works of art when he found them for Bertrand. Now, in the taxi, with her muscular thigh against his, he began to want her. But it was an odd lust, not at all like the one he felt for Jamie's soft, giving young body. He wanted to undress this phenomenon and penetrate her, in order to see what it felt like to possess a work of art, the Venus de Milo come to life.

In the bar she leaned across the table, drinking her gin, and she asked him who he was. 'You don't,' she murmured, 'look like the sort of man who works for a living. *De* Varenne. What are you? A prince?'

He smiled, vaguely annoyed. 'In Russia there are princes,' he remonstrated. 'In Paris, someone who isn't directly related to the king – or the emperor – is at best a marquis. My elder brother holds the family title. Mine is only that of count. But should I have a son before he does, my child would inherit his title. Complicated, isn't it?'

'It's the French mind. In Russia everything is simple. It is either grand, totally grand – or nothing at all. That's why there was a revolution. Your revolutions don't ever seem to effect much change. The kings go, emperors replace them, and then come strange interim republics that thrive on their deputies and senators. I am a princess. My mother was a princess by marriage and a countess by birth. And I couldn't tell you which is the more exalted title of the two.'

She swallowed her gin like a habitué, and he marvelled: A woman who drank effortlessly, like a man. He admired her large hands, her broad shoulders. 'I work for an art dealer,' he finally stated. He had meant to say, 'I *am* an art dealer,' but somehow, this woman, because of her power-

193

ful presence, made him more honest. She had practically admitted her own poverty. 'And you?' he asked.

'I? I am out of work. I am a fish out of the sea. What would Pushkin have said of me, Monsieur le Comte?'

'He would have said what he did to the fisherman: "Throw her back where she belongs." But since that can't be, what will you do, Princess? Or are you one of the wealthy, lucky émigrés?'

'My funds are sadly running out. Yet I shall not cut patterns in a *maison de couture* for Madame Chanel or Monsieur Poiret. I shall not become a governess. Tell me, Monsieur le Comte, what do princesses do when their kingdoms shrink to the size of a green pea?'

The band was playing languorous freedom blues. She needed strains of Tchaikovsky, or at least of Igor Stravinsky in his *Firebird*. She *was* the Firebird. He sighed. 'I am a count who works when he pleases, whose big brother helps to pay his debts. I'm afraid you've come to the wrong man for solutions.'

Her eyes were fixed upon him, appraising him. He felt embarrassed, wondering whether she found him wanting. Then she remarked softly: 'Not really. I could be a model, but not for rich, idle women clients at a *couturier's*. For a painter. Or – a photographer. And you might be exactly the right man to provide me with this solution.'

His heart sank. So she hadn't been looking at him as a sexual object but only as the means to an end. He was suddenly angry. She wanted to use him. And yet – she was right, of course. Chaïm Soutine would pay her great fees to pose. And he might pay Paul an agent's fee. He said a little ruefully: 'Maybe so. You are indeed a remarkably beautiful specimen.'

'A specimen, my dear count? I've been called many things in my life by many men. Never yet a "specimen".'

And then she laughed. 'You too are a wondrous specimen to behold. You are healthy and strong. If you were only your

194

rich and better titled brother, I would proffer an invitation to my apartments. But alas, you are only good-looking. And as poor, probably, as me.'

He had never been so insulted in his life. She saw his face and her eyes softened. They rested on him, caressing him. He felt his anger ebbing away to the strains of the pianist Doucet's enchanting, light touch. 'Your mistress is asleep?' she asked gently.

'My mistress is sleeping soundly at the Ritz. But that is hardly my concern. I am here, with you.'

'And I am glad of it.' Her marvellous eyes were like liquid fire, and the touch of her fingertips on his forearm was like a series of small electric sparks that thrilled him. The sun had come up over Paris, and he didn't want to leave the club. But she said, her voice husky with gin: 'Now I shall be able to sleep. I have made my first friend in Paris.'

When he came back to the Ritz with her, she kissed him lightly on the lips, by the lift cage, and whispered: 'You and I can't be, Paul de Varenne. We are far too much alike. What you need is a wealthy woman. What I need is money. For money, as you well know, is the only power that matters.'

She turned away, and he remained dumbstruck as the cage closed behind her. Elena Egorova. He had completely forgotten what time it was, and why he was standing like a fool with bloodshot eyes at eight in the morning in the lobby of the finest hotel in Paris. Only when he heard, through the swinging door, the familiar voice of his brother's fiancée, Lesley Richardson, did he regain his wits. Like a guilty child, he darted behind a sculpted panel and hid there until she too had disappeared inside the lift. And then he thought: Jamie! And he walked quickly into the sunlit morning.

195

Grigori Popov stood arrogantly in front of Paul, holding his riding crop in one hand and fingering its tip with the other. 'I think I'm making you a splendid offer,' he stated. 'One that I'm told you are in no position to refuse.'

They were in a small library of the Varenne apartment, Paul behind the small Empire desk with its inlaid mother-of-pearl top. He said, angry: 'Who is it that told you so, Monsieur Popov?'

'Everyone of note in Parisian society. You are the wrong brother, Count. You are the one who needs the funds, and besides, horses are playthings to you, and the Marquis Alexandre neither understands nor cares anything about them.'

'Yet the château, since you're so well informed, is his. Shouldn't you take your offer to *him*?'

'Until he marries Miss Richardson, he needs my business to keep his estate going. So if you suggest it, as a horse expert, he won't turn you down.'

'State your business.'

'Very well. I am a horse trainer. I possess a quantity of Russian trotters that I managed to bring over with me when I left my country, because I was wise enough to rent the hold of a ship while there was still good money in my pocketbook. You see, I escaped with my funds almost intact. But to date I have not yet found the sufficiently flat expanse of land that I need, so that its climate, the odour of the atmosphere and the general appearance may remind my horses of the Russian steppe. In Beauce, however, the fields stretch out to the horizon, and the animals would become acclimatized. Behind the park lie open spaces ideal for racing. This means that my animals would stand a far greater chance of winning races than if I trained them in some other region.

And I would make certain that if one won, the fact became known that it had been trained on the Varenne estates.'

'And you would pay me well?'

'Of course. I am a fair man. The horses shan't disturb you, nor the marquis. And with his coming wedding and the elections . . . he may not even have the time to visit his country home.'

'I shall consider your proposal and bring it to the attention of my brother,' Paul said tersely.

When the other had departed, Paul scratched his chin thoughtfully. In a few weeks Alexandre would formalize his engagement to Lesley. He had to act now, to make sure that his own livelihood was protected. Alex would have Lesley's trust and his own solid earnings, but he, Paul, would possess only a meagre salary from Bertrand de la Paume. He decided that he would accept, in his brother's name; Alex hardly ever went to the château now that he had been asked to run for the Chamber of Deputies in November, when he was also going to be married. Popov had done his research effectively. It hardly mattered, then, whether Paul asked for Alex's permission.

Paul took the pen and dipped it into the inkwell, and began to write: 'Dear Monsieur Popov,' he said as he wrote: 'You have persuaded me that your idea is a valid one. I have spoken to my brother. Your horses shall be welcome on our property.'

As preparations for her wedding began in earnest, Lesley felt for the first time since coming to Paris that she was alone. Alexandre's fine profile was like the reminder of their lovemaking at Beauce, something gentle, a bit old-fashioned, graceful but yet awkward. She watched him as, solicitous, he pulled chairs out for her, took her hand at dinner, murmured in her ear. He was part of Paris, part of an era gone by. The crowds that thronged colourfully

197

around them on the boulevards weren't like Alex. And yet she didn't feel that she belonged to them either.

To be truthful, Alex was only a partial cause of her alienation. Another cause was Jamie. They had come to Paris to be together. But since Jamie had met Paul, the two girls had hardly spent any time together. Lesley allowed Charlotte to hover over her like a watchful bird of prey, and she listened as wedding expenses piled up for her father. The old Marquise had written to Lady Priscilla, enjoining her to trust her with all preparations for a magnificent trousseau. The young woman listened and let Charlotte's voice numb her growing unease. Jamie was planning to rent a small apartment with Paul.

'He's never going to marry you,' she had said cruelly. 'Don't you see he's no better than Justin? They're the same kind!'

Jamie had shaken her head. 'Paul's been very honest. I know he doesn't want the legal bonds of marriage. But I want to be near him. I want to take care of him, to sleep close to him. . .'

'And what about Martine du Tertre? She was practically his wife before the war. Look what's happened to *her*. She lives like a recluse on rue de la Pompe, she hasn't combed or washed her hair for months, she wanders through her house like an old, abused ghost.'

'Martine isn't Paul's responsibility. He never made a commitment to her.'

Jamie's stubbornness was appalling. She didn't want to listen. Even when Bertrand told them that Martine had died in her sleep, her frail bones showing beneath her soiled nightgown, a bottle of whisky lying empty on its side by her bed with its stained satin sheets, Jamie's chin remained solidly impassive. Lesley sat at the table, her own hands trembling, with pain for the discarded woman, with anger at Paul. How could one remain cold to such a tragedy?

But Jamie wasn't cold. She was afraid. Paul needed a

198

woman's touch and vitality. If she didn't go with him now, he would go elsewhere to seek his pleasure. 'Marriage isn't important to me,' she whispered to Lesley. 'You know I don't care about formalities. But I care about love, and this is a risk I have to take.'

Lesley wondered then what risk she herself was about to take by plunging now into a union with Alexandre. Was there danger with this brother too? Alex was so decent, so kind – But he was also troubled. He'd been scarred by his mother, by Yvonne, by the war and his injury. Would she be strong enough to help him?

She thought of the enormous wedding, of the international smart set that would attend, eclipsing her in the glow of their own wealth and power. It wasn't Lesley's wedding Charlotte was planning so carefully: it was a celebration of her own status. Nobody really cared about Alexandre, about his small, red-haired bride. They wanted to see the setting, the splendour, the amalgamated richness that would gather. They would come for glamour, and she asked herself if this was really why she, Lesley, had come to Paris.

Perhaps Jamie was right. Perhaps, after all, it made more sense to love outside the bonds of society. She'd run away from home because people expected her to behave in a certain fashion, and now she had traded the dictates of Fifth Avenue for those of Alex's mother.

She had traded Priscilla's conservatism for Alex's.

Alexandre received the letter in his office and sat, perplexed, rereading it. It came from the *maître d'hôtel* in Beauce. Alex had not gone frequently to his country domain, these last few months, and so he was bewildered. The man wrote that he had reached his wits' end at the destruction of the property, that if the Marquis Alexandre did not come immediately to set the situation straight, he and the entire staff would leave. *What* destruction? Alex rang for his secretary and asked her to check the files on the Beauce property. Had anything out of the ordinary occurred? Had his mother, perhaps, ordered a transformation of the gardens, or had she wanted to build a new wing? The architect would have had to come to him for approval, as he, not Charlotte, was the legal owner of the château.

But the files revealed nothing out of the ordinary. Alexandre was unnerved. 'Cancel all my appointments,' he told the woman who served as his secretary. He jumped into the car. The metallic blue Bugatti Royale was easy to handle, like a racehorse, on the open road to Orléans. He pulled up to the gates of the château and, as he opened them, something unpleasant struck him about the grounds. The young shoots of the new trees recently planted had been eaten away. The attractive lawn in front of the main house seemed bare in patches. Suddenly anger came over him in a hot wave. The flowerbeds were all trampled, the begonias and sweetpeas mangled spots on the brown earth. He began to run, leaving the car unattended, its door still open, his eyes filling with tears of fury. He had been coming to the château of his ancestors for his entire life, and he felt the odd tie of a man to his land, a sense of binding. The devastation before him enraged him.

He pounded on the front door, and the *maître d'hôtel* opened to him, his old face haggard. He sighed with apparent relief: 'Ah, Monsieur le Marquis – '

'What's going on, Armand?'

'It's M. Popov and those horses. One hundred of them – '

'What are you telling me? Who is Popov?'

The elderly servant sighed again, the breath emerging from him like a tired sob. 'The horse trainer. We thought – M. Paul had led us to believe – that there would be, at the most, fifteen of them. There wasn't nearly enough room for them in the stable, so we had to put the rest up in the hothouse, piling the rare plants in the corners and building new stalls for the excess animals. The grassland at the back was not sufficient for their grazing needs. He let them out into the park. You should see what they did!

Destroyed the work of hundreds of years of landscaping – killed off the new trees and shrubbery – '

'I saw, Armand, I saw.' Alexandre sat down, placing his head in his hands. An immense weariness descended on him. He thought he had gained a glimmer of understanding, 'Where is this Popov?' he demanded.

'In the study, drinking the Varenne brandy.'

'Bring him here. Now.' Alexandre wondered at his strange calm. Whoever Popov was, Paul, his own brother, whom he had in some way managed to support all his life, lay at the heart of this betrayal. He looked up and saw a thick-set man with a large moustache striding in, holding a riding crop. 'Monsieur le Marquis?' he was saying.

'Yes. You will at once tell me what you're doing on my property. You – and your hundred horses.' The rage lay in control, white like molten metal. The key was in the handling of this intruder.

'But Monsieur – surely you are well aware of all this? The Comte Paul, your brother, long ago told me of your explicit permission to board my horses on his – on your – domain. I have paid him. Since you are in possession of my cheque, you have no reason to be so perplexed.'

Brazen arrogance. For a moment the desire to throttle this man almost blinded Alexandre. He restrained the impulse, but the cords of his neck began to stand out, and he felt himself redden. 'You must be joking,' he whispered.

The other laughed, hitting his muscular thigh with the tip of his crop. 'Joking about my money? No, indeed.'

'But I have never heard of you and have never seen your cheque.'

The man raised thick black brows. 'The Comte Paul – '

'How much? How much did you pay my brother?'

'Twenty thousand francs.'

Alexandre felt his jaw tightening, and he clenched his fists. He sat down once more, carefully. 'Twenty thousand francs. Well, M. Popov, where is your legal contract? You can't possibly have one in your possession. This château doesn't belong to my brother. It belongs to me, and I don't recall having signed any papers allowing you and your – animals – to occupy my grounds. By law I could have both you and my brother sent to prison for many years. You see, I am an attorney. But since this is also, unfortunately, a family matter – ' He had to stop himself. 'I shall merely throw you out this very minute. You will pack your bags, pack up your precious thoroughbreds and get out of here as fast as your legs can carry you. You will see to it that no Varenne ever hears from you again, so long as you live, which won't be for very long unless you do exactly what I've ordered!'

'The money I've paid – '

'I repeat: *You will get the hell off my property*, M. Popov!'

The man turned on his heel and quickly disappeared. Alexandre rang for the *maître d'hôtel*, who arrived out of breath. 'I'm going now, to find M. Paul,' he stated. 'Say a prayer for both of us, Armand.' And without looking back, he pushed his way out of the château and ran to the waiting car. He wanted to dismember his brother, to pound his head against a wall. Killing Paul would be an act of vengeance that purged and cleansed. Alexandre had never felt so alive as at this very minute, contemplating what he was about to do.

Alexandre walked in on his brother as he was packing books into a cardboard box in preparation for moving to Jamie's apartment. Paul was in his shirtsleeves, his fingers holding a first folio of a Donizetti opera. Surprise gave way to sudden alarm. He had never seen Alexandre like this, his eyes narrowed, his face suffused with blood, his hands clenched into fists. Before he could open his mouth, his older brother had seized him by the open collar of his shirt, and he could feel the delicate material ripping. Alex pushed

202

Paul against the bookcase so roughly that the younger man could not react, so startling had been the attack.

Alexandre could not speak. He closed his fingers around Paul's neck, shoved him once, twice against the panels of the bookcase, hearing him slam against the wood. Paul's head had been hurt, a spot of blood was oozing from his hairline. Alexandre tightened his grip on his brother's throat, felt the pulse of life there, and knew only the need to blot it out. Suddenly Paul, frightened and totally bewildered, reacted. From days of wartime conditioning to save himself, his knee shot up into his brother's groin, and it was Alex now whose eyes widened with surprise and pain. He stumbled backward, bending over, his bad leg all at once a mass of shooting stabs of pain. He felt a wave of nausea and collapsed on the carpet.

Paul, his head bloody, his shirt torn off his body, stood shaking against the bookcase. 'My God,' he said. 'What's going on? You tried to kill me! *You tried to kill me.*' There was shock in his voice and then stillness in the room. 'Why?'

'Because you're a goddamn thief, and a liar and a cheat. Because I've been working to support Mama and have given you money, and you have ruined us.'

The truth began to dawn on Paul, and his stomach contracted. 'Popov,' he gasped. 'But it was only twenty thousand francs. If you want, I can pay you from my next few months' salary from Bertrand – '

'You son of a bitch, the château is just about destroyed! It was one thing for you to breed several horses of your own, for you to indulge a favourite pastime. But to allow this man to invade our land – my inheritance, Paul, mine! He brought along one hundred stallions. They have eaten away the gardens, ruined the park – '

'I didn't know.'

'No, you didn't know. You cared only enough to take his money. That's all you ever do, Paul. You take people for what they're worth and shake off all responsibility after-

203

wards – ' His voice rose, and suddenly he stood up again, swiftly, and advanced toward his brother. Grasping him by the arms, he said, beginning to shout. 'I've heard about Jamie! You don't even have the decency to marry the girl – '

'That is none of your goddamn business!' Paul cried, pushing Alex off with a shoving motion of his arms. 'What are you going to do? Have me thrown in jail?'

At this moment Charlotte, having heard the shouting, rushed in, her face a mask of horror. She uttered a short cry and edged herself between the two young men. Her thin form was very strong, and she prevented each from once again getting at the other. 'You will both stop and explain to me what is going on in my house,' she announced.

'Your little favourite has made off with twenty thousand francs and destroyed the château,' Alex said, disdain replacing the rage and filling him now with an empty disgust. He wanted to be done with them both, to return home, to see Lesley. 'Let *him* tell you! But I'm never going to help either one of you again. I'm finished – completely wiped clean of any obligations! See if *you* can support Mama and her expensive lifestyle all by your honest earnings, Paul!' He turned his back on them and went limping out of the room.

Charlotte sat down on her younger son's bed, brushing her fingers through the sidecurls at her temples. 'Your head is bleeding,' she finally declared. Then she looked up, shook her head from side to side. 'Good God. Sit down, Paul.'

He did as he was told, beside his mother. She took a lace handkerchief from her sleeve and dabbed at the blood on his forehead. 'You have done many foolish things in your existence,' she commented. 'Alexandre is many things but not a fool. I have always needed Alexandre.'

'Alex is crazy,' Paul said.

'But which is worse? A fool or a madman? Alexandre the Great, after whom I named your brother, and Napoleon,

204

and Caesar – They were all madmen, weren't they? But not fools. What have you done? Tell me exactly.'

He told her, in a dull voice drained of emotion. 'So. We are more than ever in need of funds, just when I thought we were coming into the clear. What have you done with the twenty thousand, Paul? Not that in itself it represents a lot. Compared with the destruction of Beauce – '

'It's . . . gone. I bought some paintings. I – ' He had bought Elena Egorova a ruby. Why had he done so? She had refused him as a lover, and he had understood the terms. Yet he had purchased her this magnificent jewel. 'I bought a racehorse.'

She looked at him with withering contempt. 'Paul.' She took hold of his arm, lightly shook it. 'The answer is Lesley Richardson. And the way things are going, I'm not at all sure she's going to go through with this marriage. She seems tense, secretive.'

'I know. I've felt it too. From the very start.'

Charlotte's eyes hardened. 'We cannot,' she declared succintly, 'afford to lose Lesley Aymes Richardson.'

Paul looked at his mother, then at the unpacked boxes on the floor and at the scattered sheets of the *Lucia* libretto that had fallen when Alex had attacked him. He thought about his life, scattering around him like the sheets of the folio. Then he asked the ultimate, Garden of Eden question, which he had never dared to ask before: 'Mama, who is my father?'

Her sculpted features froze. But she replied: 'No one. You are my son and mine alone, Paul.'

He had to smile: Charlotte von Ridenour was the only woman he knew, save perhaps Elena, who would have had the style to answer him thus. He had never liked his mother, had often mistrusted her. But she was unique. Her answer had saved them both.

* * *

Lesley sat by the desk, her fingers idly playing with a pen. Something hard inside her had refused to allow her to visit Jamie's new apartment. She had behaved childishly with her friend when Jamie had stood, bags in hand, at the threshold of the suite. No good-byes. She wasn't going to let Jamie leave so easily. Paul was wrong for her, and Lesley felt abandoned. Now she was sorry. She already missed Jamie, felt alone as she never had before. The immense suite stared back at her with its luxury and emptiness. Jamie and she had been far happier in their little room at Vassar, decorated with love and originality.

Everything was falling apart. Lesley laid her head down on her arms, overwhelmed with sadness. She hadn't touched a paintbrush for days. She'd thought of Alexandre, of Paul and Jamie, of Jamie's determination to move out on her own. She too should have been doing that. Their great common dream, to come to Paris and study, and paint, and write. Jamie was already doing it all, and Lesley had only allowed floating events to crystallize about her into an engagement, an impending marriage. She'd met a man, and before she'd even had a chance to get to know him, there had been plans. Lesley sat up, suddenly angry. Why was it that this marriage was making her feel so manipulated? She wished, just now, that she could call it off.

The hotel telephone rang, discreetly, and she went to it quickly, wondering if it was Jamie. She'd apologize to her friend and go over at once with a basket of seasonal fruits, flowers, plants, as a housewarming gift. Why hadn't Jamie wanted Lesley to share the apartment with her, instead of Paul? That man, always using Alex, always despising Alex, and using Jamie too. She came to with a sudden start and thought: I'm jealous! I wish I'd done what Jamie did, what her anonymous background has allowed her to do.

She sighed, picked up the receiver. 'M. de Varenne is here to see you, Mademoiselle.'

'Send him up, please.' What would she say to Alex? She

loved him so, but sometimes the core of his being eluded her. He had his own demons to face, each and every day. Sometimes she was actually afraid of him. What would she say? 'Darling, I love you. I want you – but please, let's postpone the marriage and go to live in total anonymity in Cherbourg, or Villefranche?' One could do this if one were Jamie Lynne Stewart, daughter and granddaughter of nice simple people.

Looking at her face in the mirror, she pinched her cheeks. Why was Alex coming to her now? Probably because he wanted the cool freshness of her. That was what he'd told her once. She was his cool, fresh spirit. Only she felt about as fresh as a limp rag.

She heard the tap on the door and went to open it. Paul de Varenne stood staring at her, his head bandaged oddly, circles under his eyes, a tear in his shirt. She blinked. And then remembered: 'M. de Varenne.' Of course. Both brothers were.

'Won't you let me in, please, Lesley?' he was asking. His voice had an edge of despair to it that was in direct contrast to his usual robustness. He looked awful.

She made a gesture, stood aside while he passed inside. There was something disagreeable about him that never failed to put her on edge. She had already been so demoralized that his sudden entrance only served to exacerbate her raw nerves. She was doubly annoyed by his appearance, which seemed to demand sympathy she just couldn't muster. Feeling a little guilty, she asked: 'What happened to you, Paul?' He was, after all, her fiancé's brother.

'Alex beat me up.'

Lesley raised her hand to her mouth, stunned. 'Alex? He's the gentlest – '

'One would have thought so. Yet he tried to kill me with his bare hands. Over a silly matter of a few thousand francs, in fact. Sometimes I think he's really lost his mind!'

Lesley sat down, disorientated. Then she rose, confused,

207

and went to the sideboard on which stood a silver tray with two decanters containing sherry and Cognac. She poured a shot of Cognac into a tall silver goblet, handed it to Paul. Then, absently, she filled another with sherry for herself and sat down again, smoothing her skirt. Alex had tried to kill his brother. Nothing made sense.

'Why are you here?' she asked abruptly. 'Surely if Alexandre was this angry, he must have had a reason. You can't possibly think I'd be sympathetic.'

'Why are you so unpleasant to me, Lesley? Do you really hate me?' He sat sipping his Cognac, looking at her with wide open brown eyes, his 'candid eyes'.

She was unmoved. 'Paul, what difference do my feelings make? I don't hate you. I just don't feel there is any relationship between us. You're a member of Alexandre's family, that's all.'

'Always the proper little English girl.' He sat back, making himself more comfortable against the soft cushions. She was sitting stiffly forward, the picture of propriety. There was a pallor to her small face that lent it a pathos that intrigued him. She had always intrigued him, from their first meeting. She had such an odd, frail yet vibrant beauty, and this combination was a challenge. Elena was all overt sexuality, all hardness; Jamie all pliant female fecundity, the nurturing Mother Earth. Who was Lesley?

'You don't really love my brother,' Paul said, and for the first time Lesley heard genuine interest in his tone. She was on the verge of an outraged, loyal reply, when he shook his head and stated: 'Love is black and white, Lesley. Jamie loves me. It's as clear as day. If I were to ask her to make the ultimate sacrifice, she wouldn't hesitate.'

'But you don't love her.'

He sighed. 'I *love* her. I'm not *in love* with her. I wish I could be. Jamie is the most intelligent woman I know. But it's not quite right. Why should I lie to her?'

208

'And you didn't love Martine?' In spite of herself, Lesley leaned forward, sipping her sherry, interested.

'I was fascinated by her. She was – a bit like my mother. A woman who had fascinated the most important men of an entire epoch. They say' – he looked away, and she saw the discomfort on his face – 'that my mother had an affair with Edward the Seventh, when he was Prince of Wales. I wouldn't doubt it. Martine was kept by men of letters, men of the arts. She was clever and attractive. She had that special something that draws men much more than sheer, unflawed beauty. Martine wasn't at all a classic beauty. When I met her she was a sophisticated woman, and I, a young man with no experience, with no special talents. That she even noticed me was like a gift. That she loved me was like a miracle. Can you understand, even a little?'

She had never heard such a stream of words from Paul, and they sounded true. She nodded. 'Yes. Why is it so difficult for you Varennes to love?'

'Alex and I were reared by a stupid father who thought only of his gambling and by an extremely clever mother who thought only of herself.'

'But Alex loved Yvonne de Larmont.'

'He wanted comfort from her. Mama made life extremely difficult for him. More so for him than for me. She never even liked, let alone loved him. She doesn't love me either, but she thinks she understands me.'

How impossible this was to relate to! Priscilla, for all her neat British primness, was still a loving mother. And Ned. Lesley was homesick for Ned, just this minute, as never before.

'Why don't you marry Jamie?' Lesley asked, miserably twisting a piece of material from the sofa over and over in her hands. 'If it's so rare to encounter perfect love, why not grab it when it comes?'

'Because it's not mutual. Have you ever encountered perfect love?'

209

His brown eyes bored into her with an insistence that she sought to avoid, that probed too deeply. She looked down.

'Well?'

'I don't know. Once, before Alex, I loved a man. But it was wrong, anyway. When love is right, no one lets it go. You pursue it to the end.'

'You're a romantic, Lesley.'

'Maybe. And you're a cynic.'

They were silent, each drinking from the tall silver goblets. Lesley stood up, took Paul's from his hand, refilled it. As an afterthought she also filled her own. 'We should go to dinner,' he suggested.

She shook her head. 'I'm too tired. And look at you – '

'Yes. Well. I thought Alex might be here, that we might try to work this ridiculous situation out – '

'He must have gone home. When are you going to move to Jamie's?'

'Tomorrow.'

The sherry was warming her, dispelling some of the forlorn gloom. She thought that perhaps Alex's brother wasn't so bad. She had been creating drama in making him out to be so black. He was only a man, with his own wounds, inside and out. 'Don't marry Alex,' he suddenly said. 'Don't get married to please other people.'

'But I'm not! I love Alex deeply – totally.'

'Then why the hesitation?'

She watched her own reflection in the amber liquid in the glass. 'That's your imagination, Paul.'

'Alex never got over the war and never got over Yvonne. This is not a man to marry. He has too much of a past, too many hurts.'

'I have my own hurts. He's accepted me with them.'

'But you are, shall we say, a normal human being. Alex was never normal. Our mother never allowed him to be. Would a normal man have tried to kill his own brother? You should have seen his face, Lesley. He wanted to kill me.'

Lesley could feel the slight tremor beginning inside her. He saw it, watched the glass unsteady in her hand, and came over beside her. Gently, he placed an arm around her shoulders. She stiffened. He said: 'Lesley. Be careful.'

She looked into his face, read a strange concern, and was even more frightened. Where was Alex, now that she truly needed him? Reassurance was what she needed, his reassuring grey eyes, his love, his hands on her back, his body close to hers.

Paul bent down over her chair, and she could see the bandage and was transfixed. Everything was happening too fast around her. She didn't want Priscilla to come to meet Charlotte, didn't want Ned to sign papers with Alex – didn't want to be handed from one man to another as a chattel worth so many thousands of dollars. A surge of rebellion surfaced, and she straightened up, spilling some sherry on her skirt. Deftly, to help her, Paul took the goblet from her hand and put it safely down on the side table. She opened her mouth to thank him, but he placed a finger over her lips and shook his bandaged head. She stared at him, mesmerized.

Slowly he took her face in both his hands, brought his lips to hers, probed them softly. She tried to draw away but he refused to let her, parting her lips with his tongue. She blinked, wanting to fight back but suddenly dizzy, from the sherry and the depression and the total surprise. Had it really been such a surprise? She tried to shake herself free, but he was pushing her down on the sofa, and she was not really resisting enough, and as he unfastened her blouse she found herself crying, the tears blinding her, mingled with his kisses. How could one fight back when the world was falling apart in little bits and pieces, all around her like broken glass from a shattered bottle of *vin ordinaire*?

Suddenly vivid images of herself on the operating table, not fighting back, letting the woman cut away into the inside where the child had already been formed, flashed

211

into her dazed mind. Her blouse was already opened, Paul's hands trying to find her nipples. She cried out and pushed, her elbows flailing out at his torso, and he backed off, his lips parting. 'Get out of here!' she screamed. 'Get out of my life!' She brought her hands over her half-exposed breasts and covered them, her heart thumping wildly.

Paul had enough good grace to make a quick exit, and she didn't even hear the door close on his retreating back.

She wanted to be sick, at her own ineptitude, at her disloyal doubts about Alex, for poor Jamie, tying her life to this dreadful person. Perhaps it was her own fault. She had slept with one man, a crook, and then had had his baby ripped out of her own body; now she was afraid ever again to conceive a child. Was it Alex himself that made her afraid of marriage, or her own wish to blot out for ever the memory of what she had done in Yorkshire and, later, in Poughkeepsie? But these actions had had nothing to do with Alex, only with herself. Could Paul have suspected something about her past, or had he merely tried to avenge himself on his brother for trying to kill him?

Lesley Richardson stumbled blindly to the bedroom and fell upon the bed. For the first time in her life, she wanted to die.

When the telephone rang she had no idea what time it was. She reached for the receiver, and when she heard Alex's voice, she burst into hysterical sobs. He had wanted her comfort. He was still shaking from having tried to kill his brother Paul. She could hear his words and could only sob. When he asked her what on earth was wrong, she considered, for one wild moment, admitting the truth, ugly as it actually was. She could not speak. At length she burst out: 'Oh, Alex, I love you so much! I want us to be married *now*, and I never want to be apart from you again – '

'Yes, my darling, yes, of course,' he answered,

soothingly, not understanding at all. He would have to protect her more, to make certain that, at all times, there was safety around her.

She blotted everything out with sleep, the heavy sleep of the drugged, and when she awakened the next morning she had resolutely made up her mind to forget what had happened. If she did, if she steered clear of Paul –

And yet, agonizing, sitting at her dressing-table she knew that he would never let her forget.

Paul, watching the pigeons from an open air café, drank his morning *express*, thick and brown, and pursed his lips. He nodded, smiled to himself, and went to the nearest florist. Twelve red roses, or only one? Pensively, he considered the dark-red buds, like proffered breasts. Then he said to the attendant: 'Thirteen. To the Ritz, Suite 213. With this message: "For the one I owed you yesterday, when I imposed on you: and the dozen that represent my thanks for your tact." No signature is necessary.'

He checked his watch and paid quickly. He was late for Jamie, who would be waiting for him at the museum of the Jeu de Paume.

Chapter Ten

On the last day of November 1919, one year after the signature of the armistice and eleven months after Lesley's arrival in Paris, she was married to the Marquis Alexandre Jacques Edmond de Varenne, Deputy to the newly formed Lower Chamber of the French Parliament. She wore a white gown of silk and pearls confectioned by Worth and diamond earrings that had been her grandmother's when she was wed to the Earl of Brighton at Westminster Abbey fifty years before. At the reception at the Ritz, the mixture of guests who drank to the health of the new marquise came from both shores of the Atlantic and from across the English Channel. Many were hybrids such as Lesley herself: Wineretta Singer, the sewing machine heiress who had married the Prince de Polignac; Marie-Laure de Noailles, another American wed to the *nec plus ultra* of French nobility; and members of the British peerage who hovered near the Moët et Chandon, their lorgnettes held out to observe nubile young French debutantes in their newest outfits by Chanel and Poiret.

The bridegroom in his morning coat, his fine hair parted in the centre, his grey eyes shining in a face rendered pale by the physical strain of the religious ceremony and its aftermath at the Ritz, remained the single constant among changing groups of men discussing politics. He had been approached earlier that year to run as deputy from Eure-et-Loir, where Beauce spread its plains, and had allowed himself to be talked into this by some of his clients, conservative financiers who saw in him a brilliant young exemplar of postwar France. He would protect them from the income tax; he would protect them from the labour riots such as the one that had occurred on May Day, with open fighting in the streets of the capital; he would shut the gates of Paris to an invasion of Bolsheviks, the red menace of Europe. He had run, and, being a veteran, a wounded one at that, he had run with an advantage. He possessed the muted good looks of the old established families of France and a name that made the old guard remember his grandfather, Adrien, and forget his ill-fated father. 'De Varenne' rang of the Crusades, of patriotism, of well-balanced budgets and filled coffers. And one was willing to forgive current family debts, because to boot, this clear-headed young man had allied himself to old British peerage and new American dollars in a single stroke. Lesley Aymes was a credit to him, petite and lovely on his arm, dressed in the finest clothes and the most exquisite jewellery. The Americans had come to the aid of the French at the last possible moment. But nevertheless, the Treaty of Versailles might never have been signed if they had not sent over their armed forces. And the American girls, with their short hair and slinky figures, represented everything new and daring, a new era of jazz bands and Negro blues, of new, crisp fortunes that could be spent on the French shores and on the debt-ridden French nobility. Lesley would be the ideal partner for the new deputy. She had been told so many times, had seen serious bankers kiss her hand when they brought it to their pallid lips, had seen the glint of approval in the eyes of Hélène Berthelot, wife of Philippe, who ran the Quai d'Orsay from whence emerged all decisions relating to foreign affairs. For while Philippe ran the Quai, Hélène ran the social and intellectual side of Paris, and to be accepted, a newcomer must have passed the test at her salon.

Alexandre, while he had often toyed with the notion since his university days, had not considered politics before the war with any seriousness. He enjoyed the quietude of legal study more than he did his court appearances. He was a sober, contained man. But with Lesley he felt different,

215

renewed. She was filled with optimism about the new turn in his career, convincing him of the need for better men to reach public office. His clients used a different approach: guilt. The Bolsheviks might take over Europe. Germany might not pay back its debts, and to sit back and allow these things to happen would be an act of cowardice on his part. He knew now that he was not a coward. The war had proved this to him. Now when he looked at Lesley he was not afraid. He could become a true winner in the chess game of life.

But of course he would not follow the outdated Varenne family tradition of royalism. He believed in the Church and saw with pleasure that France was returning to a less anticlerical attitude than before the war. He believed in principles. It was not that he was a fanatic, but he had been steeped in catechism since his earliest days, and there were parts of Catholicism that still seemed important to him. He could ignore the simplistic sermons of priests less intelligent than he, but he went to Mass because the transmigration of the Host touched him and communion made him feel cleansed. He thought that institutions such as the Church were needed in society, that people of all types functioned more effectively within the security of systems and rules. He himself needed them. Lesley's mysticism amused him, but to please him she went to Mass and sat quietly beside him, her triangular face attentive. She so wanted to please him that it moved him. He had thought of joining the Catholic Right, but part of him found this too extreme, and he was a cautious man, a realist, he thought. So instead he had become a member of the moderate Right, the Fédération républicaine. His party had eventually formed a merger with the Catholics and then united with the centrists of the Alliance démocratique to create the immense Bloc National, a front of unbeatable conservatives. At that point Alexandre had felt certain that he'd made the correct political decision.

216

He would sit in his study and wonder, sometimes, about the structure of French politics. There had been many governments since the inception of the Third Republic in 1870. He had spoken to his father-in-law for hours about the American system of elections. When a senator was elected, his term was definite – six years – and no one could oust him except in the rarest cases of extreme misconduct; a President stayed in office four years and chose the cabinet that he wanted. No war, no inflation prevented this system from functioning. Checks and balances existed, but they were all more or less predictable: When there was a Democratic President and a Republican Congress, vetoes and overriding might occur. But no one lost his seat because of this, as one could and did in France.

He, Alexandre, had, like his colleagues, just been elected for a term of five years. The President of the Republic was more a figurehead than the true power of the nation. The Premier, who founded a cabinet, was the crucial person in government. During the war the nation had turned to Georges Clemenceau, 'the Tiger', who had started his political life on the extreme Left and had moved to the Right. They had called him *Père la Victoire*, Father Victory, because he had made winning the war the passion of his life, going into the trenches to encourage the pettiest soldier to vanquish the Hun, kill the *Boche*. He had been a great statesman, but he had become Premier too late, in 1917, at the age of seventy-six. Some, such as the socialist Léon Blum, claimed that he had grown senile. He had never been popular. The big question now was: When the presidency opened up in January 1920, would the Tiger be elected? Alexandre was hoping for a less controversial, more moderate candidate to win. For France was in desperate need of stability.

He looked across the great reception room filled with wedding guests, where crystal and old silver gleamed and rainbow lights bounced off tiaras perched on famous heads;

he was searching for his bride. Billowing in tulle and Brussels lace, Lesley – 'Lezlay', as his French cohorts called her – was seated in an alcove with her father, sharing a private moment with him. Alex liked Ned Richardson. He knew that Lesley's feelings for her father were a mixture of adoration and genuine friendship. They were the two originals in the family. A vague stir of uneasiness passed over him, however. Lesley had rebelled against her parents, had expressed to him various times her fear of being engulfed by the power that their wealth and position represented in New York. Now, because of the election and her dowry, they would be in a similar position in Paris. There would be a role for her to play as his wife. He'd fallen in love with her intensity, with her creative spirit – yet at the same time sometimes this spirit took odd forms of expression. For example, she would not even broach the subject of children. She wanted, she said, to be her own woman. He sipped his champagne and smiled at the Marquise Casati with her kohl-rimmed eyes, pretending to listen to her conversation about the Russian Ballet, but he was perturbed. He didn't want to crush his wife. So Lesley would have to be given room to breathe. But the question was, How much room? And would she still be able to stand by his side, seconding him as Hélène so cleverly seconded Philippe Berthelot?

She may not realize it, he thought, but I need her. I need the strength of her support. All these years, alone, no one gave me reinforcement. And in this new game of politics, I shall need to know that at all times she is with me.

'Lesley,' Ned was saying, caressing his daughter's hand, 'things will be different for you, married to a member of the Chambre Bleu-Horizon. You know this, don't you, sweetheart? The suffragette in you will have to be tamped down.'

She looked down at his large, well-formed fingers and felt the nausea of too much champagne suddenly float over her.

But she replied: 'I know. The French are a scared nation today. I don't agree with many of Alex's ideas about government – but this is his country, not mine. I'll try not to get in his way. If I disagree, I'll have to learn to speak for myself, so that no one will think I'm his figurehead.'

Her father looked doubtful. 'Alex is . . . needy. At least, in the beginning, politicians are in the most delicate position. They are exactly like advertising men, for ever dependent on the good graces of their clients. Only with a deputy, it is on the good graces of his constituency.' He motioned with his chin at the entire room, and she saw the lawyers and the bankers and the cabinet makers to whom he was referring. She was frightened, goosepimples rising beneath the silk of her sleeves – frightened at the anonymity of those faces, of their implacable conservatism that brooked no discussion.

But Alex wasn't like that. He believed in good common sense, and he would do what was right for his country. He would not follow as a sheep but lead as a shepherd. She hoped he would, and gazed through the champagne bubbles at the laughing figure of the scarlet-clad Marquise Casati, engaged in animated talk with Alex in the centre of the room. Did this bright flamboyant woman who loved the arts as much as Lesley communicate with Alex on a common ground? Lesley's own world of interests lay closer to that of the marquise than to her new husband's. During their months of courtship, they had barely mentioned her desire to break through as an artist. It was my fault, she thought. I didn't press the point, because of my own insecurity. If I had, he would have understood. She gazed up at Ned and smiled, to reassure him.

'Not so serious, my darling,' Ned said to her. 'This is your wedding day. And you are the most beautiful bride since your mother.'

She smiled, her eyes filling with tears. He was a good, strong man. He was her father. She looked again at Jamie, in her floating blue gown of crêpe de chine, and at the brown-haired young man approaching her, in his morning suit, identical to Alex's. But this was where the similarity stopped between her husband and Paul. A shiver of revulsion passed through her. How could Jamie love this man? He had stood up for his brother at the wedding, and she had wondered, after all he had done in Beauce, how Alexandre could have allowed him to act as best man. For form. For the family. I *hate* Paul, Lesley thought, amazed at the strength of her disgust. But *no one* knew what Paul had done to her, and no one ever would. She turned away and stood up. The *chef d'Orchestre* had signalled to her. 'Come,' she murmured. 'Don't we have to open the dance?'

Ned laughed. 'No. I believe it's up to you and Alexandre.'

He watched her leave his side and reappear at Alexandre's elbow, linking her arm through his. Ned Richardson saw the small, upturned face and Alex's own face bending down. There was trust in those two pairs of eyes, linked, gentle, wanting. The orchestra was preparing itself, and he scanned the room for Priscilla. She was speaking to a striking woman in purple velvet, her black hair streaming down her back, alexandrites hanging from her ears. She had come with someone infamous – Prince Felix Yussupov, who had murdered the decadent, all-powerful monk Rasputin and been exiled from Russia by the Tsar? – and Lesley had told him that she earned her living as a painter's model and had acquired somewhat of a scandalous reputation. She looked Slav, like her escort.

Suddenly the music started, his daughter was swept onto the dance floor by her elegant husband, and he saw Priscilla sailing toward him, cool and proud. In the moments it took for his wife to reach him, he saw the Chevalier de la Paume, who had escorted Alex's mother, draw the old marquise into his arms gallantly. He was a fine man, thought Ned. But Alex didn't like him. Alex didn't like his own mother either – an opportunistic, cold woman.

Priscilla glided into his arms, and he began to dance. Other couples were joining them. Lesley's face still mirrored the joy of being with her husband, her green eyes incandescent, screening out everyone but Alex. Ned felt a tightening in his chest, and Priscilla whispered: 'It's for the best, darling. She's happy again.'

'*Again*?' Lady Priscilla's light-blue eyes remained upon him. She said insistently: 'You must let her grow up, Ned.' There was something else that she was trying not to tell him. Something had happened that Priscilla knew, or thought she knew, something she had never shared with him. Were men supposed to stay out of their daughters' problems? Did mothers think that only they could decipher what lay behind a woman-child's private life? He looked at his wife, but she held his stare, unblinking. Lesley and she had never been close – yet Priscilla knew something he didn't. Then she squeezed his hand. 'They're very happy,' she stated.

He smiled mechanically and above her blonde head he saw Jamie, the maid of honour, alone. Shouldn't she have been dancing with Paul, the best man? Wasn't it true that they lived together? Ned liked Jamie enormously and wondered, watching her pretty, earnest face, still and quiet and sad. 'I must dance with Jamie soon,' he murmured to his wife.

'Yes, you must. Paul has made a dreadful *faux pas* because this waltz should have been hers – by protocol, if nothing else.' Priscilla's voice rang dry, almost haughty in his ear. He knew she disapproved of Jamie's living arrangements, and sighed. The girl deserved better. At that instant he saw the culprit, laughing, talking to the woman in purple. Lady Priscilla whispered: 'That's the Princess Egorova. Her father was a close acquaintance of Lord Buchanan, Papa's friend, when he was Ambassador from the Court of Saint James in St Petersburg.'

Ned Richardson merely raised his brow, amused. The

woman was an artists' model, who had posed in the nude for Matisse, Picasso, Soutine. But Priscilla would ignore the gossip and seize only the points of interest to *her*: Egorova's pedigree and background. She was like a well-trained racehorse who saw nothing to either side and who concentrated solely on its own course.

Yet, in America, she had perceived something in Lesley that had concerned her, something that he, blind father, hadn't even spotted. His beautiful daughter, in Alexandre's arms, was like a cloud of softness on the dance floor, all femininity and verve, her red bangs glistening beneath the veil that had been thrown back after the nuptial kiss. 'They're very happy,' Priscilla had said. Evidently they were.

Book 3

Autumn

A time to get, and a time to lose; a time to keep, and a time to cast away . . .

ECCLESIASTES, 3:6

Chapter Eleven

Jamie stared at the drawing pad in front of her. The slinky new styles of the day were definitely not attractive on her. She glanced at her calves, touched the curve of her hip that prevented the skirt from clinging in the one straight line that showed off the cleanness of the boyish figure now popular in the tabloids *Femina* and *Excelsior*. Today, 1922, the girl of the day looked like Lesley. Jamie folded her hands in reflection.

She was uncomfortable, thinking of Les. They'd drifted apart; not by planned action, not by lack of caring. Simply each had settled into a mode of living that no longer much included the other. Les was ensconced in her stone mansion on the Place d'Iéna, with its high ceilings and bevelled glass windows. Jamie and Paul were at 23 Boulevard Montparnasse, on the Left Bank, in the heart of the artistic community of Paris. It took determination to make one's way across the Seine to visit; and sometimes Les made excuses not to see her. It was as if her life had become so complicated since her marriage that any change in plans was upsetting to her.

Jamie looked around her at the apartment she had painstakingly turned into a home. To reach it, one had to climb eight flights of stairs to the top floor of an old house, decent but unpretentious. The staircase of polished wood curved upward. At each landing a large window provided light. There was no lift. From a small hallway one entered, to the right, into an immense studio with an absurdly high ceiling. One entire wall was paned with glass. The bottom was divided into casement windows. The studio encompassed two distinct areas. To the right was the living room. Near the window was a grand piano that Paul had brought.

Against the opposite wall a large, low sofa stood, covered with multicoloured cushions. Between the two armchairs were strewn more chairs and small low tables with gay cloths, supporting vases that overflowed with bright flowers and photographs in interesting lacquered frames. On the walls hung a quantity of paintings of different dimensions and different values. Braque squeezed against Marie Laurencin and Rosa Bonheur, and a small Cézanne beside a watercolour by Lesley. Jamie saw the newspaper lying on the sofa, the opened jar of bonbons from which Paul had been nibbling that morning, and her own manuscript pages next to a volume of poems by the newfangled French dadaist Tristan Tzara.

To the left was the dining area. A square table surrounded by chairs with high backs of sculpted wood, a sideboard and a grandfather clock that chimed the half hours seemed set against the background provided by a large wall hanging, really a Persian carpet of simple design, on which she had hung several kitchen utensils: metal spoons and ladles, and a huge copper measure with a handle a foot long. The walls were so cracked and old that it would have been impossible to recondition them and repaint the plaster. On the wall that was paned in glass there was a ledge, on which Jamie had arranged many green plants, which prospered. She had a knack with living things.

From the studio one proceeded to the small bedroom, taken up by the large four-poster with its scarlet cotton hangings. Then the tiny kitchen and the bathroom. Jamie had signed the lease, not Paul. One did not trap that sort of man. It was, they both admitted, her apartment. She paid for it from her small inheritance. He brought her food, took her to dinner, and had supplied much of the artwork and the elegant piano. But in no way was he keeping her. She had come to Paris to be her own woman. But, day after day, Paul settled more into her life. She loved him with all her heart, but she was afraid to cling. The entire secret to his

226

affection was that she led her own life and demanded nothing of him.

Night after night she slept, entwined against the body of a man who was not her husband. She laughed about it to herself. Marriage was not what counted. It was that Paul trusted her, wanted her. She would think, wistfully, that had he offered, she would have accepted marriage. Marriage would mean a certain respectability that she now lacked. She would have been the Comtesse Paul de Varenne, and not just Jamie Lynne Stewart. But then again – The truth was that much more than marriage, she would have liked to have borne Paul's child.

Lesley, on the other hand, lay encased in respectability. Her house was not the slanted top floor of a building: It was the building itself. All Grecian lines, four storeys tall, in the Sixteenth *Arrondissement*. Jamie found it a forbidding residence. Only in Lesley's own boudoir had Jamie felt a sense of freedom. There Les had broken free with vivid colours and delicate textures, and Matisse sketches lay next to Picasso nudes from his Rose and Blue periods. It made absolutely no sense: Les, with her short bobbed hair, her gold bangles, her short skirts, in a monument of a house that hung around her tiny presence like a ten-ton frame around a delicate portrait.

Jamie was twenty-four. She still refused to cut her brown hair, because her figure was too full and, also, because Paul liked to unwind the coiled tresses at night. They lived together openly. Friends of his, painters and art dealers, dropped in to see him at her apartment without embarrassment. Among artists there was freedom.

She set down her pencil and the pad on which she had been writing, and went to the Royal Model X she had brought to France with her from college. It was a silent black machine, with a double window on the side through which one could see the miraculous mechanism of its inner workings. When changing from capitals to lowercase letters, one had to move the carriage. Jamie was used to it and would have typed on no other. Her novel was progressing now by leaps and bounds.

She had returned to see Gertrude Stein, fascinated by the woman's style of composition. She had been most moved by her story of Melanctha, a love story odd because set in the world of the coloured people. Melanctha, the black beauty, and her doctor lover had been members of a society that lay outside the bounds of Caucasian, middle-class America. Jamie had loved it, loved Melanctha. She read Stein with interest, trying to understand the flow of rhythm that seemed more important to this writer than plot or common sense. Stein was trying to reinvent the English language, much like the British writer James Joyce, whose *Ulysses* had caused such a stir among puritans that its serialization had been stopped when it had first appeared in the *Little Review* in 1920. Since then Jamie had met Joyce, who at forty was younger and undoubtedly more brilliant than Miss Stein. Still – Jamie was fascinated by the short, middle-aged Jewish-American woman and by the artists and expatriate Americans who gathered around her for her pithy comments and incisive criticisms. Gertrude spoke to her now. First of all, Jamie was not the wife of a talented man; second, she had proved herself as a dedicated writer.

Jamie had at first felt shy about showing her poems and short stories. But she wanted to be recognized, wanted to be read. Paul had said to her: 'An unread writer, no matter how brilliant, is like a madman screaming at the top of his lungs from within a padded cell.' One had to be brave enough to risk exposure. Gertrude Stein thought that her own work was ingenious; most of her admirers thought to themselves that she was merely avant-garde and somewhat obscure, and that her particular talent lay in her coffee and Cognac conversation. But still, people showed her their creations, and she passed judgment. It was she who had first grunted approval at some of Jamie's freeform verse,

228

and who had introduced her to Jane Heap and Margaret Anderson of the *Little Review*.

This was a magazine published at various times in various places: Chicago, New York, Paris, and even Muir City, California. Heap and Anderson did not pay its contributors, but they did publish bold and innovative literary talent. Jane Heap looked like a man, but Margaret Anderson was female in every aspect, the sort of woman who luxuriated in elegant clothes and furs. Jamie had met Jane and been awed. Paul had met Margaret and charmed her. It seemed to amuse Paul to make overtures for Jamie that would then make it possible for her to achieve some success. But how far ahead all this seemed – publication, success . . . ! Jamie tucked a page of paper into the Royal X and began to type.

There were so many interesting people to encounter in Paris, who never would have found her in Cincinnati and might not have noticed her in New York. More and more Americans were becoming disenchanted with their own country. They congregated around the Steins' house on rue de Fleurus and at the libraries of Sylvia Beach and Adrienne Monnier, both on rue de l'Odéon. Sylvia Beach was an American who ran a lending library for English and American writers. It was she who had found a French printer for Joyce's huge manuscript, *Ulysses*. Heap and Anderson had been prosecuted by the New York Society for the Prevention of Vice two years before for printing the eleventh part of Bloom's saga, and hope of being considered by an American publisher had vanished for James Joyce. But one printer in Dijon had listened to the impassioned plea of Miss Beach and gone to work. Adrienne Monnier, her French friend, owned a shop across the street, and the dadaist poets Tzara, Eluard, and Aragon converged there, feeling comfortable.

Jamie drank some strong coffee. Perhaps the biggest difference between her life and Lesley's lay in the fact that

229

Les was trying, it appeared to Jamie, to become totally French. Jamie felt fine as an American. She would not have felt so fine back in the United States, but here it was forgotten that the Eighteenth Amendment had been passed, that Prohibition had turned the country into a divided camp. On the one hand were the bootleggers, the speakeasies, the illegal drinking; on the other, the Carrie Nations, the Margaret Stewarts who considered all drinking a form of evil. In France life, like wine, flowed smoothly. But she could enjoy being American. The French thought that American women were so much more modern, so much more liberated. They could vote and spoke out with such passion when their minds provoked them into action! Natalie Barney, Gertrude Stein, Sylvia Beach – they were admirable, unstoppable.

Had I been French, Paul would never have granted me a moment of his time, she thought with a start. He knew so little about her country that she still seemed mysterious. She set down her steaming cup and thought: If ever he leaves me, it shall be after I've made my mark. Because I'm going to make it, come what may.

Ernest Hemingway, Paris correspondent for the *Toronto Daily Star*, was two years younger than she. Yet Sherwood Anderson, *the* novelist of note today, had taken him under his wing, introduced him to the expatriate Americans by sending him to rue de Fleurus. She, Jamie, had thought at once that this young man, so often trying to pick arguments with everyone, so heartily disliked by Alice Toklas, would become the strongest novelist of the epoch. She'd read Fitzgerald and been charmed by *This Side of Paradise*. But Hemingway was less poetic and more vivid. Jamie would have to fit between them. Her novel was going to contain harsh reality – but with feeling, with passion, with dreams and visions.

We write what we are, she thought. To each of us our own life is unique. Had Paul loved her and erased that last

230

iota of insecurity, she would have been the most gloriously happy woman in Paris.

Lesley felt very hot, and her forehead felt humid under the bangs. From her ears dangled emerald teardrops, and at her throat was an antique choker of matching gems. Her grey silk evening gown hung almost entirely straight, and since her bust was small and her hips practically nonexistent, it presented her as a slender tubular form crowned by her red, permed hair. It curled around her face like Cupid's ringlets, and underneath her green eyes, in their gravity, belied the naughty cuteness of the hairstyle. She was clinging to Alexandre's arm, unaware that her fingers had closed tightly around his sleeve.

'*Notre cher Député*,' their hostess, Marquise Casati, was saying, laying long painted nails on his other sleeve. Her face was striking, white with an overlay of powder, black eyes ringed with kohl. She had dyed red hair that made Lesley's look almost blonde by comparison. Her black gown was highlighted only with sprinkles of diamonds.

Alexandre smiled, bent over her hand. In three years he had become more supple. His body moved with less stiffness; he was more relaxed. Lesley noted this as he replied: 'Dear friend, what a pleasure to be with you again. You are the most dramatic woman in Paris.'

'Hardly, you clever boy. There is always the Princess Egorova. She has one distinct advantage. She is younger.'

He laughed, yet Lesley could see that for a moment his eyes had frozen. Then the marquise kissed her cheek, whispered something, and disappeared among her guests. Lesley looked up, suddenly anxious, but his look had already faded and Alex was appraising the salon with interest, peering at the jade flowers in the vases, at the elaborate furniture. 'Do you like it?' she murmured.

He made a sweeping gesture with his free hand. 'This?

231

Not really, darling. You know my type: the secure conservative. I like to feel at ease, in control of my décor. This is pure rococo, don't you think?' He smiled at her, then touched her curls: 'Like this.'

'This,' she said, 'is 1922.'

'What will it be in twenty-three? God help us!'

She reddened and looked away. He was stroking her fingers on his arm, saying softly to her: 'Come now, sweetheart: I'm only teasing you. But seriously – for my birthday, please grow it out. I should like to see you with it long, straight – ' His voice trailed off abruptly, and she looked up again and saw that he was regarding an apparition that had just stepped in. Tall, with a gown of scarlet satin, she was remarkable, and her hair was exactly what he had been describing: long and straight. Princess Egorova.

'*La* Casati is wrong,' Lesley remarked. 'Among dramatic women there is no advantage to youth. They're born mature, and they never grow old.'

'Are you jealous?' His eyes twinkled at her. He had come to this reception as a political necessity, but it seemed that now that he was here, he was enjoying himself. The Marquise Casati lived in Place Vendôme, which evoked early Paris memories, and suddenly Lesley wished that Jamie were there.

'Jealous?' she echoed. 'Of Elena Egorova? Maybe a little. Women like me are "amusing", "saucy" or "adorable". Women like her are "unforgettable". But I like her.'

He raised his eyebrows. 'I'm not at all sure that *I* do.'

'You wouldn't,' Lesley remarked. 'She's too much of an eccentric. What would she do to your nice, safe décor?'

Just then an elegant man seized his hand and began to pump it. It was the Vicomte Charles de Noailles, whose American wife, Marie-Laure, threw the most fashionable parties in the city. Lesley unlatched her fingers from her husband's arm and moved forward a little, toward a low settee on which three people were smoking and holding a conversation, oblivious to other groups. There was a free space among them, at the very end, and she wanted to sit down without being noticed or hailed.

From this vantage point she could see the whole room. Politicians and artists mingled there. In a corner was Sergei Diaghilev, the Russian impresario, with his monocle and his lock of white hair among the dyed black – an imposing man. The Russians were scattered everywhere, especially during the season of the Ballets Russes. There was René Fonck, the aviator, now a deputy in the Lower Chamber of the French Parliament, a colleague of Alexandre's. Young, attractive, a friend of Paul's from flying days during the war – the breed of flying aces that had moved the nation. So many elected veterans!

The thought of Paul momentarily unnerved her. A *maître d'hôtel* in severe black tails was coming her way, and she hailed him discreetly. He was passing around a silver tray of champagne glasses and she took a *coupe* from him, her hand trembling slightly. When he had moved on she downed half the contents in swift, small gulps. Now she felt better and could continue to reappraise the room.

There was Prince Yussupov, the handsome Felix. He had become a dealer in antique furniture. Since the revolution White Russians had been flocking to Paris. Some, like this one, wealthy and the toast of Parisian society; others, destitute, driving taxicabs and carrying baggage into the luxury hotels. But Elena Egorova seemed to have made the best of her poverty.

She held her *coupe* to the light, admiring its lovely golden colour. Champagne, the liquor of love. She searched the room for Alexandre and didn't see him. She would have to get up, speak to people, be charming. That was what she was liked for: She gave parties that sparkled, where the French and the Russians and some of the Americans, though very few, mingled in spirited conversation and admired her good taste, her *joie de vivre*. The inimitable

233

Lesley de Varenne, who had become one of the celebrated hostesses of Paris.

No different, she thought with sudden depression, from my mother: The clients come to Fifth Avenue and the politicians come to us. She thought wryly that she was, after all, the granddaughter of an English earl, and the daughter of a man who sold products more successfully than any of his competitors. Finesse combined with salesmanship. One had to sell Alexandre, deputy from Eure-et-Loir. One had to sell Lesley Aymes Richardson de Varenne also. Or else why had she come to Paris? There must have been a reason. . .

There must have been a reason, she thought again, sipping the champagne. And then she felt better. Her head felt lighter, the room seemed brighter, the heat less oppressive. She wished that there were music, that she could dance. Perhaps Alex might take her to a tango place or to a jazz hall after this. The marquise was an unusual lady, but this kind of evening could become a bore, and dancing was more fun.

Elena Egorova was approaching the sofa. 'So,' the Russian said, 'you're all alone. Have you spoken yet to the Baron Brincard? He's an ardent admirer of yours.'

'What would I do with a banker?' Lesley replied, starting to laugh a little nervously. She hardly knew Elena, but found her, as did everyone, spectacular. 'I'd rather have your own ardent admirer, Yussupov.'

'Felix? A delightful man, and talented. I knew him long ago.'

Lesley saw Elena's eyes cloud over. 'Your father was the friend of the prime minister? The one that was murdered?'

Elena nodded. 'Yes.'

'And Prince Felix knew you then?'

Elena sighed. 'Prince Felix knew me then indeed . . . But since that time, many people have fallen into disfavour. The old regime is past. We have both progressed from there, *ma chérie*, and that is life.'

Lesley wondered at the grimness of Elena's tone and

234

shivered. Then she started to feel the champagne, warming her. Elena Egorova had led an enviable life – she was an interesting woman. 'You must come to visit me,' Lesley said suddenly. She was noticing the marvellous diamond ear-rings, the single diamond pendant that fell neatly between Elena's breasts, in the valley of her cleavage. Everything else was red, dark red, and black – red gown, dark hair, dark eyes. Determined eyes.

Jamie had abandoned her and the others, the Hélène Berthelots and the Marquise Casatis, were fine for an evening of pleasantry, fine for learning more about the flair of being Parisian. But she needed a friend. 'Please,' she murmured, putting her small hand on Elena's arm. 'Come tomorrow.'

'But tomorrow there is a costumed ball at Etienne de Beaumont's, and you will have to prepare for it. Who will you come as?'

Lesley shrugged. 'I don't feel like going at all. There are so many receptions, so many balls. And so little fun, so little life. Won't you please come to visit, Princess Elena?'

Elena Egorova was looking at her very strangely, almost with pity. Lesley didn't want pity. But the Russian merely said: 'My dear Marquise – Lesley – I'm bored to tears myself. Jacques-Emile Blanche was going to paint my portrait, but I couldn't care less, and I shall simply tell him that I'm tired. I'll come to you after luncheon. Place d'Iéna?'

Lesley nodded. Then Elena touched her on her bare shoulder and gave her a smile of complicity. She turned and left swiftly, a striding Minerva. Alexandre was somewhere in another room, but now Lesley felt less tense. She was alone in a roomful of strangers, most of whom she knew – a fly trapped in a web of intricate design. How much of this was her own fault? All of it, of course. But there would be a respite tomorrow.

She decided to find her husband. She touched her hair,

235

straightened her posture, looked about her with renewed confidence. In the large dining room he was standing in a group of men, all in evening dress, all speaking in hushed voices. She touched Alexandre on the elbow lightly. 'Ah,' someone said, and it was the Baron Georges Brincard, head of the powerful bank, the Crédit Lyonnais. 'The most enchanting woman on either side of the Atlantic Ocean . . .' And he took her hand and raised it elegantly to his lips.

'You are bored, my darling?' Alex asked.

'No, thank you. What were you gentlemen discussing?'

'The German reparations, *chère* Marquise. As you know, your native country and Great Britain are our creditors. They are demanding reimbursement of the war loans. Meanwhile the *Boches* are still not paying *us* – '

'But aren't you asking too high a price?' Lesley asked. She added, colouring: 'I mean . . . given the devastation of Germany today . . .?'

There was an odd silence. 'Our national debt has gone from twenty-eight million to two hundred and eight million francs. Public loans cannot carry us through,' Alexandre countered gently. He smiled at her, then at his colleagues, his eyes encountering theirs above her head. She felt as though each one were judging her, thinking her foolish: a woman and a foreigner in their midst.

'One could impose an income tax,' she suggested, her voice trembling slightly. A dead silence answered her. 'Is there any *other* viable alternative?' she added, beginning to feel pinpricks of panic.

'Would *you* favour an income tax, my dear marquise?' the baron asked, his voice unctuous with gallantry.

His supercilious smile provoked her. She held on to Alexandre's arm, feeling his support, the steady forearm. 'I think so,' she replied quietly.

'Then you would wish us all to go to the devil like the Bolsheviks,' a tall, portly man declared. 'Really, *mon cher* Alexandre – '

Her husband raised his shoulders with mock helpless-ness. 'Those are the views of my wife, my dear friends,' he answered charmingly.

They all smiled at him. Lesley looked into all their faces and saw that they had forgiven Alexandre for her *faux pas*, that they liked and respected him. He was one of *them*.

'We must go home, gentlemen,' Alex said, and she knew from the pleasantly distant tone of his voice, from the detached politeness of his words that he felt she had committed an error by not controlling her words in public. As the Marquise Casati saw them to the door, Lesley felt a wave of regret, for Elena Egorova was just then passing by, two young men trailing in her wake. Lesley raised her hand, Elena responded – and Alexandre, at her side, stiffened.

In the Bugatti she said to him, to break the silence: 'The Princess is coming to visit me tomorrow.'

'Which one? Murat? de Polignac?' He yawned absently.

'Egorova.'

He glanced at her with disdain. 'One of the many Russian princesses of Paris, my darling,' he said. 'But for the grace of the men who keep her, she would be a salesgirl at Maggy Rouff, or a hat-check girl at the Plaza Athénée . . .'

'You do her an injustice. She's the most beautiful woman I know.'

'Then, my love, I find your taste lacking.'

She leant back against the leather seat, wondering why she was for ever making mistakes. She reached out, laid a hand on his knee. In the dark night, illumined solely by a sliver of moon, he turned to her, all delicate profile. I love you, her expression told him. She said softly: 'Forgive me.'

'For what?' he asked, putting his hand on hers. His fingers rose to brush her cheek, lingered there a moment. She shivered, and he pulled the fur cape around her shoulders. Then he took hold of the wheel and began to concentrate on the road. She closed her eyes, exhausted, but

237

knew for certain that she would not sleep that night. Somehow, her actions, well intentioned, had offended him. She felt clumsy and ineffectual.

She had changed. Maybe, he thought, shedding his cravat and slipping out of his trousers and frilled shirt, it had been a bad idea to go into public office. He'd married an American girl, a spirited woman-child. She'd wanted to be a great artist, and he wondered now. She hadn't touched a paintbrush in ages. She went to all the right parties with him, wore all the new styles, and yet she was disheartened. Had he disappointed her?

He was tired, he realized, peering at the gilded brass Camerini clock on the white marble mantelpiece. It was close to one in the morning. Lesley. He wanted to go to her boudoir and make love to her. He passed over in his mind the boudoir, the soft pink silk of the coverlet, the violet of the curtains, the Chinese screen. Her little enclave.

They were different. Perhaps, he thought, rubbing his chin, they ought never to have come together. Yet the notion of being without her filled him with sudden dread. He would go to her. She was the most wonderful element of his life, yet also a woman he wasn't sure he fully understood. She wanted to please him so much that she'd stopped trying to satisfy herself. She yearned to have statesman-philosopher Paul Morand at her latest reception, and treasured personal notes from Paul Valéry, whom many thought to be the greatest existing French writer. She patterned herself on Anna de Noailles, Hélène Berthelot. Yet in so doing she was forgetting the Lesley he had chosen to marry, and he missed that woman.

He'd hurt her feelings tonight in front of those men. He hadn't properly explained to her the urgent need to make the Germans pay. She'd spoken her mind as an American, and it was his fault that he had not discussed the issue in

238

detail beforehand. She was wrong. He patronized her like a child, and there *he* had been wrong.

The truth was, of course, that he did possess greater knowledge of his country's politics than his wife. It was, after all, his business! Tired, Alexandre's thoughts drifted to the doubtful condition of France today. He remembered the presidential election three years before: the Tiger, Clemenceau, had received the greatest blow of his career. After all he had done during the war, the people had turned instead to Paul Deschanel, the dapper President of the Chamber of Deputies. Unable to face the humiliation, Clemenceau had resigned the premiership, and it had been given to Alexandre Millerand, the man responsible for uniting the Centrists, Rightists and members of the extreme Catholic Right into the Bloc National.

Nine months later Deschanel was in a mental institution and Millerand had replaced him as President. He appointed Leygues Prime Minister and kept the same cabinet. But at this the Chamber had balked: Millerand was altogether too strong a President, like the Presidents of the United States. They had dissolved the Leygues government and in doing so had committed a serious error, for there were few outstanding leaders in the Bloc National, and Millerand had the will to push through the goals dear to his party. Leygues was replaced by a remarkable statesman, Aristide Briand, but Alex, like many nationalists, had resented the new premier's soft stand on the issue of German compensation, for Briand had been afraid that France would be left in an insecure state of isolation if she stuck to a hard line.

But Briand too had come and gone. The former President, Raymond Poincaré, was now Premier. He was a solid, uninspiring man, but he represented stability and order, and a strong front against the Leftists. In France, the deputies of the Chamber were elected in direct proportion to the votes they obtained, unless they could form a coalition. Only that way could they get a clear majority.

239

The Bloc National had been founded on such a compromise. The Radicals, who represented the mainstream of blue-collar workers, along with Alex's party of conservative republicans and the ancient faction of Royalists, now all voted in a united front that held the majority. But the Left would not unite. There were those who favoured Bolshevik partisanship, and others, such as the more democratic Léon Blum, who did not. Poincaré did not fear a Left that was thus divided. Instead, he concentrated on attempting to make Germany pay her enormous war debt. That he was not strong enough with his own government seemed a minor flaw if he could get the war debt taken care of.

Alexandre had been shocked by Lesley's disagreement that evening at the Marquise Casati's. How could she not see that France would collapse if the *Boches* did not do their duty by the Treaty of Versailles? All his life he had been forced to struggle to settle his father's debts, to curb his mother's and his brother's spending habits. Conservatism made him feel secure, protected from eventual ruin. He feared taxation, thinking it the first step toward Bolshevism and revolution. Thanks to Lesley's dowry and a well-heeled clientèle, he no longer had to worry about poverty. One did not have leisure to be both a deputy and a successful attorney. He had handed over his practice to an associate, and his clients felt privileged that their lawyer was now a member of the National Assembly. But he did not feel total security – not so long as his country had not re-established its economic strength. That depended on the Germans' reimbursement, which would be like new blood pumped into a weak, sickened body.

Annoyed as he had been at her remarks that evening, he felt sorry for his impatience with Lesley. More important, he felt a simple need as a man for the woman he loved. He went quietly to her room to be with her. It was late, but he hoped to find her in bed, reading, to catch the look of sudden joy on her face when he entered the boudoir.

240

He found the room in the half light of a candle. She lay sleeping face down on the pillows. Gently he eased himself onto the bed and turned her over. The candle flickered, playing with her face, and he was moved by the small pointed nose, the closed eyelids. So young, his Lesley, his wife. Twenty-four, but with the innocent looks of a child.

He wished then, ardently, that she would resolve the issue of children with him; that since she wasn't actively pursuing her career, she would have his child. It made no sense, her reticence about children – it never had from the beginning, and it had now been three years.

He stroked her cheek, wanting to awaken her, suddenly needing to take her in his arms, to rock her back and forth until desire was born between them. But she did not react. Frustrated now, he laid her down, feeling the pinpricks of annoyance. He would blow out the candle, then, and go to his own crisp, empty bed.

As he lowered his face to the dancing light, he noticed the bottle on the bedside table and picked it up. Aspirin. What good did aspirin do, anyway? He lifted the bottle to the candlelight. Those were not the aspirin he knew, those were cachets of veronal, hypnotics. So now she'd gone from aspirin to bromides. No wonder she hadn't awakened.

Uneasy, he pocketed the bottle, blew out the candle, and left the darkened boudoir, allowing the door to swing shut behind him. Inside his pocket the bottle of veronal cachets bounced against the muscle of his thigh. He tossed off his kimono robe onto his armchair and slipped into the bed that the chambermaid had warmed with hot coals. A warmed bed was not as good as Lesley's eager, receptive body, but it was, just now, Alex's only comfort.

Chapter Twelve

Elena spent little time considering her appearance. It was her most valuable asset, and as an astute businesswoman she played it for what it was worth. She could remember with poignancy a time when her intellectual faculties had been appreciated as equally extraordinary – when she'd sat in her father's study and listened to the arguing voices of Stolypin, the Minister of Education Ivanov and the capable Kokovstev, then Minister of Finance. She'd absorbed their words and discussed them with her father afterwards. Now she relied on the statuesque proportions of her figure and the Tatar planes of her sculptured face. She sat in the studios of the repulsive Chaïm Soutine, listening with an impassive ear to savage stories of their common Russia, recounted with lascivious glee; to the outrageous Moise Kisling, rue Joseph-Bara, who drank until the wine dripped from his lips, while painting her nudity, long and stretched out, for the American tourists who purchased art like Ivory soap; to Antonio de Gandara, courtly and grand, who emphasized her dark eyes and full breasts and translated her onto his canvases as neurotic and beautiful; and to the Japanese Fujita whose good-humoured wife Fernande served her copious portions of food from her native province of Picardie. In another time and place Elena would never have encountered these people. They would have been removed from her by class, education, religion or accent. But now they provided her with funds on which to live and made her name infamous in society.

Some were quite interesting. José-Maria Sert amused her. He had painted the walls of the Cathedral of Vich and had led a life that, like his designs, was larger than reality.

His wife Misia was a lady, a Russian-Polish-Belgian aristocrat who had once been a gifted pianist and who was now best friend to both Diaghilev and Chanel. Jacques-Emile Blanche, the son of a celebrated physician, delighted her with his gossip, and she enjoyed his lively Sunday receptions. She was well paid. She was a true professional. She posed exactly as directed, didn't speak or ask for food during a session, didn't spread rumours afterwards. When a painter tried to approach her sexually, she always turned him down. It would not be politic to accept the advances of one and not another – better to be known as unapproachable when she was working.

She rented a small apartment on rue de Lubeck, off the Avenue du Président Wilson, near the Trocadéro. It was badly lit but in a beautiful corner building of white sandstone, with sculpted doors and a balcony. Elena knew that it was imperative to live in the proper neighbourhood, and although she possessed only a bedroom, living room and little dining room, she lived just blocks away from the wealthy Varennes on Place d'Iéna. She could receive visitors without shame, and her maid, though she fell short of *maîtres d'hôtel* by the simple fact of her sex, was an impeccable woman from Tours, where the best French was spoken. Elena knew what counted and what didn't. Discretion counted; distinction counted; sexual mores outside work didn't count any more in postwar Paris, but one's choice of sexual partners did. A lady of breeding slept only with her equals. And Elena knew when and whom to accept. Discreet married bankers took her to Deauville for the weekend, and middle-aged deputies took her to Maxim's and brought her diamonds and furs. She allowed them access to her body in the same spirit that she allowed a painter's brush to copy the graceful curves of her breasts and hips: with detachment, a certain boredom, and the poise of a great actress. She was thirty-two years old, an elegant candle whose wick had rarely flickered.

It was important to be seen, frequently. She enjoyed the opera. Her admirers knew that. And so, toward the Christmas of 1922, an American art collector invited her to join him for a performance of *La Bohème*. She donned her latest gown from Lanvin and a full-length coat of black sable that had been sent to her by the ambassador from Italy, who had offered to set her up in a splendid town house for his exclusive pleasure. She had considered the proposition and then rejected it. As an occasional lover he treated her magnificently and didn't take her for granted. Why exchange that for being owned?

The American was middle aged and reminded her a little of Lesley de Varenne's father. She suspected he had never heard *La Bohème*, and found it boring. In the middle of the first act he left her in her seat to smoke a cigarette; and in the middle of the second she slipped out, smiling apologetically, because she had been up all night before sitting for Soutine and her head was hurting. In the corridor she leaned against the wall and relaxed, closing her eyes and listening to the strains of Mimi's trills, which always moved her.

Suddenly a voice broke into the music: 'Elena! Are you all right?' and she felt a cool, strong hand on her bare arm. She shivered, opening her eyes with shock. When she saw Paul de Varenne, she was at once relieved and angry that he had caught her off guard. 'Are you going to faint?' he asked, concerned. 'You looked so far away . . .'

There was such a note of incredulity in his tone that she almost laughed. 'Don't worry,' she replied teasingly. 'You may affect most women that way, but not me. I know you too well.'

'You hardly know me at all,' he countered softly. He was looking at her with a speculative stare that annoyed her. He was intelligent like a street rat, and knew that he had caught Elena unaware. And he was intrigued.

She looked back, appraising his neat brown hair, his large eyes, his well-cut tuxedo. A handsome man, but one to

244

stay away from. But she envied his mistress, Jamie Stewart, because she lived by her talent alone and managed to support herself and supplement Paul's income too. With sudden jealousy, Elena thought: I'm not an artist, merely an artist's instrument, eminently replaceable. She could feel a sense of waste and homesickness for the past. Paul was saying, lighting a cigarette: 'You're a strange woman. Do you know that my brother can't stand you?'

'Why are you saying this to me?' she asked.

'Because it just entered my mind. Everthing I like, he hates. I was thinking of how much I liked you.'

She nodded. 'Thanks.' There seemed nothing else to say. She felt uneasy, wanting a cigarette. As if sensing her need, he offered her one and lit it for her. In silence they inhaled, and she felt him leaning against the wall alongside her. His presence bothered her. He was too animal, his vitality almost palpable. Although they weren't touching, she could sense his body. He was intruding on her privacy and she resented it.

'You're with Bingham tonight?' he asked casually. She nodded. He smiled. 'You want me to leave. Why?'

A vein started to throb on her left temple. 'Elena,' he said, 'I've known you for three years – or is it four? Without me you'd never have met the people who pay your stipends. Why don't you trust me?'

'For several reasons. First of all, because you're too obvious. You won't let me forget what I owe you. Second, because I don't trust anybody. And last, because you're too much like me.'

He started to laugh. 'I can never win with you!'

'And you love it. Jamie adores you and I don't. Jamie pays for your nonsense and doesn't ask you where you've been. But she's intelligent and holds your interest.'

'Jamie,' he said softly, 'only holds some of my interest. Don't forget who she is, Elena. At times I find her lacking. She lacks a certain breeding.'

245

'You can't have everything,' Elena countered dryly. But she looked at him without hostility. He was vulnerable. He led a tangled life. He was insecure. She looked at him and saw a man her own age who, like herself, wasn't an artist but made his profits from artists. Nobody knew who his father was, while she carefully hid from people what had happened to hers. Paul had been born in scandal and she had run away from it. He was, she thought, extremely attractive. There was such regularity in his features, and yet such a wild desire for living: raw and energetic. He belonged in the wilds of the steppe, or in the Caucasus. 'Paris is too civilized for you,' she remarked suddenly.

'I know. But where else could I make a living? And where else wouldn't I be bored?'

His eyes were frank. She found herself looking at his lips. He had a cleanness about him that she appreciated. She could feel her palms moistening, and so she smoked and stared straight ahead of her, concentrating on the wall opposite them. She had to think about going back inside to Mr Bingham.

All at once Paul's hands were on her shoulders, and he was turning her round. They were of about equal stature, and their eyes met. She could feel her heart beating and the silence between them. Then he kissed her, pressing her against the wall, and she dropped her cigarette on the rug and heard him crushing it out with his boot. His tongue tasted of tobacco and grass. It reminded her of the green, uncut grass of the Crimea, where she had spent summers as a child. She felt her throat constricting. She hadn't been kissed this way by anyone for a long time.

When he finally released her, he drew a question mark in the air. She understood. 'Tomorrow, at four o'clock. Come to my apartment.' Then she strode away from him, her cheeks burning and her knees shaking.

Her father had made good decisions and disastrous ones. She thought, trying to block Paul de Varenne from her

246

mind: His daughter has just made a colossal mistake. But at this point it didn't matter any more; the race had already started and the bet had been placed.

Jamie typed, her thick brown hair pinned up somewhat haphazardly, Paul's dressing-gown tied loosely at the waist. Beside her lay a ream of onion-skin sheets, and as she worked, she stopped, pulled out the page in progress, and corrected in longhand an isolated word or phrase that seemed 'wrong'. She had feelings about words, about how they fitted together. Words described an atmosphere, they mirrored it as well as the colours on a palette. It wasn't true, she thought, that music was the purest of all art forms, coming from the ears straight into the soul, and that the visual arts were second, needing only partial interpretation before conveying their intent. Writing, she believed, was the purest. Choice and positioning of words gave one an absolutely unambiguous sense of what the artist meant.

It was working. She finally knew it. The novel was taking shape, her characters living and breathing on their own. She pushed a lock of hair from her forehead, realized she was perspiring, and sat back, suddenly drained and tired, her back aching. But it was good fatigue, the fatigue of accomplishment. Melanie was real. Melanie was a little like herself; a girl from the Midwest whose father was unknown, who had created herself from nothingness, gone to Europe to 'make good', and ended up encountering the fascinating people who filled the Paris of today – the high-living Americans, the bohemian French, the exiled Russians. Melanie had no particular talent, but she wanted to arrive, to be one of the glorious and the glamorous. She had married a wealthy man without loving him and then fallen in love with a poor young artist. Jamie liked Melanie, understood her. Jamie knew that she herself had talent and also knew that nobody would ever buy her, that her own life would

247

never become a trap like Melanie's and Elena's. She'd seen Elena at parties: extraordinary in her beauty, elegant in a startling way, but not happy and always restless.

She heard a key in the front door and looked behind her, her face suddenly expectant. She stood up, feeling that marvellous quivering throughout her body that Paul's presence caused her. It was as if her entire being were stretching out to him, the blood flowing out toward his own body, nerves tending toward nerves. One could only love like this once in a lifetime. And even if the love wasn't returned, the sense of belonging was so great, so overpowering, that it made the suffering worthwhile.

'What's new?' she asked, taking a few steps toward him.

'Nothing much. Went to the Serts' this afternoon.' He appeared preoccupied, exhausted, and sank into one of the low armchairs. She went to sit on its arm, to be close to him, and ran her fingers through his hair.

'They're odd people,' Jamie commented. 'I don't feel comfortable with them.'

He looked up, smiled briefly. 'You wouldn't. Misia holds court. That isn't your manner.'

She asked: 'Do you wish it were?'

He raised his eyebrows, considered, then laughed. 'No. You are beautifully, uniquely you. The opposite of what I thought could draw me to a woman. Then why is it that I like you so much? Because I do. You know that.'

She forced herself to smile. Yes, of course she knew that – but it wasn't love. At least he was honest with her and wasn't pretending.

'What's new with *you*?' he asked, taking her chin in his fingers and looking at her with genuine interest. He cared.

'This.' She stood up, went to a small side table on which it was her custom to place the mail, and she brought back an envelope from overseas. Suddenly her eyes were very bright, as at the height of their lovemaking, and her cheeks

248

were red, as when she'd drunk a glass of wine too many. The lovely vibrancy of her.

He took the envelope, removed its contents, looked at them at first with vague boredom, then with sudden excitement. 'That's marvellous! What exactly is *The Smart Set*?'

'A magazine. A very good magazine for intellectual, intelligent people. And they've paid me three hundred dollars for my short story! Remember, Paul? It was such a nothing of a short story – just a sketch of a giddy young flapper, lost in Paris. Three hundred dollars and my name in print – can you imagine?'

He pulled her down onto his lap, and she threw her arms around his neck. 'It wasn't a "nothing" of a short story,' he corrected her. 'No words you write ever amount to nothing. You're very talented, Jamie. And I know: My own curse is to recognize true talent while possessing none of my own. You've got it. I don't always understand all the nuances of your vernacular, because English isn't my language; but when you write something, it comes to life. It's like a miracle taking place in this miserable little garret: life coming into focus through your brain. A cute little girl from some lost city in middle America, extraordinary through what she creates. There are so many beautiful women, Jamie, so many moneyed, elegant, witty and wordly women, who will leave nothing behind them when they die. But you? Just think of it!'

She didn't know quite how to react. He had paid her the highest compliment since the beginning of their relationship, yet he'd also called her apartment – their apartment – a 'garret' and her a 'cute little girl'. What she wanted was for him to finally recognize, to finally tell himself in words, that she was *the* woman of his life, that she was everything to him. But she'd never tell him about those small hurts.

'We should celebrate,' he said. 'Get dressed. Put on

249

something flimsy and colourful, a straw hat or something and let's go dancing.'

She started to laugh. 'It's almost winter,' she chided him. 'Straw wouldn't keep the wind away, my darling.'

'Then do the best you can!'

He watched her go to the cupboard, saw her drop his dressing-gown to the floor and fit a brassiere around her round, heavy breasts. She was so natural. He did care for her in his own strange way.

And then he thought of the afternoon, of Elena. Her black eyes upon him. The most beautiful eyes he'd ever seen, the most beautiful woman. All at once, watching Jamie step into a flowing skirt of crimson satin and matching high heels, he was seized with the overwhelming urge to be with Elena, to make love to her. He'd never felt so possessed before, in such actual physical need. He would have given all he had, at that particular moment, to be with her and seize her to him, tumble her upon a bed, undress her, have her. It actually made his testicles hurt to think about it.

'How important is it really for you that we go out tonight?' he asked suddenly. She had moved to the small dressing-table to apply makeup, and now he saw her turn, and the look of surprise, of quickly hidden hurt, pass over her face. The lovely blue blouse went so well with the crimson skirt, a perfect outfit for dancing. He felt vague remorse, then a renewal of desire for the other woman. One had to follow one's impulses, life was too short. Jamie had him more than any other woman in Paris and therefore had no reason to complain.

'Me? It was your idea, Paul.' She sat down on the bed, and he noticed how vulnerable she looked, her brown hair falling loosely around her hunched shoulders, her feet encased in satin pumps. He went to her, caressed her neck. 'Jamie, I'm sorry.'

'It's all right.' Too bright, the smile, too shiny, the cheeks. She still didn't know how to apply rouge and powder properly. Somehow this fact touched him and made his sense of guilt grow. She was so different from Elena, wise in her own fashion, genuine, tender. Elena was streetwise, wise in the knowledge of self-preservation and self-advancement. A hard diamond, unscratchable. Jamie was a turquoise, a beautiful gem, yet breakable.

'It's just that I must tell Bertrand about today's meeting with the Serts,' he offered lamely. He could not meet her eyes, knowing that she realized he was lying to her. Jamie always knew – she saw through him with that pure clarity into human souls that made her a great writer and not just a good narrator of tales.

And then he was angry: She saw through him, and it wasn't fair. He wasn't married to her, after all, and had never made her any promises. She had no right to bind him, especially not through guilt. 'It's got to be, and I can't help it,' he stated curtly.

'It's all right. I need the extra hours to finish my chapter anyway,' she murmured, looking down. She was slipping out of her shoes, neatly depositing them back on the shelf. Suddenly he could stand no more, and without a word he turned and left the room. On the threshold of the apartment he stopped, looked back. She had lain down on the bed, and he could see that she was crying, thinking herself alone. Always proud, never begging. He'd liked that in her, and liked it now. It moved him for a brief instant. Then he remembered Elena and forgot Jamie. He opened the door and was gone.

Lesley sat at her small desk and played with the cuticle of her thumb, picking a hangnail until the ragged skin began to bleed. She looked again and again at the hunting scene that she had painted two years before. It really was passé. Lesley was frightened. She sat there, chewing on the inside of her cheek like a little girl.

251

She was afraid to get started. So she stood up, went to the full-length mirror and thought: I am the flapper personified, the dream girl of the twenties. I have the looks and the money and the social status, the youth, everything! But flappers didn't think – she'd escaped from America because her generation hadn't thought enough. Flappers lived dangerously, and for no other reason than pure shock value. She wasn't a flapper. She only looked like one.

Therefore, there was no excuse. She could feel the faint swelling at her right temple, the warning signs of an oncoming migraine. Lately she'd felt the signs more and more often. At first, a kind of aura, then a pulsation, then the dreadful, overpowering nausea. No, of course I can't sit down and paint. I'm going to be sick! But that was absurd.

I am going to be sick, but I'm going to set up my easel nevertheless. Lesley went to the cupboard, took out the stand, unfolded it, dug out the box of paints, set them out neatly on the large worktable, the only large piece of furniture in her boudoir, and last of all brought out a medium-sized white canvas. Clean, white; so white that suddenly the entire room began to swim in white, the colour that always made her ill when a migraine was beginning.

She'd never been afraid, literally terrified, by the easel before. She'd blamed her avoidance of painting on adjusting to married life, making sacrifices for Alex, wanting to do right by him, spending her time on elaborate preparations for their receptions. Alex was inherently such a reserved person – he needed her to make that extra effort so that other people, the people essential to his political career, would be drawn to him and overlook his initial reserve. But that didn't explain her fear of painting. She'd met and married Alex too soon to have established herself in Paris in her own right. Paul, in an absurd, inverted sense of logic, had actually done Jamie a favour by not marrying her. He'd allowed people to come to know her as herself.

Lesley returned to the worktable, all polished hardwood,

252

and sat down. The room was reeling now, the mauve curtains blending with the lilacs in the carpet, and she held on to the edge of the wood, steadying herself. The pots of paint didn't seem at all inviting now. There was, she thought suddenly, a ball in two days: a benefit for the war orphans, or something like that. Marie-Laure had asked her to help. Marie-Laure de Noailles, regal yet ugly, was another daughter of an extremely rich American – a Jewish banker – who had married into an austere French clan of august nobility. Her eccentricity displayed itself in gathering to her table all the Left-wing thinkers of the day. She enjoyed shocking her contemporaries. And Winnie Singer was the renowned Princesse Edmond de Polignac, he a homosexual, she a Lesbian, each placing no demands on the other but tenderly accepting each other's preferences. These women patronized the arts and held their salons, but they had no pretensions to being great artists in their own right. Why then wasn't this enough for her? Was it that they were secure in their individuality?

She opened one of the bottles of paint, a turquoise blue, and stared at it, fascinated. She could imagine Elena's apartment all decked out in such an unusual, vivid colour. Elena *dared*. She, Lesley, hadn't dared for so long – for over three years! – that she'd almost forgotten how. And Alex, on the other hand, had grown more confident with time. She had breathed her own life into his soul.

She painted a circle, liked it. Turquoise blue on white. She laid down the brush and picked up another, and opened all her pots. She dipped the second brush in green and drew an oblong shape near the turquoise circle. Odd. No idea of what she was doing, just a child acting out her frustrations. She went from pot to pot, using every brush she had, until the canvas had no white remaining and was a mess of splotches of blending, furious colours. And then she felt an immense sense of relief. She was literally shaking. But she felt good.

253

'My God,' Alex was saying from the threshold, and his face reflected the shock he was experiencing. 'What are you *doing*?'

'I'm having the time of my life,' she replied, smiling, her pupils strangely dilated. He saw the smile and it made him cringe. There was something demented about it. 'I like it – don't you?'

'It's frightening,' he whispered. '*Why*?'

'Because this is how I feel! This is my world.'

She saw that his eyes were concerned. He came to her and placed a hand on her shoulder, another on her other forearm. 'Oh, darling,' he murmured. 'What *is* it?' And then she collapsed against his chest and burst into sobs.

Gently, rhythmically, his fingers massaged the heaving back, the delicate bones and muscles under the thin material of her silk dress. And as she wept in his arms, he wondered desperately how he might help her and to whom he might turn. 'I *do* love you,' he whispered, but even as he said it he knew that he was helpless. He wished that he could be back in the Palais-Bourbon, back in the world of reason. Still he rubbed her back.

Impulsively, Jamie threw a short skirt on and a cotton blouse with three-quarter sleeves – something simple, summery, and blue. Paul seemed to like her in that colour, and she was afraid of the daring tones sported by some of her contemporaries. She knew who she was, and she was not a flapper. 'Too serious, my little Jamie,' Paul would tease her. But it was true. She felt uncomfortable in most social situations where she did not know people and where the surroundings jarred her. Jazz bars were all right, and Paul loved them. But she much preferred out-of-the-way bistros and the small, intimate corner tables where men and women pored over the poetry they had written or exchanged ideas about the world. It was fascinating, it was Paris.

254

She hesitated, then left a note for Paul: 'I'll be home soon – not to worry. *Je t'adore*, J.' But she didn't feel like writing any more today. It was such a magnificent summer day, scented with lilacs – an early-summer afternoon, before the wealthy went off to their Riviera hideaways and abandoned the capital. Les would still be in Paris.

Jamie walked along the Seine, watched an old man with his fishing gear, wanted to speak to him, then didn't, respecting the rapturous attention he was giving to the slow grey waters and his bait. Les should have been painting people like this, immortalizing them. Paris was so unique. With his beret planted firmly on his bald old head, this man belonged here, and could never have existed on the banks of the Hudson or the Ohio river. She felt a wave of tenderness flowing through her: for him, for all of them, the Parisians in their taverns and small shops, in their suburbs and in the heart of Paris. It felt good to be alive.

She boarded a bus and smiled back when a young man tipped his hand to her in a flirtatious salute. She enjoyed it. It was pleasant, that men looked at her. She was twenty-five. Recently Paul sometimes forgot to come home, although she never asked him where he'd been. When they made love it was slow, mellow, smooth and sometimes she regretted their earlier passion, the moments of frenzied, tangled bodies one against the other. But time wore down the mechanisms of attraction.

If the ardour had toned down between them there should have been something else. He should have wanted to weld their informal union into something more permanent and solid. She wondered why it seemed more important to her now than it had before. But now she was making inroads in the world of literature. And she had become increasingly conscious of a new desire: to have a child. At first it had been a faint echo in her brain: 'Wouldn't it be nice if . . .' But now it had gone beyond that. She really wanted Paul's baby. And yet she dared not mention it to him. He stayed,

255

and her fear of his going was enough to keep all else in check. It wasn't fair. But it was the bargain she had struck, because she'd always known he loved her less than she did him.

Jamie wasn't a fool. Paul was anything but the person she needed as a husband. But the truth of the matter was, she didn't really need a husband at all. She wasn't helpless. She'd published three pieces in *McCall's* this year, at eight cents a word, and one in the more intellectual *Metropolitan Magazine*. And then there was the great news – which had propelled her today out of the apartment. Her father's bequest, plus her earnings, made her a woman of independent means. She was in that enviable position of being able to choose to love a man without needing his financial assistance.

Jamie stepped off the bus at Place d'Iéna and walked briskly to the sculptured door of the Varenne mansion. It was so long since she and Les had been together – truly together, the way they'd been at Vassar. She missed her and didn't understand the alienation – knew only that it had to do with the two brothers, with some kind of misunderstanding stemming from before Lesley's marriage, with the change in their lifestyles. She felt a pang of guilt. She'd kept away from Lesley too, because she hadn't felt comfortable with the person Les had become, months back: someone scared, nervous, always carrying a glass of champagne and trying so hard to be the perfect little French aristocrat.

The marvellously trained *maître d'hôtel* opened the door.

'Mademoiselle?'

'Jamie Stewart. *Une amie de Madame.*' Had it really been that long, that the butler had forgotten? She wondered at time, at changes – and at what changes she would encounter in the Varenne household.

She was enchanted by the beige silk walls, the Cézannes and Manets. Jamie bypassed the servant and nearly bounded into the sitting room. She saw Les raise her head, that marvellous triangular face with its translucent complexion, the straight red bob with bangs. She saw the joy in her friend's green eyes. They belonged to each other, they were sisters. Les stood up and almost knocked over the coffee table, and they were in each other's arms. She could smell the familiar scent of Lesley's Shalimar.

And then, a slight shock: Les was not alone. Jamie was taller, and over Lesley's shoulder she saw the seated figure of Elena Egorova. The Princess was staring at her, and immediately Jamie broke away from her embrace with her friend. Lesley cleared her throat, said: 'Jamie? You remember Elena?' and both the women nodded. Lesley sat down and so did Jamie. It seemed to each person in the room that the air had grown heavy with tension. A moment of awkwardness ensued as Lesley attempted to make conversation. She wanted to be with Jamie, to share, to be herself as she could only be with her – and yet Elena had become a part of her life, she liked her, was grateful for her amusing friendship.

Jamie wanted to tell Les her news, could hardly contain herself. But Paul didn't know yet, and to have to reveal it now in front of one who was not only a stranger, but a somewhat hostile one, seemed like a cheapening of what she had to impart.

'Oh, Les – the most extraordinary, unbelievable thing has happened!' she finally cried. 'Two things, actually. Harold Ober, of the Reynolds Agency in New York, has decided to represent me! And he's sent the first draft of *Promise Me Rosebuds in the Spring* to an editor at Scribner's: Maxwell Perkins! He's Fitzgerald's editor, and Hemingway's!'

'Jamie, that's sensational! Oh, Jamie – it's like a dream, isn't it? Dreams *can* really come true!' Lesley's face was a wonder to watch: the mirrored happiness, the fulfilment – but also the twinge of personal sadness.

257

'I'm most impressed, Jamie,' Elena stated. She appeared sincere and actually interested. 'I'm told that you're a most talented writer. Will you also, one day, write in French?'

'Perhaps. But at present I'm so much more comfortable in my own language. Funny, though. In a way I'd always known that this would happen; and yet – there's also this quality of disbelief, as if this couldn't possibly be happening to *me*. Can you understand that, Les?'

'You shouldn't say that, Jamie. Obviously you deserve everything that's coming to you. Talent merits praise and notice. You are cutting your own worth down by feeling like that.' Elena's voice was clear, decisive – as though there were no room for disagreement on this issue. Elena saw life in terms of earnings. One must respect a woman who had never been a girl, who never felt unsure of herself. But it was difficult to like this sort of person.

'I didn't exactly mean it that way,' Jamie explained softly. 'Miracles do happen. And sometimes they even happen to those who deserve them! But still – I'm awed, I'm thrilled. What more can I say?'

Elena thought: Jamie Stewart is not the little mouse I first mistook her for. If Paul still lives with her, she means more to him than he is willing to admit, perhaps even to himself. If only he had money . . . real money! Because he needs luxury as much as I do, *needs* the good life. If we married – God forbid! – we would not be able to keep our lifestyles. He wouldn't survive without Bertrand, nor I without my work. He couldn't be on his own. The collectors and the painters like him because he is charming, but they know that they can trust Bertrand, not Paul. Paul isn't trustworthy, he isn't responsible. If he could be an Alexandre . . . Even then I would not marry him. What we have is passion, not love, and he is not intelligent enough to sustain me for a lifetime.

After tea, Jamie stood up. She said, a bit too brightly: 'I've got to go home. Paul's on his way.'

Suddenly Elena spoke with an intensity that surprised Lesley and Jamie. 'Paul de Varenne is a will o' the wisp. One either loves or hates him. But Jamie – don't count on him. He's beautiful, he's exciting, to any woman. But don't entrust your life to someone like that. He wouldn't know how to take care of such a responsibility. He deals with all the people I pose for – I know Paul well.'

'But you know him as an acquaintance; I know him as my love!'

'Love is the most ridiculous illusion in the world, my dear. It's like the Church – all Churches: a creation to prevent us from dealing with reality. Think on it. You're not much younger than I. Don't be naïve. I'm trying to help you, Jamie. You're a nice person, someone whose work is going to count. And you're Lesley's friend. So try to listen to what I'm telling you. I like Paul. But I would never, ever trust him with my life.'

'You're not in love with him!' Jamie said angrily.

Elena smiled then and shrugged slightly. Then Jamie added: 'But I don't depend on Paul. My life is my own. I don't force anyone to take care of me. Only a child can ask this of its parents.'

'How noble,' Elena commented, with slight irony. But it was not said unkindly. Jamie sat down again, still red with emotion. Lesley placed her hand on her friend's arm, pressed it. 'I'm sorry,' Jamie stated more calmly. 'I really shouldn't have talked about any of this.'

Silence fell over the room. The butler entered, took away the tea tray as if he were a moving shadow in his black tails. Lesley was staring straight ahead, beyond the delicate tea roses in the Meissen vase, beyond the curtains. Jamie felt the after-effects of a heated argument, of torn loyalties. Lesley was no longer exclusively hers.

Jamie looked up and encountered, fully upon her, the eyes of Elena Egorova. She felt jarred. Who was this woman to her, that she should have thus expressed her opinions on

259

her private life? Sadness, bitterness flowed through her. She'd come here with her future in her hands, her marvellous, hoped-for future. Was Paul, after all, her greatest illusion? She looked back at Elena, wondered again at the coldness of the Russian princess. No, not a whore, as some people said in their envy of her loveliness. There were no whores in the twenties, only women of will. Elena was wilful, resourceful. Why was it that her eyes, so beautiful and deep, like black velvet, made Jamie feel so uncomfortable?

She could read the expression in Elena's eyes. Yes, the Russian was saying, Paul is your illusion, your fairy tale. He is the prince that will reveal himself to be your frog. Maybe so, Jamie thought defiantly. But if I love him, isn't that enough? She hadn't asked for rosebuds, or for promises.

'Jamie's novel is set for publication in the spring,' Paul announced one afternoon, when they were lying, replete after love, on the piled-up pillows. The sheet had fallen from her breasts, which lay like small melons over his arm. He was passing one hand over the left one, casually watching the nipple harden, amused but not yet ready for more sex. Her body fascinated him: the unique way it responded to his every touch, how she quivered when he made certain movements, how she grew taut and held back, how she at last let go in final release. She was always ready for him, never tired.

She said: 'So it's settled?'

'Quite. Jamie is thrilled to bits. Scribner's sent her a large advance – five thousand dollars. Harold Ober sends her love letters.'

'And you're the proud father.'

'No. I'm enjoying her thrill. It's like watching a play from the wings. They're going to print ten thousand copies to start with! Not bad for a totally unknown author.'

'She's been publishing pieces in magazines for a few years now.'

'That's hardly the same thing.'

'And so, is she going to buy you a house on the Riviera? How are you two lovebirds going to celebrate this marvellous birth?'

'I don't know. She wants a baby.'

Elena sat up, startled. His arm fell away. 'She's not . . . serious?'

'Very. But I don't want one. I've told her so, once and for all.'

'Good.' She sat back, played with a strand of her own hair, avoided encountering his eyes.

He asked: 'And you? You have no desire to procreate?'

'God, no. Are you crazy?'

He smiled. 'What would you do if Jamie were pregnant? Would it bother you?'

Elena rolled over, aware of the amusement that his questions were giving him and of her own discomfort. But she answered levelly: 'It wouldn't bother me. I shouldn't be involved.'

'And if I married her?'

'That would be your business.'

'You don't like Jamie very much, do you, darling?'

Elena sat up over the side of the bed, her muscles tensing. 'That's enough! *Enough.*' Then she turned around, facing him. Her eyes were unreadable, black, the pupils indistinguishable from the irises. 'You're a son-of-a-bitch, Paul. Perhaps we should just end this right now. Marry Jamie! She'll be successful and serve you with infinite gentleness. Leave me alone.'

She stood up, and he wanted to pull her back, because the vision of her hair falling to her waist, with her round buttocks and her streamlined legs, was suddenly arousing him. But she moved aside just as he reached out to touch her. He watched her pick up her underclothes and then he

261

said: 'I'm sorry. Jamie really means little to me any more. She's a convenience: no more than what other men are to you.'

'Then you know me very little. Other men mean absolutely *nothing*.'

'But you wouldn't want to change your nice secure lifestyle.'

She wondered then why they stayed together, because at that moment they were very close to hating each other. She needed to pull back.

What did she care about Jamie? The girl hardly touched her life. But Paul's clothes hung inside *her* cupboard, in *her* attic flat. She, Elena, felt insulted. Insulted that he still needed Jamie while purporting to be loving her, repeating the words each day when he telephoned her: 'I love you, Elena. I've never loved another person as I love you.' It was lust, but he called it love, the stupid fool.

He was standing beside her, his hands on her hips, caressing them, massaging them. She turned round, angry, and he took her face roughly in his hand and forced her to kiss him. 'Damn it,' he said, 'don't do this, Elena. We're both so irritable these days, so nervous. But I do love you.'

'Love is boring.'

'This isn't.' He held her tightly to him, and she felt his arousal against her stomach. It would be wise to make him leave now, before he did anything else. Then she felt him pressing against her, forgot, kissed him back, and put her arms around his neck. So close, so close. She wanted to forget the pain, all the other pains in her life, the frustrations of her daily existence. He was pulling her back onto the bed, and she was thinking: Why am I allowing this? It makes no sense, and there is no love. And then she wanted to cry, because he was entering her and she was willing it to take place, to be with him as one body. She'd always tried to be in control, but the pleasure was his doing, it was his technique, it was excruciating because she couldn't hold it

262

back. She hated herself and him, hated the pleasure and its consequence, that she was so vulnerable and that he could see it. She was no stronger than Jamie. Perhaps this *was* love, after all. She pushed against him, ran her fingers over his chest, shut her eyes. Wonderful, wonderful. He made it wonderful as only he could make it, and she could only whisper: 'Don't stop – make it last!'

Afterwards she turned over and avoided contact. She was ashamed. And so he said: 'May I stay a while? I've got some powder. It's good stuff.'

She rolled back to look at him. 'Cocaine?'

He nodded and went to the chest of drawers, pulled one out, removed an envelope, showed it to her. 'Pure white snow.' Then he removed a small sheet of paper, spilled some of the powder onto the paper, and took a copious dose between his own fingers. She watched him stuff the cocaine into his nostril, inhaling, and then she imitated him, sitting down naked on the edge of the bed. Almost immediately she felt exhilarated. He was pulling her toward him, and she touched his nipples, his throat, his shoulder blades. He felt good, like an athlete. She wanted to make love again. What time was it? She started to laugh.

Hours later she awakened, in a stupor. It was dark. Time had passed oddly, the paper with the cocaine powder was gone. Had they sniffed everything? Probably, because the effect of each dose lasted less than an hour. Her hands felt ice cold. The sheet had fallen off or been kicked down. She sat up, remembered frantic copulating, talking, a flurry of words and bodies. He bought it from an Englishman, but one could obtain it from any chemist or doctor. The Alexandres in the Chamber had passed or wanted to pass a law against its sale. They'd never be able to control it, the Americans would never control the use of liquor with their absurd temperance amendment to the Constitution. Since Prohibition, there were more alcoholics than ever in the United States. She wondered what time it was and what had happened to Paul.

263

He was emerging from the bathroom, freshly bathed. 'It's already eight. Jamie will be frantic. There is a dinner at Sylvia Beach's house . . .'

'She can go alone. You may as well let her get used to it.'

'Why? I like Sylvia.'

'But Jamie doesn't need to be escorted everywhere she goes. She needs a husband. Let her find one, to babysit her.' She felt irritable, angry, her nerves on fire.

'When the book comes out, so will the suitors. Are you planning to go out?'

'Would you miss the dinner?'

Their eyes met. She was testing him and also watching to see if she could detect guilt about Jamie on his features. There was none. He wanted to stay. Elena sat back, a smile spreading on her face. Why was it that she suddenly remembered what it had felt like, as a small girl, to wilfully run over a ladybird with her doll's carriage wheel? The ladybird had lain, crushed, on the handsome path, an insult to the tidiness of the gardeners. She'd felt sad – and then exhilarated. She'd won, she'd crushed the *life* out of one of God's animals, at the age of five!

Later her governess had made her feel ashamed. She'd been punished. But Elena could vividly recall that sense of having won such a great, important victory. It had been worth the punishment, which she'd long since forgotten.

Jamie was nothing more than a ladybird, an insect in the path of her conquest of Paul. She was weak and provincial, not elegant. It was so easy to make Paul forget her, to make him beg her, Elena, to spend an extra hour with him. Jamie was like the ladybird. She was *there*, in the way of the wheel of her doll's carriage.

When he took her in his arms she thought of Jamie arriving alone, late and slightly dishevelled, at Sylvia Beach's dinner party. There would be tears stinging her blue eyes, she'd apologize, a little breathlessly, to the assembled group: 'Paul couldn't make it, he's so sorry – the

264

car – you know modern machines, they're not like the Fords back in the States . . .'

And someone would laugh, to help her out, to ease her discomfort. Maybe Hemingway, perhaps Joyce. A man who'd guess at once why Paul had left her hanging. One had to pity her. Perhaps Harold Ober and that editor, Perkins, were publishing her novel out of a similar sense of pity.

But if Jamie was so pathetic, then why was Elena suddenly unhappy, thinking of her? 'I wish you could love me just a little bit,' Paul was murmuring against her ear, into the softness of her neck. She closed her eyes, pushed back the pain. No, she would not love him, it would be too easy, for then he would turn her into the ladybird that got crushed and mangled. Another Jamie. 'Not even a little bit?' he was insisting.

'Yes,' she whispered, amazed that she was mouthing the words. He hadn't heard her, her voice had been a bare whisper. But *she* knew she had said the words, and now she was afraid.

Chapter Thirteen

Nineteen twenty-four began with political unrest. Poincaré's expedition into the Ruhr Valley had weakened the value of the franc, and at last the members of the Bloc National realized that taxation, which they had ardently sought to avoid, could no longer be delayed. Their capitulation was marked by fear. The French people who had brought them to office as strong saviours now viewed them cynically as a group of conservative men of indeterminate leadership. Alexandre, tense with concern, waited for something to break, for something to happen to his government – and felt engulfed by a deep depression. He felt absolutely helpless. His country was plunging toward darkness and he would not, as he had been made to believe by the financiers who had backed him in 1919, be able to rescue it. And Lesley seemed remote, and as the months passed, increasingly nervous and walled off from him.

In the autumn he felt her withdraw even more. At twenty-six, she had thinned down until her looks had become almost severe. She had stopped wearing gold looped earrings and usually dressed in neat little tailored suits of hand-knitted wool or raw silk, in toneless beiges or dark, joyless colours. He came home one afternoon and heard voices from the salon. Lesley, her cheekbones dotted with rouge, her white lips dry, was pacing the floor in front of a middle-aged man with a trimmed Van Dyke beard and a young woman who stood deferentially aside. Lesley's voice was harsh, almost strident: 'Monsieur Franchot, this turquoise lamp doesn't belong on that Louis Sixteen side table. It simply doesn't.'

'But mother-of-pearl would clash, my dear marquise.'

'It would be perfect.'

'What do you think, Mademoiselle Markovitch?'

'I'm afraid,' the young woman said softly, her Russian-accented voice melodic and timid, 'that I agree with you, Monsieur. Turquoise makes a lovely contrast. The mother-of-pearl will clash.'

Alexandre stood in the entrance hall, hesitant. There was something awful about Lesley and these two people. She was stuffing a long, gold-tipped cigarette into an ivory holder, her hands trembling, and Monsieur Franchot, whom Alex recalled being *the* decorator of the day, hastily produced a light. His assistant seemed reluctant to speak, but Alex saw her face hardening. Then Lesley asked, with irony: 'Tell me, Monsieur Franchot: Who is paying your bills?'

'Why, Madame, you are. And the deputy.'

'Then – is there any reason to continue this argument? This is my salon. This is my Louis Seize side table. This is my lamp.' She walked over and touched the Chinese body of the lamp, all turquoise enamel, and suddenly pushed it off the table. Franchot's face mirrored the horror he must have felt – that Alex himself felt. The elegant lamp fell with a thud and lay on the Aubusson carpet, its shade tossed to the left like a discarded hat.

'Madame, this lamp is worth five thousand francs,' Mademoiselle Markovitch reproved softly.

'And I don't like it!' Lesley's chin had begun to tremble, and she stubbed out her cigarette and pulled a new one from a silver box on the side table. She went through the same motions as before, and when Franchot had lit this one for her, she began to inhale. She closed her eyes and exhaled deeply, and Alex saw her other hand clenching and unclenching. Finally she looked at the decorator and said tonelessly: 'I'm sorry.'

He appeared relieved, smiled, touched the point of his salt and pepper beard. 'Then, Madame, will you let us proceed with the room? As Mademoiselle Markovitch and I conceived it?'

Lesley shrugged. 'Do as you wish,' she replied, and put this cigarette out in the crystal ashtray beside the first. She sighed, then gave the decorator her ring-studded hand, which he raised elegantly to his lips. She withdrew her hand with a slight grimace of disgust that she hardly attempted to conceal.

Then she nodded to the assistant and left the room with short, hasty steps. Alexandre, embarrassed, walked in at once, smiled, pretended to have only just arrived. Mademoiselle Markovitch's wide grey eyes remained steady and he felt himself colouring. She was sorry for him. She was ashamed for him, for what had taken place. Clearing his throat, he said, a surge of anger rising in his body that anyone should think him ashamed of his wife: 'Thank you very much, Monsieur Franchot. I'm certain we shall both be very pleased with your work – and Mademoiselle's. Come back when you need to confer with us.' It was a polite dismissal, but he didn't want these people in the house any more. Lesley had been right – she paid the bills, and they had no right to judge her.

When the two decorators had departed, Alexandre went into his study, where a silver tray with a snifter and a decanter of Napoleon Cognac stood on a small Louis XIII table. He poured a glass for himself and tasted it thoughtfully. Again the sensation of helplessness overwhelmed him. He downed the contents of the glass in a series of swift gulps and then sat down behind his large ebony desk. He laid his head in the palms of his hands and allowed the despair to wash over him. Then he stood up and went out, up the stone staircase that curved toward the bedrooms. At the far end was Lesley's boudoir, and he tapped on the wooden door that faced him. When she didn't answer he turned the brass handle and stepped inside.

Lesley had tossed off her clothes and was sitting, in the

flimsiest of silk nightgowns, at her dressing-table, smothering her neck and shoulders with perfume. Near the perfume bottle of sculpted glass lay an ashtray of Chinese enamel, with a cigarette burning in it, and a glass beside a cordial decanter. The glass was half full. She turned and looked at him. 'You're home? Franchot was here.'

'I know. I saw. I heard. Is it really that important, darling, to have these endless discussions with your decorators?'

'Don't be so disagreeable, Alex,' she said, picking up the glass and drinking. She set it down abruptly, took the cigarette, without a holder, between her fingers. 'Franchot isn't a decorator; he's an artist, very much in vogue!'

The words struck him as false. 'Just because Hélène Berthelot and the Princess Murat have used him doesn't make his work "art". He merely puts rooms together. Other men have created the materials he works with. I wouldn't call him an artist.'

'But who are you to call him anything? You don't know the first fact about art. You're a businessman!'

Stung, he bit his lip. She crushed out her cigarette and finished her drink, poured herself another. His eyes remained hypnotized by the brusque gestures with which she was accomplishing these things. He tried again: 'Lesley . . . what's really wrong?'

She jerked her head up, stared at him. 'Why must something be wrong?'

'Because you're not yourself.'

'And who is this self? Do *you* know, Alex?'

He went to her, put a hand on her neck, caressed it. 'Sweetheart – I love you so much. I'd like to have a family . . .'

He felt her stiffening, pulling away. 'You know I don't want a baby. I never wanted one! Don't keep bringing it up – I'll keep on refusing!'

'But *why*?'

269

'Because! Just "because"!'

Her green eyes, slightly bloodshot, pierced him. He could feel the frustration mounting. He closed his eyes and fought it. His hand remained on her neck, still, its fingers immobile. He waited, opened his eyes, touched her face. The cheeks were hot. He bent down, on one knee, and held her chin. She had a feverish look about her, and her breath smelled of wine. Quickly, he kissed her. He felt her bending back her long, delicate neck, so that he could better taste her warm, moist mouth. Then, without warning, she pushed herself away from him. He stared at her, bewildered.

'You can't persuade me this way,' she said, her voice unsteady.

'"Persuade" you? I wasn't trying to "persuade" you. Only to make love to you.'

'I'm sorry, Alex. The timing is wrong.' She wasn't looking at him now but was drinking from the wine glass, peering into the golden liquid, as if fascinated by its colour.

He stood up, his heart knocking inside his chest in erratic beats. 'I'm sorry too,' he murmured, and left the room. As he closed the door, he could hear her beginning to cry. But he didn't go back. He felt a numbness, as when Charlotte had shouted abuse at him in his childhood.

In the morning Lesley awakened, her temples throbbing painfully. She put a hand out, felt for the light, turned it on. The dressing-table was messy, as she had left it the previous evening: the decanter almost empty, four cigarettes stubbed out in the ashtray, pots of makeup open. She felt her forehead, pressed her fingers against her sinuses. She wondered what time it was and rang for the maid.

Within moments she heard the knock, and then the girl, neat in her frilled apron and frilled cap, entered the room. 'Madame rang?' she asked. 'For breakfast?'

Lesley said: 'Just coffee, Marianne. A full pot, very strong.'

'Very well, Madame.' She made a small curtsey and backed out of the room. Lesley fell back against the pillows and noticed that they were streaked with the kohl she had forgotten to wipe off last night. No – that wasn't it. Alex had come to talk to her, and she'd pushed him away, and he'd felt insulted and hadn't come back. Lesley could feel drops of perspiration gathering on her upper lip. She stood up, moved unsteadily toward the connecting bathroom, splashed cold water over her temples and eyelids. Then she heard the bedroom door opening again, and she saw Marianne setting the silver tray on the bedside table and pouring out the coffee into a cup of Meissen china.

She walked back inside, sat down on the bed, ran her fingers through her short, straight hair. Marianne was about to add hot milk. Lesley said: 'Don't. I just want it black this morning.'

'Yes, Madame. Will that be all?'

'For now. What do I have scheduled for today?'

The young maid said: 'A fitting at Lanvin, at eleven thirty. Then luncheon at Sirdar's with the Princesse de Polignac. This afternoon, Madame has a tea at Miss Barney's, and a tentative appointment with the Princess Egorova to see the new Picasso exhibit at Madame Sert's, for cocktails. Madame is to telephone the Princess to confirm. Tonight – '

'Please, Marianne, stop! What time is it now?'

'Ten o'clock, Madame. Would Madame like her bath prepared?'

'Yes, yes. That would be lovely. Scent it, will you, Marianne?'

'Very well, Madame.'

The girl curtseyed, left the boudoir soundlessly. Lesley groped for the cup of coffee, drained it. She felt better. She opened the lacquered box by her lamp and took out a

271

cigarette. Her fingers were moist on the silver lighter, and the flame flickered and missed the tip. She tried again, and this time it worked. She propped herself back in the bed, poured herself a new cup of black coffee.

When the maid returned, Lesley said: 'Marianne, cancel my appointments, will you? Except the Princess Egorova. Telephone her, and ask her to come as planned, at six. When is my husband going to be home?'

'In time for the masked ball at the Comte de Beaumont's. At three thirty Monsieur Poiret is having Madame's costume delivered.'

'My costume?'

'Madame is going as Aspasia, and Monsieur le Marquis as Pericles. His costume will be delivered at the same time.'

'Oh, God.' Lesley swallowed, feeling helpless. She pressed unsteady fingers against her temples and waited. 'Thank you, Marianne.' Then she turned away, burying her face in her pillow.

As soon as Elena stepped into the Varenne hallway, and Bouchard, the *maître d'hôtel*, had ceremoniously removed her fur coat and ushered her in, she felt something odd in the household. She was wearing a black velvet suit cut like a man's and two long rows of pearls – perfect for a cocktail showing at Misia Sert's. It was strange, going to see an art exhibit. Usually her own figure stared back at her, changed through the interpretation of a particular painter, yet unmistakable. But Picasso hadn't used her. She liked going to exhibits dressed in severe, striking clothes – to shock people away from her canvas nudity, so that they became aware of her as a person and not simply as a painter's model. But Bouchard was saying: 'Madame is waiting for the Princess in Monsieur's study, if the Princess will follow me . . .'

She shrugged, surprised. She knew that Lesley didn't like

272

Alex's study, with its strict Louis XIII furnishings. But she followed the *maître d'hôtel*. He bowed slightly and opened the door in front of her, and then made a courtly gesture with his hand. Elena walked in. He was already closing the door behind her.

Lesley was seated behind the desk, absurdly tiny in comparison to its proportions. She wasn't dressed to go out. Instead, a housecoat of dark-green velvet was loosely wrapped around her, and her face showed no signs of make-up. 'You aren't going?' Elena asked. 'Is anything wrong?'

Lesley stood up, feeling lightheaded. Alex had said the same thing last night. She kissed her friend and offered her the leather armchair on the other side of the desk. Between them stood a bucket of ice with a champagne bottle wedged inside it, already popped by the expert Bouchard. She poured the foamy contents into two *coupes*, handed one to Elena. 'Everything's wrong, nothing's wrong. I just don't know any more . . .'

Elena took a sip, crossed her long, elegant legs. 'You don't feel well?'

'I'm dreadfully hung-over.'

Elena started to laugh. 'Well, then, that's not a problem we can't overcome! Is that all?'

Lesley could feel the despair again, like a horrid English fog, clamping down on her. 'Must we go? Must *you* go?'

Elena shook her head. Lesley wondered how her friend managed, day after day, sitting through those awful sessions with crude, arrogant men who shared nothing in common with her. She asked hesitantly: 'What do you find to say to someone like Soutine?'

Elena sighed. 'Nothing at all. I just look at him as if I were breathing in his words. He thinks, simply because we're both Russian, that he understands me. But I was in Petersburg, dancing at the Winter Palace, while he huddled miserably in his *shtetl*. It wouldn't be appropriate to remind him.'

273

'Aren't you ever lonely? Dreadfully, terribly alone? Feeling that nobody at all can understand you?'

'All the time. Why do you ask?'

'Because that's how *I* feel.'

They stopped speaking, each of them drinking her champagne, and the room, with its pleasant, crackling fire in the marble-topped fireplace, surrounded them like a protective cocoon. 'You don't know how ashamed I am,' Lesley whispered. 'I hate the life I lead. It's so useless! Fittings, exhibits, dinners. You forget what year it is. Every year's the same! What difference does it make that one of them had an election, or that the styles have changed again and Chanel's invented a new synthetic perfume?'

'Isn't there something *you* want, Lesley? For yourself?'

'And you?'

Elena said: 'I want to stop worrying about money. I want to stop having to work.'

'Nothing else?'

Elena poured them both new glasses of champagne. 'Nothing else, Elena?' Lesley persisted.

'Like what?'

'Like wanting to compose a symphony, or write a poem. Or – wanting a particular man to love you.'

'I specifically hope *against* falling in love. When our emotions take the lead, Lesley, our lives go awry. We make all the wrong decisions. Has any woman ever been able to love the right man?'

'I don't know!' Lesley sat, her beautiful ringed hands clasped over the stem of her glass, diminutive in the large armchair. 'I thought I loved Alex. Now I'm not sure. Everything's confused. I've made such a mess of my life, Elena. I took a wrong turn, and after that, I kept making other wrong turns. It's like waking up in the wrong country and hearing people speaking a language you aren't expecting. Lately that's all I can think of. It's like a nightmare!'

Softly Elena asked: 'And what was the first wrong turn?'

274

Lesley brushed the hair from her forehead with the back of her hand and swallowed more champagne. Elena could drink, because she was big, and also because in Russia people consumed unbelievably large amounts of alcohol and became used to it. But Lesley was smaller, and not Russian. She could already feel the lightness flowing through her veins, a giddiness. She looked at her friend and felt her throat contracting. The first 'wrong turn . . .'

'I did something terrible. Years ago.' Suddenly she was on the rollercoaster and couldn't get off. She had to finish. 'It was my fault too,' she said, her voice catching.

'What did you do?'

'I was pregnant. I had it taken care of. Just like that. I never wrote to him, never let him know – '

'Who was he?'

Lesley couldn't hold the glass any more, her fingers were shaking too much. She tried to raise the glass, drank some more, felt better. She put her head into her hands, and then, when she had finished sobbing, she looked at Elena, a strange calmness coming upon her. 'He was a thief.'

Elena stared at her, dumbstruck. She heard herself ask: 'But – what was his name? Where was he from?'

'It doesn't really matter. He was English. The son of someone who grew up with my mother. An English baronet. I loved him so much – '

'And this was . . . before Alex?'

'Yes, of course! I should have accepted him as he was. I should have let him know about the child. He would have married me – I know!'

'You can't know for sure,' Elena commented. 'Men are too elusive.'

'But it was my own stubbornness, Elena! I should have written to him! Instead I had the child – our child – killed.'

Elena said nothing. Lesley was so intent on her own memories that there was nothing she would have heard, in any case. But Elena was wondering, shocked. And she was

275

frankly appalled at Lesley's lack of discretion in revealing such a dangerous secret.

Lesley said, in a low voice: 'I could never face the idea of another child. I've always refused to discuss it with Alex. But I never knew why, till right now! I thought it was the memory of the last child. But it's the fact that I loved *him* – this other man – so much, and that it was *his* child I had ripped out. It was *his* child I *should* have borne. It was him I should have married, not Alex. I made all the wrong turns.'

Elena sat absolutely quiet, the room like a mausoleum, chilling her. She made herself say: 'Don't condemn yourself, Lesley. What's in the past can't be changed. It doesn't do any good to regret. Perhaps you didn't really love that man.'

'He was so incredibly beautiful: like a Florentine prince. He was my first lover. I was so hurt that he abandoned me, let me go home alone – that I never even considered having his child. And so Jamie arranged the operation. She paid for it too – I'll never understand where she found such money. How then, Elena, could I ever deserve to bear another child? I wasted the first one!'

'You're being sentimental, Lesley. You weren't even sure he would have married you. And you told me yourself: He was a thief. You could never live with a dishonest man . . .' As opposed to me, she thought. Paul isn't honest, but to have him, to keep him – I would do almost anything. To take him from that self-sacrificing little writer –

'He probably thought so too. But who was I to pass judgment on him? In God's eyes, Elena, his sins are venal compared to mine. I killed. I deliberately ended a life. And you know, I don't even know what happened to him. He might himself have died in the war!'

Then Lesley was asking: 'Haven't you ever been in love, Elena?'

'I don't know. I don't . . . think so.' Only *now*, of course . . .

276

'How do you do it? How do you get through the days? The men – they don't really matter, do they?'

'No,' Elena murmured. 'They don't.' Only one did.

'It would be so easy to take a lover. They're everywhere! Marianne brings me their cards on a silver platter. And it's not just the men! The women, too! Dolly Wilde. Winnie de Polignac. God – it's revolting!'

'What is?'

'The thought of having a woman touch me. Of having a woman undress me.'

'It's not really bad at all.' Elena remarked softly, getting up again to refill their glasses. She returned to her chair. 'It's much gentler, it's kinder, in a way it's even cleaner. A woman has considerations that a man can't have.'

'You mean, you've actually done it – gone to bed with another woman?'

'Yes. The first person I ever slept with was a woman. She was kind to me, and she loved me. She was the only lover I've ever been sure of. Men use us in ways that women can't. A woman will spare another woman from pain, because she knows exactly how it feels.'

It made sense then. Lesley looked at her friend and nodded. Even Alex, for all he claimed to love her, didn't begin to understand . . .

'You must never repeat what I've told you,' Lesley whispered suddenly. 'If Alex ever knew – '

'I told you my secret, didn't I?' Elena said. 'I think you can trust me with yours.'

She fastened her black eyes on Lesley, and for a moment each felt as if the world had stopped, as if the room had entombed them together. Then Lesley looked up, suddenly stirred into action. 'My God!' she cried. 'I'd forgotten all about the damned costumed ball!'

'Have a good time,' Elena whispered, and as she rose she smiled. But when she stepped forward to kiss her, Lesley noted the harsh lines of that smile, its essential grimness. She clung to Elena for a brief moment, then let her go.

Softly, Elena Egorova closed the door of the study behind her and walked into the corridor. Alexandre de Varenne was coming toward her, and she blinked. He appeared out of place there, after everything that had been said between her and Lesley. 'Good evening, Marquis,' she murmured.

'Good evening, Princess.' His voice was cold. His grey eyes concentrated on a point above her head. It was easy to see why Lesley might not love him. He was, Elena thought, singularly unlovable. Totally unlike his brother, as Paul never failed to point out.

Knowing she made him uncomfortable, she taunted him, smiling: 'I've had a lovely long talk with Lesley. She's in the study. A beautiful room, if somewhat cold. Your taste, Marquis?'

'My taste. Strange, but I've always found it the most comforting room in the house.'

'That, my dear Marquis, only points out how much we differ.' She knew that she was annoying him more with each word she spoke. Yet his marble face reflected none of the irritation, none of the hostility. He was a perfect diplomat, she thought. Her brittle smile faded, and she looked at him with a stare of unconcealed dislike. This was the man who could have paid his brother enough to keep him out of Jamie Stewart's bed. Alexandre was saying:

'You must excuse me, but we're late for a ball.'

You're late for everything, Elena thought, hearing again Lesley's confession of love for another man. With a small nod, she walked away and saw Bouchard holding her black sable. A perfect household, she commented to herself with irony.

Gerald and Sara Murphy were an elegant American couple, whom Lesley had known from New York. He was the heir to the Mark Cross leather goods store, she a blonde society girl from Ohio. They'd come to Paris much as Lesley had, to break with their dominating families and think freely. They knew every artist of merit, and Gerald who fancied himself a painter as well, was taking lessons from one of the artists of the Ballets Russes, Natalia Gontcharova.

One day Gerald took Lesley with him to Gontcharova's studio. She'd always wished to meet the Russian artist who had done so much of the scenery and costumes for Sergei Diaghilev's famous Ballets Russes. Gontcharova was a middle-aged woman with a rather flat, ugly face, but who was animated, whose studio walls breathed life. Colour sprang out everywhere, from every canvas. 'So,' she said in her guttural accent to Lesley, 'you too are a painter, it seems.'

'I once thought so.'

'Come to me some afternoon, alone. We'll have Russian tea and talk about your work.'

Lesley blushed, wanting to shrink into the woodwork, overcome with self-consciousness. But she didn't forget. She went home and sat again by her easel, and wondered. Perhaps her error lay in attempting to paint pictures. At Vassar what she had most enjoyed had been working on the backdrop for Jamie's play. Perhaps the theatre *was* the answer. She went to visit Gontcharova the very next day, arriving early. 'Would you take me on as a student?' she asked. It almost came out as a supplication.

'Maybe you don't need me. Let's first see what you can do.' Gontcharova set forth a manikin and ordered: 'Now imagine a Tatar princess from my country. She's going to dance. You'll want her clothing light, so she can move. Pick any of the materials here at your disposal. See what you can do to make her come alive.'

A Tatar princess – Elena, of course! Suddenly the blood rushed to Lesley's cheeks and a tremendous thrill pervaded her every nerve. There were so many things at her disposal!

She examined everything, enthralled like a child before a treasure chest. She selected some shawls, set them about the manikin's shoulders, changed her mind. For three hours she fussed with paste beads, with kerchiefs, with oils, painting on hair for effect, trying to capture what Elena would have looked like as a Tatar princess. She was filled with ideas.

Finally she stood back. Gontcharova, from her sofa, gulping down tea from a tall glass, remarked: 'This is quite good. You have really created a nice effect. Now what I'd do differently – ' And she rose, began to adjust some materials, moving small things around. The effect was to render Lesley's work professionally perfect while retaining its essential ideas. 'Yes.' She'd finally nodded, stepping back. 'I'll take you on!'

Lesley went back to her house with a sensation of floating on air. She called Sara Murphy on the telephone, ecstatic. Then she hesitated. The impulse was to telephone Jamie, but she hadn't spoken to Jamie for many months. Elena, then. She lifted the receiver, to tell the Russian the news and then thought again. It was really to Jamie that she wished to relate this, much as Jamie had come to her to tell her about Harold Ober and Maxwell Perkins.

Lesley slipped on a thin cloth coat and belted it. The Bugatti was gone. Alexandre must therefore have taken it to the Palais-Bourbon. It struck her then that she hadn't even thought to share her excitement with her husband. She slid into the upholstered seat behind the wheel of her new green DeDion Bouton and drove straight to Jamie's address on Boulevard Montparnasse. Tomorrow she would start work. God only knew where all this might lead!

She nearly ran up the eight flights of stairs to Jamie's attic flat. Perhaps this time they'd be able to patch things up for good, to reweave the tattered fabric of their friendship. The bell was stuck, so she knocked on the door: the old Vassar knock, three quick raps, a pause, and two slower ones. Then she tried the handle; it gave way. Jamie was the most trusting person in Paris; she never in a million years imagined that someone other than a friend might find his way into her apartment. How different from the well-protected fortress in which the Varennes lived!

The loft was charming. The shock was Paul's belongings, strewn about, much more so than any of Alex's in their own home. But that was because Jamie only had one *femme de ménage*, a daily cleaning woman, to look after her apartment. Lesley had seven servants, all living on the premises. 'Jamie?' Lesley called. 'Jamie Lynne Stewart, wherefore art thou?'

Her friend came in from the bedroom, tying the belt of her dressing-gown. Jamie had always liked to write in comfortable clothes. Her long hair lay over her shoulders, and her breasts were free beneath the loose robe. 'Les!' She was smiling, her eyes shiny. 'I thought – I don't know what I thought. It's been ages!'

Lesley looked away, playing with the long string of pearls knotted below her waist. 'I'm sorry, Jamie.'

'Look, there's no reason to be sorry. I felt you'd come when you wanted me. Or needed me.'

'So now you're a big success! Scribner's is calling you the next Scott Fitzgerald.'

'*Before* publication. Afterwards I may have to repay them their advance!'

They stood awkwardly, and then Jamie took a few steps and hugged Lesley, rocking her back and forth. It felt good. Like being back home. Jamie was so natural, so different from all the people Lesley knew. 'I'm going to tell you right away: Natalia Gontcharova is going to take me on three times a week, to study set design and costume!'

It seemed like a replay of a movie, the two friends trying not to be awkward, trying to return to their former closeness, each wanting to speak first. 'Remember when you came to me that day, about Ober?'

They were sitting down together on the sofa. But Lesley's

281

words, unexpectedly, made Jamie compress her lips into a hard line, twisting her fingers together in her lap.

'What's wrong, Jamie?'

'Paul's in love with somebody. He's having an affair, something very serious.'

In the stillness that ensued, Lesley was aware of her own heart beating noisily. 'Jamie. You can't be sure. And anyway – in Paris everyone has affairs these days. They're meaningless, usually one-night adventures.'

'This one isn't. I think this is the end. He's going to leave me, Les. As soon as the book's published, he's going to go. I know it.'

'I'd think just the opposite: You'll embody everything that's important to him. You'll be in the public eye, and money will begin to pour in. I'm sorry, but I do know him. He'd never leave you then!'

'He's in love with Elena Egorova.'

Jamie's voice, toneless, dead, stunned Lesley completely. 'No. Elena and I are good friends. She's not seeing anybody I don't know about.'

'I tell you, Paul's been sleeping with her. He's in love with her.'

'How on earth can you be so certain? It's absurd, Jamie!'

Jamie's eyes were unfocused. She said quietly: 'I know it for a fact. A few weeks ago, I saw him going into her building on rue de Lubeck. I asked the concierge if she'd ever seen him before. She said: "It's the Comte de Varenne, Princess Egorova's friend. He comes here at least twice a week." If I hadn't been in the neighbourhood that afternoon to meet Hadley Hemingway at the Trocadéro, I'd never have seen any of it. But at that point everything began to make sense. I'd felt he was in love with someone else. Now it all fell together. *Anyone* could fall in love with Elena Egorova.'

'I still think it's incredible!'

'What would you do if Alex were seeing her? Or someone like her?'

Lesley laughed. It was a harsh laugh. Then she whispered seriously: 'I don't know.' She turned to Jamie and her face was full of compressed rage at the betrayal of her friend. 'That would be *my* problem. What are *you* going to do about yours?'

Jamie suddenly looked away and said shyly: 'I'm going to have a baby.'

Lesley could not speak. She blinked a few times and finally swallowed. 'Tell me this is a bad joke.'

'This is the truth. I *want* to have Paul's baby.'

Lesley cried out then: 'But if he's planning to leave you, as you say, then that's no way to hold on to him! For God's sake! Jamie – you're not dealing with an honourable man! He'll leave you stranded – '

'I'm not going to be poor. The book comes out next month.'

'Are you . . . sure about this?'

'I think so. I'll be more certain in a few weeks. I want this baby, Les. No one, not even you, is going to persuade me otherwise. Not even Paul. I may or may not tell him. If he leaves now, I'll say nothing. If he waits – I'll *have* to tell him. But I don't expect anything from him. One day, when it's right, I'm going to tell my baby who his father is. But for now I'm going to employ a nanny to help me take care of it. I'm going to buy a little place and keep writing.'

'You're a romantic idiot, Jamie! Please don't do this!'

Lesley was shaking, wishing she might ask for a drink. It was better not to think back, but it wasn't possible. She wasn't seeing Jamie, but herself – not Paul, but Justin.

Jamie stood up. 'Look,' she murmured, avoiding her friend's eyes: 'It's not the same as it was for you. You had no choice at that point in your life. I *do*. I can live alone with a child. I'm about to lose the one man I've ever truly loved, but at least I'm going to keep part of him, part of that love, inside me!'

Lesley said dully: 'Why couldn't he have left you alone?'

'He didn't, and I let him into my heart, my life, of my own free will. Now I have to act, Lesley. I have to do something to fix the disarray before it turns into chaos.'

'Having an illegitimate baby isn't the way, Jamie.'

'What's your suggestion?'

Their eyes remained locked, without flinching. Finally Lesley whispered: 'I'm the wrong person to ask. You know that.'

Jamie placed a hand on Lesley's and answered in a low voice: 'I wish I didn't feel so strongly about this. I'd do anything not to have to hurt you.'

They remained unspeaking, until finally it was Lesley who looked up, who tried to smile. 'Well,' she declared, 'we should drink to our successes. You're going to be Scottina Fitzgerald, with baby, and I? Perhaps I'll turn out to be the next Natalia Gontcharova. Do you have something strong? To toast with?'

Jamie went into the small kitchen, returned with a bottle of gin. She set it down on the table, opened it, and poured the liquor into two unmatched glasses. Handing one to Lesley, she declared: '*A nos amours!* Here's to Love, sweet Love. Especially Elena's.'

They clinked glasses and drank. But Lesley was miserable. She wished that she had never come. If Elena was the cause of all this – how could she stay her friend? How awful the interrelationships could be that bound people together and then sent them hurtling off in opposite directions . . . ! She forced herself to finish her gin, because the liquor was calming her, and she'd been shaking.

After a second glass, Jamie stood up, her cheeks red. 'I can't have any more. I must finish a short story for *McCall's*.'

'Oh, Jamie – ' But what was there left to say? Lesley put her arms around her friend, kissed her. 'I love you. You're the only truly good person I know. You're my only friend.'

284

'And you, mine. Don't stay away. And start soon with Natalia.'

'Tomorrow.'

They lingered for a few more moments, neither wanting to break away. And then Lesley picked up her coat and bag and went to the door. At the threshold she turned, looked back at the figure of Jamie in her dressing-gown. 'How can such a wise kid be such a fool?' she asked.

Chapter Fourteen

Jamie watched everything with detached interest. Paul had wanted the supper to be served at the Tour d'Argent or Maxim's, but she'd pressed for La Coupole. It had a better atmosphere. The huge rooms, the painted walls like looming frescoes, gave the Montparnasse establishment a pleasantly informal air. She knew he planned to dazzle her with an impressive array of guests. She would have much preferred an intimate dinner for two.

She wore a soft gown made by Poiret. It had been worth the expense, because she was now no longer just a writer, but an *author*; and because Elena Egorova would be at the supper. The gown was of light-blue chiffon and covered her sloping shoulders to three-quarter-length sleeves. She had plaited her hair to the left of her face, loosely, twining silk flowers into it. The dress was indefinite enough in shape for any added weight to be unnoticeable. She'd planned that. To hide the pregnancy, even though it was only the beginning. Two months, maybe three. She barely showed.

She was carrying his child. Actually, now that she was certain that she was pregnant, it mattered much less that the child was his. She, Jamie, was going to have a child, her own child. She felt filled with the quiet joy of knowing that new life was beating inside her body. She could look at him, and care, but without the full ache she had harboured before. She could even conceive of an evening with Elena and accept it as an inevitable part of life. He didn't love her any more; actually, to be honest, he'd never loved her. And he was now in love with another woman.

She wanted her life to start anew, with a new literary reputation, with her new baby. Already there was the book.

286

She was so proud of it, so pleased. She'd hardly been able to sleep. Her own words! She'd even written to her mother: 'Mama, they are publishing thousands of copies!' She'd known that Margaret wouldn't like it. The story wasn't dirty at all, but then, in Cincinnati people thought Hawthorne was obscene.

She still wasn't sure whether she'd tell him. He'd know it was his; Jamie had not been with another man since she'd arrived in Paris in the winter of 1918. He'd so often told her that he'd expect her to get rid of it. But faced with the inescapable fact of his child's coming, would he react differently? He was the least responsible individual she knew. But also, would she want his interference? Probably it would be best not to say anything.

They arrived at the Coupole, under the gay lights, and were hailed by what appeared to Jamie to be throngs of people, some already quite noisy with drinks and champagne. Paul had placed his order for the best Dom Perignon available: 1906, the first vintage year. It flowed like rainwater. The women wore huge hats and had removed their capes, and bare shoulders shone against the frescoes. No Lesley and Alex yet. Sara and Gerald were there, she always so beautiful, with a young couple Jamie hadn't met before. The man was terribly handsome, almost pretty, with green eyes and a classical face. His wife was blue-eyed, with hair of dull gold worn in a bob, and a pleasant, full figure. Her mouth was a Cupid's pout, almost childish. 'I want you to meet Scott and Zelda Fitzgerald,' Sara said to Jamie. So *this*, then, was the author of *This Side of Paradise*! She felt suddenly embarrassed and stammered: 'Welcome to Paris. We – we have the same publisher, don't we?'

He was charming. 'And the same agent.'

'Only we're always in debt,' his wife added. Jamie smiled. Paul tugged on her sleeve and she moved on, kissing Adrienne Monnier, Sylvia Beach, and the inevitable Gertrude and Alice. Gertrude commented darkly: 'He *is* charming. But you don't have to trip over yourself, Jamison. Wait until he's had a few – he'll do it himself!'

Fitzgerald. Friend of all the intellectuals she most admired among her contemporaries. His glamorous tales of life at Princeton. She remembered having gone to Princeton once, for a ball of some sort. Her dull date. But he'd written about the 'in' crowd. And even then the name, Fitzgerald, member of the Cottage Club, secretary of Triangle, had entered her consciousness. And since that time he'd accomplished so much! So much that she herself still dreamed of accomplishing.

She'd written under the name 'Jamison Stewart'. It wasn't necessary to be too feminine. Her articles had been appearing for months; it was obvious that Jamie was a woman. But still – the people who read *Vanity Fair* and *Metropolitan* weren't necessarily the women in the small towns of middle America – those who helped to elevate a book to the top of the charts.

She watched Paul waiting for Elena. It was the first time she would see them together after learning of their affair. Why do I wish to be tormented? she wondered. At heart, she thought that some day, if she had to write a scene of betrayal, of wrenching pain, she would have had the experience herself. But she was not of those who looked for pain in order to commit it to paper. They'd said that *The Beautiful and Damned*, Fitzgerald's latest, had been closely related to his own and Zelda's early years together. But Jamie felt that one could still laugh, and breathe, and enjoy, while searching for material.

People, French and American, were kissing her, congratulating her. Paul's hand stayed possessively on her shoulder. So many beautiful women! Hélène Berthelot, Gabrielle Dorziat. Important people that her mother would never have thought would speak to a simple Stewart. Jamie felt oddly removed from it all, above the din, the lights, the congratulations. She was waiting, tense.

And then Bertrand de la Paume arrived. Paul had told her, casually, that he'd be bringing Elena. But she wasn't with him. Jamie's thoughts tumbled about incoherently. Does that mean that Paul's trying to be discreet, has asked her not to come? Could it mean that he isn't planning to leave? She could feel her stomach tighten, and sweat broke out on her forehead. She was momentarily dizzy and held on to the back of a chair in front of her. Paul drew the chair out, helped her sit down. 'What's the matter?'

'Nothing, sweetheart. Just the emotion of the moment.' Not really a lie.

He looked at her. She wondered whether he felt concern. She was shocked at her own cold appraisal of a man she had so blindly loved, almost to the point of adoration. Realistically, she knew that she'd have been unhappy spending the rest of her days married to such a person. He was, as Les had always pointed out, a hedonist and a user. He was not as intelligent as she was. He was the kind of person who'd never succeed on his own merits – he'd always need a Bertrand. She'd realized all this, but she'd refused to accept it. She'd felt such a strong tie to Paul, such a sexual longing, that the idea of ever losing him had made her, at times, physically ill. She'd been addicted to Paul de Varenne.

'How are you, Bertrand?' she asked. Offhanded but pleasant. 'Thank you for coming tonight.'

'How could I not? Paul is as a son to me. You are his beloved. Then you are my daughter-in-love, shall we say?'

She threw back her head and laughed, as she had seen Les do, and Sara. Such a casual, sexy mannerism. Great for a flapper. The pretty woman married to Fitzgerald had a deep, throaty laugh. She was a flapper, most definitely. The world had to stop to make room for her, even if it was somebody else's party. Jamie sat back, surveying the scene, the waiters pouring the champagne. Where on earth was Lesley?

'Elena couldn't come?' she asked Bertrand as casually as she could.

289

'No. She went straight to the ladies' room to attend to her hair.'

The world, slowly, stopped spinning, came to a halt. Jamie saw mouths moving, but heard no sound. She smiled, nodded. What was there to say?

Elena Egorova knew the pulse of crowd expectations, probably knew her lover very well too. When everyone had taken his place, Jamie saw the hurrying form of the Russian princess making her way past other tables, touching her hair as if nervous at being late. She wore a white gown, with a red flower in her hair, and rubies at her throat. A gown of such utter simplicity that Jamie's breath stopped. Elena went to Bertrand, kissed his cheek, murmured: 'I'm so sorry, I hope you weren't worried,' and then came directly to Jamie. All eyes were upon her. She placed a light hand on Jamie's shoulder and said, looking her fully in the eye: 'Please forgive me, Jamie.'

Jamie opened her mouth, which was bone dry, and managed to reply: 'For what, Elena? You're here, and I appreciate it.' Suddenly the dryness left, and she found a quiet strength she had not known that she possessed.

Elena smiled and then looked briefly at Paul: 'Hello, my dear. Where should I sit? Where do you want me?' It all sounded so casual, so natural. Paul was her lover, all Paris knew it. She seemed so easy, and Jamie hated her at that moment. Had she no idea that everyone knew?

Paul stood up, graciousness personified. If he was at all embarrassed, only his eyes betrayed him. The flush had left his cheeks. He was now all smooth, worldly polish: the veritable son of Charlotte de Varenne. There was an empty place between Scott Fitzgerald and Alice Toklas. 'Next to the young literary genius of America,' he announced, taking Elena by the elbow. It was that gesture, its familiarity, that hit Jamie in the stomach.

I don't want to compete, she thought. I don't really want him any more! But behind the angry determination lay so

290

much anguish that she was nauseated by the sight of the caviar canapés in front of her. She felt confused. Where was Lesley?

Just as the waiters were removing the hors d'oeuvres, Jamie saw her friend. Lesley, in a mauve gown highlighted by a fuchsia sash, was hurrying, Alexandre behind her. Lesley reached the table and pushed past the waiters. Her face was flushed. 'We had a flat tyre,' she announced. 'Alexandre couldn't find anyone to help . . .'

She was looking directly at Jamie, her eyes avoiding Paul completely. Jamie felt enormous relief. Alex was kissing her, saying: 'If walking would have brought us faster . . .' but Jamie stilled him with a hand. Her blue eyes fastened gratefully on the couple.

'Surely,' Paul said to his brother, 'it wasn't you who changed the tyre.' He was smiling, and Marie-Laure de Noailles began to laugh. Jamie found herself irritated for Alex. Paul's tone was light but mocking.

Lesley, accepting a seat between a minor *danseur* of the Ballets Russes and a jowled senator known for his depraved sexual preferences, suddenly spoke, clearly, to Paul. 'No, darling,' she stated, her voice smooth and agreeable. 'It was *I* who changed it.' Scott Fitzgerald turned his head to her and winked like an accomplice. He was sitting next to Elena, and now Lesley had to look at her Russian friend. Elena was playing with the stem of her wineglass. Lesley didn't want to speak to her. It was bad taste to have come to Jamie's celebration dinner. Lesley was angry. Her loyalty belonged to Jamie, but it was the first time she'd been placed in a situation at which they were both present.

The young man next to her had asked her something, in his heavily accented voice. She could feel her own voice trembling as she replied. Alex was beside a debutante farther down the table. She hadn't told him about Paul and Elena, nor about Jamie's pregnancy, but now she wished she had. He'd always disliked the Russian princess.

Paul was murmuring something to Jamie, and Lesley noticed that Jamie seemed removed too, like Elena. The bastard, Lesley thought viciously. Then she saw Elena stand up, bending gracefully to excuse herself to the person seated at her left. Lesley looked at Paul. As the Russian princess moved swiftly toward the ladies' room in the rear, she saw her brother-in-law follow her with his eyes. Jamie was staring at him pointedly, but he, unaware, was still focusing on Elena's tall figure weaving among the tables. Lesley ached for Jamie. Then Paul turned back to her, resumed what he'd been saying – and Lesley saw Jamie smile. It was the smile of an automaton.

And then Paul touched Jamie's shoulder and stood up. His knife clinked on his wineglass, and the guests stopped talking. He placed a hand on Jamie's arm, pressing it lightly. 'Dear friends,' he began. He had a deep, oratorial voice, and the men and women seated at the long table looked with expectancy at his handsome face. 'I have spent several years living with Jamie's book. In a sense you might even call me its father.'

Lesley searched the area for a glimpse of Elena. She found her, not far from the group, isolated in her stark splendour between two tables. Her black eyes were riveted on Paul. Her face was white. But there was something dreadful about her pallor. Lesley saw her lips parting, saw Paul quickly glance at her. He cleared his throat. 'As I was saying . . . its father.'

Lesley stared at him, hypnotized. His face had lost its healthy colour. He was almost fumbling for words. Steadfastly avoiding Elena's direction, his eyes played over the group of faces, looking at Scott Fitzgerald's amused, handsome features, his hand groping for Jamie's on the tabletop. He smiled at Alexandre, inclined his head with mocking grace. Lesley could feel her blood pressure going up, her back muscles tensing. 'Jamie's book began from her own experiences. Her heroine, Melanie, is a girl not unlike

292

herself. I think that you will all love her. Jamie doesn't seem, in her modesty, to realize that her life has changed, been transformed by the publication of *Rosebuds*. She is a star. I have never been gifted with art. But, as any father, I am proud of our child. I am proud of what Jamie has produced.'

Lesley saw Jamie's face trembling. Did he really have *no* idea? Were his words just a horrible coincidence? Elena was standing, perfectly still, in the passageway between the two tables. Paul turned, enough for Lesley to see their eyes meet and Elena turn her head away. Jamie withdrew her hand. She had sensed the interchange too.

Then Paul was sitting down, people were clapping and raising champagne glasses, waiters were rushing up with fresh bottles. Scott Fitzgerald stood up, unsteady and his voice slurred, and hailed his new colleague. Zelda's eyes were half shut; a jealous woman, Lesley thought. Suddenly chairs were being pushed back, people were mingling. Jamie was being hugged – and Lesley saw Paul look furtively around and disappear. She saw him walk toward Elena and saw the Russian princess turn her back on him and make a rapid exit, toward the front of the restaurant. Lesley couldn't stand it any more. She found Alexandre and murmured: 'I don't feel very well. Would you take me outside for some fresh air?'

Alexandre put his arm around his wife, and she leaned against him. She felt an immense gratitude: He would take care of her. Alex was holding her by the shoulders and gently propelling her toward the front of the restaurant, where an open-air café stood connected to it.

Paul was sitting toward the right, under the canopy, with Elena. Lesley saw another free table, not far away but not adjacent to theirs, and since she was ahead of her husband, she moved to it. She could feel Alex stiffen behind her. Lesley sank into the chair that Alex held out and bent her head into the upturned palms of her hands, as if to rest it.

293

'Too much smoke, too much wine,' she whispered apologetically to her husband. 'I'll feel better in a minute.'

'Jamie doesn't look well,' he commented. Lesley nodded but didn't look up. She heard the Paris night, noisy with cars and with the raucous laughter of passersby. Over the background she heard Elena's voice, cold and hard: 'It isn't my style to ask a man to choose between me and another woman. He must do so of his own accord. But I don't have to stay.'

Paul replied, but Lesley didn't hear him. Elena said: 'But I *do* have a choice: I can always walk away.'

She continued: 'This dinner has been the most humiliating experience I've gone through since arriving in Paris. Lovely words – "the proud father!" Must you go so far in your tastelessness?'

'Oh, darling – words aren't my forté, for Christ's sake! The words . . . just tumbled out. You know that it's you I love.'

Lesley couldn't bear any more of their conversation. She looked up, encountered Alex's face. He too had been listening. He stood up, held out his hand to her. In her ear, as he escorted her back to the table of guests, he said harshly: 'The bastard.'

The words were unlike her husband. Lesley stopped, turned her face to him, saw the impenetrable quality of his grey eyes. 'That's what he is,' Alex stated tightly. 'And all Paris knows it.'

She was almost frightened by the terse anger. Now she could envision Alex trying to kill Paul the day he had learned about Popov and the horses. Alex could be unforgiving. She felt a tremor pass through her. What if a man like that ever learned about her own past?

Jamie had now disappeared from the table. Lesley saw Elena returning, without Paul. Bertrand de la Paume was holding out a chair for her, bending over her with concern. Lesley excused herself to go to the ladies' room. Nobody

294

commented that she and Alex had returned only minutes ago. She splashed water on her face, waited a few moments in solitary stillness. Now she felt ready to go back. She was pushing open the outer door when she saw that it was blocked by Jamie and Paul, standing together on the restaurant side. Lesley remained with the door ajar, unable to move.

'But the words – the theme – ' Jamie was murmuring. Her lovely dress, Lesley noticed, had a stain down the front. It touched her. No matter how successful Jamie became, she would have awkward moments.

Paul said irritably: 'The words and theme just seemed appropriate, that's all. Don't read more into them. Parenthood is the last thing on my mind.'

'But you were very moving in your explanation of my book. Parenthood doesn't have to be like your mother, Paul. Or like my own parents.'

'Why are you saying this, Jamie?'

'Because, Paul, there's no going back. I'm pregnant.'

Lesley felt like a common eavesdropper on this scene. It was of such import, and of such intimacy. But she was also stunned. She hadn't thought Jamie was going to tell Paul – and certainly not on this evening of celebration. But it was true. His choice of words at dinner had led the way for a confrontation.

Lesley saw him clench his fists, hitting them against his muscular thighs. 'You should have listened to me,' he stated. His face was white, unpleasant. 'You fool,' he added, his voice chilling. 'I told you – but you wouldn't believe me.'

'I'm going to keep this baby, whatever you decide.' Jamie announced. Her own voice was soft but steady. 'It's not up to you.'

'And you're going to rear it – alone?'

'If that's how you want it.'

'I don't want a baby!' Paul cried. 'And I don't want to

marry you! I never lied to you about either of these matters. Now you think you've trapped me – '

'No,' Jamie countered. 'Never. I loved you, and I wanted a child. But I certainly wasn't trying to force you to stay with me. I've never asked you for anything, Paul. You know me well enough to realize I'll never ask.'

'What are you telling me?'

'Simply this: You don't want the baby; I do. So tomorrow we can all start new lives. You can pack your bags and leave, and I shall manage. I'm resolved to have the baby, but it doesn't particularly matter whether or not I'm married. I wouldn't have got pregnant if I hadn't wanted to.'

Her gentle, quiet voice made him blink, step back. 'You're telling me to leave?'

'No. But you won't be a father. So there is no alternative.'

There was a silence. Lesley felt it around them. Then Paul murmured, and she saw him avert his head: 'It's up to you, Jamie. I think you've made up your mind.'

'I think,' she commented, 'that *you've* made up yours.'

Jamie turned into the ladies' room, nearly pushing Lesley off balance inside. But Paul did not see his sister-in-law. He walked away, and Jamie went to stand by the washbasin, supporting herself over the edge. There were no tears in her eyes. Lesley put her arms around her from behind, felt the new swelling of her friend's stomach. She rested her face on Jamie's back, holding her tightly. Jamie hardly seemed surprised by Lesley's presence, but after a moment she turned round and whispered: 'It's all right. Don't cry, Les.'

And Lesley realized that her eyes were filled with tears.

The next day Bouchard knocked on Lesley's boudoir door and said to her: 'Madame has a caller. The Princess Egorova is here to see her.' He waited by the door, discreetly, while Lesley pinned a cameo to her silk blouse and ran a comb through her bob. She could see his reflection in the mirror, like a penguin in black tails and white shirt, deferential, almost imperceptible. She thought: They all expect me to behave perfectly.

Lesley didn't want to face Elena. She felt angry, frustrated. She'd cared for Elena. But she loved Jamie. And because of Elena, Jamie's baby would be born out of wedlock. As she looked at Bouchard, she realized how Lady Priscilla must have lived her life. To everyone she appeared as Lesley now did to the butler, her face composed, like the cameo lady she was displaying on the frill of her jabot. But inside, silent battles were taking place. She answered evenly, fearful that the anger would explode, and amazed at how easily she was controlling it: 'I can't see her now, Bouchard. Please give me my note pad.'

The *maître d'hôtel* handed her the monogrammed vellum, the gold pen, and she chewed on its end, thoughtful. Finally she wrote:

Elena, I cannot possibly continue to receive you. Your love affair with Paul is your own business. But Jamie's life is also my business. You must understand that while no one has the right to pass judgment on another human being, Jamie is my best friend, and I can't simply accept your relationship as one more inconsequential liaison. Please try to see this from my standpoint. This isn't a matter that I can handle coolly.

She reread what she'd written and handed the note to her butler. 'This is for the Princess,' she announced.

When he had stepped out and closed the door so gently behind him that she did not even hear his exit, Lesley remained at her dressing-table, feeling empty and numb. She closed her eyes. Several moments later there was another knock, and she whispered wearily: 'Come in.' It was Bouchard again. He inclined his torso, like a graceful puppet, and handed her a silver tray on which lay a calling card, earmarked according to the Russian custom. Lesley could feel her heart pounding as she picked it up. Elena had written on the back: 'I am shocked, Lesley, by your antiquated notion of right and wrong. You have hurt me deeply. But once a friendship has been ended on such terms, it has been ended for good. Neither you nor I shall ever be able to mend it.'

Lesley said, as she neatly tore the card in half and tossed it into her wastebasket: 'Thank you, Bouchard.' And when she saw the door shutting, she looked at her arms. Goose-pimples were raising the fine hairs, and she felt herself shiver.

I haven't merely lost a friend, she thought, aware that there was more than sadness in her heart. I have made an enemy.

Book 4
Winter

A time to rend, and a time to sew; a time to
keep silence, and a time to speak;
   A time to love, and a time to hate; a time of
war, and a time of peace . . .

ECCLESIASTES 3:7–8

Chapter Fifteen

Elena applied the black kohl to the underside of her lashes with a hand that trembled slightly from fury. Paul, sprawled on the bed, said quietly: 'What do you care, Lenya? She's just an unimportant little Milquetoast Miss, with great pretensions. Perfect for my brother. Let's forget them both.'

'But I can't!' Elena answered. 'She threw me away like a piece of dirty garbage. I feel . . . *used*.'

Paul said nothing. Elena was different from other people. She was feral and wild, with passions that swept over her like hot winds over the Russian steppe. The Russians – all Russians – possessed Rasputin's unbridled, elemental madness.

The sensuality around him smelled of musk, of her. She had furnished the apartment with lacquered red and black panels, and her sofa, chairs and bed had smooth, modern curves that adapted to one's body. Instead of rugs she used leopard skins. He could smell rare flowers, different species of orchids, spread out in Oriental vases, and on the various coffee tables she had disposed gilded and silver frames with photographs: all of her, taken by Baron Adolph de Meyer, in dramatic poses; and small miniatures painted by Boldini and Blanche, set up on tiny easels of dark, glittery wood or fine metal. There were coloured cushions everywhere, in contrasting shades of purple, mauve, lilac, aqua and bright turquoise. It was definitely not a Parisian apartment.

'Used,' he repeated softly. Lesley had taken sides because of Jamie. As always, he felt a point of guilt, thinking of her. He hadn't really wanted to leave her. They'd had a pleasant life. Jamie didn't suffocate a man. Elena, on the other hand,

301

was overwhelming. She used up all his emotions, all his physical juices. He loved her so totally that to give her half measure would have been cheating himself, like turning down a banquet of his favourite foods. But he'd been cornered. Everything had closed in on him at once: Elena's need for him to make a decision and Jamie's revelation. Still –

'What are we going to live on, Paul?' Elena asked. Her tone of voice was nettled, annoyed. 'You're working less and less.'

'But *you* aren't.' He felt prickles of irritation. 'What do you expect of me?' he blurted out. 'You knew my financial situation from the beginning. It was your choice!'

'It was also yours! I didn't ask you to live with me. You wanted to do it!'

They faced each other, angry voices jarring one against the other. He was perspiring now, his adrenalin pumping. He loosened his tie, opened the top button of his shirt. Undoubtedly he'd wanted to live with her. But she'd pressured him, and what else could he have done? On a wave of resentment, he exclaimed: 'Why must you needle me, Elena? Can't you love me without always thinking of your cheque book?'

'One of us has to be practical,' she said. She was pressing her lips together, ostensibly to spread the rouge, but really to still the trembling. 'You don't seem to realize,' she started again, making her voice even and composed, 'that no one will be helping me any more. We're living like a married couple, Paul. All that is missing is the licence.'

'And that's suddenly become important to you? You want to get married?'

'Of course not. But the fact is that we are now out in the open. How do you think I've paid for all these things?' She waved to encompass the room in a sweeping gesture. 'Not from my sittings alone! I've been able to purchase the basics – that's all. In future the funds for luxuries like these are going to be severely lacking.'

302

His pulse was still beating rapidly at his temples. He didn't stop to analyse why he felt insulted. But he couldn't look straight at her. The sight of her throat, exposed and white, reminded him of a forest doe, poised to run. She was a woodland animal, needing protection, and the vulnerability clothed in hardness suddenly became apparent. She posed as a predator, yet she was the prey – prey to needs that to some were luxuries but to her were essentials, like warmth and food. He stared at a small gold clock of Florentine design on her bedside table and wondered who had given it to her, and how much it had cost. It was a precious antique. Elena was the sort of woman to whom men gave things.

Now he knew why he was angry. 'I can't become a slave to Bertrand just to keep you in silks and rubies,' he retorted.

'But you need the same things! Your brother's the ascetic; he could live like a monk, yet Lesley's dowry keeps him in that monster of a house. The roles should be reversed.' She was bitter then. 'I always despised him. Now I see that they do belong together. She's as soulless as he is!'

Surprised, he noticed the sting in her voice. 'I wish,' he murmured, kind now, 'that you wouldn't take Lesley's action so hard. She's a girl who served her purpose. My mother wanted her married to Alex, so that her father's and grandfather's money could be used to maintain us all. But in her own right she's of no consequence.'

He saw Elena's eyes becoming thoughtful. There was a hardness to the look. She asked: 'Your brother loves her though, doesn't he? I mean – he didn't marry her just to please your *mother*? He doesn't strike me as all that devoted to Charlotte.'

'Nobody is,' Paul replied easily. 'But nobody quite ignores her, either. My brother is her only means of support. It's been years since she ate up what little my . . . father left her.'

'The noble Alexandre . . .' Then Elena added: 'Does he love her more than his first wife? The one who ran away?'

'Why are you so curious? My brother doesn't interest me. I

303

only care about whether he'll pay the bills. And lately he hasn't been doing it.'

'*I* only care about that too.' He saw the corners of her mouth twist upward. But it wasn't a happy smile.

'What do you mean?'

'I mean that Lesley told me something, in confidence, some time ago. But if Alexandre were to learn of it, he'd have to leave her.'

'And?'

'And you could go there tomorrow, and tell the lovely marquise that unless some . . . help . . . is forthcoming, her husband will know all.'

He'd been wrong: She wasn't remotely vulnerable, like a doe! She was the hunting dog, relentless in its pursuit. For a moment he hesitated, imagining Lesley. He'd liked her when he'd met her, had even toyed with the idea of sleeping with her. But she'd always been so obvious in her distaste for him – and later, in her outright hatred. She was Jamie's friend, judging him, condemning him. She was like Alexandre: without compassion, without breadth of vision. He said pensively: 'I like what you say. What's the secret?'

'She was involved, before their marriage, with another man – of all people, a thief. But that's not the extent of the damaging evidence. She was pregnant with his child and had it taken care of, in Poughkeepsie, when she was eighteen.'

Paul exhaled slowly. His eyebrows shot up. 'That's quite a secret. Are you certain, Lenya?'

'Of course I am. And Lesley will pay to keep it that way.' She turned her head and Paul could see her breathing deeply. He remembered her telling him about her life, its loneliness and humiliation. He felt tenderness for her. He rose, went to her, put his hands on her shoulders.

She twisted her head back to look at him from her sitting position, and he saw that her eyes were like liquid ink. It always moved him. He couldn't read her. She was, he thought, more intelligent than he, certainly quicker. But it was her passions that fascinated him, their rise and fall. She was difficult to handle, like molten metal. She burned.

'Kiss me,' she whispered, and threw back her head so that the white of her long throat lay exposed to him, the vein beating beneath the perfect skin. And so he bent down and covered her lips.

'A brandy, Lesley?' Paul strode to the sideboard where various bottles were displayed next to a heavy silver tray with snifters and liqueur glasses. It was her house, not his, but he wanted to finish things off, now that he had told her. She was standing, white, in her pale beige suit, the emeralds gleaming from her elegant fingers. She wasn't looking at him.

To fight the guilt, he poured a liberal amount of Cognac into the largest of the snifters and presented it to her. 'Come now,' he said. 'The money's nothing to you and Alex.'

'I don't control it,' she replied, her eyes vacant. 'It's all under his management. He pays the bills, he places the investments. It's always been that way.' Then she added, anguish piercing her voice as she twisted her fingers together, staring at them as if they were foreign to her: 'How could Elena do this? I can't believe it . . .'

'You hurt her,' Paul replied. He made himself a drink and went to sit on the sofa.

'I never did anything mean, anything to betray her. We were friends!'

'But you aren't now, and it's of your doing, not hers.'

'I thought she'd understand that my first loyalty had to belong to Jamie!'

'Why should she understand? One never understands rejection.'

'It's *your* fault!' Lesley suddenly turned on him. 'You've always caused us trouble! Whatever you touch – *whom*ever you touch – you dirty, you ruin! How can *you*, Paul, my own brother-in-law, blackmail me? Isn't anything holy in your book?'

'Holy? That's stupid mysticism.'

'But it's Alex's marriage! He's your brother! He's always protected you – '

'Protected me? He once tried to kill me. Don't forget it, Les. *I* can't forget it.'

'Neither can I.'

Their eyes met, each reliving the episode between them at the Ritz, five years before. Paul drank some of the gin he'd poured himself over ice in a highball glass. 'Look,' he said. 'It's very simple. You tell Alex you're planning to redecorate – and then you doctor the estimate. Elena and I aren't asking you for much.'

'Only for exclusive rights to my own past.'

'That's overdramatizing again.'

'You're the most despicable excuse for a human being I've ever met. And Elena's a coward. She should have come to deliver this message instead of you.'

'You wouldn't have received her. So what are you planning to do?'

'I have no choice.' Lesley took a large swallow of the rich yellow liqueur, felt the soothing heat going down her throat. She stared at the snifter in her hand and suddenly saw the chandelier lights reflected in it, and those same lights reflecting off her rings. In those lights she could see a myriad of other Lesleys looking back at her, their faces impassive, their small bodies erect, immaculate in their elegance. Then the fear tightened her stomach, and she knew that, somehow, she must convince Alex. She turned away from Paul and refilled her glass, and then she said, her voice unsteady: 'You've got to leave now. I'll send the money to you by special messenger within the week or fortnight.'

She wasn't looking, so she didn't see him smile. But she

heard his footsteps on the Aubusson and then on the hardwood of the hall floor. She put down her snifter and held her forehead with both hands, and let the room spin by, like hours and days and months and years of her life.

May 1924 began with scented breezes and the flowering of Paris's horsechestnut trees. The Champs Elysées abounded with young women in large flowered hats and high-heeled pumps, their cheekbones tinted with rouge and their carmine lips shaped like hearts. The lazy young men who watched them from the cafés, silk pocket handkerchiefs adorning their spring attire, thought only in passing of the coming elections. But in the Palais Bourbon, panic reigned.

With elections days away, the Bloc National had lost ground in every aspect. Its governments had been weak. The economic crisis engendered by Germany's inability to pay its outrageous war debts and the aftermath of Poincaré's expedition into the Ruhr Valley had been mishandled. The Bloc had attempted to deal with these problems by trying for an economic deflation. But this, in turn, had provoked lower wages and a wave of unemployment. Alexandre thought anxiously of the labour riots of five years before and of the Russian revolution. He could see the writing on the wall, scrawled in a bold, obscene print. There was no way for him to retain his seat in the Chamber. The Leftists were banding together under some intelligent leaders: Blum, Herriot. France was no longer at all enamoured with Raymond Poincaré.

Alex sat in his study, playing with the silver letter opener, and tried to rationalize away his fear. The Cartel des Gauches – the Leftist merger of parties now in the majority – was basically weak, like the Bloc. The Socialists still refused to participate in a common venture, claiming that the workers of France should not give in to bourgeois power, even a Leftist bourgeois power. And without the Socialists . . .

There was a light knock, and Lesley came in. He smiled briefly. She said, and he noticed that as she spoke her tongue kept passing over her front teeth: 'I've been thinking of redecorating the salon.'

'Oh?'

She saw the doubt on his face and hesitated. 'You don't agree?'

'Darling, it's up to you. I've always liked the room.'

'Then I shan't change it much. I'll call Franchot in the morning.'

He stared at her and wondered why she sounded so abrupt, and nervous. 'I didn't think you liked his work,' he commented. 'And since you've been taking lessons from Gontcharova, wouldn't it be more fun to try to make some changes yourself?'

'Myself?' She gave him a blank look. 'No. Set design isn't remotely like furnishing a house people live in. I'll call Franchot.'

'All right.'

His pleasant tone of voice set her on edge. She opened her mouth, shut it, shrugged and turned away. He wondered what he had said wrong. She'd had an idea, he'd given her the go-ahead. Why was it that he felt that his quick acceptance had been . . . *too* quick? He should have spoken to her about the elections. But she'd startled him with this request for a new salon.

Outside, Lesley felt the rush of blood to her forehead. It had been so easy. Only one tiny, inventive objection. She wished he'd opposed her. What Paul and Elena were doing was so terribly wrong. They didn't deserve to win.

Oh, my God, she thought. But if they *hadn't* won, *I* would have lost! And a flood of relief passed over her. She rushed upstairs to call Franchot. She would order two Ming vases and tell Alex she had ordered four. By the time the two were

delivered, he'd have forgotten – and would pay the decorator. A very small lie. She could handle that without feeling
too guilty.

The night of the election, Alexandre sat at the dinner table
for a long time, brooding. He moved the roast duckling
around on his plate, but Lesley, seated across from him,
noticed that his fork rarely touched his lips. She wasn't
quite sure what to say to make him feel better.

In truth, the Bloc National had disappointed the people.
She had gone to enough dinners at Marie-Laure de Noailles's sumptuous hotel, Place des Etats-Unis, to realize that.
Marie-Laure exhibited her originality by rounding up the
most extreme Leftists that she could find – much, Lesley
had thought with irony, like a rich collector of oddities
displaying his treasures no matter how outrageous. But
Lesley listened to these impassioned men.

Now she examined Alex on the night of his defeat and
knew that he took it as a personal blow. But she thought:
His party accomplished nothing it set out to do. Yet it
wasn't *his* fault. She cleared her throat and said, timidly: 'It
won't be so bad, darling, to head your own law firm again.
You're certain to have some interesting, landmark cases
that will affect the economy – maybe even more than
political office could do.'

He raised his grey eyes to meet hers. She was stunned by
the pain in them. 'Really,' she stated more strongly.
'Poincaré wasn't a good leader.'

'And Herriot will be better?'

She looked down at her empty plate, then grasped the
stem of her wineglass. 'He might be. And Léon Blum is a
brilliant man. You can't say the same about Poincaré. He's
mediocre.'

'But he believed in our country. He did his honest best.'

'It wasn't enough. France . . . was due for a change.' She

309

said these last words very gently, aware that they would hit him hard. 'Not you,' she added. 'You've just suffered along with the rest of the party.'

His eyes wouldn't leave her face. She met them slowly. Had he simply been swept away in a political tidal wave, or had he deserved to be replaced, just like Poincaré? She tried to answer herself honestly but couldn't. 'I did the best I could,' he said.

'I know.'

She rose, came silently to his side of the table. She laid her hands on the back of his shoulders, pressed them, massaged. She put her face into the crook of his neck. Abruptly he said: 'Don't, Lesley. Just don't.'

'Why not?'

'Because this is the worst day of my life.'

It was so unlike him to overdramatize that she was more stunned by this than by his earlier words. Her fingers stopped moving. She asked tentatively: 'But – your child-hood – surely that was worse.'

'My childhood was something dull and painful, lived every day. I wasn't happy. But today is a singular defeat. I had reached a goal, and now I've been dismissed like a guilty child. This, Lesley, is failure.'

His tone was cold, almost detached, and she blushed. She knew what he was going through. Yet she couldn't stop herself from exclaiming: 'You don't know anything about real defeat, Alex! This is only one event, and you've still got a successful law practice and supporters who know your worth!'

'What's that supposed to mean?'

Her arms fell by her sides. 'It means that you're still somebody.'

'And?'

'And I'm just your wife. I've never reached a single one of my goals. *I'm* a nothing, Alexandre.'

He pushed back his chair, stared at her. His intensity

310

unnerved her. 'We – we all want to become immortal,' she stammered. 'You, through politics. I, with my art.'

He looked at her, perfectly still. Hesitantly, she laid a hand on his cheek, stroked it. 'Gontcharova spoke to Edith de Beaumont,' she said. 'About my helping with the set designs and costumes for one of their *Soirées de Paris*. But – that's so little, compared with what you're doing. One evening's worth of ballet décor . . . What a small portion of immortality!'

'Jamie's achieving immortality,' he murmured in a strange voice.

'Yes. *Rosebuds* is selling by the thousands in the States. *McCall's* is running an excerpt . . .'

'That wasn't what I meant. There are other kinds of immortality, Les.'

She parted her lips, caught her breath. Her heart pounded and she could feel the blood in her eyes, hurting. Alex said: 'Lesley. Please.'

'No.'

'Later it might be too late. You're twenty-six. I'm thirty-four.'

'Surely,' she interrupted quickly, 'you don't condone what Jamie's doing. Or whose child she's going to have!' The blood still raced through her body.

He looked away. 'I'm not proud of my brother,' he whispered. 'But if Jamie wanted a child that badly – '

'It was ridiculous! Think of her future? Who'll marry her now?' She was speaking so rapidly that the words came tumbling out. Her mouth was dry.

'We're married, Lesley.'

'*No!*' She knew she was beginning to shake, that the perspiration must be obvious. She walked away from him, to the window of the dining room. The last thing she wanted to discuss just now was having a baby. She wished she were permanently infertile, that there could be an assurance of her never becoming pregnant. If it hadn't been

311

for that first pregnancy . . . She refused to think about Paul and Elena. But the anguish – she'd have forgotten Justin a long time before. Yes, it hurt to know a man didn't share one's feelings. But it was not the same kind of pain as having a knife cut into your flesh, performing murder.

'What is it?' he was asking softly. 'Is it childbearing you're afraid of?'

'I'm going to do the ballet. That's as much immortality as I want right now. Let it go, Alex. You don't really understand what it means to a woman to be saddled with unwanted children.'

'I do know what it means to be an unwanted child.'

'Then think again! The sort of mother you had, I would be, if you forced me into this!'

'I can't believe it.'

'Believe it!' Then she added: 'Look, just because it's election day and you've lost your seat doesn't mean you have the right to make me feel guilty about this issue.'

He didn't bat an eyelash. But the colour drained from his cheeks. He took a pensive swallow of wine. She wanted to cry, yet at the same time a numbness had taken hold of her. She felt completely trapped.

He stood up shakily, and she saw him walk out of the room, eyes on the floor. Then Bouchard came in and handed her a folded note on a salver. 'Madame,' he announced in his perfect, cadenced tones, 'this was delivered by the maid of Princess Egorova.'

Lesley felt the name reverberate inside her. It felt like a dagger. The butler was waiting, the salver held out in front of her with the note on it. Tainted bait. Lesley didn't want to reach out for it. She was still trembling from her discussion with Alexandre, from the bitterness of his defeat. She'd felt so ineffectual before his sorrow, and later so frightened by his new sally into the domain she tried so hard not to think about: having children. Elena was the

312

most dangerous element of her life. But perhaps this was just a 'thank you' for the five thousand francs she'd sent a few days ago. . . .

'Madame?' Bouchard pressed politely.

Her fingers took the note, unfolded it. She held it to the light of the chandelier, felt her hand unsteady. 'We appreciate your thoughtful gift,' Elena had written in her bold, masculine scrawl. 'And of course we are even more grateful for the promise of your continued help at the start of every month. Yours ever, E.S.E.'

Stunned, Lesley reread the letter. It made perfect sense. They wanted more money. Other payments. Blood money. She'd thought she'd paid, by bleeding on that table in Poughkeepsie, but the score, apparently, had not yet been settled. She couldn't breathe, and her face ached, from her sinuses down to the middle of her cheeks, like a throbbing paralysis. She put the note back on the salver, then thought better of it and retrieved it. 'Thank you,' she said to the *maître d'hôtel.* He bowed and slowly – how slowly he moved! – his small, penguin's feet retraced his steps across the vast Aubusson rug.

She tore the note up and put it in an ashtray. Then she put a match to it, watched it char. She poured some of the table wine on the flames and watched them die in the red puddle. Mesmerized, she stared at the mess.

It might never end. In ragged despair, she looked around the room and thought: The rug will have to go. Franchot could exchange it for a less expensive one. . . Or I could use clothes. A new wardrobe. Alex would notice but wouldn't care. Women were always ordering new dresses.

She sat down at the dinner table and closed her eyes, but the pain in her face persisted. She would have to take a pill. She thought: Jamie is on the Riviera, and besides, I don't want to involve her. I'm going to have to resolve this one by myself. If only Daddy hadn't left the money for Alex to manage. . .

313

She felt bitter then, for being a woman, and against the father who had not trusted her judgment to run her own trust fund. And against the husband who was doing it for her, and who had to be prevented from learning the truth.

Chapter Sixteen

The small town of Louveciennes wound down from its main square, much like the Italian villages of Tuscany. Except that Italy was ochre, sunny and redolent of the vineyard, with constant reminders of a rich medieval and Renaissance past. Louveciennes was all winding paths shaded by old trees and stone houses hidden for privacy by crumbling, picturesque grey walls.

In the early part of 1925, Jamie Lynne Stewart fell in love with a magnificent property with its own small wood that had been the hunting lodge of Madame du Barry, the favourite mistress of Louis XV. The house itself was white, Grecian, with Doric pillars in the front. Twin paths led from the house, bordered on each side by Grecian statues, to a lily pond with a white stone bench. The loveliness and the fact that this house stood far back from the town itself appealed to Jamie. On impulse, she sent a letter to Harold Ober: How much of an advance would Scribner's give her on her new work in progress, so that she might purchase the du Barry pavilion?

Her surveyor could see how much work the place needed. Inside the beams were chewed away, the parquet floors badly in need of repair. While the negotiations went on, she sat tensely in Lesley's house on Place d'Iéna. She didn't belong there. The house itself was too grand, too formal.

She didn't regret Paul – not consciously. She told herself again and again that he'd been wrong for her. Writers possessed that unusual quality of being able to distil their pain into words. She was writing her second book from a man's point of view. It was the story of a Frenchman, ill at ease in this postwar society, like Paul, unable to find out how he fitted in, how to be happy. Her character, Jean-Pierre, came from nowhere. Like Paul, like Willy, he had been born out of wedlock, and this idea pursued and tormented him through every move, through every affair. Sometimes she thought: And I'm going to give birth to a child without a father. Am I being fair?

She'd never had parents as she'd wanted them. Ned had been a father. John Stewart hadn't. Locked in his sermons and old books, he hadn't known how to relate to his small, chubby daughter. And Margaret, judging everything and everyone around her, had been a perfect example of the cold middle class, a scent of beeswax where there should have been the gentle odour of human flesh, enveloping arms, tenderness.

And so, homeless myself, I have attracted men who were also homeless. Willy, Paul. I made a home for Paul on Boulevard Montparnasse. He was happier there than ever before in his life. He stayed with me because of that. But in the end, I didn't want to be somebody's warm blanket. I want to be somebody's prize rose.

She thought of the relationships around her and wondered. Were no married couples ever happy? The Polignacs were both homosexual. Theirs, therefore, was an entente rather than a union. Lesley and Alex? She was too close to judge them, but she felt the odd tensions growing between them, and Lesley's nervousness. The Hemingways . . . on the rocks. The Fitzgeralds, brawling, drinking, fighting. Yes, they were 'in love'. But did one have to destroy and be for ever jealous of one's partner to call that 'love'? The Steins, Gertrude and Alice, were happy. But Natalie Barney made Romaine miserable with her roving eye. So even among lesbians chaos could reign.

Paris abounded with infidelities, with betrayals. A woman slipped off her chemise dress at the drop of a pin. The next day she would bed down another man and a third, both of them together, in a *ménage à trois*. Jamie found this

316

all rather revolting. How could someone respond to two lovers at once? Love was not a game. And Parisians played at everything these days.

The start of that year felt strange to Jamie. Edouard Herriot was teetering on the brink of retiring, because the franc had fallen again and too many notes were being circulated for his government to prove itself creditworthy. Jamie, feeling the life inside her ready to burst forth, felt set apart, as if politics hardly mattered. She didn't go out much, waiting for the baby to be born, for her house to be legally hers and ready to inhabit. Lesley, nerves taut, brush in hand, spent hours in the new atelier, experimenting with pastels and fuchsias, with dots and cubes and odd shapes and contours. She worked with a frenzy that somewhat baffled her friend.

At night they avoided the interminable parties with the American writers, the parties that went from bar to bar, accumulating people. Lesley and Jamie sometimes went to Montparnasse and had dinner at the Closerie des Lilas, where they'd be joined by any number of colourful people who kept them up till dawn, discussing the fate of the world. They drank absinthes and talked about art, about love – and both felt their own loss of innocence, though neither mentioned it.

Jamie watched her best friend, the sister she'd never possessed. It was the first time since the Ritz days that they had lived together. But there was a difference in Lesley that reminded Jamie of the time when she'd come home from England and hidden the fact of her pregnancy. Lesley worked, but her paintings were bizarre, like living night-mares. Jamie wasn't even sure she liked them. She worked and talked about her ambitions, but what kept recurring were material worries. She wanted to sell her work, she wanted to buy new clothes, she wanted to add a touch here and a touch there to an already complete household.

Lesley even went to see Bertrand de la Paume with some

of her paintings. He promised to sell them for her: and for a few days she appeared relieved. She had a gaunt look about her that worried Jamie. Lesley talked rapidly, in a flow of words, when they were surrounded by other people. But when the two of them were alone, she busied herself so that Jamie wouldn't ask questions.

And so Jamie began, out of tactfulness, to stay away. Instead of knocking on the door to Lesley's boudoir, holding her cup of morning coffee, she took it along to Alex's study. He was always glad to see her, and the gratitude she felt toward him was more than just friendship. He had the protective family instincts that Paul lacked, and he seemed to look forward to the birth of her baby. She'd thought him a rather cold, punctilious man and had been afraid of his reaction to her constant presence in the house, reminding him of his brother and her own immorality in having this child out of wedlock. But, unexpectedly, Alex put her completely at ease. She realized after a few weeks that he welcomed her being there, because Lesley was for ever going this way and that, hardly with him at all. He wanted a companion, a sympathetic female.

Some evenings when Lesley was out, they met in the salon and sipped brandy together, quietly. He seemed preoccupied. Once she asked: 'Tell me what's on your mind. How do you pass your days now that you're not . . .'

'Legal work. Many days in court. But most of my days I act as an adviser. My principal client is the Banque de France.'

She was impressed. She knew that this conservative institution advised the government, a government with which it was at odds except for their common concern, of assuaging the enormous national debt of more than forty billion francs. The Dawes Plan, yet another American move of intervention in European affairs, had made the French back down to a more moderate expectation of reparations from Germany.

She would lay her hand on his, and then his eyes – such sad, mournful eyes these days – would rest on her face. Then he smiled. 'How beautiful you look,' he said. 'Like a madonna.' He found her pregnancy becoming.

Only once did he sigh when he looked at her. And then, when her brow shot up, he shrugged in a gesture of defeat. 'I don't understand,' he murmured. 'You've sacrificed so much for the child you're going to have. We wouldn't have to sacrifice anything.'

Jamie felt his pain and was uncomfortable. He looked at her directly. 'Do you know what the problem is?' he asked.

She laced her fingers together on top of her stomach. Then she shook her head. 'Give her time,' she said softly.

'I thought that having you in the house would . . . you know . . . give her ideas. Instead . . .'

Jamie felt a pang of guilt. Her presence had hurt more than it had helped. She wanted to say something but knew she couldn't. Alex held up a sheet of paper he had plucked from a pile that had been lying beside him on the sofa. 'I was looking these over when you came in,' he said. 'They're household bills.'

Aiming at levity, she chided him: 'You can't work all the time, Alex.'

'I'm beginning to think I'm really going to have to – to make ends meet. Lesley's spending habits are getting out of hand.' His voice tensed: he looked away. 'My mother was like that,' he added, almost to himself.

'But Lesley's not like her at all. Talk to her.'

'I can't. She's never home. Fittings, galleries, meetings with decorators. I telephoned Franchot today, to ask him about his last bill. He informed me that he'd only replaced one armchair. He said it was a Mayfair copy, not an original Louis Seize. That one, over there. You'd never know the difference.' He motioned to a delicate upholstered damask chair, with frail armrests. 'And you'd never know it either from what he charged us!'

319

She was surprised at the vehemence, the bitterness of his tone. He composed himself and looked back at her. 'I'm sorry, Jamie. This isn't your problem. Would you like another Cognac?'

She shook her head, overwhelmed with sadness for this man who had become almost like a brother.

Alex decided to take Jamie's advice. A few days later he caught up with his wife in the hall. She was already in her coat of light-grey Breitschwanz fur, its high collar bordered with mink. 'Lesley,' he said, 'could we talk for a few moments? In the study?'

She didn't meet his eye. Although this was strange, it had been customary for the last few months. He touched her arm, and she seemed to tense from the contact. 'I'm late,' she whispered. 'Don't you have to go to the office?'

'Not until later. We should discuss some problems.'

Now she looked up at him, and there was a crease between her eyes, an intense worry that made him feel boorish about having brought up something to concern her. After all, he argued *in petto*, it was only money. But he couldn't simply brush it aside. He led the way and when she had closed the door on herself, he went behind his desk. She remained standing, her neck muscles tense, her face taut.

'Darling,' he stated. 'There's nothing fatal in what I have to tell you. But I've encountered some discrepancies in the latest series of bills. I simply can't make them tally.'

Her lips parted, and he could see the blue vein beating in her throat. She sat down, and he noticed that her nails, once perfect buffed ovals, were chewed to the quick. 'What do you mean?' she asked.

'Well, first of all, the Mayfair armchair. I – '

'*What* Mayfair? We don't own any copies! Alex, I wanted our home to be perfect. I wanted the very best, something fine, for you, for your guests . . .'

'But Franchot told me it was a copy. The armchair.'

She flexed and unflexed her fingers, then unclasped the

320

top of her coat. It fell open over a dress of soft dove-grey silk.
'*You* asked *Franchot*?'

'Yes, I was bewildered. I thought he might have cheated
us – '

She stood up, leaned forward, incredulous. 'How *could* you
have done that? Why didn't you simply ask me about it?'

He was taken aback by the outrage in her pinched white
face. He held his hands out, palms up. 'Lesley, you're never
here! I telephoned him from the office. Surely you aren't
going to take this as a personal betrayal . . .'

'Yes!' she cried. 'That's exactly what it is! You went
behind my back to question what I did with a tradesman.
You discussed matters of intimate concern with somebody
I'd hired to do a job! Alex – how could you so humiliate
me?'

'But it was just a business conversation,' he replied. Then
he felt insulted. She was taking such a small matter and using
it to put him in a role of personal, Machiavellian enmity. He
looked at her and controlled his anger. 'I didn't know you'd
think I was prying,' he stated.

'Don't you trust me?'

He kept his eyes on her levelly. 'Explain to me,' he said
quietly, 'why Franchot told me it was a Mayfair, and you
said it was an original. If the man's a liar, we should fire him.'
He paused, swallowed. 'Or you might have made an error.
In which case he's still wrong, although not actually
dishonest.'

'Wrong?'

'Yes. Doesn't it strike you as bizarre that he's charged us
for a real Louis Seize when he actually sold us a Mayfair
reproduction?'

She turned her back on him, began to pace the room. 'I
wish to God you were still in public office!' she exclaimed.
'Then you wouldn't meddle in such petty problems as our
household budget. You'd be up to your ears in the national
debt instead of our own!'

321

'Lesley,' he stated, and his words rang cold and clear. 'I spend hours of every day with the president of the Banque de France. I'm more involved than ever in France's affairs. But someone has to watch our own nevertheless. I can't let everything go to pieces here.'

'What are you accusing me of?' she asked, her voice low and trembling. 'Being a liar?'

'Goddamn it! I simply want to know what to do about Franchot!' He was really angry now too, and rose. Coming around his desk, he confronted her, putting his hands on her arms. 'What's going on, Lesley? Why aren't you ever at home? I spend all my mornings and evenings alone with Jamie!'

'That's fine!' she cried. 'You two can talk about how marvellous it is that she's going to have a baby! I'm trying to sell my art work. I have places to visit, people to meet. I'm going to do the décor for one of the *Soirées de Paris*, and I'm very busy!'

'Too busy for your husband and your best friend?'

She heard the quiet of his tone and met his eyes. It was impossible to tell him, because if she did, he'd have to know the rest. And if he knew, he'd leave.

She found herself thinking of him, of her, of their marriage. He was kind, honest. Justin Reeve had been unkind and a crook. She looked at Alex and shook her head. It was impossible to explain anything to him. Let him think what he wanted, even if it meant an estrangement from her. Let him –

'I understand your answer,' he whispered, dropping his hands from her arms. 'Sometimes, Lesley, silence is more eloquent than words.'

She opened her mouth, then shook her head helplessly. Rapidly, she clasped her coat and opened the door. He heard her bang it closed. Alexandre realized, with panic, that he was shaking. His whole body seemed out of control. And she still hadn't answered about the chair. He stood by his desk, wondering what to do about Franchot, and then sat down, wondering what to do about his wife.

She knew that somehow she had broken his trust. 'Never tell a lie.' Ned had told her when she'd been four years old. 'It's the first step to theft. If you don't lie to me, I shall always tell you the truth. It's a sacred trust between people who love each other.'

Now that the white cocoon protecting them had been broken, Lesley felt herself watching her own behaviour, and Alex's, as if she were an outsider. A continual headache nagged at her. She took aspirin, and when that didn't work, an eighth of a grain of morphine. That worked, but she felt dulled, in a world above reality, floating. It wasn't an unpleasant feeling, but it made her feel she wasn't truly there.

They circled each other, he not trusting, she guilty, afraid. If he spoke once more to Franchot, he'd be certain she had lied to him. She could never be sure he wouldn't talk, so she dismissed Franchot and hired another, less renowned decorator. It wasn't important. What mattered was that she should have the funds to pay off Paul and Elena and keep Alex at bay.

She examined their marriage, wondering why she was trying so hard to hold on to it. Wasn't it an error? I'm not in love with him, she thought coldly at dinner, watching him from across the table. He's a stranger, we don't even know each other. She felt no desire to make love to him. He lived in a different, remote world, where he met members of the Banque de France and she tried to make the set designs for one of the *Soirées de Paris*. She didn't know what he really did all day, and he rarely asked her.

She couldn't sleep. But Jamie was sleeping all the time now, her baby due imminently. In the middle of the night Lesley, restless and lonely, threw down Radiguet's satiric novel on their decadent society and went downstairs to find some brandy. Alexandre had taken the Armagnac into the study, and she suddenly had a taste for its fine apple flavour. She opened the door and was astounded to find him seated at his desk, his reading glasses perched on his nose. Both exchanged oddly guilty looks.

'What are you doing?' she asked, trying to sound pleasant and casual. But since the day he had confronted her about the Louis XVI armchair, they'd both been ill at ease with each other.

'Some paperwork from the office.'

She nodded, at a loss for further conversation. She wondered how best to ask him for the bottle of Armagnac. She stood stiffly eyeing it on its silver tray, his glass half filled beside it. Finally he saw her expression and made an offhand gesture. 'Help yourself. There's another bottle in the cupboard here.'

She turned red with embarrassment. 'I can't go to sleep.'

He shrugged, half smiling. She felt piqued by what she considered his superior attitude and said: 'You obviously aren't sleeping either.'

'I have a lot of work to do.'

She made an effort not to meet his eyes and moved instead to the desk, scooping up the nearly full bottle of apple brandy. 'If you're sure you've got more . . .'

'Be my guest.'

Her heart pounding, she turned round, left the room. On the threshold she faced him, murmured tentatively: 'If you can't sleep, later on . . .'

'Thank you.'

So much formality. It cut inside her. She went upstairs and sat on her bed, pouring herself a small glass of Armagnac. She propped herself on her pillows, took up her reading. Alex used glasses now to work. Strange how such details of daily life escaped one.

The morphine combined with the brandy was wreaking

havoc on her stomach. She turned off the light, let the book slide to the floor. The room was whirling. She wanted to breathe deeply but couldn't.

All at once she felt something breaking inside her. She flicked on the light, saw that she had drunk half the contents of the bottle of Armagnac. The nausea had passed a little but had been replaced by a great, aching emptiness. She remembered wondering about the child she'd carried. How old would it have been? And, she wondered vaguely, what ever happened to Justin?

She sat up, poured herself another glass, drank it down. And then heard the knock, a light tapping. He was coming in, his suit put aside, a neat maroon robe tied about him.

His face appeared fuzzy to her from the Armagnac, and she was afraid he'd notice the amount she'd consumed. But instead he was sitting down, putting his hands on her shoulders. Her head was buzzing a bit and she wanted to forget all the bad thoughts, forget Justin and the woman in Poughkeepsie. She put her own arms around his neck. He smelled of cologne.

'Lesley,' he was saying. 'If I run for political office next year, I'll have to leave most of the legal work to my assistants. They'll have to be paid higher stipends.'

'So?'

'So we can't go on like this.'

'You mean, not trusting each other?'

'I mean, redecorating the house every month. The market is doing all right, but it won't continue on its upswing for ever. Everyone's behaving like you: spending fortunes on consumer goods. We've got to watch it.'

She wondered how drunk she was. She wanted to cry but didn't. She pushed her face into the lapel of his robe, heard his heart beat. He smelled a little of perspiration. 'My head hurts,' she said. 'Can't we discuss money tomorrow?'

She felt him sigh. The tightness within him stiffened his body. She kissed his lips, tried to part them. At length she succeeded. He yielded, kissing her back, his arms encircling her waist. It was always better to make love when you were a bit tipsy, because then there was less pain and more flow. She couldn't respond very well but let him position her on her bed, felt with a soft moan the stroking of her breasts. They'd make love and then in the morning, the ease would return to them, the awkward, mistrustful atmosphere would dissipate.

'I'm scared,' she whispered.

'Of what?'

'Of things ending.'

'What things?'

'My youth. You. Everything. *Things.*'

She raised her face to him, and he kissed her again, and then she untied the belt of his robe. He was a singularly hairless man, with small circles of black fuzz around his nipples, that was all. Justin had had a different body. His muscles had been more obviously palpable, and he'd had more hair. She felt Alex penetrating her, but with the liquor, the pain was decreased. It was payment for the life she'd led: a selfish life. She owed him this easy access to her body. She lay back and let him move, and remembered for an instant how she had frantically moved with Justin. Now she felt no impulse to do anything but lie back and let him do all the work. He liked to work. It was part of his character. She realized suddenly how bored she was. And then the nausea came back in a sweep, and she felt sick. She wanted everything to be done with, over. She groaned, tossed her head. He stopped in his gliding motions and touched her on the cheek. 'What's wrong?'

'Hold me, Alex,' she whispered. 'Just hold me.'

She felt him slip away, and once again her body was hers alone, unviolated. How lucky men were that nothing ever touched their insides, their wholeness. He lay beside her in the dark, and she felt the warmth of his silent presence. It brought her comfort. She felt enveloped in this comfort, in this warmth. She'd felt it from the very beginning, in his Bugatti. Maybe now she could go to sleep.

'Stay,' she murmured, but the word came out a soft, unformed moan. He kissed her gently on the temple and then sat up. He was going away. She opened her mouth to ask him again, but he was tiptoeing out of the boudoir and the words stayed on her lips. He was letting himself out, and she felt the desolation of his exit. She had interrupted his pleasure, and now she was paying for it by having to remain alone in bed.

I shouldn't drink so much, she thought vaguely. Then the walls closed about her and she stopped having to feel, and to think.

In his bedroom, he pulled the blankets up, and lay naked between the cool, crisp sheets. All his life he'd been prevented from the final reward. He'd heard her tell him to stay. But for what? As an additional security blanket? I am tired of taking care of other people, he thought bitterly. Tired of their never giving any of it back to me.

And he couldn't sleep for the resentment, the sour anger. He'd always been alone.

The *Soirées de Paris* were a great success. Léonide Massine danced for the intelligentsia of Paris, and there was an aura of the forbidden about the performance. Diaghilev had many followers, many friends and admirers. Those who came to the mansion of Charles and Edith de Beaumont to watch Massine looked nervously over their shoulders and were a little afraid to clap, from a sense of loyalty. After all, the choreographer/*danseur* had been fired from the Ballets Russes after his marriage; he was the third of Diaghilev's lovers to have so betrayed him. But, argued the elegant ladies of Paris, Massine, unlike his predecessor Nijinsky, had always been an unwilling homosexual. 'Diag' – Seriozha – should have realized this and predicted his eventual defection.

Lesley sat with her husband and Sara Murphy and was

amazed at her own sense of colour, at the way her decorations blended in with the ballet. Chiffons and velvets and soft moiré silks – what fun they had been to work with! She looked over shyly at Gabrielle Chanel, severe in her black trouser suit. The *couturière* was accompanied by Misia Sert, Diaghilev's best friend. Pushing out her pigeon breast, pouting her lips, Misia, loyal, sat haughtily surveying the work before her. She wanted to disapprove. But Coco Chanel suddenly, briefly, smiled at Lesley. Then Lesley sat back, feeling proud, vindicated. Natalia Gontcharova would be so pleased . . .

At the intermission, the pagelike Edith de Beaumont, who, with her dandified husband, had started these ballet extravaganzas the previous year, strode up to Alexandre and Lesley. 'You must work for us more often,' she stated. 'I've heard whispers growing to loud cries of approval. You have a gift for costume.'

'Thank you.' Lesley blushed, aware that Edith was regarding her in a peculiar manner. 'It's Gontcharova's lessons,' she stammered.

'The results are breathtaking.'

Alexandre stood rather awkwardly, not knowing what to say. He cleared his throat. 'Lesley's been working night and day,' he commented.

'Well, then, you can take her on a lovely vacation.' Edith's eyes were piercing, unkind. He wondered why. They'd always got along well. 'Men,' she was saying, 'should be more generous with their wives.'

Why was she saying this? It sounded like a veiled accusation. 'I've never denied Les anything,' he retorted, and then stopped. He had no reason to defend himself to this woman who, after all, had nothing to do with the Varennes. But he felt piqued, his honour insulted. He glanced at Lesley and saw that her cheeks were scarlet. He couldn't help himself. 'Isn't it so, Lesley?' he insisted.

She nodded, looking at the floor. He felt a surge of

uncomprehending fury, tamped it down. Edith de Beaumont was patting her on the shoulder, moving away. Almost immediately Chanel was beside them. 'The colour combinations on stage are wonderful,' she said. 'Congratulations.'

Alex took her hand, raised it to his lips. Odd how some people, born in humble circumstances, could suddenly be elevated to positions of social standing. Everyone now received this woman, who had risen from the poorest of backgrounds to own the most innovative fashion house in Paris. She remarked: 'Well, Marquis, your wife has been hiding from us. Whatever have you been doing to her?'

Another one to use the dry, stabbing wit. 'I've done nothing,' he replied, trying to smile. 'What do you mean?'

'It's obvious,' Chanel enlightened him. 'Ever since Lesley began to work on this project, she's been neglecting us on rue Cambon. Not once has she shown up for a fitting!' She inspected his wife, touched her gown of aqua crêpe. 'Lesley comes to every one of my collection presentations,' she continued, addressing Alex. 'But she hasn't been following up with any orders. I can see why. Have you been designing your own clothes, darling?'

Lesley didn't answer. 'I like this well enough,' the pencil-thin *couturière* remarked with asperity. 'But it doesn't really have the "snap" that you need, with your red hair. Why don't you leave yourself to me, the way you used to? Ballet décor is one thing, but day-to-day fashion is another. I've worked in the field for too many years not to understand it better than any of my customers – even the most talented ones, like you.'

'I've ordered three new suits just recently,' Lesley said. Her voice shook. Coco Chanel raised her fine-lined eyebrows, cocked her head to one side. Then she shrugged.

'Very well,' she stated. 'It's as you wish, anyhow.'

When she had left their side, her erect form mingling into groups of other elegant spectators, Alex turned to Lesley.

329

She was still staring at a minute point on the floor. He said: 'Chanel's very strange, isn't she?'

'Why do you say that?'

'Because last week I saw your invoice for the purchase of seven items, besides the suits you spoke of. Yet she doesn't sound like someone who forgets what has been ordered from her house.'

His eyes were on her, his tone questioning. Lesley turned to face him, saw the doubt. She felt filled with dread. It dragged her down and glued her in place. 'Maybe she's just human,' she replied quietly, her green eyes meeting him. He held the stare in silence.

Just then Sara Murphy reached them, laughing. She spoke to Alex, and at once he turned to her, as if with relief. Lesley saw his jaw muscle, tight, outlined in his profile. The deadness was still there, and she could almost visualize herself enveloped in a cloud of distrust. She seemed to be carrying an odour of dishonesty that others could breathe in, that made them recoil.

No, she thought. Not all other people – just Alex. He is the only one who doesn't trust me.

Suddenly she didn't want to watch the end of Massine's performance and never wanted to work on another ballet production. The atmosphere around her seemed synthetic, unreal – unpleasant. Nauseated, Lesley thought: I'd rather never work again than work for these people.

Charles de Beaumont was murmuring to Alex: 'Really, *mon cher*, it was the first time a society woman accepted payment for her work. You should untie the purse strings, dear fellow. A woman needs her little luxuries, you know . . .'

Alex wheeled about, cutting off his host, and his face was ashen. Lesley noted that his pupils had gone down to tiny pinpoints. She smiled, like a mechanical doll, and took a tiny step backward. Her husband's eyes were slate grey, unforgiving. She offered limply: 'Charles doesn't under-

330

stand about the New Woman of the twenties. We don't want to be supported in our every whim.'

'Well, then,' Alex murmured, 'if that's the case, I shall let you take care of Mademoiselle Chanel and her forgotten outfits.'

Lesley saw tiny red dots on her field of vision. She groped for something to hold on to, found an arm. She felt herself being lifted away, and all at once everything was going blank. Thankful, she let herself collapse into the darkness, blotting out Alex's eyes.

Everything happened at once. Jamie's house was pronounced ready. She moved out. No sooner had she installed herself in Louveciennes than Lesley received word that she was in labour. It was morning, and Alexandre had already left for the office. Lesley packed a small bag and drove to the American Hospital in Neuilly, where she was made to wait, like a husband, for seven hours. Strong, stalwart Jamie was having a most difficult time. At the last moment a doctor came to tell Lesley that they were going to have to perform a Caesarian section. 'But they'll be all right? Jamie and the child?'

'We think so. Miss Stewart has lost a lot of blood. The breeched position of the child – and the fact that it's so large, that it was past time – '

Lesley felt her throat go dry, wished for a drink. Her hands were trembling. Never am I going to suffer this way, she thought. Nothing, no man is worth this agony . . .

Finally a nurse announced to her that everything was fine, that the baby girl was in good condition, that Jamie was exhausted but well. They've cut into her, Lesley thought. They've cut her open to extract the child – and now she's going to be scarred for life. Every lover she takes will know.

Jamie was lying on the white pillow, pale against it. Her

331

great eyes lay closed. Lesley took her hand. At this moment she hated all men, but her mountain of detestation and revulsion centred on Paul, the cause for all this, and the one who should have been beside Jamie and was not. Did he even know? Certainly he must have known he was the father. The pregnancy had been a known fact. Why hadn't he had the decency to come forward – and at least offer his support? Why hadn't he wanted to recognize the child, give it a name?

'But my daughter *has* a name,' Jamie whispered. 'I don't need Paul's. Her name is Cassandra Lesley Stewart: Cassandra, like the blind prophetess of ancient Troy, because that's what you all used to call me – and Lesley, for you. Cassie will be just fine.'

Lesley nodded, moved. 'Will you be Cassie's godmother?' Jamie asked. Lesley nodded again. 'And if something were ever to happen to me – you would bring her up? To be free?'

Lesley squeezed Jamie's hand. Then she quickly departed. Outside the nurse was arriving with the baby and stopped her.

'Don't you want to see her?'

A small face was protruding from the pink blanket, begging to be examined. Against her will, in order to avoid the disapproval of the nurse, Lesley stopped, fingered the tiny cheek. So small. So grotesquely vulnerable. Jamie might have died for you, she wanted to say. Jamie has a row of ugly stitches because of you. Jamie won't be able to walk for weeks because of you. Are you worth all this?

The world is too corrupt to bring children into it, she rationalized. And then, quickly, she ran down the hallway out of the hospital.

Alexandre waited in the living room, his back aching from the tension. Around him were clustered the absurdities of a daily, feminine existence: coloured velvet cushions, knick-

332

nacks, photographs. He didn't want to sit back and feel the voluptuous softness. It was incongruous in the circumstances. Now that he was here, he wished he hadn't come.

He heard the rustle of silk and turned his head. Elena was dressed in an Oriental lounging outfit of gold, green and orange cotton, and two long gold leaves hung from her white earlobes. Her hair was loosely piled on top of her head, held in place by two gold combs. Gold bangles cinched both her wrists. He rose and formally took her hand. He brought it almost but not quite to his lips.

'Marcelle is bringing tea,' Elena stated. 'Unless you'd rather have a brandy or a glass of whisky.'

'Tea is fine, thank you. I shan't be staying long.'

She sat down, kicking off her Greek sandals, and tucked her feet beneath her on the opposite end of the sofa. Her proximity came as a surprise to him. He could smell her, not only her heavy perfume, but also the female odour of her flesh; and he could almost feel her presence. He crossed his legs and leaned forward, away from her. 'My brother isn't here?' he asked.

'He's gone to sell a painting. I can relay any message you have for him tonight.' Her tone was aloof, matching his. He thought: I hate her.

Aloud he replied: 'I wanted to do it in person. But since I'm here, I'll tell you why I came. Jamie Stewart gave birth to her baby.'

He looked at her then levelly. She possessed the most extraordinary face he'd ever seen: Its planes were so pure, the eyes so deep, so dark, the nose so smooth and linear. It was a face that controlled its emotions. She blinked only once, and he thought that the edges of her cheekbones coloured slightly. But she replied evenly: 'Oh? You wish me to tell this to Paul?'

'Of course,' Alex said. 'It's his daughter.' He could feel the blood trying to burst out of his veins. He wanted to get up and shake her. He wanted to make her cry.

333

'It's Miss Stewart's daughter,' Elena commented. Her voice was calm, but he could detect an undercurrent of defensiveness in its tone. 'She wanted to have her. Paul never wished to have anything to do with this child.'

'Then he shouldn't have lived with Jamie,' Alex said roughly. He thought: I have never so taunted another person's feelings. Except that this woman has none, so, no matter what I say, it won't touch her. 'No man can ever disclaim such responsibility.'

'Nor can a woman. This is 1925,' Elena countered. She reached for a heavy silver lighter, flicked the light, watched the flame as if fascinated. Then she set it down on the coffee table again. At this point the maid entered with a tray of cakes and tea and set it down before her mistress. Elena busied herself with cups and saucers. 'How do you wish your tea, Marquis?' she asked.

'With lemon, please, and one sugar.'

Her dextrous hands poured tea, added a slice of fresh lemon, dropped in a coloured sugar cube. She held the cup and saucer out for Alex, who took it quickly and sipped from it before setting it down. Then he continued: 'No method is foolproof. The only one is abstinence.'

Elena laughed. 'Perhaps you are one remarkable man,' she commented. 'And that might explain why you don't yet have children. Most human beings aren't so ascetic.'

Now it was she whose eyes were on him, and he felt the blow. He sipped his tea, absolutely numb.

Lightly she said: 'You hate me, don't you? I'm everything you most abhor in a woman. Are you afraid of me?'

He glanced at the overwhelming beauty of her and recoiled. It was too much. 'I'm not the least afraid, Princess,' he answered. 'Evil doesn't scare me. I've simply learned to leave it alone.'

Again she emitted the short, ironic laughter that was like a shield against any attack. 'You're a most compelling man,' she commented. 'No wonder you were once a deputy.

334

You speak in such strong, unequivocal terms. "Evil". Which one of us is so pure of soul that he can judge another human being? You hardly even know me.'

'You're responsible for the pain of a very nice woman,' he answered, his anger rising. His voice rose slightly. He controlled it, drank some tea, reached for a small éclair.

'It was Paul's choice. No one can say who is at fault within a relationship, because only the two parties involved have lived inside its parameters. Paul is happy with me. He wasn't fully happy with Jamie Stewart, or he'd have married her, wouldn't he?'

'Is he going to marry *you*?'

Elena's eyes hardened. 'That's up to him, isn't it? Not up to you?'

Alex smiled, the tension letting up a little inside his body. 'It could be up to you too, Princess,' he said. 'Most couples decide jointly.'

'Well, then, we shall decide jointly.' She stood up, and he was astounded by how tall she was. A big, tall tower of a woman. Her breasts were unrestrained beneath the thin gauze of her cotton sheath. He found himself staring at the hardened, large nipples outlined perfectly on the cloth. For a moment words didn't come. He had to shake himself out of the daze, looking away from her.

'My dear Marquis,' she was saying. 'You are so full of preconceptions, of hatreds, of judgments. Do you ever take the time to live life as it comes? There's a sun in the sky, flowers to smell. But a frozen man cannot feel the rays, nor take in the scents. Don't waste your life.'

He heard the derision and felt the jolt of memory. The realization came to him in this swift half-second that he had always hated his mother. He could see the image of her, young, standing next to Bertrand de la Paume in her nightgown – and then the two of them taking him, a young child, into their bed. Charlotte had hated him too, her own

335

son. He'd been an interruption. All his life he had taken care of his mother, hating her.

Elena, perceptive, was murmuring, her hands on her hips: 'Women are part of life, Marquis. We exist, we breathe. Disliking us, resenting us, is actually more harmful to yourself than to us. Paul doesn't hate women, though he doesn't know how to love. But women have treated him well. Martine and Jamie loved him, and I love him.'

'But he hurts those very people who give him love.'

'One has to learn to be self-protective. I've learned, the hard way. I'd rather be loved by a man who is selfish, but who enjoys life, than live with one who doesn't know the colour of the leaves in autumn.'

'I love my wife,' Alex stated, conscious that his voice was trembling a little.

'Do you? Truly?'

She was standing above him, her breasts moving up and down beneath the orange, gold and green. Her eyes shone like points of fire, which he knew were only the refractions from the lamps and the afternoon light. Still, she was prepossessing, enveloping. Her question made him quiver inside. For the first time since he had caught Lesley in the lies that bewildered him, he allowed himself to consider, to analyse his own feelings about the situation. He was hurt; he felt betrayed; but most of all, he didn't understand what her motives were in spending as if tomorrow would never rise and then not being honest with him about her actions. A well of anger rose inside him. He wondered: *Do* I still love her? She's doing something that is surely dishonest – certainly with me she is dishonest. And she won't give me a child . . .

He was brought back to reality with a shock. 'I didn't come here for a philosophical discussion,' he said abruptly. 'A little girl was born yesterday, at the American Hospital. Her name is Cassandra Lesley Stewart. I think my brother should know that he is a father.'

336

He rose and saw the look of quiet appraisal levelled at him from her black eyes. Was his pain, his feeling of the injustice of Fate, so apparent? He needed desperately to be alone, to escape from this strange woman and from the questions she had made him think about. This time she extended her hand firmly, like a man, and didn't allow him to raise it to his lips. 'I shall tell Paul,' she said, and he saw that there was something like hurt in her face too.

Outside he breathed the air in hungry gulps and felt his heart beating. He heard a noise, and the oak front door to the building was opening. Elena Egorova, hugging her sides to ward off the wind, said to him: 'He didn't want Jamie's child. Remember that. He wanted *me*!'

It seemed an odd reason to have followed him outside. She added, almost angrily: 'When I am ready for him, *I* shall marry *him*. But I won't do it by becoming pregnant. I'm not stupid.'

'Must a woman be machinating every time she gives birth to a child?' he contested wearily. 'What about wanting to form a home, a family, out of love?'

'Spoken like a blindly egotistical male,' she said. 'Through our bodies, you control our destinies. We must either strain against childbirth, to avoid complicating your lives – or, as in your case, we are made to pay if we choose *not* to have babies.'

'And you, Princess? If you were "in control", as you say, what would you do?'

The light wind was making him hold his topcoat together, and it was swirling the gauze of her gown around her hips and ankles. She looked like a statue draped in cloth of gold. She said. 'I am a complete being, Marquis. It's quite all right with me that Paul doesn't like children.'

'But one day he may regret this and turn to his daughter.'

'That's the chance I have to take, isn't it? Life is full of risks.'

For a moment they didn't speak, but stood looking at

each other with an odd, vulnerable honesty, barely hidden by the hardness of their respective tones. She made a mock bow. 'You understand the politics of nations far better than that of women,' she finally murmured. 'In another world we would have been friends. I understand all politics.'

He smiled, in spite of himself. And she smiled back, but only with her lips. She was a sad, tragic woman, he decided, watching her entering her building again. Stronger than his brother, and in a way cleaner than Paul. At least her motives were clear, if not honourable.

Starting up the engine of the Bugatti, he thought again of Lesley, his wife for the past six years. It seemed to him as he saw the blue smoke rising around the wheels of his car that he might already have lost her. Yet what had he done but want to love her in as total a way as a man could love a woman?

I don't ever want to grow to hate her, he thought, like all the other women in my life. The only two for whom he felt a clean, untempered love were the gentle Jamie, who was the sister he'd never had, and his new goddaughter Cassandra. If he couldn't be a father, he would make up for it with Cassie – his brother's unclaimed, abandoned, unwanted child. Paul's shame would be made up for by Alex's devotion. He'd always had to pick up after Paul's wreckage. There was no escape from this; there never had been.

But this wasn't a Popov situation. This time Paul hadn't left him only with the mess. Because what Paul now didn't want, Alex desperately wanted. Cassandra, by right, should have been a viscountess, next in line after her father. By law, Alex would make her his own heiress.

Chapter Seventeen

In his office on rue La Boëtie, Bertrand de la Paume looked like a sleek, ageing greyhound, perfectly polished. His grey silk shirt hung over a chest that was now concave, and deep lines had set in around his sharp brown eyes. Lesley sat on the edge of her chair across from his desk of delicate inlays, a line between her brows.

'My friend Natalia Gontcharova is most sorry that you turned down her offer,' Bertrand stated. 'Frankly I can't quite understand that.'

Lesley reached into her bag of tooled Moroccan leather, extracted a thin cigarette, and allowed the Chevalier to light it for her. He noticed without comment that her fingernails were ragged. 'You would do well as a set designer,' he continued.

'And the paintings I brought you?'

'We each possess certain unquestionable talents. Today there are many brilliant, innovative painters. Your canvas work is good, but it isn't unique. Forgive me for being so blunt, my dear.'

'So you're not going to sell them?'

'I've sold one. To the Princess Murat. But understand that she bought it because of who you were, as a conversation piece. Your reputation isn't going to be made from this.' He hesitated, then plunged in. 'But when you work with movement – as in the *Soirées de Paris* that you did last year for the Beaumonts – you possess a certain flair that comes to life.'

Lesley inhaled, blew out smoke, inhaled again. He murmured gently: 'You've become very thin. Is there a problem?'

'No. Thank you. I'm just . . . disappointed.'

'You must learn to stick with things. How old are you now?'

'Twenty-seven.'

'You've found a niche. Don't become a jack of all trades and master of none. Not all of us can be Botticelli. Some of us have to be Gontcharova. It's an immortality of sorts. Her work will survive too.'

'And so will my father's.'

Lesley's bitterness surprised Bertrand, and he wasn't quite sure how to answer. But already she was standing up, struggling into her coat. 'You could try your hand at fashion design,' he suggested, getting up to meet her. 'Chanel was telling me you don't buy from her any more. She thought you were creating your own designs and having them made up for you.'

He had reached her too late to help her on with her wrap. She wheeled to face him, her eyes brilliant with something he couldn't fathom: anger, perhaps, or deep-seated resentment. 'Everyone is full of guesses,' she said quickly. 'Why can't they all leave me alone?'

He remembered her that year at the Exhibition of Decorative Arts, with its many pavilions hoarding all the new ideas of the decade. Fashion, too, had been represented. She'd seemed like a little girl, going from works of art to architecture, and touching all the new designs that Chanel and Poiret had chosen to exhibit. But she'd also seemed nervous. She'd seen Elena Egorova and had darted away from him to avoid her. Yet at one time they'd been good friends. He sighed, thinking of Jamie. Now he said: 'Think of what I've told you. You don't *need* to work. Therefore you can choose your medium. Choose it carefully.'

Her eyes held his, then flicked away. She said evenly: 'Thank you, Bertrand. You're a good friend.'

She was opening the door, and he let her go. He closed it behind her, then went to the window to watch her leave.

She always drove her green car now, and he saw her entering it hastily, and starting up the motor too quickly. The new generation was so impulsive. A sadness took hold of him, and he sighed as he returned to work. Nobody listened any more: not Paul, not Lesley. Alexandre had never liked him. It wouldn't do, really, for him to meddle further. I understand too damned much, he thought, lighting his pipe.

Jamie held tightly on to the little hand, marvelling as she always did at its plump smoothness, at the miracle that was her daughter in every small limb. The tug at her hand was like a tug at her heart. She could feel the warmth of that small hand clutching at her, dependent upon her, and the respondent warmth within her.

Behind her to the right was the white Grecian simplicity of the du Barry hunting lodge. Jamie thought of all the work, all the hours spent slaving over her notes and her typewriter, spent making diagrams of character development, in order to come up with the two books that had paid for this mansion. It was as far from the house in Cincinnati, with its rancid smell of wax and old candles, as this child was from who she had been at her age: also an only child, but in such different circumstances! She said: 'I wonder who you'll be when you grow up. Any ideas?'

Cassie looked up into her mother's face with that scrutiny that never failed to intrigue Jamie. Was it curiosity? Her name fit perfectly. She peered into one's face with the intensity of a seeress. 'I'll be just me, Mommie.'

Jamie laughed. 'And who will that be?'

'A fairy princess.'

'I see.' They were strolling down a small path bordering the wood, and now Jamie stopped, sat down on a bench in a cleared-out area with a broken-down fountain in the middle, and pulled the three-year-old child onto her lap. Cassie

341

wound her mother's stray hair around her pudgy fingers, then touched Jamie under the chin and started to laugh. 'Oh, Mommie.' She said it with the indulgent superiority of the worldly wise.

'"Oh, Mommie" what?'

'Just "Oh Mommie". I want you to tell me a story.'

'There was once a white elephant,' Jamie began in a singsong voice, rocking the little girl back and forth, 'whose name was Omar.'

'Why?'

'Why *what*?'

'Why was his name Omar?'

Jamie pretended to think it through. 'His mommie liked the sound of it. "*O – mar*." Now can we continue?'

'Yes. What did Omar do? Did his nanny make him take baths?'

'He didn't have a nanny. He had a nannus. A nannus is a boy nanny. And his nannus was bigger and stronger than Omar, and yes, he forced him to take baths. All babies have to take baths. All big people too.'

'Mademoiselle smells awful. I bet she doesn't make herself take baths at all. I'd rather have a nannus. Why can't we get a nannus, Mommie?'

'Because we live in France and in France there are no nannuses. Omar lived in deepest darkest Africa.'

'Can we go there some time?'

'Maybe. Anyway – '

'Oh, *Mommie*. You're such a funny mommie! I wish Mademoiselle would go away so you could always take care of me.'

Jamie smiled. 'That would be nice. But if I didn't write books, we wouldn't have enough money to pay for the food we eat. And we need food, don't we, Princess?'

At that moment footsteps resounded in the pathway and an older woman entered the clearing. Jamie bounced Cassie off her knee. 'Ah, Mademoiselle. Time for a snack?'

'Indeed, Madame. Cassie?'

The little girl peered back at her mother in accusation. Jamie shook her head. 'Come on. Now.'

Sulky, Cassandra shuffled toward her governess, and together they walked back toward the house. Jamie remained alone in the clearing. The old fountain was such a picturesque ruin, a memento of an age of elegance and grace long gone by. She sighed, rested her face in her hands. These moments of quiet aloneness did her good. Finally she pulled herself up and strolled in the same direction as her daughter and the governess.

Paul's restlessness touched every nerve ending, until he could feel his hands tensing on the wheel. On the open road away from Paris, his heart pounded at the thought of what he was about to do. He had been driving very fast. He was driving in the direction of Louveciennes.

He was going there because an inner urge had moved him. He had to admit it: He was curious. Now he was almost there. He couldn't just go back to Paris. So close . . . He might as well take a quick look at this place she had bought three years before, which he'd heard about from friends. Jamie Stewart, living now in grand style, while he struggled with Elena, on Lesley's money . . . He was all at once seized with frustration, at himself, at his weakness, and at Jamie. He pressed on the accelerator, determined to see where she lived.

The small town square of Louveciennes descended into side streets. It was a pretty town, with stone and brick houses dating back to the time of the Bourbon kings. He found where the street was. It curved away from the station, becoming more rural as it progressed. The property stood to the right, at the dead end, shut off by a black iron gate. Typical of Jamie, the gate was ajar.

He parked the car some way down and walked to the

gate. He passed inside the property. It was amazing, the quiet of the place, with birds making the only noise to be heard. They might have been living a million miles from Paris, instead of a mere fifteen or twenty. He looked ahead and saw the clear pond, with its lily pads, and the meticulously kept lawn stretching toward the house, with its two twin paths bordering each side. Drawn irresistibly, he went close to the pond, went to one of the paths, began to walk toward the house.

And then he saw her. Walking, head bent forward, hair falling from the pompadour onto her forehead. Wisps curling from the spring warmth around her face. She was walking slowly. The blue gingham dress, too long, but becoming. Her sandalled feet kicking at the gravel.

He wanted to call out to her; memories assailed him. Her face in the crook of his arm. Her marvellous eyes, examining him. Her hands, massaging his back. The soft, round, full, free breasts. Gentleness. He opened his mouth, held in his breath. How on earth could he call out to her, admit to his intrusion? But he was so filled with nostalgic longing, with need, that his whole body ached.

She'd never been beautiful. Yet at that moment, when she entered the house, going up the few steps to the Doric veranda, he knew, simply knew, that letting her go, not loving her, had been the biggest mistake of his existence.

He stayed glued to the pathway, jealous. Jealous of her belonging to this house, to this beautiful, peaceful domain. Jealous of her survival without him. She'd loved him so – and he'd wasted that love. All his life he'd wasted good things, not appreciated them. Martine, too, had loved him. He'd killed her with his neglect.

A noise startled him. The front door of the white mansion was opening again, and a small child was scampering down the steps, a middle-aged woman in uniform behind her. His heart began to beat twice as fast. The child was coming toward him, running down the path. He slipped behind a tree and as she passed by, running, he held his breath: that firm little body, those sturdy little legs, that pink face – those eyes! My God, it's my daughter.

The child was laughing, he could hear her. The governess was huffing behind her. Finally they stopped, and he strained to catch the child's expression. He felt an emotional longing so great that relief seemed impossible.

The governess and the child were walking near the pond. The child was pulling away. The governess was trying to plait her hair. Such marvellous, lustrous brown hair, with reddish tints. *His hair!* Minutes passed – endless, yet somehow static: a moment caught on the wing. Then, sighing, the older woman rose. 'Very well, Cassandra,' he heard her say in the precise, clipped French of well-mannered Parisians. 'You may stay outside fifteen more minutes. But take care of the water. You could fall in.'

'My *maman* told me. I won't lean over. But the goldfish are so pretty – '

'Just don't forget! I'll be calling you.'

The child was alone. He was alone with his daughter. *His daughter.* He stood mesmerized behind the tree, wanting to stop time so the fifteen minutes would never end. He feasted his eyes upon her, this little girl whom he had never seen before, who was of his own flesh and blood. Suddenly he wondered: Had his own father ever seen him, ever felt these emotions? Was his father Bertrand de la Paume, as some claimed?

And then he was walking, walking toward the child near the pond. He was admiring his daughter. She looked up, startled, suddenly afraid. She pulled away and he could see she was puzzled.

'Hello,' he said, his voice trembling.

'Hello.' She was standing stiffly, primly, shy, on her guard.

'Don't be afraid. I know who you are.' He sat down on the bench, and she was curious. She finally drew near.

345

'You do? But I've never seen you before.'

'That's true. Let me see now . . . Your name is Cassandra. You're three years old.'

Her face changed then, lighting up. The eyes, Jamie's eyes, dancing. 'Yes. And what's your name?'

'Paul.'

'Paul what?'

'Paul de Varenne.' He wondered if Jamie had ever mentioned his name, was suddenly afraid she had and also that she hadn't.

'That's a strange name. Very long.'

He wanted to say: It's your name too. Or it should be. 'My name is Cassie Stewart,' she added.

He asked: 'Does your *maman* always speak French to you? You speak it perfectly.'

The little girl regarded him with childish disdain. 'We speak both. My *maman* speaks French and English. With me she mostly speaks English. In English "*Maman*" is "Mommie".'

He so wanted to touch her. He held out his hand. 'I know your mommie. She and I used to be very good friends.'

'Why haven't you come to see us before? Mommie's friends come all the time. What's your name again?'

He said, through his constricted throat: 'Paul de Varenne.'

She began to clap her hands, laughing. 'That's funny!'

He looked away, away from the forget-me-not blue that reminded him so of her, of Jamie. His vision was blurred. Cassandra said: 'What's wrong? Are you unhappy?'

She was touching *him*, miracle of miracles! Her little hand lay on his shoulder, and she didn't seem afraid any more, just bewildered. Evidently grown men didn't cry in front of her every day. He made himself look right at her, felt a lump in his throat. 'I'm not unhappy. I'm not unhappy at all.'

He wondered what it was that had made him want to

346

ignore her existence until that day and what had made him harden his heart against loving Jamie. It hadn't been only Elena. Perhaps he'd been afraid to be a father. His brother, on the other hand, still desperately wanted to be one.

It wasn't the nurse who came toward them a few moments later. Jamie was coming out to get the child, and when she saw her, Cassie broke away from him and ran to her mother. He thought for a minute of running the other way, then decided to hold his ground. Stubbornness planted him there so that she would have to deal with him. I've never fought, he thought, for what is mine, because nothing I've had has ever really been mine. Alex had the château, the lands, the title – and Lesley's funds. But *he* had the child.

Jamie scooped the little girl up in her arms, and he saw, from the distance, that she couldn't move, her eyes upon him. So he walked toward her. He saw her panic. She gently pushed the child inside. 'Go on, darling,' Jamie was saying, her voice unsteady, 'This gentleman and I must talk.'

Jamie's face was very pale. Paul felt his own nervousness, yet she was so obviously upset that he knew it was the moment to make his move. He felt overcome by Jamie's face, by the memories, by the fact that the child belonged to the two of them and to no one else. In the embarrassment that followed, he tried to organize his thoughts.

She was the first to speak. Her voice came out low, in staccato gulps. 'This is my house,' she said. 'And my daughter. You must leave.'

'I'm her father. Jamie, I've done many things you can blame me for, but you can't take away my parenthood.'

'You took it away yourself,' she contested, looking down. 'I gave you your option three and a half years ago.'

'I was wrong then.'

Their eyes locked, held. 'You regret choosing Elena?' she finally asked, defiantly.

'Jamie. Please. One has nothing to do with the other.'

347

'Elena has everything to do with us. The minute she stepped into your life, our life was over. I don't want somebody else's leftovers. You chose to be with Elena more than three years ago. You forfeited your right to this child.'

'That isn't fair. What about divorced parents?'

'That's different. If you'd made an effort – married me, tried to make it work – I could have seen that the child was worth something to you. But you never came forward. You let this child exist for over three years and never made a move. I've earned the right to call her my daughter. You've earned nothing.'

She looked at Paul again, with eyes full of anger. 'You've always been a selfish, thoughtless man. But I never realized to what extent! Legally, and in God's book, she's mine. I've earned my parenthood. Ask Elena to give you a baby and leave us alone.

'Please go, Paul,' Jamie said once more in a weary, sad voice. 'This is a home, and that's something you've never understood.'

He straightened himself up, shaking, staring at her. At that moment the emptiness of his existence hit him. It was 1928, he was thirty-seven. He didn't even want to think of Elena. Lust made people hard, love made them pliable and giving. He didn't love the Russian princess, had confused love with lust. Before he turned away, feeling the greatest loss he had ever encountered, he murmured, trying not to flinch before the honesty of Jamie's eyes: 'Perhaps I'm understanding it right now.'

He found himself looking at her going back into the elegant white mansion. He felt numb. She'd said everything and he hadn't found the words to convince her. But now he knew what he had to find out. At some point one had to connect, to belong. She'll come to me one day, he thought, trying to dull the terrible pain. Everyone needs a father.

* * *

348

Bertrand de la Paume, for his sixty-eight years, walked erect, with the elegance of a man of the world who knew he had seen better days but would be damned if he'd allow the world to guess it. His hair was white, thick, combed away from his creased forehead. In his bachelor apartment, he was greeted by his manservant who at once helped to remove the stiff dinner jacket and frilled shirt, and then, without having to be reminded, brought out the warm foot bath and massaged the tired feet before placing them one by one inside the ceramic basin. By the sidetable stood a crystal glass with bromides, and Bertrand swallowed them down. His stomach these days could no longer bear rich food, and at this evening's supper in honour of a new young actress, he had consumed too much champagne and too many unusual hors d'oeuvres. He must remember to have a marvellous assortment of flowers sent to her. Then he heard the doorbell ring, and was surprised. His valet stood up to attend to the late visitor.

When he returned, he said to his master: 'Monsieur le Chevalier, Monsieur Paul is here. Shall I tell him to join you here?'

Bertrand raised his brows: Paul? So late? He felt a strange tension but nodded. He waited, perplexed and worried.

Almost at once the younger man entered, somewhat dishevelled and out of breath. Bertrand leaned forward. 'Are you all right?'

Taking a deep breath, Paul sat down, wove the fingers of both hands together. 'No. I'm really not, I had to see you.'

'You're always welcome here.'

There was a short silence. Paul could feel the lump in his throat. 'Bertrand – I must ask and you must answer. For the sake of . . . so many things. For the sake of my sanity. You've been like a father to me. *Why*?'

Bertrand smiled. 'Because you touch my heart. Because

349

I once loved your mother. Because you needed help and guidance and . . . what more can I say?'

'You could tell me, once and for all, whether you *are* my father.'

Bertrand could sense prickles on his forearms. His throat had gone dry. He could not look away from the intense, reddened eyes of the young man before him. 'What does Charlotte say?'

'That she doesn't remember. That I should be lucky not to have been born like my brother, of Robert-Achille. But that doesn't tell me who I am. Thirty-seven years of wondering . . . I need to know.'

'Why now?'

'I've wanted to know before. Nobody ever graced me with the truth. But I have to know now. Because I've seen Jamie and Cassandra.'

The virulence and passion startled Bertrand. 'Jamie? Cassandra? What do you mean?'

'I didn't think I loved Jamie. But Cassandra – I know I love her. And so I need to know who I am, for her sake too. Please, Bertrand – tell me. Tell us both.'

All at once Bertrand seemed to wither. 'Paul,' he said softly, 'there is no way to be sure. Those were heady years – the early nineties. Charlotte was the most enchanting woman in Paris. Her husband hardly noticed her. She had her own problems. A woman like that – full of lust and vanity – needed the adulation of men who could appreciate her. I was one of them. Another was Bertie – King Edward the Seventh, when he was Prince of Wales. I know that she was seeing us at the same time. Then there was an English lord – I can't even recall his name. She was ours for the nights we had her, and we never questioned her further. That, my friend, was our code of honour during *La Belle Epoque*. A child was conceived. The English Lord was sickly and blond. You were born sturdy, ruddy. You were obviously not his child. But as for Bertie and me – nobody

350

really knows. You don't look like Charlotte. For many years, while you were at the Lycée Condorcet, she pretended that you had royal lineage in you. She relished that story and probably believed it. But then – as you grew older, she became more pensive. She convinced herself that *our* love had been *the* love of her life, that the others had been meaningless flings. That no one but I could have been your father.'

'Do you believe it?'

'I suppose I want to believe it. You've wasted everything that's been handed to you. Still, you know that I love you. I've never made the mistake of marrying, so I don't know how a father is supposed to feel. But I feel strong ties to you. I hope you are my son, although it's too late to claim you. At the time I wished to do so. Charlotte was still married. Her husband took you to be his son, and that seemed best for both you and her.'

'I want to recognize Cassie. She'll fall in line to the Varenne title. Won't she?'

'Recognize Cassie?'

Paul looked away. 'Yes. She's all the good, the grace, that Jamie and I were never able to put out together except in that one being. You should see her – '

'I should?'

'If you're her grandfather, see her! She's marvellous. Bertrand – my life – it's been a ruin, you know that. I want Cassandra to be a *grande dame*. But I have nothing to offer her.'

'Jamie has allowed you to visit Cassie? Lesley always said she was vehemently opposed to it. I couldn't blame her, really. What made her change her mind?'

'She didn't. I . . . went to Louveciennes. On an impulse. I saw Cassandra.'

Shock registered on Bertrand's features. He said: 'But that's cruel! The child doesn't know who you are! Jamie must be terribly upset! She defied society to give birth to that child. That little girl is her whole life. How dare you do that now?'

351

Paul blinked back his amazement: 'I thought you'd understand.'

'When you were small, I stood on the sidelines, waiting. I entered your life slowly, step by step. We became friends when you were twenty, a young adult. You learned to trust me. I never defied your mother's wishes.'

'Cassie belongs to me as much as to Jamie.'

'Not in a court of law. You never recognized the baby, nor gave her your name. In a court of law, your rights would be nil. And for Cassie's sake, Alex would fight the toughest legal battle of his existence. He wastes no love on you, and nor does Lesley.'

Paul's face now took on an ugly, tight expression. 'How loyal of them. My own family.' He stood up, suddenly shaky. 'Bertrand, try to understand,' he pleaded. 'I need to be a part of Cassandra's life.'

The old man looked at him with some disdain. 'One pays for one's sins,' he declared. 'Illegitimacy hurts the child, but also the father. Learn to pay as I did for the carelessness of your youth. Nothing worthwhile comes easily. Let Jamie learn to respect you first. Then reapproach the child, but only with her mother's approval. Don't destroy what Jamie has built.'

'Don't ask me to destroy myself. Cassie is all I've ever had of good in the world.'

'Then make more good! Make her proud of you. Claim her only when you deserve her.'

'All these years I hoped you were my father. But parenthood isn't built on logic – it's built on emotions you don't seem to have, for me, or for Cassandra.'

'My dear boy, you're a damn fool,' the old man replied. 'A lazy, stupid fool.'

The two men stared at each other, and then, rapidly, head down, Paul walked out of the room. Bertrand watched after him, shaking his head. The pain. Exhausted, Bertrand put his head in his hands.

Chapter Eighteen

Alexandre's offices stood on the lovely rue Pierre Premier de Serbie, to the west of the Champs Elysées, in the quiet area of the Eighth *Arrondissement*. Tall, almost bare plane trees rose to the tops of the building, drawing intricate shadowed patterns across the thick Persian carpet in his private office. An enormous mahogany desk stood in front of the large window, and he sat behind it in his shirtsleeves, the cuffs removed along with the collar, and the fine fabric stained with perspiration. There was a light tap on the door, and his secretary peeked in shyly.

'Does Monsieur le Marquis need me to stay late tonight?' she asked.

He looked up, distracted. She was in her early twenties, a pretty girl. He'd never bothered to give her demure presence a second glance. He did so now, thinking absently that those with whom one worked most intimately, year in and year out, were often taken for granted. He wasn't even sure he remembered her first name. He asked her suddenly: 'Tell me, Mademoiselle Prandot, you're called ... Michelle?'

'Micheline, Monsieur.' She was looking at him with surprise. The question from such a reserved, courteous, formal boss – a question out of the clear blue sky – startled her. He was amused. He liked her because of her quiet, disciplined, unobtrusive manner, which went perfectly with the office and its reputation as a conservative firm handling only the best of clients in matters of the utmost good taste. Her little suit of dark-blue wool, with matching pumps, was modest. Certainly it was a *prêt à porter*, but one that went with an office that catered to the Baron Georges Brincard,

353

of the Crédit Lyonnais. Now he was thirty-eight . . . middle-aged, and still struggling. Only the struggles had changed. And his face was more lined, at the eyes and around his mouth, and on his forehead. He touched his hair, silver at both temples, and remembered how early his mother's had whitened. She'd been young and already grey, and had let it grow in that way, to startling effect.

The girl in front of him was hardly a beauty. But her oval face was smooth and white, her pale-blue eyes were a pleasant almond shape, and her nose, though too long, was straight and pure. Her lips were thin, and she didn't use rouge. He liked that too. Glorious painted women like Elena scared him. This girl reminded him of someone. It would eventually come to mind, he was sure. She had dark hair pinned into a modest psyche's knot at the nape of her neck.

'Yes, that's right,' he repeated, kindly. 'Micheline. Well, Mademoiselle Micheline, it's been a hard day. You deserve to go home.' He smiled, and she responded. 'Do you live with your parents?' he suddenly asked. He felt filled with new curiosity about this person who had been working near him now for three years, and something made him not wish to be alone. The tiny buds on the large limbs of the tree outside made the shadowed patterns look almost Japanese. Spring was approaching. He'd become engaged in the spring, nine years ago. He'd taken Lesley to bed then, discovered her yielding body. How long it had been since that body had yielded now to him . . . What had happened to put such a distance between them? He knew, of course. He didn't trust her any more. Because she'd changed, and he hadn't understood why. She'd become a materialist and a liar, like his mother.

He was aware that the secretary's presence underscored his reluctance to go home. He realized that he was staying there later and later, to avoid Lesley, or to avoid her *not* being there when he entered the house. The notion filled him with discomfort and unhappiness.

Mademoiselle Prandot said: 'I live with my cousin, Monsieur. She works in an office too.'

Her quiet words jolted him out of his reverie. Young girls didn't live with their families any more. He asked: 'And . . . your mother and father?'

'My father is dead, sir. My mother has a small property in the Touraine.'

'Ah,' he commented. 'So that's why you don't live with her. And it also explains your good accent. You do excellent work, Mademoiselle. Have I ever thought to compliment you on it before?'

She blushed. 'Well, sir, I know. You never reprimand me.'

'That isn't the point. One gets reprimanded for errors and sloppiness. But your work is exceptionally well done. Do you enjoy working in this office?'

'Why, sir, yes. I mean . . . it's a great honour. I'm a simple girl, from the provinces. I never dreamed I'd be lucky enough to be hired by an ex-deputy.'

He tightened his jaw with a grimace. 'Ex-deputy.' Has-been. 'I shall be changing that soon,' he said brightly. 'I think this time, when the Legislative Elections take place in April, that I'll regain my seat.'

'I think so too. Monsieur has been trying so hard – '

He asked: 'How did you know?'

'Because of the activity here. And all the talk. From the clients, and the girls in the office.'

'And tell me . . . do they seem to think I'm going to win?'

She looked at him fully, and he saw himself reflected in those pale-blue eyes, a handsome, tense man nearing forty, a man eager to hear the slightest word of encouragement even from his secretary. He was instantly shamed by this vision. He wished he could retract his question, but she was already responding, her face coming beautifully alive. 'Yes, everyone thinks so! Do you doubt it, sir?'

He shrugged, trying to appear casual. 'Everyone has doubts in life.'

'You're *bound* to win!' she cried suddenly.

He smiled. 'And why is that?'

'Because you're the best man running. And so you deserve to win.'

He was oddly touched. 'My dear Mademoiselle – Micheline, may I? – if the world were made to turn according to what people "deserved", there would be no wars, no crime, no poverty. You would be driving my Bugatti, and others I know who are now driving around in Rolls-Royces would be walking the streets. You are naïve, but that's a quality. Don't change it.'

'Thank you, sir.' She was looking at the carpet, confused by so much unexpected attention.

'The world, and human beings, will change you soon enough.' He rose, rolled down his sleeves, reached for his cuffs. She was suddenly at his side, handing them to him. He said, eyes level with hers: 'Thank you.'

She remained glued in place, her oval face wide open. And then it came to him: She reminded him of Yvonne, before the war. Yvonne, his Lost Illusion. But Yvonne had not been so naïve nor as kindhearted as this girl. She'd been tough, and sophisticated, beneath her appearance of demureness and simplicity. He found himself staring at the girl to the point where again she dropped her eyes from embarrassment. He touched the top of her hand on his desk and murmured: 'I'm sorry, Mademoiselle. I was just thinking you reminded me of someone I once knew.'

'Oh.'

'My first wife.'

'Monsieur le Marquis was married before?'

'For the length of an afternoon. It's best forgotten. I'm glad most people have forgotten it too.'

They were both ill at ease from his revelation. Alexandre cleared his throat, then realized that his hand still lay on Micheline's. She had made no move to retrieve her own, nor he to remove his. He stared at their hands and then looked at her. It was a moment filled with stillness. Finally she said: 'I'm sorry that I've caused you painful memories.'

'Oh, no,' he demurred. 'The memory was only of the outer person, which was lovely. Lovely, I assure you.' He said again: 'Lovely.' Then, plunging in and not knowing why, his heart suddenly beginning to race: 'You're a lovely girl, Micheline Prandot. May I take you to dinner?'

'Oh, Monsieur . . .'

Then he removed his hand, but to touch her chin, very lightly. A gentle soul. He cupped the soft chin in his hand and bent over the desk to brush his lips against hers. She responded. He kissed her. When he moved back she wasn't looking at him any more, but her cheeks were red. 'Let's go to dinner,' he said abruptly, fastening his cuff.

She didn't reply, but he knew that she had been expecting this, that she was happy. He hadn't made somebody happy for a long, long time. Tonight, with spring approaching, he didn't feel like going home. He felt like making somebody happy and basking in the joy of her happiness. Perhaps, he thought, it was his Last Illusion. To prove he wasn't really a has-been, not really middle-aged, and not just another disillusioned husband.

He was simply a man.

It was the first time that this had happened, and Lesley felt distinctly uneasy. She reread the note that the maid had left on her breakfast tray, from Alex: 'Please see me in my bedroom before you go out.' Such a succinct message. Years ago he would have come to *her*, and there would have been love in his eyes, tenderness in his tone of voice. She buttoned her Japanese kimono and slipped into satin houseshoes. Passing her dressing-table, she turned and seized the packet of cigarettes and her small gold lighter. The palms of her hands were moist.

She paused on the threshold of his bedroom. The massive

357

four-poster was still unmade, and he was sitting on the edge, pulling on his socks. He heard her and turned his head. His face seemed tired. 'Good morning, Les.'

'Good morning, darling.' Wary politeness as each tested the waters.

'Did you sleep well?'

She wondered what this was leading to, and also how she looked. Although tired, he appeared calmer than he had for a long time. The lines around his mouth seemed softer. She thought, on the other hand, that she was thinner, more nervous, more brittle. 'I never sleep well,' she answered, lighting a cigarette. Her fingers were trembling.

'And why is that?'

'Why ask questions?' She inhaled smoke, walked around the room, picked up a photograph of Cassandra Stewart, abruptly laid it back down on his dresser. He had a photograph of Cassie in his room. The fact hit her with something like jealousy. His niece. He must love her deeply. There were so many hidden aspects to Alex's feelings that she no longer could guess at – or gauge their intensity. He was lacing his shoes, standing up, avoiding her eyes as he fastened on his stiff collar.

'Look, Lesley,' he said, selecting a tie-pin from his jewellery box. 'The elections are seven weeks away. I can't handle our personal problems as well as the office problems and the elections all at once. I've honestly stopped caring *why* you're buying clothes every two days, or who's going to provide us with yet another antique we don't need for the living room. I simply can't afford to pay any more of the bills. *We* can't afford it. Your father speaks about people spending and spending, buying on margins, in the United States . . . and I don't like it. We must take care of our money. You're my wife, but I'm not going to allow your frivolity to ruin us.'

Her lips parted, and she could feel the stillness in the room. He turned round, looked at her. She could read

358

nothing behind the cool grey of his eyes – and this scared her. The lack of emotion. She said hoarsely: 'But Alex – '

'Darling, it just can't continue. You realize I'm right.'

His eyes took on a deeper, more pensive expression. He sighed. 'Lesley,' he murmured, 'there are so many ways a wife can tell her husband that she loves him. I haven't felt your telling me for years. We drift in and out of the same house and speak courteously to each other like well-mannered puppets. I wish I'd never married rather than have married like this, for display purposes. Alexandre and Lesley de Varenne, the perfect couple. I was deeply hurt when I first felt the rift. But now I'm numbed. So don't talk to me about the way I treat you, about the way I look at you. You never bother to look me in the face yourself.'

She sat down, stunned. The cigarette had burned down to a stub in her fingers. She ground it out. 'Come on,' he said again. 'You never loved me. From the beginning you resisted me. You didn't want me. I don't know what the story is, or why you really married me. But that isn't loving a man. Where are the children you brought to me?'

'Love between a man and a woman isn't measured by children,' she countered, stumbling over her words. She felt as if someone had hit her in the stomach. 'If so, then think how well suited your brother was to Jamie!'

'He was one hell of a lot better suited to her than to Elena.'

'So just because a woman gets pregnant, that makes their union workable?'

He lifted his shoulders one fraction of an inch, dropped them. 'I only meant that when a man wants as desperately to be a father as I did, and his wife has no physiological reason not to bear a child, the only reason she would refuse is if she weren't certain of her love for the man – of the permanence of the home.'

'Is there somebody else, Alex?'

She'd asked it mechanically. She'd known he'd give her

359

an outraged denial. When he didn't, it startled her, hit her anew. He was slipping on a gold watch and then he regarded her warily. Again, the basilisk eyes, unreadable – like agates. 'Lesley,' he stated calmly. 'You're the one who did the odd things. The one who didn't want to have a baby. Who runs off in a thousand directions, spending money that isn't explained in the bills I receive. I should ask *you*: Is there another man?'

He had the upper hand. It wasn't fair. She thought: I've done nothing wrong, except that I didn't tell him about Justin. But that was my private life before I ever met him. He has a mistress. Alexandre, who can live without sex for long periods of time, has a mistress! Who could it be? Does it matter?

'Do you love her?' she asked in a low voice.

'Who?'

'The girl.'

'Come on, Lesley.' Not giving an inch. Always the smooth diplomat.

'Be honest. I need to know.'

'I needed to understand the falsified bills too. Will you explain them right now? That last one from Doucet, for the fur hat I've never seen?'

She tried to find another cigarette, and, deftly, he reached for the packet and extracted one for her. He took the small gold lighter and lit it. Then, coolly, he handed it back to her. 'Would you like an Armagnac?'

'Yes.' Neither made any comment on the fact that it was nine in the morning. He went to a small cabinet made of chiselled rosewood, and opened the door. He took out a cut-crystal decanter and a small fluted glass. He poured out golden-brown liquid and held out his hand. Her fingers took the glass away from him, her lips drained the liqueur.

'Well?' he said. 'Are you going to explain?'

She was past tears. Elena and Paul had lived inside her head for three years, like a cancer, eating away at everything that had allowed her to think and feel as a human being. She spoke with a halting softness, an ethereal quality to her words. 'Alex, I can't explain. It isn't another man. It isn't anything I've done during our marriage. But there's no way I could make you understand.'

'No way?'

She shook her head.

'If you don't trust me enough to tell me the truth, if you must continue this charade – then so be it. I won't ask again. There are areas in each of our lives that are better left unspoken. I'd thought love was the supreme unveiler. But I was wrong. Each of us is born alone, and as we go through life, we can't share every step of our progress with another person. So keep your secret, Lesley. But know this much: I can't finance you through this little game, whatever it may involve. You're on your own now.'

'What does that mean? I have nothing "on my own". Every penny is under your control.'

'Then take it from there. You've been selling your paintings. I must protect our assets. It's bad enough that Paul can't meet his bills half the time – '

'You're still paying his bills?' Her voice had risen to shrillness.

'Not very often. But if I weren't here to "come through" once in a while on some gambling debt or other, he'd have become an embarrassment. That would hardly help our reputation, would it? I don't see how he and Elena live. She's just about stopped working, and he doesn't seem to be helping Bertrand much these days.'

'You shouldn't pay!' she cried. Her voice shook.

'Tell me about it,' he commented dryly. He ran a comb through his hair, checked himself for final effect in the mirror. 'My entire family bleeds me dry. Nobody works. Nobody cares. But everybody begs for financial assistance.'

'I'm sorry, Alex.'

'Sorry doesn't seem to be enough.'

361

'What is it you expect of me?'

He looked at her, and there was a set to his jaw that made her nervous. 'Nothing any more,' he replied.

She wanted to cry but couldn't. She wanted to will herself out of the room, but her knees wouldn't work. She could only stare at him as he moved with quiet grace, getting ready to leave for the office. So cold. She tried to speak but didn't have anything to say. 'Will you be home for supper?' she asked finally. She was proud of the control in her voice, of the casual, wife-to-husband question. As if the previous scene hadn't even taken place.

'I might work late,' he replied, equally casually. She thought: There *is* another woman. And the fact registered on her dulled consciousness as just another bruise on her battered emotions. It was almost laughable. Alexandre, the image of the faithful husband, taking a mistress because his wife had lied to him in order to protect him from learning a painful truth.

No, she thought, it's not that. I'm protecting myself. A mistress is one thing. Being abandoned is another. And he'd leave in a minute. She couldn't bear to think of being left, as she'd been left by Justin years ago. That wrenching pain had maimed her deep inside, left her afraid to be alone. Better this flawed marriage than total bereavement. And she loved Alex. She loved the honour of the man, his basic dignity. She'd loved him when they'd married, though she hadn't then understood that their union transcended the quicksilver lust that had been the basis of her relationship with Justin Reeve. If only she had known how to express her love, how to hold Alex to her. But she'd been afraid to give in to her emotions. The last time she had let herself be controlled by her feelings, she had become pregnant. She wanted to prevent this from ever happening again. Now there was also the terrible, ever present fear of being blackmailed. The tension and deception had created a wall between Lesley and her husband. They barely communicated at all. At the top of the staircase she clung to the wrought-iron rail and looked down as he moved away from her. Despair filled her. She leaned over the stairs and cried, suddenly, just as she saw him emerging into the hall. 'Alexandre!'

He wheeled about, turning his head upward to look at her. She thought: He is a beautiful man; I have never fully appreciated him. 'Yes?' he called up to her. She thought the taut lines of his face were relaxing into hesitant expectation. But perhaps she was only hoping that they were.

She wanted to say: Stay, I need you. We'll talk if you wish. We'll do whatever you feel might make things better. But his eyes were too far away for her to really decipher. She became afraid, afraid of confrontation, afraid of telling him the truth. It would have to come out, in any case. She had run out of steam, like an old car out of petrol on a deserted road. Paul and Elena would have to tell him, because he'd stopped their funds now by cancelling her access to extra money. She thought: All right, soon enough he'll throw me out. Just now I still am married to him. And so she shook her head and said, barely loudly enough for him to hear on the ground floor:

'Have a good day, Alex.'

When he had disappeared from view, she leaned back against the railing. The world seemed to have stopped. Nearly ten years of marriage. Her face felt paralysed, her stomach twisted. What's been my life? she asked herself. Paintings that sell for half of nothing to a few kind friends? I could have been a great set designer, but *they* wouldn't grant me the peace of mind. No one can create in a panic! I could have been a good wife, but the memories of what happened before were just too much of a burden. She'd had the misfortune to make a mistake – and then to have lied about it.

* * *

363

Elena Egorova watched him sleep and thought that age, for women, was implacable. Thirty-eight. He was thirty-seven, but in sleep his face was unlined, the mouth softened into a half smile, no tension lines around the eyelids as delicate as a bird's wings. An overwhelming sensation of need came over her. He was a child, with no sense of tomorrow, with no purpose in life. She'd loved that about him. She was so driven that his simple desire for comfort, for more time in which to live out his passions, had seemed a blissful counterpoint. Now she wondered. He'd always been the man of the moment. But in reality, the past, *his* past, had been haunting him. He'd felt such an urgency about understanding who he was, where he came from, where he was going, that in his quest he had destroyed their equilibrium.

It was Jamie Stewart's fault. He'd gone there and seen the child and found that she looked like him. He wanted the child now. But the child was also *her*. The child had her eyes, and Paul had always talked about Jamie's wild, blue eyes. Like a clear sea. Elena hated the child.

He stirred, moving the satin sheets, and sat up, brushing the hair from his eyes. She went to him, naked, her large breasts pressing against his arm to bring him to full consciousness. Consciousness that she willed to be of her, of his need for her.

There were so many needs inside her: the need for him, for his body; the need to feel quenched of revenge on Lesley, who had done to her what all her friends had done after her father's arrest – dropped her. No one was going to dismiss Egorova again. There was also the need to keep Paul here – away from Jamie and Cassandra. Without money, how could she accomplish this? She looked into his waking eyes and wondered whether to tell him about Lesley's note. Then she decided not to. Instead she slipped under the sheet beside him and touched the tips of his nipples with her fingers. 'Paul,' she murmured. 'Paul.' She bridged all gaps between them and pressed against him, wanting him.

While he was inside her it occurred to her that things weren't going quite right: He'd moved too quickly. She tried to make him hold back, but it was almost as if he weren't aware of her. Perhaps he hadn't awakened properly. She felt a wave of frustration and whispered: 'Say something, darling. Love me.'

She'd now done something terrible – she'd begged. She could feel the sense of her own mental recoil, yet she held on, tightly. He said, 'Of course I love you, Elena.' But she wanted to cry. Egorova didn't cry. She choked both on her tears and on her insatiable desire for more of Paul.

At length he sat up, plumping the pillow, and she snuggled into the crook of his arm. 'What's on the agenda for tonight?' he asked.

'Nothing. Too many champagne dinners make us society cats, and I wanted to save you for me alone.'

He didn't answer, and she felt the absence of his comment as a personal rejection. 'Foie gras, with caviar, to begin with. Then roast quails in juniper sauce with potatoes *à la Dauphinoise* and baby peas, and an endive salad with watercress. And for dessert, *bombe glacée*. You can choose the wines.'

He smiled. 'A beautiful menu, Elena.'

She'd wanted him to say: I'd rather have *you*. She asked, teasing the hairs on his stomach: 'And me? Before or after?'

'Whenever you'd like.' He smiled at her. I want that smile, indelible, for ever.

'Bertrand,' he said, 'doesn't understand. Something has changed between us. It's as if years of a tenuous, unspoken bond had suddenly been shattered by the question, asked and unanswered. He doesn't understand about Cassandra.'

'What's there to understand? He doesn't want you chasing rainbows. I don't want you to be hurt either. Jamie holds all the cards and you can't keep bashing your head against the wall. It's futile!'

'You can't be sure of that,' he answered. 'Elena: She's the

365

only child I have! Suddenly I've been made aware that all my existence has been spent in waste – total, utter waste. I feel a failure. No wonder Jamie doesn't want Cassandra to know me.'

'And I? Would I have you if I considered you a failure?'

'Oh, Elena . . . I don't know. I can't think.'

'I thought we were happy, until you decided to go hunting and made that senseless trip to Louveciennes.' She turned away from him, her bitterness on the verge of exploding. 'Damn it! Why, Paul? You didn't want her to have that child! For three years you ignored her existence!'

'For three years I spent day and night with you, thinking this was Life. I love you, Lenya. But my life isn't just you. I ran round wearing blinkers in order to pretend I had no daughter. I can't do that any more. I want her to be recognized as a Varenne.'

'Supposing we had a child?'

'Lenya – a child of ours still wouldn't erase Cassandra. She's my daughter.'

Elena stood up, so that he would not see the tension in her white face. She wanted to hurt him for having hurt her. But if she hurt him – then what? If she turned round and slapped him on both cheeks, raised her knee to his groin – then what? She'd be showing her hand. That she needed him. So she said coolly: 'We received some news today, while you were sleeping. It seems that Alexandre has caught up with Lesley and isn't going to give her any more money. She's desperate. But I think if we let her stew until the elections, she'll be near breaking point, and we'll be able to use her in some new fashion we haven't thought up yet. It will give us time, and her worry. Don't you agree?'

'And in the meantime?'

'We still have enough from the last cheque to last those few weeks.'

'If she cracks completely, she might tell him herself. And then where would we be?'

'Lesley will never tell. At heart, she'll be praying and hoping we won't carry out our promise to blackmail her. She'll be waiting – but she won't tell. Not with the elections around the corner in April.'

'How you think quickly on your feet,' he said with admiration.

She turned to him, triumphant, and waited for him to call her back to bed. But instead he sighed and murmured: 'When does it all end? When can we all have peace?'

'*You*, Paul, want *peace*?'

'I'm thirty-seven. I'm useless. I possess no talents. Perhaps one day I'll wake up in the morning and want to feel one tiny bit of self-respect. Don't you ever wish for an end to the struggle? For something you could be proud of?'

'You're beginning to bore me, darling. Remember which brother you are before you turn completely moral on me.'

He stood up, and she saw the elongated, firm chest, the long, strong legs. He stretched. 'Elena, it isn't a question of morality or immorality. Bertrand said I'd have to make Cassandra proud of me. How the hell do you propose I do that? By telling her I've been blackmailing her godmother and my own brother in the process? By explaining that I can't support myself?'

'The child is three. You won't have any explaining to do for years.'

'But to Jamie I will. She'll be watching my every move to make sure no "person of my ill-repute" ever again crosses paths with her daughter. How do I win on that one?'

'Perhaps,' she remarked softly, 'you *don't*. You tell yourself Cassandra's all right, that she doesn't really need you. Sooner or later Jamie will marry. And you can have other children if you still feel this urge. Don't become obsessed, Paul. It'll ruin your life.'

He said, so harshly that his tone jolted her: 'Is obsession ruining yours, Lenya? Years and years of not forgiving the world for what it did to you when you were eighteen? Years

367

of unfocused vengefulness that have now become focused on Lesley?'

She couldn't reply. He moved to the window, looked out at the small back garden surrounded by stone. Then he turned round. 'I'm sorry,' he whispered.

She was standing naked by the bed, her chin slack, her eyes unreadable. He'd always been able to read the beauty in Jamie's eyes. Paul felt his own sense of alienation right there in that room, his sense of not knowing where he belonged. Was Elena really saving him? And from what? From poverty. From working for Bertrand.

From making a connection with his daughter.

'You hate Lesley too,' Elena was saying.

'She's too insignificant to hate. I hated my brother. But Bertrand says that Alexandre has made Cassandra his heiress. I don't hate Alex. We're just not the same.'

'But don't you see that we need the money?'

'Yes. That much I see. Still, Elena, I didn't enjoy having to blackmail Lesley. You'd have enjoyed it. To me it was like stepping on a wounded bird.'

'And you think I obtain my pleasure from crushing defenceless people?'

'I have no idea. I see Les as a source of money, but you also see her as a means to your revenge. I don't care, Lenya. I don't care what you do to Lesley. She's unimportant to me. But if Cassie learns of this whole thing one day, do you think for an instant that her mother would let her forgive me?'

Elena uttered a strangled, animal cry, a cry of such passion and helpless rage that it frightened him. Her face was twisted into a grimace that was ugly. He felt the force of it and his stomach twisted. He said, trying for gentleness: 'Lenya . . .'

She made a move, like a jungle panther, and leaped at him. She slapped his cheek, then slapped the other cheek. There were tears, odd, feral tears, on the edge of her lashes.

Her face was frightening. Suddenly they were entwined on the carpet and she covered his mouth with hers, plunging her tongue deep into his throat. She bit his neck. She found his penis and rammed it inside her, and rode him, like a stallion, her eyes closed and her hair swinging in rhythm. Nothing had been left to him, and he felt that this must be rape.

When it was all over, she collapsed against his chest, breathing in uneven gulps. He touched her hair, tried to hold her. She was trembling in every limb. 'This is what you want,' she then said, with a fierceness that came at him like a cold, harsh wind.

But he wondered, as he carried her to their bed, whether he had not changed a little. Jamie would never have assaulted him this way. Jamie had bored him. But too much of Elena was perhaps not enough of something else . . .

What, or who, did he love? He loved himself. He thought he loved Elena. He loved Cassandra. Covering his mistress with the sheet and blanket, he felt a new wave of hopelessness. He was caught not knowing where he wanted to be, by choices he had made three, four years before. He inched closer to Elena, to her warmth, and for the first time it repelled him. She was too strong, too definite, too unbridled. His neck hurt from the bites and his penis felt sore. She made a moaning noise and groped for his hand, and he let her take it, mutely.

She watched the gardeners tidying the flowerbeds beyond the porch, her long, cool hand poised on the soft silk curtain that framed the bay window. Numbly, she gazed down at the coral gloss of her nails, now no longer chewed and ragged. The neat enamel reflected back all her outward perfection, the same perfection that mocked her in the three panels of her boudoir mirror. She was thirty years old, and Dolly Wilde had said of her the previous night that she

369

seemed the flapper personified: modern, fluid, boyish. Dolly liked boyish women because she was a Lesbian. But what she really would have said, had her proclivities been different, was 'sexless'. The erect back, the small bone structure, the smoothness of her pallid skin. There was always a perfect dress to hide the jutting shoulder blades and the flat, empty breasts: a dress of pure silk, or of the new synthetic jerseys made famous by Chanel, a dress with raglan sleeves that were tight around the wrists, then flowed in a single line to the waist and in another to the neckline. Dresses like the one she was wearing today, in a soft pastel blend, depicting abstract globes of romantic purity. A package well wrapped but containing used goods.

He came up behind her and she felt him move beside her, his shadow filling the space next to her. 'I was writing to your father,' he said. 'About the stock market. I've pulled all your funds out of stocks for the moment. I think he should do the same. The European market hangs in such precarious balance that the American one, be it later, can't help but eventually be affected by our world's economic fluctuations. It's politics that make economies change: faith in governments, wars, peace. After our war there was a resurgence of faith in the world, in a new society – and so everybody celebrated by spending. Now . . . I foresee a darker future.'

She turned a little to look at him. Such a long speech for him, her husband who did not trust her. She'd once accused him of patronizing her about politics, of wanting her to be a carbon copy of himself and his beliefs. Now the thought filtered through the dreadful numbness to the core of her. He was protecting her assets, which was, of course, also protecting his own; but he was, in addition, sharing his advice with her father. She was touched. 'Are things so bad?' she asked faintly.

'I'm not sure. I could be wrong. But buying on margins has always seemed to me to be an unsafe risk. I thought I

370

should pass on my ideas to Ned so that, when he makes up his own mind, he can think about them too.'

'But my father's taken risks all his life. He lives that way. His profession is risk-orientated.'

'Not necessarily. He doesn't take on new business unless he believes the client will be successful. Other advertising firms are notorious for gambling. But your father is cautious. Once he is committed to a client, yes, he will push as hard and as flamboyantly as he can to produce the most sensational campaign. But that comes later.'

She thought: I'd never seen Daddy as 'cautious'. I suppose, all these years, I saw Mother as holding him back, the driver pulling the reins. Alex, however, had never seen him this way. He visualized her father as a man not unlike himself – willing to take some educated risks and only then plunging in. She looked more fully at her husband. Yes: He, whom she'd always categorized as afraid of risks, wouldn't have entered the political arena, especially now, after one loss, unless there was a certain daring, a certain breaking of conventional fears, in his own making.

'Why are you staring at me?' he asked her. 'It's as if you were seeing a stranger.'

'We're all composed of onion layers,' she whispered, looking quickly away. 'Every now and then one of our layers peels off and there's a new one to examine. In that sense we're all strangers, even to ourselves, at the various stages of our lives.'

She saw his grey eyes fasten on her pensively. He was someone to be valued. She'd misunderstood who he was, fundamentally, from the beginning. He wasn't, after all, only a figure etched in black and white. And yet . . .

She felt she was always waiting. Waiting for one of *them* to send a letter to him, revealing all the sordid events of 1916. Waiting with her heart in her throat every time the mail came. Supposing the letter came to the office? Supposing he lost the election because of this? Learning about what she had done, feeling so distressed that he gave up . . . Or they might come in person. She refused to go out, spending her days in the salon, waiting for the doorbell to ring when he was at home, so that she would be the first one to reach Paul, or Elena, and stop them before they told him. Hanging on one more day.

She couldn't eat, couldn't sleep. Abruptly she needed a glass of something strong and left the window, going to the sideboard. He watched her pouring whisky into a tall glass, without ice. He made no comments, but she saw him watching her. Almost defiantly – defying his silent reproach, and defying those two who sought to ruin her – she swallowed once, twice. She liked the strong taste.

'Thank you,' she said, her voice catching, 'for writing to my father.'

'It's only natural.'

'You're a good man, Alex.'

Fumbling with the cord of the curtain, he murmured, his own voice unreadable: 'But "good men" are not often the ones that are loved.'

She hesitated, her lips parted, wanting to say: But I do love you. She'd thought he was stiff, pressing her about babies. That he could not understand her. In reality, had she ever tried to understand him? Once, she thought, feeling the ache as if it had happened anew, I thought that love was magic. Perhaps love is having a man who gives advice to one's father, who stays even though I won't do what he wants. She felt a new ache, an ache to touch Alex, to bridge their gap. 'Alex,' she began, touching his arm.

He looked at her. She stammered: 'Alex. Kiss me?' So many months of absolute emptiness and distrust. And she knew, the way one always did after ten years together, that he had someone else. It had come as a natural consequence to the distance between them. She could hardly blame him, given her part in causing their rift.

He took her whisky glass and set it aside, and put his

372

hands around the delicate oval of her face. She couldn't stand the intensity of his eyes on hers – the probing. He wanted her eyes to tell him why she'd lied. 'Do you still love me?' she asked feebly.

He ran a finger down her nose, and she felt his pain, caused by the rejection she had made him endure: rejections of truth, rejections of a family, rejections of sharing. 'I'm not sure, Lesley,' he answered softly.

'Do you love another woman?'

'I'll never love anyone as I loved you.'

Past tense. She'd ruined everything, with her dreams of English abbeys and moonlit seductions that had led to Justin. She hadn't seen reality. She cried for her youth, for the aborted pregnancy, for what *in her dreams* might have been. She'd confused book romance with real life and a real man.

And now he spoke to her in the past tense. Letting her understand that she had wasted the greatest love he'd ever feel for a woman. In the end, women were the stupid ones. They went after a rainbow even while happiness beckoned. He dropped his hands, gently. She thought: Anyway, what good would it do for me to make it right between us . . . even if it weren't too late? How many days would we be happy before the news came to destroy us?

She picked up her glass and drank. It was like counting moments before one's execution: One wasn't dead . . . yet. But outside the world kept up its careless pace.

373

Chapter Nineteen

Elena sat at a table at Fouquet's, sipping an *express*, the black pillbox hat planted firmly on a tight coil of black hair, the veil pulled down to the tip of her nose. Thus she could observe without being observed. It was the millinery of flappers, and she had spent a lifetime shunning hats, except for the generous, broad-brimmed extravaganzas of the *Belle Epoque* that she had worn to flaunt her disrespect for the dictates of *couturiers*. But now she wondered whether women had adopted this kind of demure apparel, with a veil, in order to hide their real selves. It was the hat of sad women who hid their eyes and of jealous women who looked for their men without wanting to be found out.

'Another, Madame?' She nodded to the young waiter and thought of anonymity. She had been defying it, creating immortal images of herself through her clothes, through her friendships, through the brushstrokes that had captured her. But if she didn't want to pose any more, it wasn't, as she'd told Paul, because she found the process humiliating. She'd felt less used, less of an object in a painter's den than she had in the Orient – less used, perhaps, than she would have been if she'd married a young count in St Petersburg before the *débâcle*. It was her beauty that had inspired these artists. Lesley, on the other hand, was being used by Alexandre. He used her money, he used her grandfather's peerage, he used her as a hostess. No, she hadn't felt abused. She was afraid of ageing. She'd simply grown worried that her voluptuous breasts had started a slow process of loss of tone in the ligaments, and that her hips had rounded, her eyes had creased. An old model wasn't usable. She'd wanted to stop before Kisling told Boldini that Egorova was finished – old.

The women who were ageless suffered just as much as those who looked like young elves, like Lesley, when thirty-five was viewed from the upward climb of the peak of life. Ageless women 'matured'. They 'ripened'. But nevertheless, the euphemisms didn't hide the truth. The veil did. That morning she felt old. Thirty-eight and thirsty, thirty-eight and frantic, and sad. I'll leave him before he thinks of me as a tragic old mistress, the way he thought of Martine.

His obsession with the child at first amused her. Now she had to admit that she felt a gnawing concern. He'd never wanted to procreate, so what sense was there in the child's mystique? Supposing he'd asked her, Elena, to bear him a child? Supposing he'd asked her to marry him? Comtesse Paul de Varenne. Not so bad. But he'd never broached either subject. She hadn't had a chance to decide whether her lack of maternal instinct might be overcome for him, to please him. Jamie had had a child to please herself, risking the loss of him. She'd thought Jamie pathetic. Yet Jamie, in her white mansion with its clean, Doric columns, was happy. She wasn't married, but she had lovers now and then. She'd survived Paul. She'd had a relationship with Pavel Tchelitchew, the painter. She'd been, on and off, sleeping with that strange Hilaire Hiller, the dark-clad, ugly American painter who owned the Jockey Club. She had odd tastes to have been attracted to him, but he was amusing, he was soulful, he was tragic: perfect material for a writer who once had lived the cloistered existence of middle-class Cincinnati. Elena had to admire her for having reached freedom to live as she pleased. She defied society without having to wear outlandish clothes and without brandishing scathing memories of a grand past. She still wore her skirts too long and her hair carelessly. But she was *somebody*. And she was only thirty. Young, wide-eyed. With the child *he* wanted, who looked like the better part of both of them.

375

Anguish was feeling you were losing hold on the man you loved – wondering whether you were paranoid for nothing. Being in pain all day, all night, even with him beside you. Having tight ropes on both sides of your spine, because he wasn't thinking of you as he once had. Living together was a bad idea. It allowed men – all men – to take women for granted. Their rare beauty became common. And then they began to notice the small flaws, the creases, the laugh lines. But to give up the communal life? Then she'd be taking a foolish risk that, at thirty-eight, given his proclivities, his enormous sexual need would take him that much more away from her.

He'd forgiven Jamie for having had the child; yet if she, Elena, were to do the same thing, he'd turn away in disgust: Egorova at two years before forty, imitating the innocence of Jamie Lynne at twenty-six. She didn't want a child at all! She wanted Paul, the sexual thrill of him in her bed, his odour on her sheets. Money. If she could find a way to squeeze money – a great deal of it – from that little bitch, Lesley, then if he wanted the child, she would accept their taking her with them. There were ways by which he, a Varenne, might win custody in court against a libertine American unwed mother novelist. If need be he could woo his brother into changing his opinion of them. They could get married and persuade Alex of their great desire to prolong the Varenne dynasty. Alex, she had been told, had someone now. Marie-Laure de Noailles had told her that she'd glimpsed him in a remote tavern in Montmartre with someone sweet and young. That would definitely be his *modus operandi*. Sweet, young, adoring. Not an Egorova, figure of scandal. But in any event, they could, with money, obtain Cassandra for Paul. It was insulting, it made the blood pound against her forehead, to think that this hedonist, this user, this amoral man, had turned soft in the head over a three-and-a-half-year-old child.

The *express* was bitter, and she drank it down, appreciat-

376

ing its acrid taste. Suddenly she saw, scraping a chair to sit at a table ahead of her, a tall, good-looking man with glossy black hair, a thin nose, dark eyes. Odd: Didn't she know him? He turned, feeling her eyes upon him, and she thought: *do* I know him? I can't remember. He had a Van Dyke beard, very trim, very dashing, and a moustache. A Florentine figure of the Renaissance, dressed in the best of Savile Row. Elegant way of sitting.

He smiled, and she felt chilled. Men had spent twenty years smiling at her with desire. This one was merely trying to be polite. Through the veil he had caught her expression of question. And so he stood up, bowed: very British, smooth. 'Madame,' he stated. The voice. Memories. 'I don't believe we've met. Although you think we have?'

'My name is Princess Egorova,' she declared, realizing her voice was strained.

'Ah, I am honoured. Daniel MacDougal, of Scotland. But I am right, aren't I? You're such a lovely woman, I'd have remembered meeting you,' he said.

'Thank you, kind sir, but it was my error. I thought you looked familiar.'

'I'm fairly new in Paris. In Parisian society. I sell art works to a select few.'

'Oh. Then you must know Paul de Varenne, the man I live with. And our friend Bertrand de la Paume.'

'I've met the Chevalier, but not your friend. As I say, I travel a great deal. It takes a while to establish oneself in this city.'

'I know the feeling only too well. I came here ten years ago, after the armistice. But I shall never be Parisian.'

'Russian?'

'Yes.'

'Unmistakably so.'

He was smiling, but she was thinking: My hair is coiled. I'm wearing a demure little black hat and a veil. I'm sitting

377

down. Now is one of the few times I can be sure I don't look Russian. Vaguely dark, yes. Slav? Perhaps. But not 'unmistakably Russian'. He was watching her and she couldn't read his eyes. Like her own, they had a bottomless blackness. Suddenly he stated, with a charming, self-deprecating smile: 'I forgot that I had an appointment. It would have been a pleasure to pursue our acquaintanceship. Some other time, perhaps?'

'Absolutely.'

He pulled a card from a thin wallet of Cordovan leather and handed it to her. Embossed, in black lettering, was his name: Daniel S. MacDougal, and below, in smaller letters: art consultant. So this was what he called himself: a consultant. There was an address on Avenue Montaigne – a business address? She wondered why he didn't know Paul and why he made her uncomfortable. He'd been smooth, poised, eloquent. Yet she knew he was lying. Suddenly she felt a flash of recognition. He was bowing, bringing her gloved fingertips to his lips. Then he was weaving out among the tables, disappearing into the morning throng of Parisians passing by.

Elena Egorova held the demitasse of *express* and felt the world blurring around her. There was only her hand, the whiteness of the cup – and the eyes of the bearded man. She could feel her heart pounding. Staring at the business card, she touched its corners as if discovering that they'd been dipped in gold. She stood up, stunned. And she was young again, and remarkable, and clever.

'Russian?' 'Yes.' '*Unmistakably so.*'

His mistake. He was the fool who would allow her to build her house, the house where Paul would find her once again his miracle worker, his enchantress. He would have to say to her again: Thou hast ravished my heart with one of thine eyes, with one chain of thy neck.

She put down the change for the coffee and left the table. The day smiled at her and so she threw back the veil from her forehead and met it straight on, like a happy woman.

Bertrand de la Paume scrutinized the card, peering at it through his bifocals. Then he looked at Elena with a half smile. 'Yes, I've met the man. Young: mid-thirties? Dark, with a beard? From Edinburgh? He's only recently come to Paris. I can't tell you much about him.'

'But surely, in art circles people have heard of him.'

'Oddly, no. He says he's been travelling. The Orient. Now he's settled on something he enjoys – but more as a dilettante than as a professional. He's bright, he's polite – he'll be good with the ladies of Paris.'

Elena stood up. 'That's most informative. Of course, my reason for asking . . . Paul never mentioned him, but today this MacDougal looked at me as if he knew me. I was bewildered. Since I was at Fouquet's, in the neighbourhood . . . I thought I'd drop in to ask you. It gives me a chance to sit with you for a while. We rarely see you, *cher ami*.'

'Beautiful women are always intrigued when strange men pretend to know them in order to start a conversation.' He was looking at her with the amusement of an older man, and suddenly she felt the weight of her years fall away. To him she was still a young girl. But he hadn't responded to her comment about visiting them. Bertrand, who might or might not be Paul's father. Elena knew that Paul was to blame for the rift between the two men, once so close.

She walked around the office, fingering various precious knicknacks, a vase, some flowers. Admiring the Cézanne on the right wall. When she felt that she had remained long enough to convince him that her questions about MacDougal had been simple curiosity, she bade him good-bye with a kiss on the cheek. He was, she knew, partial to her. Perhaps, she thought wryly, I made a mistake in 1925: I could have married Bertrand and lived a life of quiet luxury.

379

When she returned home, Paul lay stretched out on the sofa, his red silk cravat loose around his neck. 'You look most sedate,' he commented with good humour.

She tossed off the black velvet pillbox hat. 'It's my disguise for the day.' She sat down beside him, loosening the coils until her hair came bouncing down her shoulders. She snuggled next to him, smelling the cologne, the slight animal perspiration that always clung to a man's skin. His hand rose and, with careless ease, touched the silken hair, her cheek. Wandered to her breast where the nipple hardened. She bent over to cover his lips with her own. She felt his tongue, lazy, playful. Her own tongue fought hard against it. But he didn't push her back, didn't muster desire in the way he reacted. It was exactly that: He was kissing her *back*, responding to her initiative.

It had been so different that first time in the hallway of the Opéra, she remembered. Sadness enveloped her and she pulled gently away. Smoothing down her skirt, she said, her voice falsely bright: 'We have a piece of extraordinary news. I have found the crack through which we can get to Lesley.'

His face came alive then, and she knew, as she had suspected would happen, that she had lit a magic fuse – greed. After a few years one had to resort to outside means in order to keep the relationship alive. One had also to possess the financial capacity to feed one's fire. It was an insulting reality, but Paul was not hers as he had once been. He was pawned goods that had to be redeemed.

'I have found an old Ashley Taylor, an old friend from Singapore,' she announced gleefully. 'And we're going to use a perfect stranger to blackmail him: Lesley!'

Paul stared at her, dumbstruck. 'What on earth are you talking about?'

She touched her hair with an air of pride. 'Ashley Taylor is *here*! *I saw him*! And he recognized me too. He pretended not to know me, but then gave himself away. It doesn't matter how, but he knew me. Do you remember what I told you about how I came to Paris? About the della Robbia forgery that fell into my hands? It was the same Ashley Taylor who gave it to me!'

Paul's eyes were interested yet also wary. He interjected: 'But the man did you a favour. Because of him, you had funds to leave that hellhole and come here. Why would you want to pay him back this way?'

She said, insulted, jarred: 'Because he's the only means we have for obtaining money! I don't want to harm this man – he was good to me long ago. But still – he's insignificant in my life, and you're everything. I'm doing it for *you*, Paul.'

He moved uncomfortably on the bed. 'And? How are you going to blackmail him through Lesley? Why *her*?'

'Because he already knows me and has nothing to fear from me. You've got a bad reputation. But she's clean – and a total stranger. He could never do anything to her – whereas he could, to us. She's the Marquise de Varenne: the wife of the deputy. He has nothing on her, but on me – so much! He could hurt me by spreading the truth about the manner in which I earned my living in Singapore. And our friends – society – would drop us at once. Paris is strange, my love. The same people who accept courtesans like Chanel – like *me* – like your mother – in their midst, would never be seen with a call girl. They have an odd sense of values. On the outside, one must look clean. I'm the Princess Egorova, and you're the Count Paul de Varenne. If I pose nude and you provide your acquaintances with *coco*, it's all right – so long as it's done behind closed doors. Do you understand now?'

He nodded, slowly. 'Yes. You're right. I feel sorry for him. Lesley will have to do it. She's the ideal instrument.'

'And so,' Paul said smoothly, finishing off his gin and tonic, 'it's really very simple and uncomplicated. Think of it as helping out society. He's a con artist, Lesley.'

381

She sat, very still, in the winged velvet armchair. In front of her was a member of her own family. Alexandre's brother. And then she saw, in her mind's eye, the young man who had taken her in his arms, her, his brother's fiancée. The young man who had smoothly swindled the family out of thousands and thousands of francs, who had connived to destroy the family domain in Beauce. She remembered the day of their meeting, at Gertrude Stein's: He had liked her and caressed her with his eyes, silken brown eyes, moving over her body like a hand, softly seductive. Then he had taken her best friend to bed and lived with her openly. He had betrayed her friend with another friend – Lesley's only other *real* friend – and had allowed the first one to have a baby that he'd never claimed. And now this new betrayal. He cared about nothing and no one.

'So this wasn't even your own idea?' she asked in a low voice, sarcastic.

He looked down into the ice cubes in his glass, silent.

'You're such a coward, Paul. You can't even think up your own cons. *You're* the con artist personified, but you don't even realize it. You're too stupid.'

He still said nothing. She was afraid to rise, for fear that the contents of her stomach would come up. If she stayed completely motionless, perhaps the nausea would seep away. Then he said: 'It's so easy, Lesley. None of us cares about this man. He takes advantage of rich women. Your friends would bless you if they could find out.'

'Then why don't you do it?'

'Because I'm not the Marquise de Varenne. You're everything he will fear: the wife of a powerful attorney, a rich woman with connections and an unblemished record. And a total stranger. He'll never work out how you discovered his secret. He'll be frightened, and he'll pay.'

'Just as I was frightened, and paid. Only it wasn't enough. Now you expect *me* to become the blackmailer.'

382

'We feel your name and prestige give you a better chance of success . . . You know,' Paul continued, 'Elena always finds out what's important to her.' He spoke almost as if he felt awe. Lesley thought: He doesn't love her any more. The realization was chilling, as chilling as anything that had taken place that evening. She asked: 'Why, Paul? You had everything a man could hope for with Jamie. No one will ever forgive you for leaving her when she was pregnant. She has so many friends. Because she knows how to give, and you can't even receive with a little grace.'

'Nothing we do in the heat of passion can ever be laid to rest. There is always someone who will hold it against us later.' His eyes had become opaque, and she thought: He wants what isn't his. That's the only *real* passion this man has ever felt. He wanted me because I was Alex's. He wanted Elena because everyone else wanted her.

'You, of all people, should understand that,' he continued. She didn't want to look at him; he was so foreign to her, to the emotions she knew, that it was impossible not to examine him as a fluke, a fault, a crack in an otherwise perfectly crafted ceiling. 'You loved: you were going to have a child. Apart from the fear of Alex's learning what you did, don't you ever feel the remotest regret?'

She remembered once, when her sister Emily had been fourteen, that a houseboy had fallen in love with her. He'd followed her up the stairs one afternoon and had abruptly seized her from behind and clasped her in his arms. Emily had been frozen with shock. Their worlds, so totally separate, had been like oil and water. That he had even dared to conceive of their mixing had been beyond her imagination, and so she hadn't been prepared to fend him off. He could have raped her. He could have done anything he wanted, her mind had been so completely numb with surprise. This was what was occurring now. She steadied herself, stood up. She couldn't speak, and so she simply walked out of her own living room, one foot in front of the other. She would think when her mind unfroze. Emily had screamed *afterwards*, long after the cook had grabbed him and he'd been taken away, struggling – fired on the spot.

In her room she sat on the edge of the bed, fingering her quilt. Then she did something she hadn't done in years. She sank to her knees in her silk stockings and thought: I can't pray, I've forgotten how.

Dear God. Help me. Or take away my life. In two weeks Alex would either be elected or defeated, and Paul would pick that moment to crush him by exposing her. The deputy's wife is a whore, a murderer. She killed her own child.

Alex had asked her for a child, had asked her for a real marriage. She'd been cheating him for ten years: one of engagement, nine of marriage. She'd cheated him out of a present, out of a future. If she'd let him go in 1919, he'd have found someone else. He *had* found someone else, at last. She should write him a note, letting him go. You deserve somebody clean, somebody who will give you a son, a beautiful daughter. You deserve a fresh start.

But then she remembered that during her childhood, the nuns had taught her that suicides always went to hell. The Bible said that life was a gift from God, and that taking one's own life was stepping into God's domain, trespassing. God never forgave. No, she didn't want to die. She was afraid of what came after life. She hadn't meant to hurt the baby – it hadn't been a baby to her. She'd been conscious only of her parents, of what they would say and do: her mother's cold eyes, her father's disappointed face, etched in the pain of bewilderment. How could she have done such a thing to them? And then there had been the shame of Justin's lack of caring. She couldn't have gone back to a man who hadn't loved her enough. He'd taken her as lightly as she had shed her clothes to be with him. But she hadn't meant any *harm*. She'd done something joyful, by making love to celebrate being alive. God had

384

already punished her for it. Why, why did she have to keep on suffering?

She felt a sudden wave of pity for the poor stranger whom she would have to confront, because she had no choice. She respected Alexandre, and there was no way in which she would hurt him beyond what she'd already done. He would have been free if it hadn't been for the promises she'd made when she'd accepted his marriage proposal. She'd married him for peace, to escape from the pain of her failed affair with Justin and the lost child. And to escape from the control of her parents. She hadn't loved him. She'd liked him, felt comfortable with him. And he had been good to her. She owed it to him to protect his career.

Dear God, she prayed, forgive me. There's just nothing else I can do. I've run out of energy.

'You don't understand at all,' Elena said impatiently, fastening her dark eyes on his face. 'She won't give in. She's absolutely frightened to death. And she's the one person he would yield to. She is too important for him to ignore her. Because of Alex, her family, her social standing. She's the perfect pawn for us to use.'

He didn't answer. She sat up in bed, the sheet falling away from her large, pear-shaped breasts. 'She won't remember us,' she said. 'She'll be doing it for herself – to save her marriage and her dignity. To think she'd be willing to blackmail a stranger, just to prevent our revealing an act she had no choice but to perform. Whoever he was, the man who seduced her was the criminal – not Lesley.'

'You feel such sympathy for her?' Paul stared at her, shocked. 'But – '

'She's a woman!'

'Then why don't you leave her alone?' he asked, incredulous. Fascinated by her eyes and this new revulsion he felt toward her.

'She's the key to money – Alexandre's and Ashley Taylor's.' Her eyes hardened, her mouth twisted. 'Because she was my friend. She had no right to cut *me* off! How did she *dare* not understand? She too was a woman!'

'But Jamie was her best friend.'

'Jamie was useless to everybody. With me Lesley had a powerful ally.'

'Jamie is a woman also. Don't you feel sorry for *her*?'

'My compassion doesn't stretch that far,' she replied, and her voice was flat like a steel-edged knife, uncompromising. Paul thought of Lesley and felt a surge of unusual pity. She'd become a means to an end. She added: 'Ashley Taylor has a lot of money, Paul.'

'But he's the only man who's ever helped you!'

'That's too bad for *him* then, isn't it? He's another man who abuses women! Not me, but perhaps I'm the woman who can make him pay. If I weren't here, he wouldn't be blackmailed. He could repeat his con, safe under his beard. It's incredible what a simple beard and moustache can do to change a man. And his hair is different. Only the eyes are the same.'

'But – supposing Lesley is different from you? Not everyone,' he added, 'can act in cold blood and hurt someone for no personal reason.'

'Lesley has a lot to lose. She won't fail us.'

Lesley's hair fell to her shoulders now, because women were wearing it longer again, but also because she hadn't bothered to go to the *coiffeur* in some time. Her maid had trimmed the ends and Lesley had been growing out the bangs. She felt old. The mirror reflected back small creases in her forehead. The bangs had hidden them, but now that two pearl combs held back their too-long wisps, she was struck by these sudden age marks. She thought her skin was sallow and that her face looked skeletal. She had carefully

decided how to present herself to this man, Daniel Mac-
Dougal. She would hide behind her most conservative,
modest exterior, not for him but for herself, to bolster her
through this ordeal that would be as dreadful for her as for
him. Perhaps, if he looked deeply into her eyes, he would
sense the truth and not judge her. Somehow she hadn't
been able to convince herself that he was a dishonest man
who needed exposing. She saw herself as the guilty party
about to perpetrate a criminal action against an innocent.
For, after all, what had this man done to hurt her?

She was wearing a simple black sheath dress with
enormous sleeves, that made her look like Elizabeth I, the
Virgin Queen. At her ears she pinned two diamonds, and
on the dress, a diamond brooch. The severe colour contrasted with the clinging tightness of the material, which
emphasized her curves. She'd become so thin that the
round breasts were really more padding than flesh, and as
she examined herself critically she wondered whether she
should have worn a less fashionable dress that would have
made her seem more anonymous and sexless. But it was too
late. She dabbed some rouge in the middle of her lower lip,
powdered her nose and cheeks, and went out into the hall.

As she walked down the stone staircase, she could feel the
beginnings of perspiration gathering in the tucks of the
material. She almost turned back then, remembering a
small enamelled box in her boudoir where she kept a
measured quantity of snow-white cocaine, with a golden
spoon the size of a large hat pin. It was there in case she
needed to fortify her spirit. But Bouchard was waiting for
her. She saw, through his eternally discreet eyes, her own
self, her figure. He approved. She looked the part he wanted
her to be, the Marquise Alexandre de Varenne. And this
too was who this man was expecting to see. She had sent
him the note on her finest, official stationery, asking him to
come for tea to discuss a painting that she wished to
purchase through him. She'd heard from friends that he

was a specialist in little-known masterpieces. Her hand had trembled and she'd made a mess. He undoubtedly thought her one of the drunks of Parisian society. But today he would find her most sober. A dry, withered flower whom no man had touched for too many months and whose only recent emotion had been gut-wrenching despair. But she was not, after all, in the business of seducing this stranger. She wanted only to get rid of him quickly and with as few complications as possible.

Feeling her heart pounding, she took a deep breath and stepped into the subdued, elegant salon where Bouchard had settled the Scotsman. She could see him standing by the bay window, looking out into her rear garden. It was difficult to tell about his build, for he was wearing a jacket with padded shoulders. Close-cropped dark curls contrasted with the white of his shirt collar. The jacket was of navy-blue material, and his legs were long. She remained glued to the floor, small waves of strangeness passing over her. There was something about him that was wrong. Or perhaps it was simply her own guilt and fear. She tried for her voice, found it, said: 'How do you do, Mr MacDougal. I am the Marquise de Varenne.'

He turned round, and his movement was quick, graceful, pantherlike. She couldn't breathe. A stillness had gathered that was like death. She was staring into his dark eyes, noticing tired lines around them. His nose seemed fuller. He wore a beard and moustache. But it was he. She knew it the moment he faced her, the moment his eyes, politely, sought hers. And she could feel her own shock passing through him. He hadn't known either!

He was the first to break the ghastly silence and the first to compose himself. He walked. He took steps that led to her, and as he approached she felt panic, the desire to run. Dizziness swam around her, like the dizziness of being drunk too quickly on champagne, without food to offset the effect.

'Lesley.'

'Justin.'

Now she wanted to cry, to *do* something, but the knot inside her throat felt like a cancer, swelling. 'Really,' he began, 'I didn't know who you were. Or I wouldn't have come . . .'

She couldn't swallow. The knot began to throb. He was almost stammering. 'I mean . . . not unprepared. It's unfair this way, to both of us.'

'Fair.' She repeated the word, rolling it around in her mouth as if it were a slice of potato, to be tested for heat, texture and flavour. There was something jarring about the word in his mouth: 'fair'. She finally found her legs, went to the sofa, sat down without having made the slightest motion to invite him. She was oblivious to him except in the sense that he was *there*, in her house. Her stomach sent shooting spasms through her.

'I didn't know you were the wife of Alexandre de Varenne,' he said, his voice dull but controlled. 'I knew he had an American wife, but Paris is filled with expatriate Americans . . .' The words stumbled out, almost incoherent.

'I've been married to him for nine and a half years! Surely a man who cons rich women doesn't miss such intercontinental gossip?'

He blinked and his lips parted. He swallowed. She felt breathless, her cheeks blazing from the outpour of twelve years' anger. Then he said: 'After you left, I enlisted and spent some years in the Far East. I've been travelling ever since. I knew of the Varennes. I had no idea you had married one of the brothers. You must believe me.'

'Why? Why should I believe anything you say?'

He couldn't reply. So she asked: 'And why the new name? Why "MacDougal"?'

This time he answered, composing his expression: 'For business reasons.'

She laughed, and the laughter was tinged with hysteria.

' "Business"? You mean, of course, forgeries. Is Tommy still your partner?'

'Don't, Lesley, please.'

He tried to meet her eyes, but their fire unnerved him completely. He made a move, stopped. 'I'll go.'

She rose, and felt the sudden shot of adrenalin pumping through her system. 'That's always been your manner,' she stated, her voice low. 'You make a mistake and then you run away. I wish you'd died, Justin.'

She thought, amazed at the strength of her words: I meant it. I wanted him dead.

'That's cruel, Lesley,' he replied, his voice trembling.

'You deserve worse.'

He licked his lips, and she remembered that he used to do that as a young man, when he was considering possibilities, unsure of how best to proceed. 'Lesley,' he said. 'The feelings we had – twelve years ago – they were my feelings too. Don't hate me because I was young and ended a relationship. I couldn't handle my feelings for you.'

'That was *your* problem.'

'I can't believe that after so long you haven't forgiven me. What we had was a lovely episode, but surely there were other men between our time and your marriage. We thought we were in love. We probably were. But one of us would have ended it sooner or later, don't you think? We were too young.'

'You were irresponsible. There were so many other girls you could have slept with – why me? I was a virgin. Was that part of your male egotism: to look for "unconquered territory"?'

At that moment they both saw Bouchard entering, pushing before him the tray on wheels with the Meissen teapot and three platters of delicate finger sandwiches. Lesley passed a hand over her brow, pressed two fingers against her temples. The *maître d'hôtel* stopped in front of her, and she addressed him with a voice that suddenly shook: 'Thank you. I'll take care of it.' Now, after the initial reaction, she was feeling the release, as if her stomach muscles were letting go, as if she would be able to weep if she tried.

The servant bowed, made his retreat, and Justin said: 'Lesley. It was a wonderful, emotional holiday. We were discovering what life was about. I don't think, in all honesty, that either of us was trying to find a partner to last us through our lives.'

'What you mean is, you wanted free love without commitment.'

'What did *you* want?'

His black eyes were riveted to her, and she suddenly rose, went to him, stood before him. 'I loved you. I wanted it to continue.'

'You were going back to America. We both knew it.'

'You could have stopped me!'

'I didn't have the courage. Marriage seemed an enormous step to take at the time.'

'But making a baby seemed less crucial?'

She saw him flinching and strengthening himself. 'I was pregnant,' she whispered, looking directly into his eyes.

His right hand clenched, unclenched, and he was very white. 'Why are you saying this?' he whispered. 'It isn't true. I'd have heard of a child!'

'Do you want proof? I had it taken care of in Poughkeepsie. My friend Jamie knows all about it.'

This time he looked away, turned round to avoid her piercing green eyes, the accusation in them. He walked to the window again and stood there alone for a long moment, his hand steadying his body on the curtain sash. 'Look at me,' she commanded.

He faced her. She wasn't sure what she read in his features, but he looked older, beaten. She saw the purple rings around his eyes, thought it strange that she'd failed to notice them before. Her anger was ebbing. In its place came the old sick despair, only worse, viler. She felt extremely ill; the room was tilting on its side. 'It's all true,' she murmured. 'I couldn't have had the child. I had it cut out of me by a cheap woman in a side street of Poughkeepsie. You've forgotten me, but I've had to relive every minute of that event, and of our time together, for twelve years.'

'Why didn't you write me?'

'To have you propose under duress? I had more pride than that.'

'I never thought – '

'That's right. *You never thought!* And I shouldn't blame you. What you did, I wanted. I just never wanted it to end. I loved you so much – '

And then the pain returned, and she twisted her fingers together. 'I married a kind, gentle man I didn't love. For peace. And you? Are you married? Do you have children?'

He shook his head. Tentatively he touched her shoulder. The wells of anguish all at once spilled over, and she couldn't see him any more through the glaze of tears. But she could feel his hand. She remembered its touch, and it hadn't changed.

He tried to pull her gently against him, and she didn't resist. He put both arms around her, and she wept against his jacket. She could feel his chin on the crown of her head. At length she looked into his face. 'Were you ever sorry you sent me away?'

He nodded again, silently. 'Talk to me,' she insisted.

'I felt tremendous emptiness. I did care, Les.'

'I felt you cared. Or it wouldn't have hurt so much. That you simply didn't care *enough*.'

'It wasn't exactly that. I was . . . caught between too many things. You can't understand.'

'No, I can't.'

'There was the war. I felt . . . panicked. I had no room for the gamut of emotions you were expressing. Most men were like that, in those days.'

392

'That's a convenient excuse. You had ample time to work on your forgeries.'

'The forgeries were *because* of the panic.'

'No,' she answered. 'You're still forging.'

His face seemed all at once to harden – to close. 'You're like my brother-in-law,' she continued, relentless now. 'He takes advantage of moneyed people. I think you enjoy it, Justin. To you it's become a game.'

'You don't know what you're saying.'

'No? Would you like me to say it more loudly – so that my friends could all hear me? What would happen to you then?'

'Lesley . . .'

'I loved you twelve years ago. I went through an ordeal because of you. I loved you, and then I hated you, and I hated myself – for not having told you. I was sorry at times that I'd married Alex instead of you. But I was shocked, Justin, at the kind of work you did. I'm still shocked. You haven't changed. You might have married me, but only to avoid being banned from society by my grandfather. And I would have suffered far more than I did when you left me. A lifetime of sleeping with a thief, of lying with him and for him – '

'Stop it, Lesley!'

' – of smiling at his colleagues and pretending I wasn't retching – '

'*Stop it!*'

His face had reddened, and he had dropped his arms from her. She saw the compressed violence in his eyes and yet felt impelled to push forward, to crush him in order to equalize their pain. But nothing would ever equal what she'd lived through on that table. Suddenly she felt absolutely in control. The ache, the memories had disappeared. The wound had finally closed. She'd just buried a corpse, and she felt relieved, almost exultant. 'Why should I stop it, Justin? I'm telling the truth.'

She smiled at him with an odd, detached sadness. Then she turned away and went to the serving tray. 'Our tea must be cold,' she announced. 'Sit down, Justin. We still have another matter to discuss.'

He went to the sofa and sat down, crossing his long, elegant legs. He was wearing a double-breasted blazer from which a cravat flashed, and his shoes shone. As she poured tea, she looked at him covertly. He was attractive; he had changed very little. There was a litheness and natural grace in every one of his movements. How did one outgrow one's first, traumatic love? He was sitting there opposite her, and her hands on the Meissen china were quick, expert, no longer trembling. She thought: We've both aged. Now her composure had returned. She saw him clearly now. He'd never loved her. He'd had some fun with her. She asked: 'Milk or lemon?' and he replied: 'Lemon, please.' She dropped the slice in the cup, asked about sugar, dropped a brown sugar cube after the lemon. Then she raised her eyes to him and handed him the cup. I've recovered, she thought, and sat down, emptied out but whole. He waited, while she stirred the liquid in her own cup and drank from it.

'Lesley,' he said, 'I never knew anything about the baby. I swear it to you.'

'Many women die when they go through what I did. I was very lucky.'

'You have no children now?'

She said evenly: 'It's just like you to ask. For years you might have kept up with what I was doing. But I was merely a single episode in your life. Why did you bring up love? It would have been better to be honest with me.'

'There is no logic between men and women. We act according to our feelings of the moment.' He looked at her seriously. She thought of Alexandre, of his pained, kind face. He had no poetry in his soul, only prose. But it was the prose of an honest man. Why had she preferred the rogue?

She was, then, like Jamie and Elena. Milton had made his point about the power of evil over good. Women especially fancied evil as strong, intriguing, and good as boring, commonplace.

What I have to do now means my survival, she thought. If I can put it off, my marriage will be safe. But what then? Will there be sufficient ties to keep us happy, after all that's happened? Or shall I still long for that secret something that I once imagined I possessed with this man here? She cleared her throat. 'Was it that you didn't want a wife, Justin?' she asked. 'Or was it that you were finished with me, that the fascination of the moment had been used up? Was it my innocence you wished to break through?'

'You want answers for what I did twelve years ago. I was taken by your loveliness. You are still a lovely woman. You don't look your age.'

'If you had met me now, would you be wanting more?'

'You said you married your husband for peace. Why, Lesley? You never wanted peace as a young girl.'

'Perhaps I'd had my fill of excitement with you. But it was unwholesome. What we had was heightened by the fact that it was forbidden. If you'd married me, and I'd had the child – we might have become bored with each other. And . . . our values are too different. We're not of the same world, Justin. And in marriage, that's what's important.'

'You and Alexandre are of that "same world"?'

'I'm not sure. But I know you and I aren't. You're of Paul de Varenne's world, and Elena Egorova's. A world of quick passions and no remorse.'

'Elena Egorova,' he repeated.

'Do you know her?'

'I knew someone of that name, during the war, in the Orient. I thought I saw her again the other day. A beautiful woman with dark hair. But she didn't recognize me, and I wasn't absolutely certain.'

'What was she to you?'

395

'What does it matter? Someone whose life crossed mine for one brief instant.'

She stared at him, understanding. She'd told Elena everything except the name of her lover. She'd been stupid enough to reveal all but his name! But how could she possibly have imagined they'd both have known Justin Reeve? So all her problems now, as then, had come from him. Elena had capitalized on Lesley's mistake as a young girl to torture her now, as a married woman, without realizing she'd set her up for the shock of her life. 'It's no use.' Lesley sighed. 'I'm going to have to do something extremely repugnant to me. You are, and always have been, a man who used rich women. You are selling forged works in Paris, to my friends. If you wish to continue, I could stop you. But why should I? You'd only start again in some other part of the world. But I have problems of my own. My dowry is controlled by my husband. I need money. Do you understand, Justin?'

His face was totally devoid of colour. 'You want money from me?'

She suddenly enjoyed his shock and the role she was playing. 'You thought me simple and naïve, and honest. I'm honest – but I'm not going to waste my honesty on those who have abused me. I want you to pay me a certain sum, against the promise that I shan't tell anyone who you are or what you're up to. I'm going to play Robin Hood, Justin.'

He licked his white lips, and his eyes turned hard. She could feel her heart beating in her chest and was light-headed from the boldness she had just displayed. Now if he refused, she'd be backed against the wall. One had to hope she had bluffed her way into frightening him, into his taking her seriously. He asked: 'And if I don't pay?'

'Then I shall start by telling my husband.'

He bit his lower lip, chewing on it pensively. Abruptly he stood up, pressing his clenched fist against his teeth repeatedly. When he turned, it was with sudden force, and his face frightened her. She hadn't expected the set lines on his face, the coldness, the anger. 'No,' he told her, 'it isn't going to be like that. *You* are going to do something for *me*. You're right: Your husband *should* know! You're going to tell him that there's a special file in the Ministry of Justice that I would dearly love to see destroyed. It concerns a case against me, years old. That's really the reason I have to operate under a different name here in Paris. I don't want to have to do that all my life. Like you, I don't wish to run away from my past like Jean Valjean. Tell the deputy that if he doesn't obtain this file, I shall warn the press about your affair with me, and the, shall we say, aftermath. He's running for office in this election, isn't he?'

She could hear the two of them, breathing in the silent room. It was as if she'd never met this man before – as if they'd never shared any tenderness, any past. She couldn't verbalize the incoherence of the moment – the complete effect of shock to her system. She would have to reply. She tried, but no sound emerged. And then she heard the voices in the entrance hall: Jamie's, Bouchard's, and Cassie's. Waves of relief and terror, simultaneous, washed over her. She knew she was perspiring, that the sweat was making her dress cling to her breasts and hips.

Then her friend came in, holding her daughter's hand. Jamie's hat was a becoming array of blue flowers, with a small brim and a short blue veil. Her spring suit was of the same periwinkle blue. Cassie's hair was in pigtails, the red tint enhanced by bright red bows. Her smock of checked red cotton was splattered with chocolate marks. Around her mouth were the same brown stains.

'We just thought we'd come for a visit,' Jamie announced. 'We had to come to town, and Cass wanted to see the puppets at the Rond-Point. We bought ice creams. You can see the results!'

Lesley willed herself to sit up, to kiss her small niece. She

397

tried to smile graciously. 'Jamie,' she said, wondering how much her voice was shaking. 'This is Daniel MacDougal. My friend, Jamie Stewart, and her daughter, Cassandra.'

Justin was rising, ceremoniously taking the hand that Jamie was offering, a pleasant smile on her face. 'Everyone has heard of you, Madame,' he said, raising the gloved fingers to his lips. 'Your books have rendered you unique among your contemporaries.'

'Thank you,' Jamie said. She looked at Lesley, and her eyes were question marks that Lesley avoided having to answer. She was praying for Justin to leave, right away, before her composure disintegrated completely. Jamie sat down, drawing Cassie close to her, and for a moment Justin drained the contents of his tea cup, as if nothing were even slightly amiss and he were only a casual guest in her home.

Then he stood up. Lesley felt as if hours had gone by, not minutes. Smiling, he went to her, but she made no motion to put out her hand. He bowed. How supple and smooth he was! 'It's been such a delightful afternoon,' he stated. 'Thank you, Marquise, for the delicious tea and the enlightening conversation.'

He waited, but Lesley answered nothing. And so he looked once again at Jamie, and at the child. 'Good-bye, Madame Stewart – Mademoiselle . . .'

When she heard the front door closing behind him, Lesley shut her eyes and slumped against the cushions, Jamie asked: 'And so who *is* he? He's terribly handsome.'

'No one important,' Lesley replied.

'But something's wrong.'

Lesley hesitated. It would be such a blessed relief to blurt everything out to her best friend. She opened her mouth, then stopped. Alex's future lay in her hands. She couldn't speak. 'No,' she said. 'He's an art dealer of sorts. I just . . . didn't like him very much.'

He'd been there, he'd gone. Her past had been totally erased and in its place had come new anguish. She couldn't associate the man who had just left with the young man with whom she had made love, whose baby she had carried, however briefly. She'd never make that association. It was better that way. Justin Reeve would remain a memory, etched in the sepia colours of long ago, and Daniel Mac-Dougal would never be confused with him. He was a dangerous, cruel individual whom even Elena and Paul had misjudged. Their plan had backfired.

Chapter Twenty

In the evening, Lesley knew that she would not be able to tell Alex. He sat across from her in the formal dining room, the crystal chandelier gleaming rainbows onto the bone china of the dinner plates, and his face showed the extent of his exhaustion from the pile-up of work before the election. She couldn't eat. He couldn't either, but his reasons were different. His cheeks were white, tinted with evening stubble, and his eyes were bloodshot. She wondered why he thought it worthwhile to continue. Pushing away her salad, she asked him.

'There has to be something to believe in,' he replied. She read the sadness in his voice, felt the blow.

'Alex,' she began. 'Do you want a divorce?'

The grey eyes quickened. 'Why? Do you?'

She said, before she had thought through her answer: 'No.'

The focus of his eyes became more pronounced. She felt them piercing through her. She stood up, went round the table, hesitated behind his chair. He had half turned to stare at her in surprise. She touched his forehead, caressed it as if to iron out the creases. Such smooth, fine-grained skin. He was an aristocrat to the bone. Tired, unsure of his future, he was bearing up to his burdens, facing her. She thought, almost with amazement: I love him. Not like a brother – like a man! His physical frailties appeared dear to her, and also appealing. She felt a wave of tenderness and weakness inside, a melting. Was it desire?

'No,' she repeated. 'But you've found someone else.'

She'd tried to bring up this question once before, but the poignancy of her tone struck him now. She half hoped he

400

would deny it, then found herself praying he would. Instead he looked into her eyes, lines jutting out around his mouth – lines of vulnerability. 'Who is she?' Lesley asked. She had to know.

'Is it really important?'

'Is *she* important?'

Alexandre licked his lips. 'She's kind. She's young. I never wanted to hurt her. I didn't do it to hurt you either, Lesley.'

'Then why?'

'You know. There's been nothing between us but distrust. Why did you marry me?'

Her hand still lay on his forehead. She pondered the ridiculousness of the situation, their conversation, her sudden rush of jealousy toward this unnamed woman. 'I'm not exactly sure,' she answered. 'But I do know I don't want it to end.' And at the same time, she knew that it had to. If Elena and Paul kept their silence, now there was Justin, a far more severe threat. But he might have been bluffing. She could picture him again in her mind, sitting opposite her, so close, and looking at her without anything but cold ruthlessness. When it came down to the razor's edge, nobody had any emotions but that essential one of wanting to survive. But what would her life be like without Alex?

If I tell him, he won't steal the file, she thought. He's much too honest. But if Justin reveals what took place between us twelve years ago, Alex will be ruined anyway. If I can only stall Justin until the election, I can conveniently disappear, and the scandal won't be so bad for him. Everyone will feel perhaps sorry for him and blame *me*. He'll suffer. He'll have to relive the shame of Yvonne. But it was different with them; he still loved her. It took years for him to get over the rejection. And she left with another man . . .

He was reaching up to encompass her hand with his, and for a long moment, they remained liked this, feeling the

401

warmth in each other's fingers. Then he whispered: 'I can end it, Les. I'm not in love with her. I still want you to be my wife.'

The suddenness with which she turned about, bursting into tears and running from the room, left Alexandre wide-eyed and concerned.

Paul's fist came slamming down on the table, and Elena saw the wine splash over the rim of her glass. 'Of all idiotic mistakes!' he cried. 'I can't understand you! Her grand-parents were members of the British aristocracy – Couldn't you have checked? Goddamn it, any child would have given the notion a possibility. Her lover was English, she *told* you! And Taylor is a baronet. They're of the same generation, social class, lineage. And you never even imagined they could have met?'

'You knew the same facts,' she countered. 'You didn't work it out either.'

'But it wasn't my idea! The one who thinks up a con has to put two and two together! That wasn't my job – it was yours!'

'Why? Why does everything always have to be up to me? I was the one who first thought of blackmailing Lesley. She supported us for a long time. Where else would we have turned? You alienated Bertrand to the point of losing his precious help. Now where are we?'

'Bertrand alienated himself,' Paul stated tightly.

'But at least when he loved you and considered you his son, he was on your side! Now he hasn't given you any jobs, and we're running out of funds. How could I possibly have known that someone I met during the war, in the Orient, would turn out to have been Lesley's lover?'

Paul looked at her, and she felt the coldness in his eyes. She was chilled by it, and panicked. Blood rushed to her cheeks. She tried to put her hand on his, but he withdrew it, and his eyes narrowed. She thought: Not only has he stopped loving me, but he actually hates me! And I've been the greatest fool in Paris: Ashley Taylor, Lesley's lover . . . Using her to blackmail the one person who has as much evidence against her as she does against him! A Mexican stand-off.

'Darling,' she said, 'we'll think of something. *I'll* think of something.'

His jaw stood out against the light, and she saw the muscles contracting.

'It's all right,' he retorted, not looking at her. 'Your tastes were always more extravagant than mine. It's you who's going to have the problem, Elena. You thought up this crazy idea. Alone I can manage, somehow.'

She couldn't believe it. 'You aren't serious?'

'Come on . . . Let's face it. We've been together for more than three years. It's been good at times. It was even grand at the beginning. But passion has to die at some point, doesn't it? We'd be far better off going our separate ways before we really hate each other.'

She couldn't speak. He said, looking at her again, his eyes expressionless: 'Elena, it wasn't love. Love is something that binds people in subtle, emotional ways. We had a very good affair, but it was always tinged with violence. We ravaged each other. We left each other empty hulls. After sex we felt depleted. Not *com*pleted. *That*'s love.'

'You don't even understand what that word means!'

He sighed, and she ached with the need for him to meet her eyes with the old desire, for whatever it had been worth. She asked again: 'Paul? You can't really be serious?'

'I am. Our lives no longer have a common purpose. There are other ways to earn a living than to blackmail people.'

'You're becoming moral?'

'No. Simply practical. You're a year older than I am. I,

403

at least, have a few basic skills, thanks to Bertrand. And I have a daughter.'

She turned very pale. 'What does Cassandra have to do with anything?'

'She's Alexandre's niece. My brother isn't like me; he's extremely moral. He'd like nothing better than for me to mend my ways. Jamie hasn't yet married anyone. And everyone in Paris knows I'm the father of her child. If I were to right this wrong and take up my responsibilities with them, Alex would surely support me.'

The scream died in her throat. She stood up and threw the wine she'd been drinking in his face. While, stunned, he sat gazing at her through drops of absurd red liquid, she smashed the crystal on the tablecloth and snapped the stem off the glass in a single gesture. Red seeped around broken shards, soaking into the tablecloth as if it were a blotter.

'You're mad,' he whispered. 'Absolutely, dangerously mad. I should have stayed away from you from the start, Elena.'

He heard, before he saw, the crash of glass against the wall, inches from his head. The hair around her shoulders bounced with life of its own, wild and free. He stared at her face as if he'd never seen it before, and she saw, reflected in the brown irises of his eyes, her own ugliness.

Jamie Stewart, who had never been beautiful, was only thirty years old, and she was Cassie's mother. And Jamie Stewart lived in a white stone mansion protected by the security of her talent.

'Madame Egorova?' he asked, his hand reaching out for hers and lifting it like a swan's feather to his lips.

She sat down in the Louis XIV armchair opposite his, and from behind the netted black veil, she took in the luxurious surroundings of his suite at the Georges V Hotel. He fitted into it like a smooth suede glove, his trim beard hiding the point of his chin, his moustache hiding the fullness of his arched lips. His civilian attire, brown suit and brown-and-red tie, gave him a totally different appearance from his military demeanour of 1918.

Elena raised the netting over her small pillbox hat and looked at him. There was kohl around her black eyes, and the carmine of her lips matched the colour of her blouse, under the Patou suit of elegant black velvet. She said: 'It's "Princess", Monsieur MacDougal. But I think you remember that.'

'I'm terribly sorry. Of course: You told me so at the café.' He smiled, inclining his head. She thought: I can understand why Lesley wanted to make her life with such a man. He was possessed of such innate finesse and grace that, with a few more Italianate touches, he might have appeared a dandy. His fingers were perfectly formed, long and almost delicate. He was slender and lithe, and his clothes were moulded around him as if they were a second skin. Polished brown boots finished off the picture.

'I believe you knew it before. In Singapore, at the Little Club, just before the armistice was signed. Or rather, just after. Only we were too busy dancing to realize it had been signed.'

She watched for an expression of surprise, but his eyes were too much like hers: impenetrable through their blackness. His head tilted to one side, and he stroked his beard. Then he smiled. 'Indeed. But a gentleman waits for the lady to acknowledge him first in such delicate situations.'

She made a small clapping gesture with her gloved hands. 'Bravo. *Touché*. Nevertheless, Ashley, we meet again. Or rather, we already did. I think that there were other reasons for your refusing to reintroduce yourself – Monsieur MacDougal.'

'The della Robbia sold well?'

'Extremely. I thank you again, my dear. That was a

405

beautiful gift, and because of it, I'm here today. It paid for my passage and the first few months I lived here.'

'Then this is a visit of gratitude?'

She noted the wariness of his tone. 'This is a visit of reacquaintanceship. We were lovers once, in the Orient. I came to propose a new venture. But first, don't you feel we should toast the future together, along with the past?'

He clicked his fingers, all graciousness again. She watched him ring for a bellboy, and when one appeared at the door, heard him order a bottle of Dom Perignon champagne from 1926 – an excellent year. She rested on the back of the armchair, and half closed her eyes. It was all going to work out.

'You seem somewhat nervous, Ashley,' she commented when they were alone again and she had unbuttoned the jacket of her suit. 'But of course, it's normal. Monsieur MacDougal doesn't wish to be confused with the art forger Ashley Taylor, or, to be more accurate, Justin Reeve. The one whose reputation was tarnished by the sale of a William Blake whose authenticity was highly contested at the time. Leo Stein's word meant a great deal, didn't it, to the French authorities? Were you actually brought to trial?'

'Don't be absurd, Elena.'

'Oh, don't be concerned, dear. Poor Lesley de Varenne. Apparently it's an old story.'

This time he did blanch. He sat down. There was a knock at the door, and he started. The bellboy entered, with the champagne on ice, and they both watched him intently, not looking at each other, while he uncorked the bottle and poured. After he had served them, Justin dismissed him. He remained with face half-hidden by the wine, his long fingers clasping the glass. Finally he said: 'Lesley de Varenne. How do you know her?'

'Never mind. What are your feelings about her now, Ashley?'

A glimmer of understanding flickered in his eyes, but he kept silent.

'What do you know about her husband, Ashley?'

'Just what I've recently discovered. He's from an old, once-wealthy family, but it's her money that helped launch him. He was a deputy for five years, and then he lost his seat when the Left took over in twenty-four. He's up for re-election in two weeks.'

He continued, 'And, Princess, if I may ask, what exactly is *your* interest in this whole affair?'

Elena's expression hardened. 'Look, Ashley . . . Justin – we're both too clever to mince words. I admit that Lesley's little blackmail scheme was my idea. I put her up to it. She was indiscreet enough several years ago to admit to me that she had once been pregnant and had the matter, shall we say, arranged. I naturally promised to remain silent. But dear Lesley was foolish enough to end our friendship soon after. And my vow of silence ended with it. She has been . . . helping me financially for some time. But the well has run dry. When I saw you in the café the other day, I recognized an opportunity. And Lesley seemed the perfect pawn. Obviously I had no idea that you were the very man she had her unfortunate affair with. Life does play such unexpected little tricks, don't you agree? But, frankly, my dear, I have a plan.'

Justin's face remained impassive. 'Exactly what do you propose?'

'I am a realist. Paul de Varenne and I are near a parting of the ways. All my life I've had to struggle. And the Varennes are going to be my passport to a life of ease. Paul is the father of Jamie Lynne Stewart's baby. And, as you also may know, Alex adores the child. In fact, he has made her his heiress. I propose that you, let us say, remove Cassandra for a brief period of time. The ransom shall be twofold. For you, dear Ashley, a certain file in the Ministry of Justice, obtained by Alexandre. For me, hard cash.'

His eyes remained upon her, hard and unblinking.

Since 1926, Raymond Poincaré had been the premier for the second time, replacing Edouard Herriot, the Radical Socialist who had taken over the government for two years in 1924. Alexandre had to admit to himself that, in spite of his earlier misgivings, tax collection seemed to have saved France from the national bankruptcy that had threatened. Poincaré, solid, conservative, hard-working, had, in his own steadfast manner, moved his country into a new prosperity. And, riding on the coat-tails of this perennial leader, Alexandre felt a new surge of confidence that, on this twenty-eighth of April, with the buds coming alive outside the window of his office, he would be re-elected to the *Chambre des Députés*.

Micheline Prandot, a modest pink flower in the psyche knot of her hair, knocked lightly on the door and opened it with shy familiarity. It was late afternoon, and shadows of golden light were streaking Alexandre's crimson and blue Persian rug. He gazed at her, found her touching in her light beige suit, and felt at once a renewal of his constant guilty feelings about her. 'Hello, my dear.'

'How do you feel?' She sat down in the client's armchair, an upholstered Louis XIII, and crossed her shapely legs.

He smiled. 'It's going to be a precarious victory. Not like the one in nineteen.' He thought briefly of Lesley, of the last election that he had won. It reminded him of his wedding, of the dual celebration. The girl looking at him so earnestly was like this new election: less grand, less startling than the last. But genuine and meaningful.

'If the Communists had formed a coalition with the Cartel des Gauches, do you think the Left would be winning?' she asked.

'Absolutely. The Communists, by holding out, are forcing the Right back into focus. We shan't win a clear-cut majority, but by forcing two ballots the Union Nationale is definitely going to return to control. The Communists must surely realize that by pretending to hold themselves aloof from any bourgeois business they are giving their greatest opponents a majority they wouldn't otherwise have achieved.'

'Are the two ballots really necessary?' Micheline questioned.

'For forming a united block and making compromises, yes. That's why we have to vote today. The first round, six days ago, didn't give us our hoped-for majority.'

'But six days ago, your seat was won.'

'Perhaps mine was – but in a powerless Chamber, what good could I do? I need to be elected with a strong party behind me.'

'The Union Nationale isn't quite so strong as its predecessor, the Bloc,' she commented, and he thought: She's intelligent. She's well informed. She cares about me. That last idea made him both happy and sad. If Lesley had felt this way, how many problems could have been avoided . . . And yet things had recently become different between him and his wife. There was something new, something hopeful, in the manner in which Lesley spoke to him these days, in the turn of her head, in the brightness of her eyes. It was almost enough to make him believe she might love him. But – had she ever? Micheline did.

I can't continue like this, he thought, squirming slightly in his armchair. Micheline is too good, too young, too kind. She's not anyone I would ever marry, even if I were free. She knows that. Our social backgrounds are too dissimilar. But if I let her go free, she could fall in love with another man and make a decent home for herself. It's time. I've risked a lot to win this election. I can take a risk here too and try to make Lesley understand how much she means to me, and how important our future is. For this I must be clean.

409

'Your wife is giving you a fabulous celebration party,' Micheline was saying, as if reading his mind, and he heard the trembling behind her words.

'Yes.' They hardly ever discussed Lesley. Now he cleared his throat. 'She's made a great effort, Micheline. This seat has preoccupied her almost as much as me.'

The delicate chin steadied itself with some difficulty. 'It's been uppermost on the mind of anyone and everyone who loves you.'

'Thank you. I know how much you've supported me, Micheline – you've been wonderful. Without the strength of your gentle words of encouragement . . .'

'But Alexandre, something is wrong.'

He nodded, slowly. 'My sweet Micheline, you've given me months of loyalty, months of something I desperately needed . . .'

'Love.'

He looked away. 'It's not right for me to pursue this affair with you. You deserve better.'

'You've told me that many times! I think what I have is the very best. I love you so much, Alexandre.'

The earnestness in her blue eyes was so painful that it seemed to turn his stomach inside out. 'I care for you too.'

'But "caring for" isn't the same as "loving".'

'I know. And that's what I'm coming to. Micheline, you're very dear to me. Too dear for me to lie to you. I still love Lesley. In spite of all the years of problems between us, if there's a chance for us to be together, I want to take it. She's my wife.'

He couldn't look at the tears in her eyes, but he felt them. She stood up. 'It's all right. I do understand. If ever you should need me, Alexandre . . .'

Then he met her eyes. 'Thank you. For everything. For – '

'Don't.'

She turned around, went to the door, stopped. 'I'm going

to stay long enough to train someone new,' she said softly. 'You're going to need an excellent secretary. Please don't be afraid I'd let you down now.'

His throat felt so knotted that the words came out raw, hoarse. 'You've never let me down. I want you to realize that of all the people who've been in my life, you alone stood by me without fail. All the time.'

She floated out of the office, and he laid his head in his hands. The election was over; there was relief but also sadness. The sadness of what had just taken place. Sometimes honour was difficult to come by. It would have been such an easy thing to keep her near . . .

He rose, shuffled the papers around his desk, and put on his jacket. He would go to Lesley now, and celebrate.

There had been but few words between them, before the party. He'd entered, and she'd looked up and backward, from her mirror: her green eyes softening, stroking him. She'd had her hair newly bobbed, and it framed her small features like a bright, copper cap. 'How handsome you look, Monsieur *le Député*,' she had murmured. 'Tired, but handsome.'

'I wanted to tell you something, Lesley.'

Her brows had risen inquisitively, a half smile illuminating her triangular face.

'Darling, you were asking me about . . . there being someone else in my life. I want you to know that there is no one. Only you.'

He'd watched a shadow passing over her expression. 'Thank you, Alex. We've been through so much, haven't we? And yet nothing that anybody could put his finger on. No major traumas. Just the erosion of ten years of knowing each other. But it's in the small battles that a war can be won – or lost.'

'And our personal war?'

'Was it a war? Or just a parapet that grew up between us?'

'I don't know any more. I thought today about you, about our meeting, our wedding. You're the most important thing in my life.'

'And you're the centre of my being. I once believed that those early moments of excitement were what made a woman love a man. But excitement is in confronting one's daily existence and still pulling through on the same side. I don't want to lose you, Alex.' And the party that followed had rung with celebration. He'd felt joy, hope – until the footman had come with news of Cassie's abduction. Now he could think only of his niece, and of her mother.

He remembered Lesley's words as he entered the crowded drawing room, as he bent over Jamie's collapsed form and gently placed her on the love seat. It couldn't be possible that someone had kidnapped Cassandra. Jamie had suffered so much already. It couldn't be happening to her – to *them*. His brother had moved up and was sitting down beside Jamie's head, and his brown eyes were accusatory. He said tightly: 'Alex, anything about Cassie is my business. It's time you understood that she's *my* daughter – not yours.'

Lesley placed a restraining hand on Paul's arm. 'Please. This is hardly the moment. Cassie is a concern to all of us. And so is Jamie.' She raised her head to the liveried servant. 'Madame Stewart should be put to bed in the blue guest room,' she stated quietly. 'And see to it that the glasses are kept filled, that the party is kept going. The Marquis, the Comte and I want to see the nursemaid in my husband's study. And I don't want any word of this to leak out.'

Paul rose and made room for two men to carry Jamie away. Alexandre's jaw set nervously. It would be impossible to keep Paul out of this. 'Come on,' he commanded abruptly. He led the way out, his wife following, his brother taking up the rear. Turning round, he saw Elena Egorova

412

staring after them. Thank God, she had made no move to join them.

Once behind the closed door, Alex took his seat behind the large desk and looked at the nanny. Her middle-aged features were ashen.

Lesley was standing behind him, her hands on his shoulders. Protecting him? On the opposite side – always on opposite sides, he remarked bitterly to himself – sat his brother. The nursemaid took the chair nearest him, sat with her back hunched over. 'It wasn't my fault, Monsieur le Marquis,' she began.

'Never mind. What happened?'

'Cassandra was by the lily pond. I let her stay outside for a few minutes. No more than ten! And then she was gone. I came out, looked everywhere. Moments later the *maître d'hôtel* came running in, with this note – ' Tears welled up in her pale eyes and her chin started to tremble. She handed Alexandre a folded piece of paper – a common piece of bond stationery, without identifying crest, initial or monogram.

He felt Lesley's fingers tightening over his shoulder blades. She was reading too. In large block letters, somebody had written: 'The Marquise de Varenne knows why Cassandra Stewart has been taken from her home. It concerns a matter discussed in her house, concerning a certain file. The child will not be harmed unless the Marquise and her husband refuse to co-operate.' There was no signature.

Alex asked, his voice hoarse: 'What's this all about?'

'I-I don't know,' Lesley stammered. Her face was very pale, her eyes translucent. He could see her withdrawing into herself, the fear spreading around her mouth and nose. 'I can't think . . .'

'Paul,' Alexandre stated. 'You're going to have to leave us alone. If there's anything to report, I'll let you know.'

'I'm not leaving!'

413

'You are. This is my house. You're leaving or being thrown out. And understand that this is a crisis in which your presence isn't needed. You've never cared about Cassie – and it's too late now.'

'She's mine by rights! Jamie knows that! Jamie's welfare too is my concern!'

'You lost all rights to Cassie when she was born, and to Jamie, long before that, when you took up with Egorova. I want you out. And take Mademoiselle François with you. Ask the butler to give her a brandy. She looks as if she needs one. We all do.'

He stood up, and all at once his straightness, his tallness, was formidable. Lesley, behind him, was like a pale blur. Paul glowered, but turned on his heel. The nursemaid followed him out, carefully closing the door behind herself.

They were alone now, bound by a common tension. Alexandre pounded the desk once, twice, then regarded Lesley. 'A file?' he asked. '*What* file?' His tone was sharp, and there was a coldness in his eyes that frightened her. 'Everything is going to have to be cleared up now,' he declared. 'All the little subterfuges, the doctored bills. I'm sorry, Lesley. But the words you told me this evening mean nothing to me. They're empty. Cassandra's life may be taken if you don't start admitting the things you've been holding in all these months and years.'

'But Alex – '

'*Now*, Lesley.'

She stared back at him like a trapped animal. The rims of her eyes were red, and her fingers twisted together unconsciously. She pressed against the rear wall, raised a hand mechanically in front of her, as if he were about to strike. Alex felt his anger mount. 'Damn it!' he cried. 'This isn't the time to be thinking of yourself! Nor of our marriage! Think of your best friend's child, for God's sake, if not of me!'

'I have no idea what you're talking about,' she answered.

Suddenly all the life appeared beaten out of her. 'I've got to go upstairs, Alex. Jamie may need me.'

'Are you planning to tell her about the note? Because if you don't, I will!'

'No!'

They stood defiantly facing each other. Her cheekbones gleamed bright red. 'Then you do know,' he whispered.

She turned her back on him, held up the hem of her skirt, ran out of the room. He sat down again, his mouth dry.

He wondered then, as he had for so long, what it was that she was so intent on hiding from him. And he realized that as much as she seemed afraid and unwilling to tell him, so much did he feel about hearing it.

Lesley sponged Jamie's forehead, then passed the hot, soiled cloth over her own face. Kohl came off, and she examined the flannel with absent query. 'Why?' Jamie was repeating. '*Why*? It's not as if I had a lot of money . . .' Tears were streaming down her face, filling her eyes and then spilling out over the lashes again. Lesley sat mutely beside her, dry-eyed. She tossed the cloth down on the floor and raked her scalp with her fingernails, until it tingled with pain. Strands of sweaty hair stuck together over her eyes.

'Don't worry about money,' she murmured. 'Money . . . that's the one thing I've always had too much of. And yet . . . it's never enough . . .'

Jamie looked at her. 'What do you mean?'

'Nothing.' She wished that this time she could weep, to release what she had built up inside her. Jamie had saved her life. If it hadn't been for Jamie's sacrifice, she would never have found the money to save herself. The shame of the pregnancy would have been unbearable. What would have happened to her then? What would she have done without Jamie?

415

She took Jamie's hand, stroked it. All through their important years, they had stayed close. Jamie was the strongest person she knew. Lesley thought of Cassie, of Jamie's determination to give birth to her, against all taboos. Odd, how the turn of one woman's life had been determined by a pregnancy she didn't want, while another's now was being held together by one she had planned, hoped for. Still, in both cases the men had left. Men never stayed. Alexandre wouldn't stay.

How could Justin do this? she thought. Her predicament was so awful that her mind couldn't grasp it. Justin, whom she had loved. He'd lied, cheated, and now he might murder. She thought the unthinkable.

Would he really *murder*? she wondered. Was he that evil? Perhaps he wouldn't, she reasoned. He'll get scared and return her. And I won't have to tell Alex to steal the file from the Ministry. If I told him, would he do it? For Cassie?'

He doesn't love me any more, she thought, her despair suddenly coming into focus. That evening she had realized how much he meant to her. It didn't matter now. He would surely leave her.

He'll go back to the other girl, whoever she was, Lesley said to herself. And eventually she'll be willing to have his child. And whether or not he steals the file, he'll continue in politics. It's his lifeline. He *could* find the file and get away with it. Justin didn't think I'd ask him to. He didn't think his threats were sufficient for me. Perhaps he was right . . . I wasn't going to tell Alex, I was going to wait and see whether Justin, whether Paul and Elena, were bluffing. Or at least I didn't want to think about it . . . about the roof caving in over us. Yet it was bound to happen: Too many people knew.

And what now? she asked herself. She stood up, went to the connecting bathroom, poured herself a glass of water, drank it. She wanted something stronger. From downstairs, echoes of noise, of music, floated up. A band had started to play, a jazz quartet that she had discovered at Le Boeuf sur le Toit, hoping to impress all of Paris with them. But would anybody dance if she and Alex were absent at the key moment? Had Alex returned to his guests, or was he still alone in the study?

Jamie's child was gone. Her old lover had taken her. It was her fault. If she'd done as he'd asked her to, if she'd told Alex long ago, none of this would be happening.

Jamie was sitting up, her lovely brown hair falling over the pillow like a soft cascade of autumn leaves. 'Les,' she was saying. 'I love my child. I've got to find her.'

'It's my problem too,' Lesley replied. 'I love her very much.'

They fell silent. There was nothing left to say. Jamie turned over, burying her face in the pillow, and began to sob, very softly. Lesley watched her and felt herself being torn apart.

Only I can really do something meaningful, she decided. I've got to tell Alex about Justin – about all of it. And even though he'll throw me away, he might take the risk of stealing and destroying the file, for Cassie's life.

Jamie had helped when she was desperate, and now she owed it to her to help save her child. Lesley took Jamie's hand, squeezed it. 'I'll be back,' she promised. 'I must go and talk to Alex about something.'

Her friend's eyes, searching, insistent, followed her out of the room.

Chapter Twenty-One

The crowd had thinned to a trickle of gossipmongers and close friends, who were still sitting around the reception room, gingerly holding on to *coupes* of champagne in which the bubbles had died. Somehow, word had leaked out about the kidnapping, in spite of Alex's strict injunction against this. Misia Sert was there, plump breasts pushing out of her violet gown. Sylvia Beach and Adrienne Monnier were sitting on a love seat, talking quietly, and Lesley saw Elena, her features white against the darkness of her costume, talking to the Baron Georges Brincard of the Crédit Lyonnais.

Bouchard was passing out a tray of fresh coffee and snifters of Napoleon brandy. Another valet was bringing in light tea cakes and newly baked brioches and croissants, puffed to a golden brown. Lesley hesitated on the threshold. After all, these were her guests. Misia sidled up to her, laid painted fingers on her arm. 'How is Jamie?'

'Managing, thank you.'

Natalia Gontcharova, looking like a crimson cardinal, approached, her flat Slav face alive with concern. 'Nobody knows anything?' she asked.

'Not yet. But thank you.'

She could see the blonde Sara Murphy from the corner of her eye, speaking to Paul. She decided that here, things were in sufficient control, and so she pressed Misia's hand and tiptoed out into the hall. She felt a terrible stillness. But now it was compounded with fear, with anxiety, with the dread of the unknown. Alex.

He was in the study, drinking coffee, his hair, grey at the temples, clumped together from being raked in nervousness. His eyes were bloodshot. When she entered, closing the door behind her, he looked up, and the vulnerability of his face aroused her compassion. She went up to him, put her hands over his face, pressed him against her breasts.

'I have something to tell you.'

'About the note?'

She nodded. She moved away, went to the other side of the desk, sat down in the armchair. Her dress felt wet beneath the arms, and her temples were pounding with a dull, terrible ache. She found it impossible to face the questions in his eyes. 'I'm going to tell you something, but after that you will find it impossible to love me.'

'I can't love someone who doesn't tell the truth,' he replied.

'But you have never done anything you'd need to hide. I have.'

He stared at her, disbelieving. She bit down on her tongue, took a deep breath. The pain inside her body was concentrated in her nerves. She felt ill because in her heart there was sickness. I don't want to lose him, she thought. Not now that I've only just begun to find him and myself too . . . Then she recalled Jamie's sobs upstairs, and she plunged in, desperately. 'When I was eighteen, I went to England with my mother. We stayed at my grandfather's estate in Yorkshire, and I met a young man. I thought he loved me. I believed him when he told me that he did. I was certain I loved him too, as much as I'd ever thought it possible for a woman to love a man. I was very young, Alex, and inexperienced.'

'And?'

'He promised to make his life with me. But when we returned to London, he didn't call on me. I was bewildered, hurt. I was sure there had been a mistake. I went to see him, and I happened to stumble on a revelation that shocked and startled me: He made his living by selling forged paintings. He didn't try to hide it from me. But he

419

wouldn't marry me. I couldn't understand – that he didn't love me, that he wasn't honest. I still wanted to be with him in spite of everything. But you see, *he* didn't want *me*. The love wasn't mutual.

'Then I went back to Vassar for my sophomore year. I discovered I was pregnant. By November there was no way I could deny it. And so I told Jamie.'

'You were *pregnant*?'

She felt very strong now, because she'd told him the first part without flinching. Her eyes stayed on his, and she read his astonishment. 'You had a *child*, Lesley?' he finally asked, his voice hushed. 'Where is it?'

'I didn't go through with the pregnancy. Jamie helped me to arrange to . . . have it taken care of.'

His stunned silence told her all she'd feared. He didn't love her any more, and he never would again. His respect for her had died, because she hadn't ever been the girl he had imagined. It was too late now. Only Cassandra mattered. She continued in a hushed voice: 'Nobody else knew. I won't go into details now, but it was a terrible business. It was horrible. But I lived on. I knew I couldn't have done anything else.'

'Your parents never knew anything about the courtship?'

'My mother did. But when nothing came of it, no one ever mentioned him again. He was British. His family knew ours. They could, I suppose, have forced us to marry. But that would have been a very bad solution.'

'And what you did was better?'

'I was Ned Richardson's daughter. The scandal would have hurt his business. And my parents might never have forgiven me. You know about these sorts of things . . . about the way people pass judgment on the actions of others . . .'

She was making an appeal to him, but his eyes remained hard. She cried: 'But I didn't do anything wrong by loving Justin! And I hadn't planned to become pregnant. You may feel you're in a position to condemn me, but you're not.'

420

'Your never telling me was unforgivable,' he said. 'Why?'

She looked away, became quiet again. 'I couldn't. You wanted me to be spotless. I wasn't strong enough to destroy your illusions. I think I wanted you to continue to see me as you hoped I was.'

'And now? What sort of illusions are you leaving me with?'

The harshness of his tone brought tears to her eyes. 'I don't know, Alex. It was my life. I made my mistakes. The worst part was what happened to us because of it. I never could think of having a child because the idea of it was just too painful – the way the other pregnancy ended. I couldn't face it. It was easier to pretend I just didn't want children.'

He wasn't looking at her, but she saw the lines of his face, the set of his jaw. 'Alex – I'm so sorry – '

'But what has all this to do with Cassandra? I don't understand!'

Lesley concentrated on a nub of silk on the curtains. 'Once, when I was feeling very lonely, I confided in Elena. Of course it was at a time that we were still close friends, and I could rely on her discretion. But then I had to make the decision to cut her out of my life – because she'd begun to live with Paul, and Jamie was pregnant. I had to make a choice. She was very angry. And also, she and Paul couldn't pay their bills. They blackmailed me, Alex – and that was why I forged the bills for you. When you put a stop to my spending, they became desperate. Elena had known Justin in Singapore, under a different name: Ashley Taylor. She recognized him in a café. She knew his past. She resolved that I was the one person who could be successful in blackmailing him – because I was a stranger, because I was your wife. She had no idea he was the same man I'd told her about. I asked him to come here and did what they'd told me. So that they wouldn't tell you anything then in their desperation. But you see, he turned the tables. He thought that *he* would be able to blackmail *me* and force you to steal

421

the file on him, the file on his criminal activities before the war, in return for never divulging to the press what I had done twelve years ago. I thought he was bluffing, that we had reached an impasse. But he's gone one step farther and taken Cassie. He meant what he said: You will have to comply, or . . .'

She looked at him, pleading with her eyes. Both of them were completely drained by Lesley's revelations. After several moments, she said wearily: 'We look awful. My clothes are clinging to me, and I'm exhausted. I need to have a bath, sleep a little – if I can.'

'Yes,' he replied. 'I need some time alone. To decide what to do. About Cassie. About us. About our whole life.'

'What do you feel for me at this moment?'

He shook his head, sighed. 'I don't know. Honestly, I don't. I feel . . . dead.'

'But if it helps . . . I know now I love you. When you told me tonight that you were alone, that there was no "other woman" any more, it was as if a whole new world were opening up to me. I felt . . . happy.'

He half smiled. 'You and I are the less important concern,' he commented. 'I must resolve the issue of the file. I have never, Lesley, disobeyed the law. I am a lawyer. Just now I can't even understand what this person expects me to do – to violate everything I've ever held sacred! To steal a file from the Ministry of Justice!'

'But Cassie – '

'Cassie. Our only heir. Jamie's daughter.' He looked down, fumbled with a cufflink that he had removed. 'My brother's child . . .' Then his grey eyes went to her face. 'Besides, I could so easily be caught. The Minister of Justice isn't a friend of mine – I'd have to think of a reason to go there. And there are always secretaries around at all hours of the day . . .'

'You could go at night.'

'I don't have the key. And I have no inkling of where the

file might be kept. No, I'd have to pray, and bluff my way through, during office hours.'

She nodded. The enormity of the situation made their own personal dilemma seem unimportant. She wondered, briefly, whether Jamie had felt the same way when it had been a question of money for her next semester and she'd suddenly been faced with Lesley's problem, that November so long ago. Jamie had sacrificed, Jamie had never thought of *not* coming through for Lesley.

I am too tired to reason properly, she thought, welcoming the end to all the secrets. It's in Alex's hands, and God's.

All his life he had lived by the rules. Now he was suddenly face to face with a reality that had nothing to do with codes and honour. A man had taken his niece from her home. And he, Alex, was the only one with the power to save her life. In order to do that, he would have to break the laws of his country.

And what of Lesley? He felt anguish in every muscle and vein. Lesley's confusion had ruined ten years of living together – the delicate framework of ten years of respect, of caring, of building confidence in each other. He would have given his life for this woman, and now, ten years later, he was finding out that he had really been living with a fantasy. Perhaps it was his fault after all. Perhaps he hadn't shown her how much he really loved her. What examples had he had? Charlotte? Yvonne? I have no marriage left. Perhaps I never really had a marriage.

He wondered what he was going to do. But was there really any question? He had to find a means to locate the Reeve file. After that, he'd worry about Lesley.

As he was pressing his fingers against his temples, he imagined himself divorced. He pictured this house empty of her, of her scents, of her paints. Another empty house, without dreams. Lesley hadn't even loved him. It had all been pretence on her part and hope, eternal, stupid hope, on his.

He knew she thought he was rigid, pretentious. He supposed she was right. But what difference did her labels make? He was who he was. For years he'd tried to be a son his mother might love. From now on he would be responsible to himself.

And Paul? Such fury rose in him that his fingers began to tremble. Paul had betrayed him so many times . . . His own brother had known about Justin Reeve and used the information to make them pay. And Elena . . . ! How did this Justin Reeve ever decide to kidnap Cassandra? he wondered. It doesn't make sense . . . He must have done a lot of research on my family – or someone told him what he needed to know. If so, *who*? Lesley loved Cassie; Paul would not have hurt his own child. That left only Elena.

I am beginning to imagine things, he told himself. Probably the man simply asked around. Everyone knows who Cassandra is – and that I will go to any length to get her back.

Jamie sat in the back garden of Lesley's mansion, a shawl over her knees. Neatly trimmed hedges stared at her from the sides, and a fruit tree in blossom. The most beautiful time of the year was spring: the only moments when Ohio had seemed bearable. Moments of honeysuckle and mimosa, of lavender coming into bloom – of the clinging scent of the hydrangea, its white, blue and pink petals welcoming the sun like thirsty lips. She shivered. Louveciennes was bursting with signs of spring, but she wouldn't be able to return there until she had Cassandra back.

She heard a footstep on the porch, turned round. Paul was coming toward her. She noticed that age had caught up with him; there was a puffiness below his eyes that showed the strain, and his body wasn't so trim any more. It was difficult to look at him without feeling old sensations of loss, of regret, of anger. He'd never leave her cold. There was always the reminder that he'd left for another woman. She wondered if she'd ever be happy again, as she'd been when they had lived together in her loft.

'Jamie,' he said softly. There was another wrought-iron chair next to her, and he drew it up, sat down. He crossed his legs, and she felt his awkwardness. Suddenly he bent toward her and touched her gently on the cheek. 'How are you doing?'

'As well as can be expected, thank you.' She didn't want to help him, but at the same time had not the strength to send him away. Just now she needed company, and as she looked at him, she could see Cassandra in the set of his jaw, in the shine of his hair. She knew why she had loved the perfection of him, and once again, it hurt.

'Even with all that has happened, you are beautiful,' he commented.

How many times had he told her that before? She was wearing a simple dress of pale-yellow cotton and hadn't pinned her hair up. She looked down, embarrassed, a little annoyed. 'How's Elena?' she asked sarcastically.

'Jamie, I made a lot of stupid mistakes. Elena was one of them. I should never have left you.'

'That was a long time ago, Paul. You were right: You didn't love me, and you loved her. Don't feel guilty now.'

'But the truth is, I no longer love her.'

'And so Jamie seems to be the only one to understand you,' she said bitterly.

He sat quietly, his face lost in thought. She wondered why she wasn't reacting more strongly to him. Ten years ago she would have been excited, moved. Instead she thought poignantly of her daughter and wondered whether she would ever see her again. What was the identity of the person who had taken her? She turned to gaze at Paul's face in three-quarter profile, soft shadows falling over his nose

425

and cheek. It was Cassie's face, except for the eyes. Such beauty, such virility. Yet Paul, inside, had always been weak. She'd been living without him for over three years and had felt strong in spite of his absence. Other men had made love to her, had found her amusing, intelligent, pleasing. Brilliant men, like Pavel Tchelitchew, whom she had met through Jane Heap of the *Little Review*. Men who had won in the game of life, while Paul hadn't even dared to play. Paul was the kind of man who always sat by the sidelines, smiling at the women who played in his stead.

'Cassandra is my daughter as well as yours,' he was saying. 'I want to wake up to her cries of laughter. I want to watch her grow.'

'Stop!'

Their eyes met. 'She'll be brought back to us, Jamie,' he whispered. 'I know it.'

'You don't know that! Please, Paul, don't talk about her.'

'Then tell me that if she is returned, we can be a family. Tell me, Jamie, that you'll marry me.'

To spend the rest of my days supporting him, she thought, and supporting the women who would hang on to his arm while I'm looking? She remembered the loft, her robe falling open, his hands finding the secret softness of her stomach, the tenderness of her nipples. Making love while piles of onion-skin papers danced down to the floor, un-numbered. Later, the two of them laughing, trying to sort through the mess. Eating sardines and Camembert, with day-old bread and strong coffee. A lifetime of that, even if there were other betrayals . . .

'You've never loved anybody else,' he said.

'But it doesn't count now. I've made my own way. Cassie has been reared without a father. She doesn't know what it is to have one. I don't need you any more either.'

A breeze had risen that was blowing tendrils of her hair against her cheek. She brushed them away. He sat mes-merized by her great blue eyes, by the grave, pensive

426

expression on her plain face. How different from the Tatar geometry of Elena's features! But how much more poignant was Jamie, in her sincerity. 'Don't send me away,' he said quietly.

There were tears on the edges of her lashes. He reached for her hand, and she didn't withdraw it. 'I'm making you an official proposal. It doesn't matter that we already have a daughter. This is 1928. The point is that, finally, we shall be legalizing our situation. You're the right woman for me, the only one who ever cared to understand me. Bertrand and you were my only friends. Both of you abandoned me. Perhaps with your help, I can return to his good graces too.'

'It wasn't he who abandoned you,' she countered gently. 'It was you who moved out of his sphere. I too tried, but you wouldn't let me stay close to you.'

They remained still for several minutes. Finally he raised his eyes to her, asked: 'Will you consider my proposal?' She didn't answer.

She asked instead, her voice tremulous. 'Who has taken Cassie? Do you have any idea?'

'It has something to do with my brother,' he replied, bitterness lacing his words. 'Something to do with his political influence.'

'So it's not me they're blackmailing? It's really Alex?'

'That's how it appears.'

Paul was Cassandra's father. When she'd given birth to her, when the doctors had opened her up because the baby hadn't been able to exit from the birth canal by her own power, Jamie had prayed. Jamie had prayed for Paul to come forth, to declare to everyone that this child of her sacrifice was his as well. But he'd stayed away. Only Lesley and Alex had claimed Cassie. She looked at Paul and she felt a great emptiness, a great loneliness.

'Paul,' she murmured. 'You say you want me. But you're only saying that because, just now, you want Cassandra. You want what you can't have.'

427

A bird sang in the fruit tree, and above their heads, small white clouds moved in the sky, grouping and regrouping like dancers in a rhythmic ballet. He was looking at her, his brown eyes intense. She shook her head and touched his face. The tears fell down her cheeks.

'Why are you crying?' he asked, in a hushed voice.

'For all of us. For what we want and can't have.'

She withdrew her hand, and he stood up. By her chair he lingered, a strange light alive in his eyes. Then, abruptly, he went out of the garden and back into the house, his shoulders stooped.

She understood that whatever chance they might have had had died, that she had starved it, consciously. But what would have been the point? He was, she realized, beyond change.

It had been nearly ten years since they had confronted each other, and both Paul and Alex could recall those terrible moments when, in Charlotte's apartment, they had struggled and brutalized each other over the property at Beauce, and Popov's horses. When Paul came out into the hall after leaving Jamie, he was lost in thought, in regrets, in the mourning of the past. He didn't look up, didn't think to find his brother there. Alex was coming out of his study, and when he saw Paul his footsteps quickened. He caught up with him in front of the salon.

'I want to talk to you,' he said curtly. He felt tense, about to explode.

'You have news of Cassie?' Paul's face suddenly looked hopeful.

'In a sense. But not here. Bouchard is by the door.'

Paul shrugged, followed Alexandre back into the study. As soon as he had closed the door, Alex turned on Paul, his face contorted. 'You goddamned son-of-a-bitch!'

Paul felt goosepimples rising on his skin. Fear crept into

428

his body, and for a moment he couldn't move. 'What?' he whispered.

Alex grabbed Paul and shoved him against the closed door. 'What do you want?' Paul breathed.

'You went after her for three years. What else have you done?'

'"*Her*"?'

Alexandre began to lift him by his shirt, and Paul could feel the fabric giving way, ripping. 'It wasn't my idea,' he stammered, trying to look beyond Alex.

'I don't care! You're my brother! You're the one who went against me at every turn. Why? Why did you hate me enough to blackmail my wife?'

Paul began to shake uncontrollably. Alex let go with one hand and hit Paul hard in the face. Paul jerked away, but Alex's hand went up again, hitting him a second time. 'You hated us both,' Alex whispered, his pupils tiny dots in the slate-grey irises. 'And for this a man has seized your daughter. You say you want her. I'm never going to let you come near her! She's all the children that I never had – that *you* prevented me from having! *You*'re the cause for the breakup of my marriage! You were blackmailing her, and she couldn't face me. *For three years!*'

'She was never in love with you! Ten years ago I nearly went to bed with her. It was an accident of chance that it didn't happen.'

'You pig!' Alex went to choke him, but caught himself.

'You shouldn't be going after me,' Paul said. 'It's been Elena! She was the one who wanted revenge. I didn't care! You've never understood, but you and Lesley were foreign to me – people who didn't matter. I didn't hate you – I didn't love you. You were – you *are*! – nothing to me! The only family I have is Cassandra.'

'But I felt differently. In spite of who you were, I still never acted against you. You were my brother! Never mind who was your father. We had the same mother. Your child

429

became my child – she was my blood! It was Jamie who bound Cassie to Lesley, but it was you, you bastard, who made her my niece!'

They remained inches from each other. Alex finally let go. He said. 'It doesn't matter. But when this is over, I want you to leave Paris. I don't want Cassandra to know you, and I want you out of my life. I'm going to change my will, Paul, to cut you out permanently. What Elena chooses to do is her business. *You're* the one who was my family. I gave you one final chance, ten years ago. I should have disinherited you then!'

Paul didn't speak, but the blood left his cheeks. He felt his body sag. 'Get out,' Alex said, and he went to the door and opened it. Paul stared at him, speechless. Slowly he walked out of the room and Alex closed the door.

Paul stood in the hall, feeling the chill of the spring day, the chill of the great old mansion and of emptiness.

The telephone call came at eleven o'clock on the morning of 1 May, and Micheline herself came into Alex's office to tell him that it seemed urgent. She did not go out, but remained by the door, waiting, as he picked up his extension. He knew, before he spoke, who the caller was. The line was garbled, sparked with electric interference, but he heard the precise, elegant British voice on the other end, and it gave him a jolt. This was not only Cassie's abductor, but Lesley's old lover. As his hand, damp with perspiration, closed over the receiver, he tried to picture the man. He must be different from himself – delicate, but powerful, to please Lesley. Probably dark, with a fine nose. But not feminine. Had she said so, or was it just in his imagination? He said: 'I know who you are, Sir Justin. My wife relayed your message.'

'And you will comply?'

'That depends. How is my niece?'

'Very well. In good spirits. Now, Marquis, I want you to remove the file and to place it in a certain deposit box at the Gare du Nord. If this is done today, I shall verify tomorrow whether you have obeyed my orders. Then, if all has gone according to plan, Miss Cassandra Stewart will be returned to her mother's house the following day, in the afternoon. Do you understand me?'

'You expect me to risk my reputation without seeing the child first?'

'You have to take my word for it that she is safe. But it's up to you.'

The words chilled Alex. He listened to the details, wrote them down on a slip of paper, and hung up the receiver. Micheline said: 'It was he?'

He nodded. She hovered near the door, unsure whether to leave or go to him. But suddenly he was galvanized into action. He straightened his tie, slipped on his jacket, ran a comb through his hair. 'It's almost lunchtime,' he declared. 'Don't wait for me. If anyone rings – '

'I shall say you'll be back when?'

'In two hours. Eat something, meanwhile, Micheline. Go out if you wish.'

As he passed through the door, his side brushed hers. He hesitated for one moment, his eyes softening. She touched his arm, her face tense. 'Take care.' He patted her hand and strode out, into the clean crisp day, and stepped into the first available taxicab. 'The Ministry of Justice,' he stated. He hadn't wanted to take his car, because the new Silver Ghost Rolls-Royce was fairly well known around the city. Its custom-made seats of metallic blue, its unique solid silver bonnet ornament had already come to be associated with the Varenne house. It had replaced the Bugatti, which he missed but which had been growing old, less dependable on the road. The taxi driver turned to peer at him: 'You're not the *Ministre*, are you, Monsieur?'

Alex smiled, shook his head. On the seat lay a discarded

431

copy of the early edition of *Le Matin*. He opened it, scanned the first page. Good. There were still no headlines about Cassandra. He'd begged Numa Baragnon, chronicler of judicial matters, and Henri de Jouvenel, the editor-in-chief, not to feed to the public this tragic event in their private lives. He was afraid that the more was written, the more harm might come to his niece. But on the second page, discreetly to the right, the words hit him: 'Still no news of the député's niece, abducted on 28 April. She is the three-year-old daughter of Jamison Stewart, author of . . .'

He stopped reading. Things like that were impossible to keep out of the hands of reporters. Piranhas – all of them! They came in handy when it was election time, and it behoved one never to alienate them. But they were a rare breed, feeding on the wounds of others. He tossed the tabloid aside in disgust and realized that they had almost reached Place Vendôme.

As he paid the driver, and stepped in front of the Ministry, memories assailed him. The octagonal piazza, with its noble dwellings designed by Mansart in the seventeenth and eighteenth centuries, made him think of Lesley and Jamie during the days when he had first paid court to the twenty-year-old heiress from New York. He and Lesley, marking time till the wedding, had been seen in public places smiling at the *tout-Paris*. Paul and Jamie, passionate, hiding away in taverns and bars of Montmartre and Montparnasse, had all but taken over the hotel suite for their *amours*. So much had happened that first winter, when Paris had spread its arms vainglorious, after winning the war! He shook his head as if to clear his thoughts and entered Number 11–13, which had housed, since 1915, the Ministry of Justice. It had been built nearly a hundred years after Mansart's death, but the architects had followed his original design. Alexandre hardly paused on the landing, but climbed the stairs rapidly, his pulse beating in time.

He knocked on a large oak door, opened it. Behind a partition, several secretaries and clerks were at work. One of them, a pleasant young woman with blond hair, looked up, smiled, said: 'Monsieur le Député! What brings you to our offices this morning?'

'I wanted to look for an item of information in one of your files. Would you give me some help, mademoiselle? Your wartime files, please,' he added, pleasantly casual.

'That's an enormous dossier,' the woman stated. She stood up.

'Not anything to do with war activities,' he reassured her. 'It's a certain criminal case that has intrigued me. Nothing conclusive was ever proved, but much work was done . . . We're doing some legal research for a client.'

She smiled again and led him through a series of doors into a white room with high ceilings. File cabinets lined the walls and continued into the centre of the room. Several swivel chairs provided the only other furniture. The secretary went to a far corner, motioned with her hand. 'If I can be of further use . . .'

'These are the years in question?'

'Yes. But the cases are in alphabetical order. The problem is that sometimes they are labelled with the name of the victim, at others with that of the accused. But we have court transcripts – '

'It never reached court, thank you, Mademoiselle Jeanson.'

'Well,' she said vaguely, 'good luck.'

When she had departed, Alex crouched near the enormous cabinet. Where to begin? He wiped his glasses on his linen handkerchief, put them over the bridge of his nose, and opened the first drawer. It wouldn't be there. He was looking for the R's. Dust floated up from the yellowed folders as he flipped them through his nervous fingers. And what if there were several copies? Well, that would be Reeve's problem. He'd asked for the original, and nothing

433

else. Because in a court of law, only the original document counted.

An hour later he was wiping the sweat from his brow, still making little progress. He hadn't even found the name 'Reeve'. He was growing desperate. Collectors ... He flipped to the S's, located 'Stein, Gertrude and Leo'. The information gathered wasn't much, as the Steins had apparently been leading charm-filled lives on the right side of the law. Then he saw, as a mere footnote: 'Leo Stein ascertained that in the case of the William Blake *Tiger*, the canvas was not an original. It had been sold by Sir Justin Reeve, British art dealer, who swore to its authenticity . . .'

Alexandre's finger remained holding the papers in place in the folder. With great care, he removed only the sheet on which the footnote had appeared. Then he closed the drawer, wiped off the handle with the handkerchief, and stood up, feeling the sweat glistening on his forehead. It was two thirty in the afternoon.

He passed through the doors and into the widely-lit front office. The blonde looked up, solicitous. 'Did you find what you wanted?'

He shook his head regretfully. 'No, I'm afraid. Are there any copies? Perhaps the original has been misfiled.'

'No, that wouldn't be the case. The war files have been completely gone over by the Minister's staff. The important things would be duplicated, of course. But the ones on which there was inconclusive evidence . . . I doubt it.'

'Well, I'll come back another time to double check,' he declared, smiling. 'You've been most helpful.'

'If it's important I could try to find it for you,' she offered. 'Or you could send Mademoiselle Prandot.'

He remembered now. This girl and Micheline were friends. So she knew, probably, about their affair. He frowned slightly, 'Mademoiselle Prandot is leaving my employ,' he stated somewhat curtly. 'But if it's necessary, I'll send one of our other secretaries.'

'Certainly, Monsieur le Député.'

He inclined his head and left the room. Only the cases with conclusive proof had been duplicated. That's what she'd said. Perhaps it was true, perhaps it wasn't. But Justin Reeve would go on what Alex would tell him.

He called for a taxi and gave the Gare du Nord as his destination. Outside, playful spring leaves were waving in the sun on the limbs of the plane trees, like bangles on the arm of a graceful flapper.

The Doric columns of the du Barry mansion rose tall and cool against the sudden heat of the May afternoon as the butler came out with his salver of iced tea and cakes, discreetly moving from one person to another. There were only five people on the patio. Jamie sat near the steps, Lesley standing behind her and to the side, alone, Alexandre leaned against one of the columns while Paul stood in the shadows close to the house. Nobody spoke, but they waited tensely, minutes passing by like hours and weeks.

Lesley was thinking: Nobody knows what Alex had to do. He did it for his niece. If I had told him before, might he have been willing to forgive me? But it was too late. When he had returned from the Gare du Nord two days before, his face had looked haggard, white and drawn, and she hadn't dared approach him. He'd gone into his room, shut the door, refused dinner. Jamie hadn't asked. She was too subtle, too tactful to pry, but in her eyes had come a glow, a compassion. Had she known then that Lesley's marriage was over? They still hadn't discussed it. Alex had later knocked on Jamie's door, lingered an hour speaking to her. Lesley didn't know what they'd discussed. But she thought: If it hadn't been for me, for the mess of my life, none of this would have happened. Alex wouldn't have had to do something repugnant to him. Jamie wouldn't have been deprived of her daughter.

435

Something rebelled inside her. She'd led her life as anyone might have, only she'd had the misfortune to be caught with a pregnancy. Alex was holding himself aloof, judging her. But she hadn't really done anything! Elena and Paul were the criminals. What they'd been doing was cruel, illegal. They'd been living off her for three years, making her relive a nightmare that otherwise she might have forgotten. Eventually she and Alex would have been able to live on, to be happy. *They* hadn't let her.

All at once there was a noise, a crunching of gravel. Jamie uttered a small cry, rose in her chair. Lesley's arm tightened around her. Alexandre came close to them, his foot scraping Jamie's chair leg. A small form was coming up the path, in a red-checked dress: Cassandra, carrying a small doll, her reddish-brown hair tied back into a pony tail. She was coming from far away, from the gate, but Jamie shot up from the chair and started to run, her own hair loose over her back, flying. Lesley moved forward, but Alex laid a hand on her arm: It was Jamie's child, Jamie's moment.

The three people on the porch watched, mesmerized, as Jamie bent down and hugged the child, as they heard her sobbing against her daughter. Then Lesley saw Alex. He slipped out to the right, disappeared among the shrubs and trees that separated the right flank of the house from the road. Her throat tightened. Part of her wanted to watch the reunion, the other part wanted to follow Alex. She was suddenly afraid. Out of the corner of her eye she saw Paul coming by her, running to the woman and the little girl. He was crouching down by them and lifting Cassie into the air. Jamie was standing now, looking at him. Lesley turned round and went where she had seen Alexandre go, into the small wood. Her chest felt painfully constricted.

There was no sign of Alex. Lesley walked along, then lifted her skirt and began to sprint, reaching the gate just as she saw him passing by, running. She'd rarely seen him move so quickly. Her heart pounding, she ran after him.

The cul-de-sac seemed empty at first, a beautiful, shaded road bordered by disintegrating stone walls. She turned her heel, cried out, fell down, stood up again, holding her ankle, tears of pain in her eyes. But the concern seemed greater than the bruised ligament and the broken heel of her shoe.

To the far left there was a parked car, a red Citroën, and she heard noises coming from its vicinity. She tried to run, but her ankle hurt too much, so instead she limped along toward the car. She approached it and then she heard the yells. In the ditch, next to the wheels, two men were fighting, their arms around each other, fingers around each other's throats. Alex and Justin.

Lesley stood transfixed, watching them. She looked on in horror as Justin's fingers tightened around Alex's neck, squeezing the breath out of him. Then Alex reacted, shoved the other man off him with all his might. But instead of fighting back, Justin began to run toward the car, leaving Alex in the ditch, stunned, his hands touching the bruises on his throat. Justin slammed the door, turned the key in the ignition, and revved the engine. The car took off with screeching tyres.

Lesley ran to her husband, knelt beside him. 'Call the police!' Alex ordered, breathless and in pain.

But she shook her head, tears streaming down her face, tears of relief as well as of fear. 'Let him go,' she said in a hushed voice. 'He's never going to hurt any of us any more.'

It was very late. In Louveciennes, he had left Lesley sedated, and Jamie and Cassandra finally asleep. Alexandre drove up in his Silver Ghost, the tyres screeching as they came to an abrupt halt in front of Elena's apartment building.

She opened to his ring herself, wearing a black satin robe. Her hair was plaited and hung over her left shoulder, and her eyes glowed like a panther's at night. 'What do you

437

want?' she asked him, her voice hoarse from cigarettes. They moved into the hall, but the front door remained ajar.

'What role did you play in this abduction?' he demanded.

Elena shrugged, and the plait moved along her broad shoulders. 'What a stupid question.'

He leaned closer to her, and she shrank away. His eyes were narrowed to slits of grey metal. 'It isn't so stupid,' he said smoothly. 'Because Lesley told me everything about your blackmail scheme. And Reeve wouldn't have known enough to blackmail me through Cassie. He was a newcomer to Paris. He would not have known how important she is to me.'

Elena's body tensed, seemed to pull together. She said nothing. Alex's hand suddenly grabbed her elbow. 'You told him,' he whispered, 'and you engineered it with him. I have no proof, but I know what I'm saying is the truth!'

'Don't be ridiculous!'

'Don't lie to me! Rumour has it that you and Paul are finished and that you need money.'

She regarded him without expression. 'There's nothing in what you say but empty words.'

'Maybe so. But you and I know the truth. And I think Paul should know too. I'm sure he suspects it.'

She sprang forward, her great lithe body bounding out of his grasp. Before he was prepared, she had flung herself at him, her nails clawing his face, her fists beating his chest. He struggled with her and grasped a wrist. He twisted it, and tears came to her eyes. 'So,' he murmured. 'We have it now.'

They stood glaring at each other, her wrist in his hand.

A voice came from near them, and they both turned, startled. In the doorway Paul now appeared, his face distorted, his shirtsleeves rolled up, his brow wet with perspiration. He said: 'I can't believe it, Elena. That you would go so far . . .'

Her nostrils flared once, and her skin, white and taut, made her look like a painted statue in the hall. 'Paul – '

'There's nothing left for you to say to me,' he replied. 'My brother said it all.'

Alexandre looked at them both, the woman next to him, who had lost her war, and the man who stood framed in the door, who was bound to him by blood but for whom he felt nothing. He sighed and pushed past Elena, his steps resounding on the parquet floor. 'I'm going home,' he announced without looking at either of them. He pushed past his brother and they heard the car door slam.

Elena continued to stare at Paul, her lips parted, the pulse pounding in her throat. And Paul stared back at her, his features contracted in a mask of disgust, of revulsion, of horror. In his Silver Ghost, Alexandre slipped into his coat and revved up the engine, welcoming the breeze, the sound of a city at night. For human beings were beyond his understanding.

439

Epilogue

Jamie's villa in the hills above Cannes was threaded with
bougainvillaea, their crimson and purple flowers growing
like vines over the covered patio and over the sides of the
ochre walls, like a patchwork of brilliance. The July sun
gleamed, caressing Jamie's skin. She adjusted her hat and
continued to trim the roses in the flowerbed in front of the
door.

She heard Alex's voice before she saw him, and she faced
him, her tanned features opening to him, her eyes bright
with pleasure. 'You?' she asked.

'Paris was abominable. Poincaré's illness is worse. He's
going to resign any day now.'

'And then what?' She wove her arm through his, sat
down with him under the covered porch.

'Aristide Briand. But it's the end of an era, Jamie, you
know that.'

'What you need is a glass of wine.' She stood up, and he
watched her form going into the large, cool house. She
returned with a bottle of white wine that was still frosted
from the icebox. A small, dark maid followed her out,
carrying a Florentine tray and two glasses. 'It's only a little
vin du pays,' Jamie said, pouring and handing him his glass.
'But it's good, and it's cold. Are you coming to stay for a few
days? Perhaps a few weeks?'

He looked down, kicked a small pebble. 'I can't, Jamie.'

'We're bored here. Zelda and Scott are drinking and
fighting all the time. She's become so thin, it's pathetic . . .
But you haven't come all the way out here to listen to me go
on about the Fitzgeralds. It's time, you know, Alex.'

'For what, darling?'

440

'For you and Lesley to talk. To discuss things.'

He avoided the azure eyes. 'Do you think there's anything to discuss?'

'Love doesn't just disappear overnight. It's been fourteen months, Alex.'

'Fourteen months we've lived without each other.'

They were quiet, and the crickets hummed around them. He sipped his wine. 'You never have regrets?' he asked her.

'About Paul? I can't, Alex. He gave me Cassandra. I care about my books. The new one's coming out in the autumn. I'm not really alone. If I want a man, there's always one available, isn't there?' She smiled at him, and he was struck by the infinite sadness of her eyes, by their wisdom.

'You don't want to go through life growing older, with the men for ever getting younger,' he remarked, taking her hand, 'You deserve something better than that.'

'I don't depreciate my life. I'm thirty-two. Somehow, when I imagine myself as an older woman, I see wide-brimmed hats, lively eyes. Success. And maybe young men, and an older man here and there to take me to dinner. But the good ones are all married, or homosexual. I'm not looking for a husband, Alexandre. I never did, I loved two men, and that was enough.'

He didn't answer. 'Paul did what he had to do,' she continued. 'It's better for me, now that he's gone to London. I don't have to worry about how I'm going to feel if I should run into him at a party. And until Cassie's grown, he won't become an issue in her life. Later she'll want to know her father. If he still feels like it, he can come to see her.'

'One never knows how Paul will react.'

'Do you ever hear from him?'

He could read the wistfulness of her eyes and raised her hand to his lips. He shook his head. 'Not directly. Bertrand gets news of him once in a while. He gets along. Men like Paul always get along. There are always people to take care of them.'

441

'Women?'

He shrugged. 'Don't ask me. All I know is that I haven't sent him a *sou*. We were never really brothers. Now it's official.'

'And your mother?'

'She's immortal!' He laughed, and she joined in, shaking her head.

The crickets sang above them, and she asked, in a voice that was suddenly hushed: 'And Egorova?'

His lips tightened. 'You didn't hear? She's living with Bertrand de la Paume. I never thought it possible. He's such a decent man, and she's such a vulture. To think that when I was little, I hated him.'

'Because he'd loved your mother? Because of Paul?'

'Yes.'

'But it's good to love! Perhaps he was the only person who ever really loved Charlotte. You must understand about Elena. She's beautiful, and she's strong, and she's been terribly wounded by life. I think she loved Paul as much as I did. When he left her – after Cassandra – '

'She can't be living with Paul's father out of revenge. Nobody's that vindictive. He's an old man, Jamie!'

'And that's why she's with him. She's thirty-nine. To him she's still young, vibrant. There are those like me who enjoy younger men and then there are the Egorovas. They need men to adore them, or they can't survive. Besides, Bertrand, as you say, is Paul's father. Paul's good side comes from him.'

'She'll have one thing she's always gone after,' he remarked bitterly, accepting another glass of wine. 'Because when he dies, he'll leave her money. And then she'll be able to do what she wants.'

'But Paul will never love her again. He won't ever be able to forgive her.'

'And you, Jamie? Why is it that you can forgive so easily? Even Elena?'

442

She said, staring into her wine: 'Not "easily". Not easily at all . . . But I just can't see life the way Egorova does: hating and always thinking of vengeance. On Monday you have to think of Monday. You can't be planning Tuesday based on what happened on Sunday. That may seem like a simplistic philosophy, but it's the only one that I can abide by. *Today*'s important.'

He turned his face to her, in all its grief. She rose, laid a hand on his cheek. 'Come,' she whispered. 'It's time.'

Jamie left Alexandre inside the stone living room, in front of the unlit fireplace. The simple wicker furniture was comfortable, like Jamie herself, he thought, sitting down on the soft chintz. There were fresh flowers in an unglazed ceramic vase, and he could smell them, rich and mature. In his chest his heart beat rapidly, and he drank the cool wine. He didn't want to think. He'd come here to find her, of course, and there was no way he could have avoided it. Fourteen months.

After Cassandra's return, she hadn't come back home. She'd sent for her clothes and had moved in with Jamie. And he hadn't opposed this. He'd watched the maids packing her clothes and had known what it was she'd felt: utter, abysmal emptiness. And horrid guilt. There was no way for them to patch things up, not after all they had been through. He hadn't understood, and she hadn't told the truth. It hardly mattered who had been more to blame. In his heart he hadn't forgiven her for having been pregnant by another man and for never having wanted to bear *his* child.

'Hello, Alex,' she murmured, and he stood up quickly. She had let her hair grow again, and it fell to her shoulders, soft and glowing. Bangs still fringed her forehead, above the incredible light-green eyes. She was wearing a peasant dress of simple gingham, in a green and yellow weave, and there

443

were gold loops in her ears. Somehow she reminded him of the girl he'd met, and yet she was different. But who, he wondered, had she really been in those days after the war? It was 1929, and he'd known this woman for eleven years, without ever knowing her. He had married a scarred child who had felt pain as deep as his. He had wanted balm for his sores, when in fact she'd needed it for her own as well.

'You look fine, Lesley.'

'Thank you. Sea and sunshine become us all. Cassie's grown tall and strong. You'll see her at lunch . . . if you'll stay. The Fitzgeralds have taken her for a swim.'

'That's nice.'

She fumbled with the corded belt of her dress, then sat down, near the fireplace, in a large armchair. Winged armchairs always made her look so small, he thought, and so vulnerable. 'Will you stay?' she repeated.

She had the cool poise of her mother, the cold politeness. He said, 'I'll stay if you invite me. I went to the *Colombe d'Or*, in St Paul-de-Vence, before coming here, just to deposit my bags. I thought that I might take a few days off, relax for a while.'

She nodded silently.

'Lesley,' he asked, 'are you happy here?'

She shivered slightly. 'Yes. Don't I look it? Jamie and I have always known how to live well together.'

'And you and I haven't?'

Her eyes met his probingly. 'What do *you* think?'

'That there was love. That neither of us was mature enough to know how to handle it – and each other.'

'But that was how it was, nonetheless. You can't repair the past, Alex.'

'But one can go forward.'

She stood up, clasped and unclasped her hands, went to the window. He let her silence stay for a minute, then rose and went to her. She felt his presence but didn't move. He

444

laid a hand on her shoulder. 'Lesley, there is no one else. I've been alone since you left me.'

She looked at him fully. 'I'm sorry if I caused you pain. But what else could I do? You thought me immoral. How could we have continued to live as man and wife?'

'That was then. Jamie says I have to learn to forgive. You must too.'

'I'm not the one who has any forgiving to do. You were always immaculate, Alexandre. You never did one thing to hurt me. That woman would never have entered your life if I hadn't been the guilty party, over and over. I realize that. But I can't keep on, for ever, blaming myself for what happened. The sins of the past must lie, like old corpses, and be given a decent burial.'

The bitterness of her tone stung him, pierced him to his core. But he kept his hand over her shoulder. 'I'm not so "immaculate",' he whispered. 'I harmed you by my aloofness, by my own past. I didn't know how to love you properly, because no one had ever loved *me* before. But I was telling Jamie: This is the end of an era. Don't turn me away this time, Lesley. Come back, live with me.'

Her eyes were moist, and he tilted her head upward with his hand. She didn't push him away. 'I'm thirty-one,' she murmured. 'A little old to begin a family. A little used and threadbare.'

'You're *you*, and I love you.'

She closed her eyes, and he knew that she was trying to blot out all the pain of eleven years, all the mistakes, all the rancour. At Christmas they would have known each other for eleven years. 'Do you want to come home?' he asked.

In the palm of his hand, her chin quivered. He bent forward, tasted her lips, pressed his own against them. Her tears were like salt water on his tongue. Suddenly he clasped her in his arms, felt the power of himself with her, holding her against all odds, all people. Her hand moved to his face, her finger touched his nose, passing lightly over his

445

eyelids. 'I can't promise you anything,' she said. 'Because I don't know anything myself.'

'I don't want a promise. Just you.'

She raised herself on tiptoe, kissed him. Then she leaned against him, breathing quietly. 'I'll try,' she whispered, 'if *you* will.'

In the distance, a church bell started to ring, the sounds breaking on them like waves, perfect in the symmetry of their plaintive cry. But it was not a sound of sadness. It rang through them like an omen, like a good-luck charm. It rang eleven times, for their eleven years.

Author's Note

The Eleventh Year was first conceived as a story about the apathetic seventies and was to be set in Los Angeles. The problems confronting my generation after the debacle of the Vietnam War fascinated me: I had lived through it, had witnessed the devastation and disillusionment that had beset my comtemporaries during the Nixon years. But my editors at Delacorte had been hoping for a somewhat more exotic decor, in a somewhat more removed period. And so I decided to place my characters in Paris during the Roaring Twenties; no other time can compare so well to the American seventies. World War I brought to the youth of France the same dispirited decadence, the same lack of moral standards, the same turning to drugs; and in politics there existed a version of Nixon's silent right majority – with some of the identical corruption on high. So my flower children became flappers, rock and roll became Negro blues – with the added advantage that in Paris, after the war, three disparate cultures had come together: the expatriate American artists; the exiled white Russians; and the French, who were searching for outside stimulation to relieve their boredom and lack of ideals.

This book went through many arduous changes and evolved with the hand-in-hand assistance of Charles Spicer, my editor at Delacorte, an extraordinary partner. Overseeing our work was Jackie Farber, Editor-in-Chief, who never abandoned us. Ellen Edwards of Jove Books first started on the project with me and saw me through the initial revisions.

I wish to thank the following people for their invaluable help and expertise: Stewart John Hyde, who gave me my material for the Oriental passages; Dr Morris Wolfred, of Beverly Hills, for the medical information; Daniel Crump and Debbie Webb of the Pasadena Public Library, for unfailing footwork and research on the political systems of France and the United States; Ed Bigelow of the Pamela Reeve Agency in Los Angeles, for help in tracing the beginnings of his field in New York and Chicago. My best friend, Debbie Schwartz, a Vice President at Grey Advertising, proofread the manuscript for me in its several versions, and many helpful suggestions came to me from the Hungarian-French film director René Gainville.

My agent, Roberta Pryor of International Creative Management, was the single person who stayed with me from the earliest conception of *The Eleventh Year* to its final stage. Her support saw me through the most difficult times. She is as much a friend as a valued business associate.